"A writer of mult⋯⋯⋯⋯⋯⋯⋯y displayed in this brill⋯⋯⋯⋯⋯⋯⋯⋯
　　　　　—M⋯⋯⋯⋯⋯⋯⋯⋯⋯*views*

"I was mesmerized."
　　　　　　—Jordan Rich, *The Jordan Rich Show*

"A violent, sex-obsessed tale from prolific historical novelist Thomas Fleming. A search for the Irish American soul."
　　　　　　　　　　　　　　—*Kirkus Reviews*

"The tension mounts to an almost unbearable rate, exploding
in a physical and emotionally violent climax. Fleming carefully interweaves the strands of several parallel plots into a
stunning, multilayered thriller."
　　　　　　　　　　　　　　　　—*Booklist*

"Fleming weaves together these racial and ethnic themes
which resonate in the American psyche. . . . The reader
daren't miss a paragraph."
　　　　　　　　　　　　　　—*Library Journal*

"Mobs, Reds, IRA mix nicely. . . . In a mere 308 pages,
Fleming packs the issues of hyphenated Americanism, the
limits of family loyalty, the Vietnam War, patriotism, and
corruption. . . . The pace and the body count are more remi-
niscent of a Quentin Tarantino movie than of a John LeCarré
novel."
　　　　　　　　　　　　　　—*Flint Journal*

THOMAS FLEMING

HOURS OF GLADNESS

TOR®

A TOM DOHERTY ASSOCIATES BOOK
NEW YORK

This is a work of fiction. All the characters and events portrayed in this book are either products of the author's imagination or are used fictitiously.

HOURS OF GLADNESS

Acknowledgments: Lines by W. B. Yeats. Reprinted with the permission of Simon & Schuster Inc., from *The Poems of W. B. Yeats: A New Edition* edited by Richard J. Finneran. Copyright © 1983 by Anne Yeats.

Lines by Dylan Thomas from *The Poems of Dylan Thomas*. Copyright © 1946 by New Directions Publishing Corp. Reprinted by permission of New Directions Publishing Corp.

A Tor Book
Published by Tom Doherty Associates, LLC
175 Fifth Avenue
New York, NY 10010

www.tor.com

Tor® is a registered trademark of Tom Doherty Associates, LLC.

ISBN: 0-812-56677-7
Library of Congress Catalog Card Number: 99-33598

First edition: November 1999
First mass market edition: February 2001

Printed in the United States of America

0 9 8 7 6 5 4 3 2 1

To Dave and Sharon

I am of Ireland,
And the Holy Land of Ireland

—William Butler Yeats

A LITTLE NIGHT MUSIC

"Mick. Rose just called. You better go get 'im."

It was Tom Brannigan, the night sergeant. Michael Peter Ignatius O'Day, known to everyone in Paradise Beach as Mick, was checking the last empty house on Leeds Point. A northeast wind was coming off the ocean, carrying icy rain and spray with it. He could see the combers lifting their white manes in the darkness. It was cold enough outside to freeze your hand to the metal skin of the police car, if you were dumb enough to touch it for more than twenty seconds.

Was Brannigan okay? Did he have the tape off? All radio communications of the Paradise Beach Police Department were recorded. It was one of many ways that Chief William P. (for Patrick) O'Toole guaranteed that nobody was on the take from some Mafia slime or one of their casino front men in Atlantic City. Being Irish, O'Toole understood that there were times when the equipment should be turned off, and he made sure it contained the appropriate switches.

Mick decided Tom Brannigan was still okay, in spite of having a wife who had joined some sort of charismatic Catholic group who thought you could talk directly to Jesus. She had been going nuts ever since their oldest son, Jack, got it in the Granada show.

"Where is he?"

"At Rose's place," Brannigan said. Even with the tape off, he was taking no chances. Three or four retired bozos listened to the police radio on shortwave sets.

"I just checked Leeds. Everything's like a cemetery as usual."

"No sign of the devil?"

"He moved to Atlantic City ten years ago."

According to a local legend, a devil lived on Leeds Point, a leftover from Revolutionary War days, when deserters from both armies caroused there, screwing whatever the tide washed up. One of the whores had supposedly given birth to a creature with horns and cloven feet.

"I'll have Yummy cover for you."

Yummy O'Keefe was curled up in the back of his squad car behind the regional high school. Only guys like Mick, with trouble on their records, guys who owed something for their jobs, got the beachfront patrol in the winter. Mick could practically hear Yummy cursing.

It was 3 A.M. He would be in Atlantic City in fifty minutes, if the Garden State Parkway was not iced up. He drove slowly through Paradise Beach, a habit inflicted by the summer months, when you never knew whether a drunk or several drunks would come roaring through an intersection. At Maryland Avenue and the Parkway, he slowed almost to a stop before a big, two-storied house with an open porch in front and a glassed-in sunporch on the side. It had prestige written all over it, even if it was not one of the huge piles sitting out on the dunes south of town.

Although the house sat in shadow, beyond the glow of

the corner streetlight, Mick could see it as vividly as if it were high noon. He had grown up here. He remembered when its bright green color had been a defiant announcement to the WASP natives and their mostly WASP summer visitors that the Irish had arrived to stay.

For a moment Mick's head was filled with music. He was remembering the family parties on the Fourth of July and Labor Day. Inevitably they ended with everyone grouped around the piano, singing Irish songs: "Danny Boy," "The Rose of Tralee," "I Met Her in the Garden." The parties always ended with his grandfather "Sunny Dan" Monahan singing his favorite in a rich baritone.

> Oh the days of the Kerry Dancers!
> Oh the ring of the piper's tune!
> Oh for one of those hours of gladness
> Gone! Alas, like our youth, too soon.
>> Oh to think of it!
>> Oh to dream of it!
>> Fills my heart with tears . . .

Now more than youth was gone. The house's insolent green had bleached and faded and peeled in the heartless summer sun and cruel winter wind. It had been five years since the house had been painted, five years since there was any reason to rejoice in being Irish in Paradise Beach.

Mick sat there remembering what had happened five years ago. It was the reason why he was going to Atlantic City. Five years ago, two cars full of U.S. Treasury agents had pulled up in front of the house. Mick had answered the door. He had been working nights as usual and he had just gotten up. It was about three o'clock on a hot afternoon in May.

The lead guy looked like he had seen too many reruns of the Eliot Ness TV show. He did not smile. He did not introduce himself. He just said, "Is this the house of Daniel Brendan Monahan?"

"He's not home," Mick said.

"We've got a federal warrant," the lead said. "We're going to search the place."

"Let me see it," Mick said.

The guy produced the warrant. It looked legal all right. What the hell were they looking for? "You guys wait here while I talk to my uncle. He's the chief of police," Mick said.

"Look, pal," the lead said, "we're in a hurry. We want to be back in Newark by five o'clock to catch a plane to Washington. We don't care what your uncle says. This thing is signed by the U.S. attorney for New Jersey. You try to stop us and you'll go to Newark with us—in handcuffs."

"Gee, I'm real scared," Mick said. "Wait here anyway."

He slammed the door in their faces and called William O'Toole at police headquarters. When Mick described the visitors and their warrant, Uncle Bill almost gave birth over the wire. "Is your grandfather there?" he said.

"He's at the Shamrock playin' poker. Mom's at school teachin' the remedials."

"Keep those guys out. I don't care how you do it. Keep them out until I get hold of Dan. We'll be there in five minutes."

Mick came back and put the inside chain on the door. He opened it a crack and said, "My uncle and my grandfather'll be here in five minutes."

"Open this door, wise guy," the lead said.

"Five minutes," Mick said. "Set your watches. Guaranteed."

Mick stepped back about ten feet. Two of them hit the front door and tore it off the hinges. They landed on their knees in the hall. Mick kicked the first guy in the teeth and the second one in the belly. The other guys swarmed him. He got off one good punch before they had him on his back. They kicked him and rabbit-punched him a few times to get even for the two door crashers, who were moaning low in the corner of the front hall. They dragged him into the parlor and handcuffed him to a chair.

"Find the cellar door," the lead said.

"Probably in the kitchen," someone else said.

Mick noticed two of them were carrying shovels.

In about five minutes the grandfather's clock in the hall bonged 3 P.M. All 250 pounds of Bill O'Toole charged into the front hall in his gold-braided chief's uniform. After him labored Mick's tall, beak-nosed grandfather, Sunny Dan Monahan, gasping and wheezing on his cane, his pale old man's mouth working spasmodically. The two door crashers were on their feet now, discussing what they would do to Mick when they got him to Newark.

"What the hell's going on?" Bill O'Toole shouted.

The door crashers just looked contemptuously at him. Even under ordinary circumstances, federal cops found it hard to talk to small-town cops. *What the hell's going on?* Bill shouted again.

"Yeah," Sunny Dan Monahan said in his old man's croak. "What the hell is goin' on?"

The lead appeared from the kitchen carrying two canvas bags. Dirt dribbled off them onto the floor. He had a pleased smile on his television face. "What the hell you doin' with that?" Dan Monahan said.

"I'm taking these bonds to the U.S. attorney's office in Newark," the lead said.

"Those bonds belong to me!" Dan said.

"I doubt that very much," Eliot Ness Jr. said.

Bill O'Toole and Dan Monahan stood there while agent after agent paraded past them with bags of bonds, dribbling more and more dirt on the parquet floor of the front hall. They each made two trips. They must have taken out at least fifty of the things. Dan Monahan stood there quavering about "my property." Toward the end he started calling them thieves. "I earned that money! I put in ten thousand days and nights earning that money."

Through it all Bill O'Toole said nothing. But halfway through the parade, he started to crumble. His huge chest sank first, then his marine spine sagged, then his linebacker's shoulders slumped. By the time the last bag man left, he was looking more like a stuffed dummy than a commander of men.

Eliot Ness Jr., returned and said he was going to give them a break. He would not take Mick back to Newark. That might save them some attorney's fees. He took the cuffs off Mick and left without another word. Mick sat there, rubbing his wrists. Outside the feds started their motors and pulled away.

"Oh my God, Bill," Sunny Dan Monahan said. "Who could have done it? Who ratted?"

"I don't know," Bill O'Toole said. "But if I ever find out, he's a dead man."

That was how the Monahans, the O'Tooles, the O'Days, and the rest of the clan became $5 million poorer in a single afternoon. That was why Bill O'Toole was playing craps in Atlantic City. It was not the only reason why sadness seeped into Mick's soul like the winter chill, in spite of the full blast of the heater in the car. But it was one reason.

UNREELING

In another six blocks of cautious driving, Mick reached the west side of Paradise Beach, where houses clustered along the shore of the great bay, and the slope-roofed bulk of the Paradise Beach Yacht Club, shuttered for the winter, loomed against the expanse of dark whitecapped water.

Over the causeway Mick boomed and down the straightaway through the pines, letting the motor's rpms mount, his mind deep in the engine he had rebuilt to Ferrari specifications on his own time. His gift to the Paradise Beach Police Department. Had anyone even bothered to say thank you? Of course not.

About ten miles down the road Mick slowed the car from its 90 mph pace. It gave him time to glance through the pines at a white mobile home there in the moonless, starless darkness. Trai was sleeping beside Phac inside that freezing tin box. Where he would never sleep, thanks to the Catholic Church and the Communist Party.

Hit it, Mick told himself, slamming the accelerator to

the floor. Get out of here, out of the past, the stupid double-crossing past. Into the double-crossing present.

It did not mean anything anymore, Vietnam. It was gone like World War I and World War II and Korea. Like high school football and basketball. Only the trophies were different. The high school gave you golden statues for your mother to park on the mantel. Vietnam gave you a dishonorable discharge. That was what everybody had gotten, when they finally figured it out. Only some discharges were more dishonorable than others.

Up the parkway ramp Mick roared onto a sheen of ice. The squad car slewed like a boat in a heavy cross sea. Mick rode it out until he found concrete under his tires and headed south for the devil's new playground, Atlantic City. A four-year-old could drive the parkway, with its wide empty lanes and carefully calculated curves.

In the monotonous darkness, memory stirred like a VC in the bush. Slowly, inevitably, Mick was in Binh Nghai again, twelve thousand miles and fifteen years away from this frozen Atlantic landscape, strolling across the dusty, sunbaked marketplace with his M16 on his shoulder.

There sat Trai in her father's doorway with that round straw hat on the back of her neck. "What's up?" he said.

She giggled, revealing the whitest, brightest smile in Quang Tri province. "Nothing is up, Marine," she said. "But something is soon down."

"What?" he said, already knowing the answer.

"Soup, hot soup is soon down, Marine."

He hunkered beside her in the doorway and she gave him a bowl of fish soup, full of shark's fins and octopus eyes. Incredibly delicious. While he ate, he practiced his Vietnamese with her. "I hear you're going to marry President Thieu."

More giggles. "Oh, no. I must save myself for the marine who kills Le Quan Chien. In Vietnam, you know, we believe the gods come down in human form to play the part of heroes. I want to marry a marine god. I will know who he is when he brings me Le Quan Chien's head."

"Why don't you sell my head to Comrade Chien? He'll pay you five thousand piastres for it."

"Oh, no. Then who would drink my soup?"

Those delicate hands fluttered, the slim body beneath the black cotton tunic moved in small, subtle ways. Mockery danced in those almond eyes. Woman, whispered the voice in Mick's body, his mouth full of soup, yet somehow dry with desire.

Stop, stop, stop, Mick told memory. But memory was impossible to stop. It kept unreeling like an old movie on television. He had seen it 120 times but he could not stop looking at it.

Worse, you never knew where memory's movie was going to start. Sometimes it was in the middle. Sometimes it was at the beginning, sometimes at the end.

The wind boomed against the squad car's windows, the sleet crunched beneath his tires. Winter sounds. In Vietnam there were other sounds. The swish of a bush, the crack of a twig in the darkness, the splash of a foot in a rice paddy. Each meant death was out there in the night.

He was back in the cemetery, the night they killed Lam.

Ap Nguyen Lam, the tired, chain-smoking joker who had given Mick his first training as a cop. Lam, who taught Mick that a good cop never lost track of himself. He always held something back, no matter what he was doing—kidding, arguing, even screwing. A cop was always watching, analyzing, judging. If Mick had remembered that lesson with Trai, his life would be a lot different. But that white smile, that small, lithe body, had blown it out of his mind and he was paying the price.

Lam had also taught Mick the kind of war they were fighting in Binh Nghai and a thousand other villages like it. Mick would never forget the night Lam showed him his doomsday book. It contained the names and ranks of sixty-nine VC leaders that he had personally killed in the previous five years. On the next page was a list of eighty-nine friends and relatives—village headmen, schoolteachers, aid workers—that the VC had assassinated.

That night while Mick crouched among the graves with Sullivan and Lummis and Page and the two Popular Force Vietnamese, Khoi and Luong, Police Chief Lam was having dinner with his mother and nine leaders from nearby villages. Mick had objected to the visit. He said the VC were probably watching the house. Lam said his mother was old and sick and would not live much longer. She was his only living relative. Besides, the marines had the Cong on the run. The night no longer belonged to them.

For once in his life, Lam was being too optimistic. The night belonged to no one now. The VC were surprised to find the marines, the PFs, challenging them for it. But they had not yet surrendered it. Scarcely a week went by without a firefight between a marine patrol and a VC detachment.

Mick had no authority over Lam. Mick only commanded the eleven marines who had volunteered to join him in Binh Nghai as part of a program to beat the VC at their own game instead of in set-piece daylight battles—the army's approach to winning the war. They had spent the last three months living in the village, patrolling the roads each night, ambushing the startled VC a half dozen times.

Among the Vietnamese, Lam had been one of the strongest supporters of this new policy. That—and his doomsday book—made him a primary assassination target. Lam was just beginning to slice the juicy duck his salary had enabled his mother to buy when the four-man VC team came in the door shooting. Lam was the only man with a gun, and he could not fire because he was afraid of hitting his mother or one of the guests.

Lam was hit by at least ten bullets. For good measure, the VC dropped two hand grenades on his body. Mick was on his feet, starting to run for the house, when the PF, Luong, grabbed his arm. "No. Ambush," he hissed.

Nobody had much use for the PFs. For one thing, they had M1 rifles, unable to fire more than one bullet at a time. Most of them were terrified of the VC and ready to do almost anything rather than fight them. Mick had discovered Luong was the exception. He was a potbellied little guy with protruding teeth, not much bigger than his rifle. He had fought the Japanese and the French on the Cong side and had for some obscure reason switched to the Americans. He was a PF for the $20 a month he got paid, which enabled him to avoid farming or fishing, both of which he detested.

Mick followed Luong out the back gate of the cemetery down another path that took them to the river. They got there in time to hear the assassination team paddling away. Mick fired sixty rounds in their direction, the M16's red tracers winging over the dark water, Luong's M1 banging beside him.

Back in the cemetery, almost in syncopation, Sullivan and the other marines opened fired on the VC detachment who had been waiting to cream them if they had charged down the main street to help Lam. The VC had tried to come through the cemetery and use the same path to the river Luong had used with Mick. The marines had four bodies to display in the marketplace the next morning. Around noon, one of the assassination squad washed up with the high tide.

None of that brought Lam back to life. His body was a piece of mangled meat. They buried him in the cemetery while his mother wept and clawed at her eyes. The VC had now killed her husband, all four of her sons, and five of her nephews.

Ten days later, Nguyen Thang Phac arrived to take Lam's place as district chief of police. One look at his elongated frame and lean, haunted face and Mick knew the jokes were over. Lam was a killer who had laughed at death. Phac was a killer who no longer laughed at anything.

WELCOME TO ATLANTIC CITY. The billboard displayed towering casinos, a sun-swept beach and ocean, svelte women and handsome men beside gaming tables. Past more billboards urging you to lose your shirt at individual casinos Mick roared, his mind, his body, recoiling from what he was going to see and hear in this bedeviled town. But it was better than the unreeling. Better than another night in Binh Nghai.

TINSEL TOWN

The clock on the dashboard read 4 A.M. as Mick rolled into Atlantic City's wet, deserted streets. The usual dozen bums were huddled in doorways freezing to death. One or two of their ragged friends rooted in garbage cans looking for Christ knows what.

The last time Mick had come down here, he had spotted an ex-marine, Minus One Haines, around the garbage cans. Minus One was the nickname the drill sergeant had pinned on him in boot camp because he could not do anything right. Mick had tried to help Haines, a runty loser from Bayonne who thought becoming a marine would make him six feet six. Mick had gotten him through boot camp. He had learned a lot about being a leader, working on Minus One.

Haines had wanted to come to Binh Nghai with Mick, but he had turned him down. Mick had picked only the best for Binh Nghai. He remembered the hurt look on Minus One's face. He had stepped forward with twenty other volunteers when he saw Sergeant O'Day was in command. Was that why Minus One was rooting in garbage cans? Did he have him on his conscience too? Mick wondered.

At the boardwalk and Delaware Avenue, Mick parked the car and took off his badge, slung a shoulder holster under his arm, and shoved his .38 in it. Without his hat and with his dark blue jacket zipped, he might have been a bus driver. Sometimes in the summer, ferrying drunks to Paradise Beach police headquarters, he felt like one.

In the casino, the freezing wind and rain that had lashed him on the boardwalk ceased to matter. He was in the warm, glowing world of the Arabian nights. On the ceiling were a million tiny, twinkling stars; in a dim corner a swing band blared and a fat black singer in a white sequined gown wailed about her lack of love. She was singing to mute rows of blank-eyed slot machines, like a humanoid performing on a *Star Wars* asteroid. The slots sluggers had long since boarded their buses and rolled home to Allentown and Paramus. Only the big bettors were still on duty, watching the cards slither from the draw poker machine, the roulette wheel spin, the craps dice dance.

Not a few of these insomniacs were women. It was amazing how many women came here alone. In front of the first baccarat table, with a pile of chips high enough to ski down, stood a shapely blonde about forty in another all-white outfit, down to her shoes. What was her name? Mick reached into his cop's memory and produced it: Jacqueline Chasen, granddaughter of old Marcus Teitlebaum, who had once owned all of Leeds Point. His heirs had subdivided it into sleek, modern houses on tiny lots and made a bundle.

Jacqueline Chasen looked at him and some sort of recognition seemed to flicker in her mascaraed eyes. She had been a brunette the last two times Mick saw her. Remember me, baby, from your beach-blanket-bingo days? Mick was tempted to ask the question but he decided against it. She was class. Everyone in Paradise Beach had talked about making a pass at her, but no local had ever got close. She was still looking classy, if a bit long in the tooth. The white outfit, the pearls, probably meant a heavy escort was around somewhere.

"Hey, Mick, how you doin'?"

The voice forced Mick to turn his head to the left. He did not want to do it. He did not want to see the owner of the voice. He was the main reason why Mick hated to come to Atlantic City. At another baccarat table, beside a pile of chips even bigger than the one Jacqueline Chasen was handling, sat Mick's father, Harry Alexander O'Day, known to everyone as Buster. Every time Mick came to Atlantic City, Buster was at the baccarat or the craps table, dropping another twenty or thirty thousand as if it were Monopoly money, sneering drunkenly that there was lot more where it came from.

There was too. Back in Jersey City, the northern factory town where Mick had been born, Buster ran the biggest numbers operation in the state. He had inherited it from his father and built it even bigger with help from the Mob. But Mick was never going to see any of the money. Neither was his mother. About a year after he was born, Barbara and Buster had gone their separate ways, and neither had ever explained why to him.

Not that he had ever asked. He had been taught to despise this small, balding man with the mouth that twisted into a sneer even when he tried to smile. It had been easy because as far as Mick could see, there was nothing about Buster O'Day that anyone could like. All he had was money, piles of it that he waved in Mick's face every time he saw him.

"Hey, you wanna try your luck?" his father said, clutching a wad of $100 bills.

"Nah. No thanks," Mick said. "I'm here on business."

Buster sneered. Not even a try at a smile this time. "Yeah. I know. He's playin' craps."

Mick's cousin Rose Gargan grabbed his arm. Her

crotch-tight, feather-trimmed dress looked like it was going to split her in half. Mick still wasn't used to seeing Rose Gargan wearing that kind of dress. Rose had been pretty when she was in high school. She did not seem so pretty now. Her red hair was twisted into something that looked like the strands of a mop. She had about three inches of lipstick on her mouth.

"He's down at least twenty thousand," she said. "You better get him out of here."

"I'll see what I can do," Mick said.

Mick knew exactly where to go, the craps table nearest the casino credit window. There sat three hundred pounds of Irish beef known as William P. O'Toole. Lately, he seemed to get fatter every time Mick looked at him. A bar girl was serving him a dark brown Scotch. Mick took it out of her hand and drank about half of it. He grinned and patted her sequined behind. "I'm a relative," he said.

Mick watched Bill O'Toole lose $2,000 on a pass nine. "Not goin' too good," Mick said.

"It'll come back," Bill said. "It always comes back." There seemed to be some truth to that. Uncle Bill had won amazing amounts of money at these tables last year. But nothing had gone right since September. This was the third time Mick had been told to ride to the rescue.

"Maybe you ought to give it a rest," Mick said. "Maybe the date's against you."

"What day is it?"

"March thirteenth."

"That's my mother's birthday, you idiot."

"Maybe you still ought to give it a rest," Mick said as his uncle bet another $2,000 on a straight seven and lost so fast it sent needles of pain dancing through Mick's forehead. He knew exactly what Uncle Bill got paid to be chief of the Paradise Beach Police Department, $26,000 a year. Mick also knew how much he got paid—$16,000. Uncle Bill had just blown a quarter of Mick's salary.

He was tempted to throw an arm lock on Uncle Bill and drag him out of the place. He was messing up what was left of the small but beautiful deal the Monahans and the O'Tooles and the McBrides had worked out in Paradise Beach. Even without Dan Monhan's $5 million in bearer bonds in the cellar, it was a lot better than no deal at all.

"Hey, Chief, how's it goin'?"

Joey Zaccaro inserted his swarthy fox face between Mick and his uncle. Joey's eyes were straight from the zoo, glittering, wary, stupid. But his mouth smiled in a way that was almost human. According to the laws of New Jersey, Joey was not supposed to be allowed in the door of any casino in the state. He had Mob connections two pages long in the FBI printouts. But New Jersey tended to stop enforcing the laws after midnight in Atlantic City. Maybe even before midnight when a guy rolled as high as Joey Zip.

"I'm goin' lousy. How you goin'?" Uncle Bill said.

"Couldn't be lousier. I'm down forty."

"See what I mean?" Mick said. "It's a bad-luck night."

"Who's this?" Joey Zaccaro asked.

"My nephew."

Joey introduced himself. It was the third time they had done this turn. Joey had a lousy memory for faces. He slapped Uncle Bill on the back. "When this guy's hot, he takes the joint home. Never seen nothin' like it."

Suddenly Joey's eyes jumped from the craps table, where Uncle Bill was losing another $2,000 on a pass four, into the middle distance. "Jesus Christ!" Joey snarled.

He hurtled away from them as if he were on wheels—across the carpet past the roulette tables and the draw-poker players to the baccarat table where Jacqueline Chasen was still playing with her mountain of chips. Without even breaking his stride, like a quarterback throwing a pass on the dead run, Joey belted her in the face.

She flew about twenty feet and landed on her back under a draw-poker table. Joey Zaccaro went after her like a linebacker going after a fumble. She rolled away, out the other side of the table, and started running, total terror on her face. Nobody so much as moved. Nobody wanted to mess with Joey Zip even though he was obviously about to commit murder.

As Joey passed the craps tables, Mick stuck out his arm and the Zipper stopped like a man running into a turnstile from the wrong side. His legs churned, his arms flailed, but he did not go anywhere. "Lemmy loose!" he screamed. "I wanna kill that broad. I wanna wipe her out."

Mick looked over his shoulder. Jacqueline Chasen was semi-collapsed against a pillar, sobbing hysterically. Security guards were lumbering toward them from three directions.

"You better get the hell out of here," Mick said to Joey Zaccaro. "We better do the same thing, Unk."

With a half nelson on the flailing, cursing Joey Zip, Mick guided a lurching Bill O'Toole across the block-long swath of gold carpet to the door. Buster O'Day watched from the baccarat table, his sneer practically neon across his puffy face.

In the lobby Mick released Joey. "You got some muscles, kid," Joey said. "You got any brains to go with them?"

"A few," Mick said.

Joey had regained his self-control. "What the hell did that dame do to you?" Bill O'Toole asked.

"Never mind," Joey said. "Hope the old luck comes back next time."

"Same to you," Bill said.

"I never worry about luck," Joey said. "When I need it, I make it."

"That proves you ain't Irish," Mick said.

Mick drove home slowly, carefully. He always drove slowly and carefully when he had Uncle Bill in the car. He had taught Mick to drive. He was the closest thing to a father Mick had ever had in his life. At the same time he was not his father. Mick used to wish he could forget that.

He used to wish there were no real son in Uncle Bill's life, no family golden boy, no James Patrick O'Toole, known to everybody as Ace. Even before he became a marine pilot, he had been called Ace, because he did everything right: hot student, great athlete, devout altar boy. Jimmy had been shot down over Hanoi in his F-8 Crusader in 1969. Mick had joined the marines to avenge him.

"How much did you lose tonight?" Mick asked.

"Don't worry about it."

"Just interested."

"It'll come back."

"Sure."

Silence until they were off the parkway, driving down the road through the pines. Lights were on in Trai's house. Phac was up, stumbling around the kitchen, hungover probably. He drank hard during the winter. You could not blame him. He worked on the SS *Enterprise,* Paradise Beach's biggest commercial fishing boat, owned by another of Mick's uncles, the mayor of Paradise Beach, Desmond McBride.

Crazy, the way a man gets stuck doing things. Phac had started out as a fisherman in Vietnam. The war turned him into a cop. When he makes it to the United States of America, land of freedom and opportunity, what happens? He goes back to fishing.

"I'm down sixty grand at least," Uncle Bill said as they roared over the causeway.

A reddish glow was tinting the gray sky over the Atlantic. Out to the horizon the ocean was flecked with foam. The northeast wind was still churning down from the Pole. Mick wondered what Phac thought about that wind when the SS *Enterprise* dug its nose into the freezing swells. There was no wind like that in Vietnam. Over there, things cut to the bone in other ways.

Phac did not deserve that wind. Trai deserved it. She should be out there on that icy, pitching bow, gaffing tuna, for what she had done in Vietnam. But Phac froze instead.

That was the way the world turned. Women got away with things because they were women. Maybe Joey Zip had a reason for belting Jacqueline Chasen.

"But I'm good for it. They know I'm good for it," Uncle Bill said.

"Sure." Mick did not know what Bill was talking about. Did he think old Dan had another stash of bearer bonds somewhere?

Whuuuuuh, moaned the northeast wind as Mick drove over the causeway that separated Paradise Beach from the rest of New Jersey. At the end a big sign urged everyone to vote for Walter Mondale for president. "Goddamn Democratic Party," Uncle Bill said. "Collection of shit shoveling draft dodgers."

Uncle Bill talked that way a lot. He had a whole library full of books on Vietnam. He could tell you how Kennedy screwed it up and how Johnson screwed it up. He particularly hated some guy who had gotten a Pulitzer Prize for a book that claimed the South Vietnamese deserved to lose because they were corrupt. That idea would naturally blow the mind of anyone from Jersey City (or Boston, Philadelphia, Pittsburgh, Chicago, Kansas City, San Francisco, and New Orleans, to name a mere handful of places where chicanery is as American as apple pie). Mick tried to tell Uncle Bill it was better not to think about Vietnam, but he never listened. Mick finally realized it was the only way Uncle Bill could feel close to Jimmy.

Mick turned into Delaware Avenue. All the shore towns had named their streets Atlantic City style. Marie O'Toole opened the door as they came up the steps. She had obviously been awake most of the night. Exhaustion had sunk deep lines into her once pretty face.

"Jesus Christ," Marie said. "I can't stand much more of this."

"I blew another twenty," Bill O'Toole said. Mick sensed Uncle Bill enjoyed making this announcement.

"That makes sixty thousand dollars!" Marie screamed.

"Where are we gonna get sixty thousand dollars? Daddy can't do anything for you anymore. Do you expect him to mortgage his house?"

"There's lots of ways to make sixty grand," Bill O'Toole snarled. "Lots of ways that don't have anything to do with kissing your father's ass. So why don't you shut your goddamn mouth for once in your life?"

"I'll shut my mouth when you tell me what happened to your wonderful *connections* in the federal attorney's office who didn't pick up a phone when those bastards were on their way down here to grab those bonds."

"I told you a hundred times they weren't from New Jersey. They came direct from Washington, D.C.," Bill roared.

Most of the time Mick tried not to think about the arguments in the family. Since they'd lost the bonds, Uncle Bill had taken a hate to Sunny Dan Monahan. Bill had always hated Desmond McBride and his wife. They had made a lot of money from their fishing business and took trips to Ireland and Florida and Bermuda and were always talking about their son Leo, who was the right testicle of their district's congressman, the Honorable James Mullen, chairman of the House Appropriations Committee, no less, and one of Senator Ted Kennedy's playpals.

Leo still wanted Mick to sue the Marine Corps for giving him a dishonorable discharge. He wanted to smear the Corps and turn Mick into a media hero. Leo was a liberal asshole.

Was Uncle Bill a conservative asshole? Was his brother-in-law Desmond McBride with his shamrocks and leprechauns and his blathering about the ould sod an even bigger asshole? Mick went back to the squad car trying to avoid answering these questions.

HAPPY DAYS ARE HERE AGAIN

In Mick's squad car, the radio was squawking. Tom Brannigan was getting pretty upset. He had an emergency call from Leeds Point and Yummy O'Keefe had gone back to his snooze behind the high school. Mick took over and headed out to the Point. It was unusual to have anyone in those houses during the winter.

The call was from Number 13, at the very tip of the Point. That house belonged to Jacqueline Chasen's mother. But she had not lived there for years. She made a nice dollar renting it in the summer and usually closed it for the winter. Mick had not noticed any signs of activity around the place during his midnight house checks. Whoever was there must be living a quiet life.

Out on Leeds Point, while Mick was en route, Jackie Chasen was flushing $500 worth of cocaine down the toilet off her bathroom. She was angry with herself—and also very frightened. Going back to cocaine was alarming proof that her rehabilitation program was not working. Meeting Joey Zaccaro was exactly the sort of reminder she needed.

Suddenly Jackie was back six months, ruefully, wrathfully, hatefully, lovingly, fearfully, carefully, carelessly, calmly rubbing creamy oil on Joey Zaccaro's olive skin as he lay facedown on the deck of this house in the September sun. All those words describing the way she was rubbing on the oil were true. They were all alive in the theater of Jackie's mind.

In that place of untime the audience was always the same. Her grandfather, Marcus Teitlebaum, sat in the first row wearing a Harris tweed suit and a dark blue club tie. Beside him sat his tearful, frightened wife. Grandfather glared at Jackie on the stage, his brush mustache twitching with rage. Behind him sat Jackie's mother and father and her great-grandfather. Her mother, pearled and jeweled for an evening out, was reading a book. Her father had his eyes closed. Great-grandfather Yid in his smelly old coat and dirty, tieless shirt and yarmulke gaped. His mouth was a round *O* in his Hasidic beard.

The sun was over the ocean. It slanted down on Jackie's tanned breasts and belly. It filled her thighs, the inky black hair of her pubis, its blank, blind heat swarmed in her belly, its fierce whiteness permeated the theater of her mind, x-raying the faces of the audience, revealing the hollow gourds of their skulls. Her mother's pearls were black around her proud neck, like a noose.

Joey Zaccaro turned over. On his back he became someone. His face spread, the cheeks loosening with forty-five years of time and tumescence, the hair thinning at the forehead, the ears weathering. His thick lips had dozens of little cracks. Black veins protruded in the lids of his closed eyes. The hairy, bulky chest had developed folds that intimated androgyny (the ultimate secret?), the slack belly protruded, the penis was a crumpled stump.

Jackie poured on more oil and rubbed it down the belly

through the shiny, matted hair around the penis and down the shrunken thighs to the spindly shanks, strangely blotched and pale. Then she coated both her hands with oil and began massaging the penis back and forth between them.

"Hey," Joey said, shoving her away. "What ya tryin' to do? Didn't you get enough last night?"

Jackie fell on her back. She raised herself on one elbow. "I told you, I never get enough."

"C'mere."

"You c'mere."

He lay there, blinking in the sun. "I said c'mere."

Jackie's eyes drifted past him to the sliding glass doors that led to the living room. One door was half-open. In the dark rectangle stood a thirteen or fourteen-year-old girl in a white linen dress. Her hair fell in a dark cascade down her back. Her lips were parted in a half-sad, half-mocking smile. She was incredibly beautiful and proud and fine, like Elizabeth Taylor before she bloated. In her eyes was a glow worthy of Anne Frank before she went to the death camp.

It was not the first time Jackie had seen her. She had appeared in a half dozen recent dreams, looking at Jackie from a great distance, standing on a sand dune at the southern end of the beach or at the far end of Ocean Avenue, Paradise Beach's main street. The sun had glared on her white dress, creating an angelic, almost a demonic aura.

Her appearance here made perfect sense. She was telling Jackie that Joey had to be the last one. Maybe, in a desperate, inverted way, Jackie had done the right thing, choosing someone like Zaccaro, someone totally repulsive. Maybe she was trying to make sure he was the last one.

Jackie tried to tell this to the girl in white. She tried telling her about the two months of midnights she had spent here with Dick Stapleton. The WASP prince, scion of the most powerful family in New Jersey, had talked about divorcing his wife, about moving to Hawaii with Jackie. Then one midnight instead of Dick there had been a voice on the answering machine, a robot from nowhere-space telling her in glottal tones he was *sorry as hell but this wasn't gonna work.*

The girl in white did not seem to be listening. She stood there, perfectly still, the half-sad, half-mocking smile intact, like a painting. She only made Jackie resolve to find someone, somewhere, who would let her tell him about Dick Stapleton. The girl in white made it clear it was not Joey Zaccaro, whose only recommendation was his access to free cocaine.

Jackie thought of all the men she had balled since 1968, the year the world had exploded. The long-haired, golden-eyed war protesters in Chicago, the manic rockers at Altamont, the boastful junior professors at Brandeis, the failed poets in Greenwich Village, the sneering black-power put-on artists in Newark, the panting Jewish princes in Glen Cove. She saw the curve descending from ecstasy to pleasure to boredom to loathing. First for the men and then for herself. It was the self-loathing that the girl in white was telling her she could stop, if Jackie would only listen to her for a while. If she would follow her into the dark rectangle of the past where she was waiting.

"Get out of this house," Jackie said to Joey Zaccaro.

In memory now, the new theater of her mind, Jackie strolled across the deck and entered the living room. The girl in white was not there, of course. Jackie knew she was not going to find her that easily. She paused in the center of the dim room—iron gray drapes were drawn against the sun—and listened to the purr of the central air conditioner. Yes, she thought, yes.

Jackie padded past the Lucite furniture and dropped a record on the stereo. Mick Jagger began howling mockery about love and lust. In the huge master bedroom, where similar drapes were drawn, Jackie popped two Valiums and pulled on a pair of tan Gucci slacks and a white blouse. Sunglasses.

Back in the living room she encountered Joey Zaccaro, still naked. His slumped chest, his potbelly, his spindly shanks, were even more repulsive when he was standing up. He looked like a defoliated orangutan. "I want you out of here when I come back," she said.

He grabbed her mane of black hair and spun her around. "Who the fuck do you think you are?"

"I don't know. Bianca Jagger. Yoko Ono. Princess Leia."

He tried to drag her against him for a kiss. Jackie drove her knee into his crotch. Joey's eyes bulged, his jaw went comically askew. Clutching himself, he sank to the rug in marvelous slow motion. "I'm coming back here with a cop," she said as he writhed at her feet. "Make sure you're gone."

Outside in the hot sun, the Valiums took hold. Jackie smiled at her electric green Lamborghini Miura P400 SV glistening in the sun, waiting for her orders like an obedient animal. She slipped into the driver's seat and savored the view for a moment. The curve of each front wing cradled the top of the low, gleaming snout. The stainless-steel figure of a naked Greek athlete raced into the distance on the tip of the hood.

Like most Italian cars, the Miura was well adapted to a woman driver, a being with short legs and moderately long arms. Jackie turned the key and the twelve-cylinder engine rumbled into life. Even on a crowded highway, the Miura could make you feel as if you were sharing the road with the sun and wind. That was what the copywriter wrote. As the Vals took deeper hold, Jackie believed it. She saw the Miura catapulting her into the past like a time machine. . . .

Jackie could barely tolerate the rest of the memory. The way the Miura, the copywriters, the Valiums, had betrayed her, the way she had missed a curve on the Garden State Parkway and ended up at the bottom of a ravine, smashed, broken, an object that took almost a million dollars' worth of medicine to re-create.

* * *

When Mick arrived, Jacqueline Chasen was in the living room, which was full of modern furniture that bent and curved in all sorts of weird directions. "I thought I heard a noise," she said, pointing upstairs.

"I'll check things out." Mick flashed his light around the two upstairs bedrooms and the attic. When a woman started hearing noises, she often wanted a cop around for more than protection. Last year, there was a redheaded divorcée out on Maryland Avenue who kept hearing noises and only calmed down when Mick started visiting her regularly off-duty. The year before that he had calmed down two of them, both blondes. A lot of divorcées with kids rented houses in Paradise and worked in Atlantic City.

Except maybe this dame really needed protection. When she recognized Mick, she started to cry. "You saw Zaccaro try to kill me tonight. What can I do? I'm afraid he'll come after me here."

Mick knew that was a needless worry. Hoods like Joey Zaccaro stayed out of Paradise Beach. They wound up with busted jaws and maybe fractured skulls if they tried any loan-sharking or drug peddling in Bill O'Toole's bailiwick. But he did not tell this to Jackie Chasen. Instead he played worried investigator.

"Why's Joey got it in for you?"

"I was his girl for a while. He didn't like the way I walked out on him."

"Why the hell were you fooling around with a piece of slime like Joey Zip?"

"I was mixed-up for a long time. I'm not anymore."

Mick liked the way she said that, head up, eyes bold. At the same time, he was listening with his cop's ears, noting the holes in Jacqueline Chasen's story. People with straight heads did not play baccarat at 4 A.M. in Atlantic City. Joey Zip did not beat up every woman who walked out on him. Otherwise he would long since have become a permanent resident at Trenton State Prison.

"There's only one way to stop worrying about Joey Zip. You gotta keep a cop around the house." Mick was smiling now. Making his move.

Jacqueline Chasen got the message. She thought it over without the slightest hint that she considered it an unreasonable suggestion. "I haven't . . . in a long time. While I was straightening myself out . . ."

"I'm in no rush. I've been wanting to meet you since I played lifeguard while you and your sister swam at Havens Beach back in the sixties. I remember you and your grandfather on the boardwalk—always in white."

Jacqueline Chasen stared and things connected. "You're the famous Mick O'Day!"

"Once upon a time," he said, concealing how much the words hurt. "I've got to take the car back for the next shift. I'll see you in about a half hour."

In exactly thirty minutes, Mick gunned his white 1970 American Motors Rebel, with a rebuilt engine that put it in the Lamborghini league, back to Leeds Point. Jackie Chasen was in a negligee in the master bedroom, which had a pair of sliding-glass doors onto a deck overlooking the ocean. The surf thundered on the sand, the northeast wind moaned like the voice of the devil in the dawn. Jackie lay on the bed, watching with obvious approval as Mick slung the shoulder holster with the Colt .38 in it on the back of a chair.

"Maybe fate is at work here," Jackie whispered as Mick lay down on the bed, his big body gleaming from the shower.

"Maybe," Mick said, untying the negligee, letting his hand curve down the firm belly to the warm hair, the liquid flesh beneath it. He believed in preserving the spirit of romance as long as possible.

"I've been wanting to meet someone who could take me back to the person I used to be. That girl in white on the boardwalk."

"Anything's possible," Mick said, though he had no desire to go back to that airheaded athlete on the lifeguard stand, the dum-dum who had fallen for Trai's brilliant smile in Binh Nghai.

"Oh. Oh," Jackie whispered as his finger found that special place. "I'm beginning to realize . . . how much I need a cop around the house."

It was a nice ending to a lousy night.

DAMSEL IN DISTRESS

Trai Nguyen Phac awoke to the sound of sleet slashing against the windows and metal walls of her mobile home. She was lying on the metal floor, curled in a fetal position. Waves of cold penetrated the cheap cotton blanket on which she lay as well as the blanket that she had pulled around her. A few feet above her in the narrow bed, her husband made odd sighing whistles when he breathed.

Trai always awoke at dawn, especially in winter. In the gray light, sadness seeped through her soul. She had dreamt again that she was back in Binh Nghai beside the river and Ha Chi Thien was making love to her. The air was thick and warm, the water gurgled through the reeds, and Ha whispered a poem against her throat.

In April, when the river rises again, will you remember
My hand on your heart?

In April when I am far away in the city
Of doubt and despair?

Trai wondered if Ha Chi Thien was still alive. Three
years ago, the newspapers had published a story about
him. Friends had smuggled some of his poems out of
Vietnam and published them in a book. They said he had
been jailed by the communists. He was in the Hoa Loa
Prison in Hanoi. Trai had wanted to buy a copy of the
book of poems, but Phac had said Ha was still a communist.

Father Nhu had said it was wrong for her to give herself
to Ha Chi Thien. God had sent her a baby to punish her
and then killed the baby to make her sorry for her sin. Trai
had never understood his argument. All the village girls
had little love experiments with men their age. Sometimes they had babies, but their families raised them. Perhaps Father Nhu meant it was wrong for her to give
herself to an outsider, a teacher from Saigon, like Ha Chi
Thien.

Later, when Ha's brother, Le Quan Chien, became the
Viet Cong district leader, Trai's love for Ha seemed an
even worse sin to Father Nhu. When he said mass in Binh
Nghai, he pointed to Trai on the bench beside her father
and called her an unclean woman. That meant she would
never marry. Father Nhu's interference filled Trai's father
with rage. He stopped believing in the Catholic God and
became a secret follower of Le Quan Chien, who said
God was a capitalist lie.

Sadness swelled in Trai's soul. It was bewildering that
so much evil could be born from an act of love, so much
ugliness from a moment of beauty.

Trai threw off the blanket and slipped her feet into rubber thongs. She hurried into the tiny kitchen and turned
on the oven. Soon warm air began to circulate. She began
boiling water for tea and frying bacon and eggs. She
thought it was disgusting food, but Phac insisted on eat-

ing it. Bacon and eggs was a favorite American dish.

Suong came into the kitchen, his face heavy with sleep. Some of the sadness in Trai's soul was replaced by joy. He was growing into such a handsome young man. He was going to be tall like his father. He was even more intelligent. He spoke beautiful American. "Morning, Mom," he said.

"Gude . . . morring." Trai liked being called that American name, even if she was not his mother.

Patiently, Suong made her repeat the phrase until she almost got it right. American was such a hard language. When war had invaded Binh Nghai in 1960, Ha Chi Thien had fled to Hanoi, leaving her pregnant. The VC killed the schoolteacher who succeeded him. Trai was never good in school anyway. She was always looking out the window at the sampans on the river. Ha Chi Thien had called her Miss Poppy Flower. He had asked her what she was dreaming about when she looked at the river. She said she dreamt of being a white swan, paddling through the reeds with her mate.

Trai poured a glass of orange juice from a carton for Suong. She put a dish of cornflakes—a collection of dried bread chips on which Americans poured milk—in front of him. Such awful food! But Suong loved it and grew tall and healthy on it.

Phac was awake. She heard the water running in the bathroom. Soon he came into the kitchen, wearing his fisherman's boots and rubber pants. A red woolen shirt covered his thin chest. He was so tall. When she first met him, he was the tallest Vietnamese man she had ever seen: six feet. Tall and thin, even back in Binh Nghai, with knobby wrists and ankles protruding from his black cotton clothes. He had the same angry look on his face then that he wore now.

"Good morning, Father," Suong said, staring at his cornflakes.

"Good morning," Phac said.

The sleet slashed against the windows and walls. In the

distance, they could hear the roar of the ocean. "Maybe they won't sail today," Trai said to Phac in Vietnamese. "The wind is so strong. There seems to be ice blowing on the wind. What do they call it?"

"Sleet," Suong said.

"Seet," Trai said.

Phac smashed her in the face. Usually Trai saw the blow coming and was able to raise her hand. But this time he caught her by surprise and her head whirled to one side so hard she thought her neck was broken. Even though Phac was thin, his arms were fearfully strong.

"Give me my food, cunt," he said in Vietnamese.

Suong glared at his cornflakes. Trai was afraid he would protest. That would only enrage Phac and lead to a worse beating later in the day.

"I'm so sorry," Trai said. "Did I say something wrong?"

"You are putting a curse on us. You want us to starve to death. If the boat doesn't sail, I won't get paid."

Phac was a Buddhist. He hated Trai's Catholic God. He believed in devils and evil spirits and had begun to think the ones that were tormenting him had come from the pope.

"You misunderstood me, dear husband," Trai said. "I was only concerned for your lungs. I lay awake for a long time last night listening to you breathe. You seemed to have a difficult time. The cold has gotten into your lungs and I—"

"Shut up and give me my food," Phac snarled.

Trai set the bacon and eggs in front of him and sat tensely at the table while he ate them. "I am so stupid," she said. "I never realize how important it is to think realistically. Soon you will have your own boat and you will be able to stay home if you choose on miserable days such as this one. I would cook you something tasty for lunch. We would have a pleasant time."

She was showing him that though she might be a cunt, she was a well-trained Vietnamese woman who was mistress of the art of *cong,* versatile ability in the home. Desperately, Trai clung to the hope that eventually her other gifts, *ngon,* soft speech, and *hanh,* gentle behavior, would soften Phac's bitter soul and make him glad he had decided to take her with him to America. If he let her buy the proper clothes and makeup, she might even regain *dung,* subtle beauty.

As soon as Phac finished the bacon and eggs, Trai sprang up and poured him a cup of tea. He gulped it without a word of thanks. "What are you learning in school today?" he asked Suong in Vietnamese. Phac too found American a difficult language.

"We are having mathematics and social studies this morning," Suong said. "We will study the history of the American Revolution, which happened two hundred and eight years ago."

"What about the Vietnamese Revolution?" Phac asked. His voice was bitter.

"Our teacher says we will study it later. We have many other wars and crises to study first. But he says there is a similarity between the American Revolution and the Vietnamese war. He says the Americans in Vietnam were like the British in 1776, fighting guerrillas they could not conquer."

"Tell your teacher he is spreading duck shit," Phac said.

"Oh?" Suong said, looking dismayed.

"Guerrillas in tanks. Tell him that is what conquered Vietnam."

"Maybe he could write an essay on it. You could help him," Trai said.

"Shut up, ignorant cunt," Phac snarled. He gestured to his cup and she poured him more tea. He gulped it again, although it was almost boiling. Perhaps he was trying to set himself on fire inside so he could endure the sleet and cold on the ocean.

"Ignore what I just told you," Phac said to Suong. "You must pretend to admire your teacher's wisdom. That way he will give you higher grades and you will have a better chance of a scholarship to the college of Princeton. A degree from there will enable you to become a rich man."

"Yes, Father," Suong said. Trai sensed that he did not believe this. He was learning more about America than Phac. It was such a confusing, complicated country. Men like Mick O'Day, who had strode through Binh Nghai like a god, who had fought the Viet Cong and smashed them, were not wealthy. An American policeman was paid little, and people did not give him presents and money like the police in Vietnam.

Mick still gazed at her with hungry eyes. He still remembered. But there was no forgiveness in those eyes. Sometimes Trai dreamt of him in her arms beside the river. It was different from the dream of Ha. There was deceit and evil in it. But there was also a kind of love. Such dreams only proved Father Nhu was right, she was an unclean woman. Perhaps when she prayed before the crucifix today, Jesus would come and console her.

Phac put on his yellow slicker and fisherman's hat. He pulled on thick gloves to keep his hands from freezing. "Good-bye, Son. Work hard today. I will do likewise."

"Yes, Father."

Every day for seven years Phac had said the same thing to Suong—every day since they had come to Paradise Beach after a year in the refugee camp in Hong Kong, where Phac could not work and the Vietnamese government demanded he be sent back to Vietnam to stand trial for murder.

Phac departed without even looking at Trai. She waited until she heard him start the old car, which Mick kept repairing for him. Then she got out some rice and poured *nuoc mam*, the pungent sauce made from sun-ripened fish, over it. She poured tea for herself and Suong and let him have a few bites of the rice. A taste of home.

He thanked her and then frowned at his empty dish of cornflakes. "I hate it when he hits you like that."

"I deserve it. I am a very ignorant woman. I've committed many sins. I am paying for them."

"I don't believe that! Everyone commits sins. Why do you have to pay for them all your life?"

"I don't know. Go study your lessons now until the school bus comes."

Suong retreated to his room. He arose in the dawn with his father because Phac insisted on it. He said it gave Suong more time to study. Suong complained that he did not have to study so much. He was already getting the highest marks in his class. But Phac told him to study anyway. Suong obeyed. He was the hope of Phac's life. His only surviving son.

Suong was why Phac had brought Trai with him from Binh Nghai. Their marriage had been entirely political. But he expected her to embrace Suong as her only chance to practice *phuc duc,* the creation of family strength through descendants. He knew how deep this instinct was implanted in her. She would be a good mother to Suong, no matter how much she hated Phac.

When Suong left for school, Trai cleaned the house. The other four rooms were freezing, but she cleaned them anyway, scrubbing the icy floors and walls, wiping the insides of the windows. Phac did not let her turn on the heat in these rooms because he was saving money to buy a boat of his own. He had saved almost $20,000 in seven years. It was extraordinary because his employer Desmond McBride paid him only $90 a week.

When she finished cleaning, Trai turned on the small television in the kitchen and listened to a man named Phil Donahue. He had a number of women on a stage; they talked about sex. That was an easy American word to understand. The Americans used it a lot. Trai was not able to understand what they were saying about it, but it seemed to be serious. One woman on the stage wept. Phil Donahue talked in a strange, rapid way. Trai could not understand a word of it, but it was all about sex. He waved his arms and rushed up and down asking people to talk into a microphone about it. The Americans were strange. No self-respecting Vietnamese man or woman would ever discuss sex in public.

A knock on the door. Who should be standing there in the blowing sleet but Father Philip Hart, the pastor of St Augustine's Church in Paradise Beach. Father Hart was tall like most Americans, but he had lost some hair, an oddity for a comparatively young man. He had a long, earnest face and a nose that turned up at the tip and pale blue, anxious eyes. He was not at all like Father Nhu, from Binh Nghai. He had been like a stern grandfather. Father Hart was like a worried brother.

"Trai—Mrs. Phac—how are you today? I just thought I'd drop in to see if everything was all right."

"Oh, all fine. All okey doke." With Father Hart, Trai relapsed into the pidgin she had learned when the marines had come to Binh Nghai.

"You're sure?"

"Oh, yes. Tea?"

"Why, thank you. I could use a little internal heat."

They sat down at the kitchen table. Father Hart talked about Vietnam. He did not approve of President Ronald Reagan's refusal to open diplomatic relations with the communist government. Father Hart thought Mr. Reagan was a terrible president.

If America had diplomatic relations with Vietnam, people like Trai and Phac might be able to go home. Trai nodded and smiled. She was obeying Phac's orders to agree with the Americans no matter what they said. The idea of Phac, a man with *Sat Cong,* "Kill communists," tattooed on his chest, going back to Vietnam was ludicrous.

Father Hart reached across the table and took Trai's hand. "Mrs. Kilgore told me what you revealed to her. About Phac beating you."

"Beat-ing?" Trai asked, although she understood.

Mrs. Kilgore was the social worker for the Catholic agency that had settled the Phacs in Paradise Beach. Mick was the reason they had come here. He had joked about "his village," which was also on the ocean, and when the refugee authorities in Hong Kong had asked if the Phacs knew any Americans, Trai had blurted out Mick's name and the name of the town. Phac, in his rage at the Americans, had forgotten it. Phac had wanted to go to France.

When Mrs. Kilgore had visited last week, she had amazed Trai by asking if Phac beat her. A study of Vietnamese refugees in Los Angeles had discovered a high percentage of wife beaters. Taken by surprise, Trai had admitted Phac beat her. She did not tell Mrs. Kilgore why.

Now, here was Father Hart, determined to put a stop to it. Trai was terrified. Phac was perfectly capable of killing her. She had seen him kill many people, men and women. She had seen him kill her own father.

"Oh, no." She smiled. "Is confusion. I . . . no understand."

"You mean you didn't understand Mrs. Kilgore? She asked if he hit you. Like this."

Father Hart slapped himself in the face. "You have a bruise on your cheek right now."

"Oh, no. Oh, no. Mistake. I bump face in dark."

"You're trying to protect him. You tell Mr. Phac I want to see him at the rectory tonight. I'm going to warn him if he so much as touches you again, he'll be on his way back to Vietnam."

"What? Oh, no," Trai gasped. She understood the word *back*. It had the clang of doom in it.

"You don't have to worry. You've got a friend here, Trai. A friend who cares about you and your country."

Father Hart talked about how much, how deeply, he cared for Vietnam. The more he talked, the more Trai saw that he was talking about a country that had never existed, except in his mind. His intentions were noble but his knowledge was nil, and the combination was deadly. Only one person could help her in this emergency. She dreaded even speaking to him, much less asking him for help.

Trai nodded and smiled as Father Hart wrote out the

request for Phac to come to the rectory. Suong could read it to him if he had trouble understanding it.

Father Hart squeezed Trai's hand again and departed. Trai flung on the cheap blue winter coat that the Catholic relief agency had given her and rushed into the wind and sleet. A half mile down the highway stood a lonely telephone booth. She was drenched and shivering violently by the time she reached it. On the way she had repeated the number over and over again. She dialed it and a woman's voice answered, "Hello?"

"Mick. Can I speak Mick?"

"He's sleeping. Who's this?"

"Oh, please. So—urgent."

It was a word Trai had heard on the Phil Donahue show.

In another minute, the deep voice spoke in Trai's ear. "What's up?"

For a moment, surrounded by the sleet-drenched American pine forest, Trai was flooded with incredible warmth. She was back in Binh Nghai, sitting in the doorway of her father's house, watching the big, yellow-haired marine saunter up and say those very words.

"Oh, Mick," Trai said in Vietnamese. "You must come see me right away. I'm in terrible trouble."

WELCOME TO PARADISE BEACH

Not bad for an amateur, eh? My friend the reporter, who is helping me write this tale, opines that by now you will be intrigued, hooked, sucked into what happens to everybody in this interesting clash between good and evil. He has begged me not to intrude my opinionated commentary.

The reporter, who yearns like every newshawk to become a novelist, believes the artist should stand outside the story à la James Joyce, cleaning his fingernails (or was it trimming them?). I say bushwah. I am writing history here, a yeasty slice of the American past—and a tragedy in the bargain. Moreover, in the marvelous way that America crosses breeds and mingles races, I am part of the story. Although I do not have a drop of Irish blood in my veins and can confidently trace my ancestry back to the first criminal who wandered to the wilderness of South Jersey, I have breathed the rank odor of this tragedy, tasted its brutal flavors, wept over its incredible mixture of heroism and stupidity, love and hate, sacrifice and venality.

Ultimately, like most historians, I am not telling a comprehensible tale. I am exploring a mystery. For the idiots among my readers who think history should be comprehensible, I recommend a close reading of the papers of the Continental Congress in the American Revolution. He or she will discover a tale of blunders, self-interested intrigues, blind idealism, and wild-eyed ignorance of military realities that will make our victory in this eight-year struggle totally mysterious.

In this excursion into the intricacies of Paradise Beach, I may even be creating a parable. Have you ever tried to make any sense—real sense—out of the parables Jesus told, or Buddha? They speak to the higher reaches of the soul, beyond the brain stem. Parables are necessarily opaque. If you stay with me long enough, you may become that most dolorous of beings, a metaphysician, searching in a darkened room for a black hat that isn't there.

I stole that line from G. K. Chesteron, the kind of hearty optimist and glib apologist for orthodoxy that I despise. That may give you a glimpse of my philosophy. If it does, that puts you one step ahead of me.

Alexander Oxenford is my name. I am better known to Mick and other patrons of Paradise Beach's premier bar, the Golden Shamrock, as the Professor. During the daylight hours, when I manage to maintain a precarious sobriety, I teach history at the Island Regional Senior High School in Paradise Beach. They don't call it history anymore, of course. It is now called social studies, a weird mixture of paeons to democracy and misinformation about everything from slavery to women's liberation.

I am a lineal descendent of Octavius Oxenford, who arrived on this impudent strip of sand between the Great Bay and the Atlantic Ocean about two hundred years ago. He was probably a deserter from the Continental Army of

George Washington. Family legend maintains that Octavius enlisted three or four times in various regiments to get the handsome bounty they paid the suckers to risk their necks for life, liberty, and the pursuit of happiness, freezing their toes and fingers off at Valley Forge and Morristown, while 99 percent of the population stayed home and made money.

You think our fondness for sending the dumbest and dullest to fight in Vietnam was an exception? Tell it to the poor Irish immigrants who were paid by heroic abolitionists in Boston to replace them in the draft for the Civil War. Either Octavius the first got wise to this scam or he felt the hot breath of the inspector general on his neck. At any rate he equipped himself with a complaisant camp follower and headed for South Jersey, where miles and miles of pine forests enabled a man to disappear with impunity.

There Octavius encountered a rabble of fellow deserters from both armies, wandering whores, and an occasional honest fisherman. The ex-soldiers supported themselves with a desultory combination of piracy and highway robbery. When the war ended, the more unregenerate among them wound up on the gallows, but Octavius reformed sufficiently to escape the noose.

Translating his doxy into a wife, Octavius began producing little Oxenfords. For the next century, their descendants settled into an Edenic existence. Fish flopped into their nets summer and winter, and ducks darkened the skies each spring and fall. Back in the pines, on the other side of the bay, it was a simple matter to build invisible distilleries that produced from the juice of apples and peaches a substance capable of inducing trances and hallucinatory states. Some people called it Jersey lightning.

Perhaps this trance state had something to do with the passivity with which my immediate forebears and their friends permitted some real estate developers from North Jersey to rename our town in the 1920s. From Havens Harbor it became Paradise Beach, a detestable moniker reeking of grandiosity, promotion, and the fast buck—the trinity of values that has made America what it is today.

The Oxenfords were mute witnesses of this debacle, as they have been of all the other catastrophes that have engulfed the continent, from the Revolution to the Civil War to the mass slaughters of our glorious century. For some reason we have never mastered the greatest of American arts—making money. Honesty was never our problem. We just never produced anyone with the ambition to get ahead. A skeptical streak inclined us to ask: Get ahead of what?

Perhaps that was why we welcomed with surprising tolerance the post–World War II arrival of Irish-Americans who came, not to pay the outrageous prices we charged the wealthier members of their tribe each summer, but to join us permanently as voters, neighbors, fellow inhabitants of Eden.

Like us, they seemed to have no strong desire to pile up mountains of pelf. Their priests, whom they brought with them, counseled resignation and acceptance of the world's cupidity and corruption. They also preached a sexual purity and an elevated view of women that we descendants of whores and buccaneers never espoused, except for a week or two in the fervor of a camp meeting.

They were fascinating creatures, these Irish-Americans, who called themselves Irish, a cognomen we readily accepted. They were knowing in one way that we, with our stubborn isolation and bizarre individualism, had never achieved. They were all politicians. It was born into them, a combination of clan spirit and a readiness to accept the monotony of the civil service. In five years, they had taken over the political apparatus of the town. We had an Irish-American mayor, an Irish-American police chief, and a mostly Irish-American police force.

In school I occasionally tried to teach them the truth about the ambiguous country to which their great-grandparents had emigrated. But they seldom listened. Their patriotism was as compulsive as their Catholicism. They did not know how to think about America anyway. Their minds were lost in a dream of somehow regaining the northern city they had ruled for forty years.

Few of them had ruled personally, of course. Others, shrewder or tougher, had grabbed most of the power and the cash. But they had all felt the pride, the swagger of ruling. Call it political or ethnic solidarity, call it atavism, it had been real. The proof was the existence of their chieftain, Sunny Dan Monahan, in his bright green house on Delaware Avenue. The rest of them lived in amateurishly insulated summer cottages, but Dan, with his green Cadillac at the curb and his hospitality on St. Patrick's Day, was proof that the years of glory had been real.

For forty years the Irish had ruled the other emigrants in their native city. They were led by a chieftain named Frank Hague, who summoned all the detritus of Emma Lazarus's incantation to the Statue of Liberty to join him in a titanic struggle to get their slice of American action from the smug bankers and the mealymouthed Protestant ministers who justified the WASPs' grasping supremacy. They had succeeded to an almost unparalleled degree. Frank Hague became as rich as any Wall Street tycoon and proportionate amounts of cash descended to some of his followers such as Sunny Dan, who ran Jersey City's waterfront Second Ward.

I have interrogated witnesses who saw Dan in his days of power, sitting in a railroad car on an obscure siding in Jersey City, while shipper after shipper, labor leader after labor leader, deposited mountains of money on a crude table, a door stretched over two wooden horses. On any day during payoff week, a half million dollars would be on that table. Most of it went down to City Hall, but Dan took his slice and, with the help of some gentlemen on Wall Street, put his share into bearer bonds—a wonderful device invented by the American banking community to permit people to steal money without the trouble of carrying it around. A bearer bond is, as the term implies, translatable into cash no matter who happens to possess it at any given moment.

When Hague's hegemony collapsed in the early 1950s, Sunny Dan had accumulated an astonishing number of these bonds. He took them south to Paradise Beach, where they enabled him to remain the chieftain and assured his daughters and sons-in-law that their future was rosy and that even their somewhat constricted present was capable of being gladdened by sudden infusions of cash.

Still, for Dan and his daughters and their spouses, a canker never ceased to gnaw in their well-fed bellies. Puny Paradise Beach could never be Eden for them. Nevermore could they roll up the killer majorities that had brought presidents and senators slavering to their doorsteps. But for their children—or some of their children—Paradise came close to living up to its extravagant name.

I am thinking now of Mick in the glorious summers of his prime. He would come floating into the Golden Shamrock around midnight and tell me about his latest conquest. It was the sixties, 1967 to be exact, and all the girlies were eager to discover the Experience in those BHA (Before Herpes & AIDS) days. I had played some part in freeing Mick from his compulsive Catholicism, enabling him to accept their eager offers.

My God, what a beautiful creature he was in those days. He sat on that elongated green lifeguard's chair at Havens Beach, the blond hair cascading to his shoulders, muscles rippling on his golden brown torso. He emitted sexual attraction with the intensity of an atom smasher spitting particles into a centrifuge. Nobody knew they were responding to something elemental, a piece of history emerging from the void with the same inconsistency atoms display to our baffled physicists.

Mick was a warrior, spawned by His Incomprehensibility in our supposedly modern world for reasons we cannot begin to understand. Maybe by the time I finish this story we will understand a few of them. But I doubt it.

One night in 1970 just before Mick went into the Marines, I hypnotized him in the Golden Shamrock when we were all drunk. I regressed him through several irrelevant lives, which included at least two deaths by starvation in Irish famines, back back into the Celtic mists where the Firbolg and the Tuatha da Danaan wandered and chanted and fought. He wailed a song in a language that no one in New Jersey had ever heard before. He crouched by a nonexistent peat fire to warm his hands and backside.

Then he stripped off his clothes and wound the bartender's rag around his neck in a remarkable approximation of a Celtic torc. The light of ancient battle fury danced across his face. Both hands gripped the hilt of an invisible sword, and he hacked and thrust and whirled it around his head exactly as his ancestors had wielded the weapon at Arretium in 285 B.C. where they annihilated a Roman legion.

Think about that while I relapse into the third person and get back into the story.

HOME THOUGHTS FROM ABROAD

As usual, the Aer Lingus 747 took the better part of forever to get its hulking immensity into the air. Dick O'Gorman felt sweat gluing his Taiwan-made undershirt to his Oxford Street shirt as he gazed down on Ireland through the inevitable gray drizzle. A line from William Butler Yeats caromed through his brain: What shall I do for pretty girls, now that my old bawd is dead? O'Gorman took a quart of Jameson from his flight bag, filled a paper cup to the brim with the brown whiskey of his native land, and drank it down in one swift swallow.

O'Gorman filled another cup and handed it to a scrawny, red-haired man in the seat next to him. He had an ugly set of bare patches in his hair, like mange on a cat. Billy Kilroy imitated the older man's dispatch of the Jameson and held out the cup for another round. O'Gorman filled it reluctantly. But he filled it. "We're on duty, you know," he said.

"Fook dooty," Billy said in the nasal whine of the

Belfast proletariat. In the dangerous alleys of the Bog-side, Billy was known as the Eye, for his ability to put a bullet through the slit of a Saracen tank with an ArmaLite rifle or in a man's head with a Zastava pistol.

It was going to be a desolate two weeks with this sod on his hands, O'Gorman thought gloomily. The IRA's chief of staff was still at it, making his life miserable.

The pilot began droning his message of phony reassurance to the passengers, telling them that they were trapped in his infernal machine for the next five and a half hours, during which they would hurtle over the wintry Atlantic at forty thousand feet with a tailwind pushing their ground speed to 620 miles per hour. Kilroy held out his cup again. O'Gorman filled it. The quicker the little back-talker shut his fabulous eyes, the better, as far as O'Gorman was concerned. But the liquor only seemed to make Billy garrulous.

"Why the fook we gawn to the States?"

"That's where the money is," O'Gorman said.

"I'd rather go to Sofia."

"Sofia is no longer an ally. The Russians have sold out them—and us—to extract their tits from the Afghanistan wringer."

This enormous fact did not even register on Billy's small brain. The staggering changes in the globe's political landscape since Russia's disastrous plunge into Afghanistan and the election of Ronald Reagan to the American presidency meant nothing to him. The world barely existed beyond the borders of Belfast, and even there he saw things through the telescopic sight of an ArmaLite. Compared to Billy and his kind, men with tunnel vision were broad-minded.

"Last time I was in Sofia, they gimmy this Bulgarian bitch. Christ, she had an ass as wide as a Saracen, but she made up for it with her mouth. Anything like that in America?"

"In American you have to persuade them."

"Fook that." Billy held out his cup again.

O'Gorman poured himself another drink too and pressed the oversize button that released his seatback. He sipped his whiskey reflectively, out of Billy's line of conversational fire.

Dick O'Gorman was good at persuading women—Irish, English, American, French, Italian. Even an Arab or two when he'd jetted to Beirut to promote an alliance between the Palestine Liberation Front and the Irish Republican Army. But he was not good at persuading the people who knew him best, the members of the IRA's ruling council. They went right on bombing and maiming and assassinating enemies real and imaginary. After thirty-six years he was thoroughly sick of the whole business.

More and more O'Gorman relived those months in 1972 when he and William Whitemore, the British secretary of state for Northern Ireland, had met almost every day to negotiate a settlement that would have made the IRA a powerful force in Irish politics, north and south. But the stony-eyed men around the chief of staff had found the mere idea of talking to a British politician treasonous. O'Gorman and Whitemore had been within days of an agreement when the orders to break the truce went up to Belfast and the bombs began exploding, the snipers' bullets whining again.

Now it was too late to negotiate. The world had made one of its incomprehensible turns. The governments that had pledged their allegiance to socialism, to the classless society of O'Gorman's youthful dreams, were floundering, while the resurgent capitalists gloated in London and New York, Bonn and Tokyo.

He should have quit in 1972 and gone to England with Moira and told the whole disgusting story to the newspapers. It would have put the IRA out of business in a month. Instead he let Moira go alone and sing her pathetic solo to the Brits. Sweet little Moira with her burning idealist's eyes and overheated thighs. The chief of staff himself had made a pass at her, the horny puritanical bastard, but she had belonged to him. To Black Dick O'Gorman with the belt of scars across his belly where a burst from a Sten gun had hit him during the first battle of Belfast in 1956.

He could still remember the pain that had raged in his body until whiskey and hypodermic needles quenched it. But it was not as acute as the pain that had coruscated through his mind in 1972 when his chance to become a political leader of international stature had vanished because his fellow revolutionaries had no ideas in their thick skulls beyond the one enunciated by the glorious, brainless Easter martyrs of 1916, the gun and the gun's best friend, death.

What should a man with a belly full of Sten-gun scars do about this discovery? Moira knew the answer. Walk. Tell the truth and stop the killing. But Moira did not understand Deirdre. His dear Deirdre of the Sorrows. It was she and her heroic lineage of IRA heroes who had seduced Richard O'Gorman, son of an English mother and a neutralist father, into the patriot game.

Since 1972, he had persisted in returning to Deirdre again and again for expiation and forgiveness. She was the only fragment of meaning he had left, his only link with mythical, mystical Ireland, the Kathleen Mavourneen of his student days. Perhaps he confessed his infidelities to her to avoid thinking about the other things on his conscience. The shopgirls blinded by the bombs on Drumlin Road. The informers kneecapped with Black & Decker drills.

O'Gorman remembered the chief of staff weeping, almost hysterical, in 1969, when he was told that they had shot two rural policeman, the first of hundreds. "What will happen to their wives and children?" he'd cried. That was the moment when Black Dick O'Gorman had decided the Englishman (as they secretly called him) was not tough enough to be chief of staff of the Provisional IRA. After all, what had he done besides spend eight

years in a British jug for getting caught stealing guns
from a military school? He had changed his name to the
Gaelic spelling and learned their mother tongue to pass
the time behind bars. But he still spoke Gaelic with an
English accent.

At the next meeting of the council, Black Dick had
made his move (after killing a bottle of Jameson to steady
his nerves). He had proposed Joe Cahill, a man who had
actually seen some fighting in Belfast, as chief of staff.
But the vote had gone humiliatingly against him. The
Englishman swiftly concluded he must never show emotion again—above all to "the Politician"—the nickname
he had instantly fastened on Dick O'Gorman, his enemy
unto death.

"Hey, come on, where's the stoof?" muttered Billy Kilroy, his cup empty once more.

O'Gorman refilled it again, resenting the way this little
Bogside twit talked to him.

They told him at headquarters to treat Billy like a wired
can of sodium chlorate, the marvelously potent explosive
the Russians had once shipped them from Prague. "Tip
him the wrong way and he could go off in your face," Joe
Cahill had warned his old friend.

Bad nerves were one thing. Billy's obnoxious assumption of superiority was another matter. Had they sent him
along to mind the Politician the way the Russians used to
send keepers when anyone about whom they had the
slightest doubt went abroad? That would be a hell of a
thing. Black Dick O'Gorman, fifty-four-year-old veteran
of the first Belfast offensive, former member of the Irish
Revolutionary Army Council (he was ousted by the chief
of staff the day after the 1972 truce blew up). A man of his
distinction guarded by a violent child like Billy Kilroy?
Could the chief stoop that low in his determination to
destroy him?

It was hardly the same war in Belfast these days. So
many of the old faces were gone, caught by Protestant

death squads in their houses or cars or walking home from a pub. The Prods had learned to imitate the IRA's tactics with incredible skill and savagery. Not really surprising. They were Irish too.

"How we gawn to get the money?" Billy muttered.

"Cocaine," O'Gorman said. "But we won't have to touch it. The Americans are going to handle it for us. The Cubans have got it all lined up. All we've got to do is stand around and look heroic for the sods."

"Didn't know they snorted mooch in Booston," Kilroy said. For him, like many Irish his age, the United States and Boston were synonymous.

"We're not going anywhere near Boston," O'Gorman snapped. "Don't you remember what you did in Boston?"

They had made the mistake of sending Billy to Boston four years ago, alone. He had gotten drunk and tried to rape the forty-five-year-old maiden daughter of the president of the Ancient Order of Hibernians. The Americans had poured him on a plane singing the "Internationale."

"I dawn't remember a bloody thing about that trip," Billy said defiantly.

"We're going to New Jersey. Down on the seashore. The Irish-Americans are still thick down there."

Billy's head drooped. In five minutes he was snoring. A small recompense for wasting a half bottle of whiskey on him. O'Gorman contemplated the mange patches on Billy's head. Joe Cahill said Billy got them from scratching his head too much. It looked as if the sod had clawed the hair out by the roots.

Suddenly Billy's legs shot straight out. His feet rammed into the seat in front of him, practically sending the occupant flying headlong into the cockpit. Billy was rigid. The sweat was pouring off him like a waterfall. O'Gorman could hear Billy's teeth grinding. His eyes were bulging under his squeezed lids. "Ah, naw," he was whimpering. "Naw. Naw. Naw."

Above the rear of the rammed seat rose the large gray

head of an outraged Irish-American tourist. "What the hell is going on?" he rumbled.

"I'm so sorry," O'Gorman said. "My son here is having a spell. We're taking him to the States to see the doctors."

THERE WILL ALWAYS BE AN ENGLAND

Through a fine mist, Captain Arthur Littlejohn of Her Majesty's Royal Yorkshire Rifles swung his red Triumph onto the ancient bridge over the river Ouse. Ahead of him were the sloping roofs of York, capital of his native province. In the center loomed the immense bulk of York Minster, the great cathedral, visible witness to God's transcendence.

For five centuries, Littlejohns had walked these twisting streets, worshiped in York Minster before it was lost to the Protestants, drunk toasts to the cleverness and wit of themselves and fellow Yorkshiremen beneath the splendid timberwork of the Merchant Adventurers Hall. Captain Littlejohn never missed an opportunity to visit York.

In a few minutes he was parking his car on the quiet side street a few steps from the regiment's Officers' House. New recruits were being drilled by a sharp-tongued sergeant on the smooth bricks of the parade ground formed by the House and the barracks. Upstairs in the anteroom, old friends were sipping port before the huge fireplace. A surge of nostalgia swept over Captain Littlejohn. For a moment he felt as if he had died and were returning to the scenes of his former life.

"Littlejohn, what a nice surprise," said Colonel Richard Hadley, holding out a slim, manicured hand. Simultaneously his cool gray eyes were studying the captain for signs of strain. No one spent a year in Northern Ireland without some strain.

"I've got a bit of leave. Thought I'd drop in on the family," Littlejohn said. "Just driving by so . . ."

"Of course, of course. How was it over there in Belfast?"

"Rum. But very enjoyable in the end. I found intelligence a fascinating business."

"That's more than I ever found it. But I was always on the receiving end. Always telling me there were twenty thousand bloody wogs out there in the jungle when it turned out to be twenty."

The colonel had helped suppress the communist insurrection in Malaya.

"We've gotten much better at it," Littlejohn said. "It's really the leading edge of the army these days."

"Oh? You sound like you've all but defected to them, old chap."

"They want me to stay on. At least for another assignment. I hope you won't object."

"Excitement. If I was your age, I'd probably feel the same way. Where will you be going?"

"America."

"Really? I don't imagine you can exercise certain privileges over there, can you?"

Colonel Hadley was recalling in fairly precise detail the request he had received from army headquarters. They wanted him to recommend one of his officers for detached duty in Northern Ireland. The brisk ADC at headquarters had added that the assignment would include an M-5 classification, a license to kill the enemy in ways that would at best be unorthodox and at worst might be illegal. The colonel had chosen Littlejohn because he was a Catholic and presumably had at least a glimmer of what was going on in an Irishman's head. He was also the best marksman in the regiment.

"The Foreign Office is working on a clearance," Littlejohn said.

Colonel Hadley felt a flicker of alarm. Something was wrong with the expression on Littlejohn's face. Was he starting to like shooting Irishmen in the middle of the night? That was not good for the service—or for Captain Littlejohn. But what could the colonel do about it? The icing was already on the cake. He was being given a taste in this visit—and all he was supposed to do was smack his lips and murmur, "Delicious."

An hour later, warmed by a Scotch and soda and some easygoing banter with old friends in the anteroom, Captain Littlejohn eased his Triumph to a stop in front of Hazelewood Hall. His mother was saying good-bye to a clump of Americans who had just completed their tour. There were about twenty of them, all middle-aged or older. Littlejohn saw nothing in their lumpy faces but vulgarity and self-satisfaction. Every time he thought of his mother shepherding these gawkers through rooms where he had eaten and slept and dreamt of a future dedicated to God's glory, Littlejohn had to suppress a terrific rage.

With impeccable grace, his mother kissed him on the cheek and introduced him to the tourists. She was looking older, but her face remained rich in the plangent beauty that had inspired his youth. Her tawny hair was still streaked with reddish gold, her lovely neck was as unlined as a girl's. In another time, she would have sat for Gainsborough or Sargent. But the barbarians who controlled the art world today were not interested in beauty.

"Arthur's been on duty in Northern Ireland," she said.

"Oh, yeah?" said one of the Americans, a hulking bruiser with a face Littlejohn had encountered a thousand times in Belfast. "If I'da known that, I wouldna paid my dough. My name's McCafferty."

"My name's Maloney," said another man, taller and more mild-mannered. "It doesn't bother me at all. You've got a lovely home here, Captain. Thanks for telling us so much about it, ma'am."

"You're quite welcome," said Amanda Littlejohn, the eighteenth Lady Moorfield.

The Americans trooped toward their bus, McCafferty arguing violently with Maloney.

In the timbered entrance hall, beneath the portraits of a dozen notable ancestors, his mother took Littlejohn's hand. "Shall we make a visit?" she said. "I'd very much like to thank Him for your safe return."

They walked through the sixty-foot-long dining room, with its mahogany table at which a dozen kings had supped, to the chapel beyond it. The small stone room, the oldest structure in Hazelewood, displayed the bare, powerful architecture of the crusader chapel in Jerusalem. Mass had been said here almost daily since 1239. They knelt together, as they had knelt since Arthur Littlejohn was a boy. But were they praying together? For the first time in his life, Littlejohn doubted it.

His mother was thanking God for her son's return from a land of murder and mayhem. He was thanking God for keeping the IRA's best car bomber, Jimmy O'Hara, that extra five minutes in the house with red-haired Peggy O'Dowd, who they had paid £500 to betray him. Captain Littlejohn was thanking God for giving him a steady hand and a cold heart when at the last minute Peggy had changed her mind and screamed a warning. That gave him a license to kill her too. It was much neater that way. He might have killed her even if she had not screamed. But God was good enough to provoke a scream and solve a nice question of conscience.

The captain did not thank God for protecting him from the fusillade Jimmy O'Hara fired at him with his AK-47. Whether Arthur Littlejohn lived or died was entirely up to God and a matter of utter indifference to him. That was part of the bargain he had made with God. It was a good bargain. It had enabled him to become the most effective special-intelligence officer in the British army.

An hour later, bathed and unpacked, Littlejohn sat with his mother in the Nook, the small study off the great hall. On the wall above the fireplace was one of the most popular paintings of Victorian England, *When Did You Last See Your Father?* It portrayed a young boy being interrogated by frowning Puritans during the English Civil War of the 1640s. The boy might have been a Littlejohn. After the battle of Marston Moor, which was fought only a few miles from Hazelewood Hall, the Littlejohns had been on the run, living in the woods and in peasant cottages.

Now, with the sort of irony that history seems to favor, Captain Littlejohn was playing the interrogator, asking similar questions of eight-year-olds in Ireland. But their answers were not the polite evasions of the frightened boy in the painting.

We wants the army out. We'll stone 'em out and burn 'em out and murder 'em and tar and feather 'em. They're gestapo. They're pigs. There's no bacon in England because all the pigs is here. We'll give the bastards cheap haircuts. We'll melt 'em down into rubber bullets. We'll gelignite 'em. Do you 'ear me? We'll gelignite the limey bastards.

That was the answer Littlejohn had got from Jimmy O'Hara's eight-year-old son when he was asked if he had heard from his father lately.

"I've invited Alice to dinner."

"Oh, good."

"I really do think it's time you married, Arthur."

"I'm afraid it's out of the question as long as I'm on these special assignments."

"Alice is not going to wait forever. She's close to thirty, Arthur."

For a moment Littlejohn almost told her the Secret. His vow of celibacy. But he could not quite manage it. She wanted grandchildren so badly.

He had intended to be a priest since he was thirteen. He

had confided his ambition to Father Kinsella, the rector of Stonyhurst, the Jesuit preparatory school. With no warning, the day before he returned to Stonyhurst for his senior year, his father informed Littlejohn that he was going in the army. There had been a Littlejohn in the Yorkshire Rifles since 1745. Arthur had told his father he wanted to be a priest. His father had dismissed his vocation with a wave of his hand. He had never been very religious. "The army's not that much different from the Jesuits," he said.

Arthur had been filled with cold anger. He had walked to the family chapel and taken his vow of celibacy before the tabernacle. He knew it was a promise that any confessor would dismiss, virtually on request. It was a gesture of retaliation, almost of disobedience, against a father who was now dead. But he could not let go of it. In Ireland the vow had acquired a meaning that went deeper than his understanding of it. Somehow it had become part of his personality, part of the inner gyroscope that steadied him in moments of danger or stress.

Alice arrived. She had come up from London on the train the previous night. She was working for the BBC. She was his mother's opposite, small, dark, compact, her hair in a pageboy on her forehead. His mother left them alone in the Nook while she caught up on her correspondence with the Tourist Board.

"You look peaked," Alice said.

"I am a bit. You don't get much sleep in intelligence."

"That must make it difficult."

"What do you mean?"

"To be intelligent. I presume that's why you're in it."

"The old brain does creak a bit."

"Anything else?"

"Creak? Oh. My conscience, sometimes. For not writing."

"I'm not talking about that. You never have written. The year you spent in Hong Kong, I got exactly one letter. I mean about the things you're doing in Ireland."

"I can't talk about that."

"I don't mean your work. I mean the whole operation. Shooting women and children."

"The troops get out of hand now and then. But that's not policy. We only fire when fired on."

A lie. But an official lie was not the same as a personal lie. The Jesuits had taught him that. His father had been right about one thing. The army and the Jesuits did have a lot in common.

"We've been working on a documentary at the BBC. I've seen footage. It's so beastly."

"You mean the IRA bombs. I should say."

"I mean the whole thing. I think we should withdraw and let them fight it out. I found a wonderful quotation from Shaw."

"Oh?"

"'After all, what business is it of the British if we Irish want to slaughter each other? They were glad to have us slaughter their enemies when they needed us.'"

"Doesn't make much sense, does it?"

"I think it makes marvelous sense."

"Makes me glad I didn't go to Cambridge. They didn't teach Shaw at Sandhurst."

"Perhaps they should."

"Perhaps."

"I'm going with someone. A producer from the BBC named Dolan. He wants me to marry him. Should I say yes?"

"I didn't know they had Irish at the BBC."

"His family's been in England for fifty years."

"Well . . . I won't let any understanding we have—"

"Father's upset. He sent me an army motto: 'Money lost—little lost; honor lost—much lost; heart lost—all lost.'"

Her smile was forced. Alice's father was the former colonel of the Yorkshire Rifles. He had been even more instrumental than Amanda Littlejohn in fostering the engagement to Alice. Littlejohn sensed that all he had to do was take Alice's hand and this BBC Irishman would evaporate. But he could not make the gesture. He sat there, frozen, his mind slipping out of Hazelewood Hall, across the Irish Sea to bomb-ravaged Belfast.

His mother beamed in the doorway. "I hope you've had time to lay some deep-dyed plans," she said. "Dinner's ready."

The meal was a struggle. Littlejohn's mind had shifted into doublethink, the intelligence mode. He was talking on one level to his mother and Alice about the royal family's latest scandal, the future of the Liberal Party, while the other half was analyzing data. Was the Irishman at the BBC part of the apparatus? Were they trying to harass him by taking his fiancée away from him?

He realized now that Alice was important to him. She was a reward that awaited him after a long upward struggle, as at the Irish shrine at Knock, where the pilgrims ascended the mountain on their knees. He was a pilgrim struggling toward some sort of illumination that would include Alice's generous arms. Now they had taken her away. The stage was bare, leaving him in bitter soliloquy.

It made him almost regret the information that was sending him to America. It had begun with a rumor picked up in a pub by an informer, confirmed by a second informer, who was supposedly in deepest cover. But it would never have become solid enough to send him to America if Littlejohn had not confirmed it personally in one of his reconnaissances.

Littlejohn fondled that word in his mind. No one knew about his reconnaissances. Sometimes he thought God did not know about his reconnaissances. The things he did on reconnaissance were not done by Captain Arthur Littlejohn. They were the acts of another person, an ur-soul brewed out of terror and Irish mist. His reconnaissances took him into the deepest, deadliest parts of Belfast and Londonderry, into Bogside whorehouses and pubs where a British officer would be killed in the slowest, most painful way the IRA's diseased minds could devise.

There he had confirmed the information from their own beery, unsuspecting tongues. And reconfirmed it with his favorite prostitute, blond, bitter Maeve Flanagan. The IRA was about to buy a million dollars' worth of sophisticated weapons in America. They were sending two of their best men to handle the operation. Aside from the desperate need for the weapons, they wanted to prove their boast of new American cooperation. It would have its usual magical impact on the waverers and quitters in the Belfast ranks.

"Arthur." His mother blinked back tears. "Alice tells me you've decided to break your engagement."

Even now, he saw that all he had to do was feign surprise, laugh, and protest that Alice had misunderstood him—and they could set a wedding day. But again, he could not speak. He wanted to see if she was part of the murderous game he was playing.

"It seemed the best thing to do under the circumstances."

America was going to be very interesting.

A THOUSAND WELCOMES, ALMOST

"Well, well, well, well," Hughie Mc-Ginty said, showing his crooked, yellow canines. "Old times, old times indeed, Dick."

"Old indeed," said Richard O'Gorman, raising his glass.

"Slainte," said Desmond McBride, making the word sound like a TV ad for a mouthwash. He had already mangled beyond repair the Gaelic for a thousand welcomes. McBride was the mayor of Paradise Beach, the dismal shore town to which they would soon be transported. He was a smiling vacuum, one of those American lightweights who thought they knew all about Ireland because they had visited it two or three times for a total of six weeks and had an Irish grandmother who mispronounced a half dozen Gaelic phrases.

McGinty was a colleague from the early days in Belfast. He had lacked the stomach for the bombing and had decided to walk. They had let him go without prejudice, believing he could be useful in America. But he was neither a likable nor a trustworthy fellow. A whiner from start to finish.

There should have been a third welcomer—even a fourth—whose absence set O'Gorman's teeth on edge. McBride's son was the link between the IRA's leadership and the rest of the scheme. He worked for a congressman from New Jersey who was close to Senator Teddy Kennedy.

All things considered, the congressman should have been present too. Maybe even his spherical friend, Senator Ted. After all, O'Gorman was a man who had sat down to couscous in Yasir Arafat's tent and talked world historical balderdash with Che Guevara. Certain former members of the Irgun, the Israeli terrorist group, also spoke of him with respect.

Yet in America, the handful of Irish politicians who supported the IRA did so behind closed doors, through third and fourth parties, as if they were dealing with moral lepers who could infect them with that most fearsome of American political diseases—the loss of a voting bloc. Gone were the days when Irish-Americans rose in the Senate of the United States and roared, *"Britannia delenda est."* In the first place, there weren't five people in the country who could get the reference, thanks to America's abysmal school system. In the second place, once it was translated, the British propaganda machine would serve the speaker up, macerated and broiled on TV for breakfast the following morning.

All of which meant that if Black Dick had to forgo the pleasures of celebrity, he was determined to console himself with another pleasure, which was unquestionably available in Babylon on the Hudson. The great metropolis blinked its millions of inviting eyes at them through the bar's twilit front window. But they might as well already be incarcerated in Paradise Beach, as far as responding to these enchanting signals was concerned. There had to be a way to lose these two millstones and give him and Billy at least a single night of pleasure.

"I think it's time we discussed our plans," McBride said. "McGinty and his fine friends have kept me more or less in the dark. He said the final orders had to come from you."

"Oh, it's very simple," O'Gorman said. "The Cubans are bringing a million and half dollars' worth of cocaine with them. We're going to sell the dope to your brother-in-law O'Toole's Italian friends and run the money out to the Cubans and get the weapons. It'll all be said and done in twenty-four hours."

"Cocaine?" McBride said. "I've never heard a word about cocaine before. If something went wrong—if the Coast Guard—we could all go to jail for twenty years."

"It's a goodly stretch you'll get if they find you with the weapons," O'Gorman said. "You agreed to bring them ashore. The cocaine is just a detail."

"I thought you were bringing the money," McBride said. "Didn't you say that?" he asked McGinty.

"I said I hoped he would," McGinty said.

"We don't have a tenth that much cash in the whole command. This is a big shipment of weapons. The biggest yet."

"Does Bill O'Toole know about the cocaine?" McBride asked.

"I should say he does," McGinty said. "He handled the whole thing with the Italians. He's lined up one of their high rollers from Atlantic City. The fellow owns half the boardwalk, Bill says."

"I don't want to hear any more about the cocaine," McBride said. "You can use my boat, but I don't want to hear any more about it."

In Ireland, McBride had promised them his boat and himself as captain and navigator. Was the deal about to fall apart? McGinty let O'Gorman take charge.

"Well and good, well and good," O'Gorman said. "We can understand how you feel, Des. We're still grateful and then some, right, Billy?"

"Yah," Billy said, his nose in his drink. Even his pea

brain could see it was too early to put pressure on this papier-mâché hero.

"How's Nora?" O'Gorman asked McGinty.

"Just fine. We've got two lovely kids."

"Good news."

Sweet little Nora, the rose of Kilwickie. In 1975, she owned the softest rump, the juiciest knockers, in the Six Counties. O'Gorman had passed her on to McGinty somewhat the worse for wear. That was part of the reason for the anguish in Hughie's voice.

O'Gorman liked the whine of supplication that only he could hear. It meant McGinty knew that if things went awry, Dick O'Gorman could arrange to have a killing machine like Billy Kilroy on a plane to America in twenty-four hours. That was always implied in their original arrangement to let McGinty walk in good health, unkneecapped, with both eyes still in his head.

You wouldn't kill a man with two lovely kids, would you, Dick? That was what McGinty was saying. He knew it was a waste of breath, but he said it anyway. Irish.

"If we get going, we can be in Paradise Beach for dinner," McBride said. "It's only two hours from New York. We get quite a lot of New Yorkers in the summer."

In the winter, O'Gorman thought, you get penguins and seals, neither of which will be inclined to cooperate with what Kilroy and I need to ease our distress.

"I was thinking of staying the night," O'Gorman said. "There's some people in the Irish Mission at the UN that are looking for a word from me."

"Them fookers can wait," Billy said. "The weapons is more important."

"The weapons won't be seen for weeks perhaps," O'Gorman said. "The Cubans have very little use for schedules."

"I don't like doing business with communists," McBride said to McGinty. "I thought you said the guns were coming on a Japanese freighter."

"So I did, so I did," McGinty said. "It would have been

a better dodge, wouldn't it. But the Japanese wanted tons of money. The Cubans are providin' the ship free of charge. In this business you sometimes have to make bargains with the devil."

He glared at O'Gorman. "Thank God for Ireland's faith. With it for protection we can dance with the devil without a bit of fear, right, Dick?"

"Right."

O'Gorman did not know who infuriated him more, McGinty with his drooling religiosity or Kilroy with his sudden assumption of command. Between them they were going to let Ellen O'Flaherty, redhaired and worshipful, pine by the telephone at the Irish Mission. She had begged him to call her after the recruiting weekend they had spent together in Mayo. He was only two years behind schedule.

"Shall I get the car?" McBride said.

"By all means. The Irish Mission can wait. First things first," O'Gorman said.

The moment McBride left the room, McGinty all but sprang at O'Gorman's throat. "Jesus, Mary, and Joseph. Don't you know better than to talk about the motherless Cubans in front of a Yank? They're still the communist enemy, for Christ's sake."

"We oughter change their minds about that," Billy said. "They oughter know we'd be left thrown potatoes at the fookin' Saracens if it wasn't for the Bolshies."

"You're not gonna change their minds, so skip it," McGinty said. "Take my advice, skip it entirely."

"Did you get that message, Commander?" O'Gorman said.

"I got the message that you need watchin'," Kilroy said. "You ain't off the plane four hours and you're chasin' snatch."

Someone in Sofia or Belfast had fumigated Kilroy's brain. He had acquired the trappings, if not the essentials, of intelligence. Even more incredible, the brainwashers had convinced him he was worthy of respect. It almost made a man believe in indoctrination.

They exchanged telephone numbers with McGinty. He told them to rely on O'Toole, the police chief at Paradise Beach. He was tough and dependable. McBride was necessary because he owned the boat. He had been recruited in Dublin on his last visit to Ireland but was, as anyone could see, a timid fish. He would have to be handled with care.

"Right, right," O'Gorman said, jet lag gnawing at his nerves.

They said good-bye to McGinty and crawled into McBride's green Cadillac. He inched out of New York in the rush-hour traffic. It took them an hour to get through a tunnel under the Hudson River. On the other side they picked up speed and were soon zooming along an overpass surrounded by decrepit houses and random church steeples. It looked like a city that God had forgotten.

McBride lectured them on the glorious political past of this decaying metropolis, called Jersey City. Here the Irish had ruled for decades. Now it was in the hands of the Italians and the Poles. It made no sense whatsoever to O'Gorman. He gazed longingly at the soaring skyscrapers of New York on the other side of the Hudson. Ellen O'Flaherty, what I wouldn't give for a touch of your willing thighs.

McBride talked on. The jet lag gnawed. O'Gorman was tired of being transported. He seemed to have spent his entire life being transported from airports, train terminals, bus stations, while some foreigner talked at him, presuming he understood why the Lebanese hated Gemayel or the Libyans adored Qaddafi or the Algerians yearned for the return of Ben Bella. It all came down to boredom and transportation. Some earlier ancestor, perhaps transported in chains to eighteenth-century Georgia or Australia, must have left an antipathy for the word in his genes.

Soon they were hurtling down an immense highway called the New Jersey Turnpike. It had six lanes on either

side, and the cars and trucks drove like the devil and all his
angels were crawling up their exhaust pipes. The trucks
were gigantic roaring monsters that looked as if they could
thunder over a car without even noticing it. McBride drove
blithely beside one whose wheels were so huge, they were
spinning at the height of the car's windows.

"Holy Jesus," Billy said in the backseat. He was shaking all over. It was the roar of the truck motors. It was taking him back to Belfast, to the sound the Saracens made
in the streets. "Holy Jesus, can we stop somewheres and
get a drink?" he cried, the sweat pouring down his
scrawny cheeks.

"There's a bar back there," McBride said, and told
Billy how to liberate it from its hiding place inside the
seatback. Billy downed a whole glass of something and
passed a half up to O'Gorman. It was Scotch. Good stoof,
as Billy would say. They hurtled on, past a landscape full
of dark factories emitting the most god-awful stench
O'Gorman had ever inhaled. He put his nose in his
whiskey to escape it.

"You'd swear they forgot to bury a fookin' British regiment," Billy said.

They finally escaped the stench, and after another hour
of boredom on a parkway mercifully free of trucks, they
purred sedatcly down the broad streets of Paradise Beach.
The place was not quite as deserted as O'Gorman had
feared it would be. There were plenty of automobiles,
many of them quite expensive looking. The houses were
all well painted. Prosperity had apparently come around
the corner some time ago. McBride eased to a stop in
front of a large, green corner house with a substantial
lawn around it. "Here's where you'll be staying," he said.

Inside, he introduced them to his father-in-law, Dan
Monahan, a tall, shriveled old man on a cane, almost
totally bald and not a little gaga. "Always glad to see a
friend from Ireland," he said. He repeated it three times as
if they were deaf or stupid. "Barbara?" he called. "Meet
my daughter Barbara O'Day."

Out of the kitchen, wearing tan slacks and a white blouse and an apron that said *Three Cheers for the Cook* came a smiling redhead with a sexy swinging walk and a figure to match it. She was no youngster but neither was he, O'Gorman reminded himself. She held her head high and smiled boldly into his eyes. "I've always wanted to meet a real Irishman," she said.

Paradise Beach might be well named, after all.

LONG LIVE THE REVOLUTION

Braking, double-clutching, changing lanes without even a blink of a tail-light, Melody Faithorne thrust the red Ferrari through the swarming rush-hour traffic at the southern end of the New Jersey Turnpike with the insouciance of a Formula 1 champion. Beside her in the death seat, Leo McBride chomped a mouthful of Maalox to dull the twinges in his aching stomach. "Take it easy," he said. "They'll wait for us."

Melody ignored him. She shot around a sixteen-wheeler, hurtled past a Dodge van crammed with middle-aged commuters, and cut back two lanes to pass another sixteen-wheeler on the right. The trucker gave her a blast of his horn. Melody dangled her delicate wrist out the window and replied with an upturned middle finger.

Leo McBride gazed ruefully at his wife. She was wearing one of her sixties specials, torn blue jeans and a faded denim workshirt. Her flower-petal face was devoid of makeup. Yet the glossy blond hair, the breasts pressing against the shirt, stirred desire in his groin.

"Let's get one thing straight," Leo said. "No fooling around with this guy."

"Black Dick O'Gorman?"

"Yeah. Didn't you tell me he was famous for his sex appeal?"

"I don't remember saying any such thing."

"Maybe I read it in the CIA report on him."

"Now you're getting me interested."

"Melody. I mean it. I won't let you embarrass me in front of my parents, my relatives. It's a capital no-no. I'm serious."

"Do I complain when you prowl?"

"I haven't prowled since Jennifer what's her name in London—two years ago."

"Poor dear. I'm using you up? Is that your complaint?"

"It's a nice complaint," Leo ruefully admitted.

"There's something else a lot more important to get straight: deniability. I want you to drill it into your clunk-headed relatives' heads. They never heard a word from us about this gambit. In no way, shape, or form can it be linked to the senator."

"But it's okay to ruin the congressman?" Leo snarled.

"Of course not. He's out of the loop too."

"Gee, thanks."

Melody worked for Senator Teddy Kennedy. At times Leo wondered if she did more than work for him. She was one of the girls who had been partying on Chappaquiddick Island the night the senator drove Mary Jo Kopechne off a bridge and himself into becoming a political pariah outside Massachusetts. Leo had tried more than once to get Melody to tell him what had really happened on that historic night. But her lips were sealed, even to her husband, even when she was sloshed or high.

Melody's status as a Chappy girl guaranteed her a job for life in the Kennedy apparatus. That suited her perfectly. Having graduated first in her class from Wellesley in 1969 and first again from Yale Law in 1972, she had absolute confidence in her destiny. She was born to raise hell, publicly and privately. The sixties zinged in her bloodstream and she was still determined to make the rest of America get the revolutionary message—or else.

Leo McBride had met Melody at Yale Law, to which he had fled to escape sudden death in Vietnam. In the hyper-temperature of her acrobatic bed and neo-Marxist head, his summa cum laude Georgetown diploma had turned into Silly Putty. For a while Leo was only one among a circle of lovers. But his persistence and a certain ability to cajole her into the wisdom of playing the political game in order to accomplish revolutionary goals had won Melody's grudging attention.

Melody was even more impressed when Leo landed a job in Congressman James Mullen's office with his grandfather's help and swiftly became Mullen's chief of staff. Along with screen-star good looks, Leo had a natural ability to flatter and persuade. He was also a drudge—a combination that virtually guaranteed success on Capitol Hill.

When Mullen rose to the chairmanship of the powerful House Appropriations Committee, Melody decided an entente should be sealed with a wedding ring. Henceforth, if Senator Kennedy or one of his friends wanted anything from Washington's cornucopia of political pork, Leo saw that it got pushed through the committee, no matter how malodorous it was. The senator frequently used the connection to persuade other solons into voting his way on the liberals' agenda. Mullen, a moderate Democratic, seldom objected.

As his reward, Leo McBride got Melody every night—theoretically. But he had signed aboard an open marriage, and he soon discovered that Melody was more inclined to play the field than spend much bed time with her husband. At first he had retaliated with liaisons of his own, but his Irish-American psyche found little satisfaction in these one-and-two-night stands—and he was further wilted to discover that Melody did not give a damn.

Only one thing mattered to Melody—the oncoming triumph of the world revolution against capitalism, which would usher in an era that guaranteed abundance, gender equality, and the pursuit of sexual freedom for everyone. She was undeterred and undiscouraged by the election of Ronald Reagan. She dismissed him as a dotard and an airhead and remained ferociously committed to supporting what she called "vanguard movements" everywhere. This was not difficult, working within the aura of the Kennedy name. If she managed to get the word *liberal* into Senator Ted's head, he was ready to endorse almost anything.

"You don't have to worry about anyone from Paradise Beach shooting off their mouths," Leo said. "They're used to keeping their traps shut. It's part of the code."

"Oh, I forgot. The wonderful code. The existence of honor among your ancestral thieves."

Pain gyrated in Leo's stomach. At times he grew weary of Melody's contempt for Irish-Americans and their politics. From her *Mayflower*-descended viewpoint, the Irish were nothing but a tribe of crooks. The quicker their remnants were expunged from the nation's politics, the better. She carefully concealed this opinion from Senator Kennedy, of course. His Harvard diploma and his blind devotion to the tenets of liberalism gave him a temporary exemption from extinction. But she made no secret of her generic detestation when she was alone with her husband.

More than once, Leo had tried to convince Melody that the old Democratic Party and its political machines were not all bad. Their ability to steal elections had put John F. Kennedy in the White House. Their solidarity had provided a haven, a sense of community, in the urban wilderness. Melody had dismissed his argument with a sneer. She had called him a sentimental recidivist, an atavist.

"Now that we're into rule making, here's one for you," Leo said. "No booze. You tend to shoot off your mouth too much after three drinks."

"Yes, dear."

One of the more unpleasant surprises of his marriage

was Melody's fondness for hard stuff. Her Boston-born mother and father were two of the worst drunks Leo had ever met. It explained why they barely had a nickel left in their trust funds. At the moment they were living aboard a cabin cruiser in Fort Lauderdale—the last piece of property they owned.

"I mean it, Melody!"

"I *promise*."

Encouraged by this concession, Leo could not resist renewing his criticism of this latest collaboration with the IRA: "I'm still not enthusiastic about giving these micks surface-to-air missiles."

Melody had put the deal together through her contacts with the IRA's American front groups and clandestine Cuban agents operating out of their UN mission in New York. She had persuaded Leo to approach his father and arrange a meeting with an IRA spokesman during his annual pilgrimage to Ireland. Leo had reassured Desmond McBride that loaning one of his boats was a noble, even a patriotic, gesture of support for a good cause.

Too late, Leo learned that the scale of the operation was far beyond the usual few hundred rifles and grenades and ammunition that IRA sympathizers bought from gun merchants—many of whom turned out to be FBI agents in disguise.

"Why not?"

"I'm afraid they'll use them on civilian planes."

"As long as they're British, who cares?"

"Your lack of interest in history is one of your primary flaws, Ms. Faithorne. Did you ever hear of the *Lusitania?* When the Germans sank that ship in 1915, they killed a hundred and twenty-eight Americans—and turned the United States against them. The same thing could happen if there were Americans on any British plane the IRA shot down."

"The IRA will issue a warning to stay off British planes. Any Americans who choose to fly on them will be doing so at their own risk."

"The Germans issued a warning like that just before the *Lusitania* sailed."

"Oh, go fuck yourself and your historical research. Nobody gives a damn what happened seventy years ago."

Melody pressed the pedal to the metal and the Ferrari accelerated to a 110 in sixty seconds. She knew exactly how to unravel Leo. He chewed another Maalox and struggled for some usually unreachable level of calm.

"I've been doing research on the history of the IRA. This habit of blowing people up is an Irish-American idea. They picked it up from German anarchists in Chicago in the 1880s. When they went to Ireland and proposed it to John O'Leary, founder of the Irish Republican Army, he said there were some things a man must not do for his country."

"Are you related to him?" Melody said. "That sounds like one of your noble-sounding wimpish ideas."

"The Irish-Americans ignored him and started blowing up London with nitroglycerin and dynamite. It was a public relations disaster. When they attacked the House of Commons, the U.S. Senate passed a resolution condemning them by a vote of sixty-one to one."

"So? Wimps obviously predominated in those days."

"They lost the support of most of the Irish-Americans too."

Melody zoomed past a half dozen sedans plodding along at the legal fifty-five. "The IRA doesn't need mass support," she said. "It's a vanguard organization. All they need is the backing of a handful of wealthy or politically well-connected people to disrupt the British repression machine. Once that's accomplished, they'll devote their energies to leading the Irish people."

"Stuff," Leo said. "Whenever they run a candidate in the south, he gets about two percent of the vote."

"That's because the capitalist government of the south hasn't been disrupted—yet. They'll get to that as soon as they acquire power in the north."

"Bullshit. I'm beginning to think your revolutionary

dreams are the political equivalent of smoking dope."

"You son of a bitch!"

With the speedometer at 105, Melody slammed on the brakes. The Ferrari fishtailed all over the highway. The stench of burning rubber poured into the interior as the tires virtually disintegrated. Leo writhed in his seat as sudden death unmanned him.

They wound up sideways in the breakdown lane. Through a haze of terror, Leo heard Melody screaming, "What I care about doesn't matter, is that it? I'm just another hysterical woman, is that it? A stupid cunt who gets her way on her back, is that it? Your great male brain, packed with historical bullshit, should be our censor and guide, is that it?"

"No—nothing of the sort," Leo mumbled.

Tears were streaming down Melody's china-doll face. In some part of Leo's brain beneath the level on which he had been trying to operate, he knew this was a performance, the ultimate resort by which Melody always got her way. But he was helpless to resist it. For the thousandth and first time, he surrendered.

"You know I love you. You know—I'm just as committed," he said. "But giving these things some thought—"

"Thought. No one ever got anywhere on thought. Acts are what win wars. Acts are what change the course of history."

What about old Karl Marx? He never performed an act in his entire life. Unless you call taking another book off the shelf at the British Museum an act. The subterranean Leo was still there. But he was helpless, extinguished, if not quite extinct, by the combination of pity and pathos and sexual promise that was engulfing him.

Leo got out and examined the Ferrari's tires. They had lost some treads but their air was intact. They resumed their journey to Paradise Beach at a more subdued pace.

"The next exit," Leo said.

Melody spun the Ferrari into the exit lane, passing a pickup truck on the right. Leo handed her the money for the toll and they roared down the long, straight road through the pines at a swift but not quite suicidal pace. In twenty minutes, the 240-horsepower motor purred to a stop in front of Sunny Dan's faded-green mansion. Leo left their bags in the car—they were sleeping at his parents' house—and followed Melody up the steps.

Inside, they were greeted by a party in progress. Sunny Dan was in his BarcaLounger, a brown bourbon and water in his hand. In the corner sat Leo's first cousin Mick, looking morose as usual. A nice combination of guilt and family solidarity had prompted Leo to offer his services to expunge Mick's dishonorable discharge from his service record. He was a victim of the cover-your-ass psychology that had permeated the officer corps in Vietnam. They had let him take the rap for the brutal policy of repression and murder that characterized America's so-called pacification program. But Mick had told Leo to get lost. Mick had transferred to the Marine Corps the stoic pride and sense of solidarity that had made the old Irish political organizations so potent.

In another corner of the room sat a smooth-faced, dark-haired Irishman with a face that rivaled Richard Burton's for charm—and dissipation. The world-weary eyes belonged to a man who expected no surprises from life. A suggestion of contempt shadowed the proud mouth. This had to be Richard O'Gorman.

Leo McBride instantly sensed a rival. He was the local matinee idol, suddenly facing a man with an aura of larger fame. Beside O'Gorman sat another Irishman, a creature who looked as if he had recently been dug out of a Donegal bog after a sleep of ten centuries and restored to life by a local McFrankenstein. Was this what the Irish looked like before the Normans and the Spanish arrived to give them a decent bloodline? Billy Kilroy's hunched, scrawny frame and bleak, stupid visage were enough to drive romanticism out of anyone's soul. That commodity had been eroding in Leo's psyche for quite a while.

"Here he is!" Sunny Dan shouted in his old man's

cackle. "The only guy in the family who's still in politics. I mean real politics—not the penny-ante game you play, Desmond."

There was his father, hunched against the wall, fingering his drink, which was as dark as Dan's. That meant he would never drink it. The rest of the family kept trying to get his father drunk. But Desmond McBride was a cautious, careful man who simply refused to buy the raucous lifestyle of the Monahan clan. Leo admired him for it. Desmond had kept his head clear and refused to let their exile to this seashore town stop him from making money. His tuna-canning factory was the biggest business in South Jersey. His fishing fleet had grown to over a dozen boats.

But at times Leo wished his father would get drunk and talk to him man to man. Did he know what the rest of the clan called him—"the altar boy"? Did he really love his wife, whose incredible avoirdupois overflowed the chair beside him? Was his enthusiasm for Ireland a genuine passion—or a way of lording his money over the less affluent members of the family?

"Hello, Son," Desmond said.

"Hi, honey," his mother said.

Leo kissed them both—and noticed disapproval darken Mick's eyes. He would never kiss his father—if he had one. But Desmond McBride had kissed his father and from Leo's earliest memory had insisted on a kiss from his son.

Leo shook hands with Mick and turned to Dick O'Gorman and said, "Leo McBride from Congressman Mullen's office."

"Ah, yes. And this is your wife—from Senator Ted's?"

Melody was kissing "Mom" and "Dad" McBride and "Grandpa" Monahan. She was incredibly mushy when she donned her family persona. But when she heard O'Gorman refer to her, she whirled like a ballerina and gave him a smile that went considerably beyond family affection.

"So this is the famous Black Dick O'Gorman!" she said.

"Not around here," O'Gorman said.

"Oh, we're among friends—aren't we?" Melody said, swinging her sheen of blond hair like a swatch of gold. She turned to the rest of the room. "This man has done more to free Ireland than anyone alive today," Melody said. "There are people at the State Department who revere him. People in the CIA who can't wait to see him become the first prime minister of a united Ireland!"

"Well, I'll be damned," Sunny Dan Monahan said.

Maybe we're all damned, Leo McBride thought as he watched his wife begin seducing O'Gorman in public. Gazing around the room, Leo saw no recognition of what was happening on anyone's face—except perhaps Mick O'Day's. But he had the cop's habit of presuming the worst about everyone. He could be discounted. The only person who mattered—the only one who knew what was going to happen and cared about it—was Leo McBride, the son of the altar boy.

Was he going to do anything about it?

Probably not. But the subterranean Leo could not help wondering if there was a limit to how much humiliation his psyche could swallow. He knew something about his reckless wife that she did not want mentioned in Paradise Beach. The mere threat to reveal it might make her behave. The mere thought of her pleading for mercy—even for a few minutes—was an incredibly delicious sensation in Leo McBride's scarred soul.

SHOOT 'EM UP

With the arrival of the VIPs from Washington, all concerned sat down to a feast—a fine chunk of roast beef, gravy, mashed potatoes. O'Gorman sat next to Melody Faithorne, struggling to conceal his distaste. Her bone-china face, her blond hair, might have stepped out of an ad in British *Vogue*. And her name! There had to be a Lord Faithorne somewhere in the British peerage.

Her eyes, her manner, kept telling him she was his for the asking. She would have to find out the hard (or should it be the soft?) way that Dick O'Gorman preferred to do the seducing. Women who flaunted their availability stirred some primitive disapproval in his Celtic soul.

As for her pretty-boy husband, something was eating him. O'Gorman could only hope it was not second thoughts about their joint enterprise. They needed his federal bona fides in Boston to get the weapons out of the country with properly forged documents. Sitting opposite him were Desmond McBride and his wife, who was almost as wide as she was tall. They could safely be dismissed for the time being. Not so Barbara's brawny, blond, six-foot son, Mick. He explained why Old Dan had made a point of introducing his daughter as Mrs. O'Day.

Mother and son did not seem to get along well. Mick answered most of her questions about how he had spent his day off with surly monosyllables. O'Gorman found this almost as encouraging as the absence of Mr. O'Day. He was unmentioned; a casual exploration of the house had revealed not a trace of him in a picture or any other memento.

A chance remark shocked O'Gorman out of his erotic daydream. "I keep hoping he'll get off night duty. Maybe then he'll find a nice girl and settle down. But I think he actually likes driving that police car around in the dark."

The glaze of hostility on Billy's face had to be met without an instant's delay. "So you're a policeman?" O'Gorman said to Mick. "That means you work for your uncle. Desmond here's told me all sorts of good things about him."

O'Gorman was reminding Billy that they had the chief of police in their pocket, so there was no need to worry about living in the same house with a mere patrolman.

"Uncle Bill's okay," Mick said. "But I've never heard him say a word about Ireland."

"A man may keep some of his deepest sentiments in the silence of his heart," O'Gorman said.

God how he loathed the part of the sententious Irish philosopher. But Barbara O'Day's eyes filled with tears. Was she hiding something in the silence of her heart? Something more pertinent than love of Ireland?

"The Irish are the natural vanguard of resistance to oppression," Melody Faithorne said. "The British began our era of capitalist subjugation. It's only just and right that the Irish should be the ones to give them the coup de grâce now that America has knocked them flat."

The creature talked nonsense almost as brainless as Kilroy, O'Gorman thought. But he raised his glass and solemnly avowed they were in the fight to the finish.

Old Dan told stories about Democratic national conventions he had attended, all the way back to Al Smith, whoever that was. In spite of his name, the fellow was apparently Irish-American and had once been nominated for president.

In his cover role as a professor of Irish literature, O'Gorman told stories designed to make Ireland and its four-hundred-year struggle for freedom seem like a historic vaudeville act. He loathed each and every one of these tales. Naturally, Old Dan and Desmond McBride and his fat wife loved them.

So did Barbara O'Day. When she laughed, she wrinkled her nose in an utterly charming way. Her breasts danced beneath her white blouse. Only Mick was unamused. Boredom, even a patina of hostility, immobilized his strong-jawed, stubborn face. What was wrong with the boyo? Perhaps his unhappiness had nothing to do with Ireland and things Irish, but O'Gorman disliked anyone who resisted his charm.

After dinner, Old Dan slipped Mick some money and told him to take O'Gorman and Billy Kilroy down to the Golden Shamrock. Desmond McBride said he wanted to go home to work on his taxes, but Dan said, "Jesus Christ, have some fun for once," so he tagged along. So did his son Leo and his wife, who offered them a ride, which squashed O'Gorman and Billy in the suitcase-sized rear seat of their Ferrari. But it gave them a few minutes for some frank talk.

"Here's the name of the customs inspector you need to see in Boston," Melody said, handing him the envelope. "Also the name and address of the warehouse where you can stash the weapons while you work out the details. There's five thousand dollars in there for incidental expenses—a gift from the senator."

"Thank him for me. I hope we can meet someday."

"When you become premier," Melody said.

"It might be better to lay off that stuff. I'm just a traveling lecturer as far as the Monahans are concerned."

"Old Dan's too gaga to notice. Mick and his mother are too dumb," Melody said.

"One important point," Leo McBride said in his reedy voice. "Deniability. If anything goes wrong, you never met us."

"Jesus God, what do you think we are? In the IRA if a man blabs, he's dead in twenty-four hours," O'Gorman said.

"Yah," Billy said. "And he means dead." Billy put his finger against the back of Leo's head in the shape of a make-believe gun and clicked his tongue.

"You don't have to worry about us," Leo said. The shrill tone only further convinced O'Gorman that he was not to be trusted.

The Golden Shamrock turned out to be a bar whose walls were papered with, surprise, golden shamrocks. The proprietor, William Gargan, known to one and all as Wilbur, was the fattest man O'Gorman had ever seen. Wilbur slapped his immense belly and blamed it on the famine of 1847. He said the Gargans had been hungry ever since.

Gargan kept calling Desmond McBride "Big Brother" in a sarcastic way. Eventually O'Gorman figured out that they were brothers-in-law. They had each married daughters of Dan Monahan's. Gargan dispensed Guinness and Irish-whiskey chasers with a munificent hand. He barely noticed Billy and O'Gorman.

O'Gorman told some more vaudeville stories. Billy drank the whiskey and Guinness and was soon snookered. That meant he started telling stories about the Belfast wars. He bragged about the eighteen notches in his ArmaLite rifle and the way he dodged the hot pursuers. O'Gorman decided it might be best to manufacture a hero out of the blithering Patriot Boy and confirmed his claims, though O'Gorman made a point of declaring he personally abhorred the violence and had persuaded Billy to abandon his ArmaLite. But O'Gorman confided to one and all that Billy was the best shot in the Six Counties, and probably in all of Europe and possibly in the world.

"He can't be better than Mick," growled a voice on the outer fringe of the circle of listeners. "There isn't a stinking communist in the world who's a better shot than Mick."

The circle parted, giving O'Gorman a chance to confront his antagonist—a lean, red-haired man roughly his own age, with a cynic's mouth and knowing, bloodshot eyes. He cradled a dark glass of liquor on his chest as if it were a newborn child. O'Gorman had met his like in a hundred bars and pubs. He was the local self-appointed expert on world politics and history.

"Now, now, don't use such a term for an Irish patriot," O'Gorman said.

"'We must hate. Hatred is the basis of communism.' That's what Lenin said to the commissars of education. Is there any difference between that and the IRA's creed?"

"What is your name, sir?"

"Oxenford."

"I'm amazed that Celtic blood tolerates an Englishman in this bar, much less your opinions," O'Gorman said.

"Englishman?" taunted his opponent. "The Oxenfords have been Americans since 1665."

"The Professor knows what he's talkin' about. He's read more books than everyone else in the whole town put together," Wilbur Gargan said. "He teaches history in the high school. If he wasn't such a lush, he might be teachin' at Princeton."

O'Gorman cursed himself and the Irish whiskey in his belly for failing to anticipate the power of local custom. These Irish-Americans took both sides of their hyphen seriously.

Unbothered by any compunctions about local custom or hopes of popularity, Melody Faithorne scornfully attacked Oxenford's credentials. "My family arrived in 1620 on the *Mayflower.* But that doesn't prevent me from supporting the poor and oppressed around the world.

That's America's mission! Its reason for existence!"

"Your half-baked New England righteousness won't
fly in New Jersey," Oxenford said. "This is Middle America, where we worship money without hypocrisy. Americans have never pursued anything but the fast buck.
That's the real translation of 'Westward ho.' The only reason why every immigrant ever came here."

"Hey," proprietor Gargan said, bored with ideology.
"How about a friendly contest? See who's a better shot,
the IRA or the U.S. Marines."

"Have you got your gun with you?" Oxenford asked
Mick.

"Sure," Mick said, and unzipped his black jacket to
reveal a shoulder holster with a Colt .38 in it.

"Let's go down in the cellar and have a match," Gargan
said.

"My lad's a bit tipsy," O'Gorman said.

"I can outshoot a fookin' cop drunk or sober," Billy
said.

They all adjourned to the cellar of the Golden Shamrock, which had apparently been used as a shooting
gallery to settle similar contests. Gargan bragged that
Mick had outshot all comers, from fellow ex-marines to
ex-paratroopers to visiting New York detectives. A mat-
tress on the far wall had a paper cutout of a man pinned to
it. Standing at the far end of the cellar, Billy put six bullets
into the head. The shredded cutout was replaced and Mick
took the gun and put six bullets in exactly the same place.

Upping the ante, Gargan ordered the contestants to
stand with their backs turned while he moved the target to
the far right corner, then the far left. Both times, firing as
they turned, Billy and Mick put six bullets into the head.
They turned the target upside down and the result was
exactly the same: a dead heat.

"Let's try it in the dark," Mick said.

"In the dark?" O'Gorman said.

"That's the real test of a marksman," Oxenford said,
smirking at Mick like a lunatic parent.

"It'll take thirty minutes," Mick said.

"Why?" O'Gorman said.

"That's how long it takes to get night vision."

O'Gorman was forced to acquiesce. They trooped out of the bar and across Ocean Avenue to the beach. Oxenford pinned the target to an oar someone had brought along and plunged it into the sand, just above the high-tide mark. Proprietor Gargan kept the chilly offshore wind at bay for the required thirty minutes with hefty slugs of Jameson.

"I'm ready," Mick said.

He fired six times at a hundred paces. They examined the target with the help of a flashlight. Each bullet was in the same place. The head.

Mick handed the gun to Billy. "I can't see a fookin' thing. I don't get this shootin' in the dark."

"Give it a try," O'Gorman said.

Billy fired six times. The bullets went whistling out to sea. Oxenford declared Mick the winner and lurched home, well satisfied with his night's work. O'Gorman wondered how the Americans lost in Vietnam with that kind of marksmanship in their ranks.

Melody suggested a walk on the beach. O'Gorman said he had no interest in freezing to death. She went home in a huff, dragging her pretty boy with her. O'Gorman shuddered at the demands she was going to make on his equipment before midnight.

Back in the Golden Shamrock, O'Gorman was soon cursing Oxenford under his breath. No one was impressed by Billy's Belfast stories anymore. They had decided he was a joke. Billy did not like it. He drank until he was blotto. Mick O'Day poured him into his car, which had a motor that rumbled like a 747, and they drove back to Sunny Dan's house. O'Gorman lugged Billy upstairs and dumped the sod into his bed. He lay there going, "Naw, naw, naw," his teeth grinding.

From the second-floor landing, O'Gorman could hear Mick's deep voice downstairs. "The Professor says that little guy's a goddamn communist. What the hell is Uncle Desmond up to?"

"I told you a long time ago to stop listening to that man," Barbara O'Day said. "The whole Oxenford family are a bunch of godless atheists!"

"I don't listen to him very much, but he knows a lot about world politics."

"He's full of it! I've told you that a hundred times!"

"I gotta go to work."

"Work. I bet you've got another divorcée on the string. Someone told me they saw your car parked out on Leeds Point for most of the morning."

"Mom. That's none of your business."

"I want to see you get married. Settle down!"

"Yeah. One of these days I will."

"You don't listen to me. You've never listened to me."

"Sure I do. I just don't do what you tell me."

O'Gorman descended the stairs like a man walking on broken glass. Barbara O'Day was in the living room, watching TV. A talk-show host was listening to an actress explain why she had been married five times. Mrs. O'Day told O'Gorman that she was the star of the highest-rated soap opera in the country.

"Would you like a drink?" Barbara asked.

"No, no. I've had more than enough. Mick and his friends were grand hosts. Almost too grand for poor Billy. He's not used to such generosity, growing up in Belfast."

"Ummm." She had no interest in Belfast.

"Does your husband travel for a living like many Americans?"

"My husband?" The word made her stiffen in the chair. "No."

"I hope I haven't asked a painful question. Was he perhaps killed in one of your wars?"

"No. We're separated."

"Ah. I'm sorry."

On TV, the actress went on explaining how she had yet to find the perfect man. He had to be someone who appre-

ciated her intelligence as well as her body. The talk-show
host thought this was a marvelously original idea.

"I can't believe he was unfaithful. Unless he was blind
as well as deaf and dumb."

Barbara blushed like a schoolgirl of eighteen. "He
didn't want to live down here. We . . . didn't get along."

She continued to stare at the TV but she was no longer
listening to it.

"I understand, I understand," O'Gorman said. "I've had
a similar marriage, for twenty years now."

"Really? Why—How?" No doubt she assumed that
everyone in Ireland sang turalooraloora all day long and
never had a quarrel.

"Politics. My wife's family is one of the richest in the
Republic. They want no trouble about the poor Catholics
in the north. When I vowed to devote my life to their rescue, they showed me the door. She . . . stayed behind."

"Oh."

"It was difficult at first. But . . ."

He let the implication of his suffering drift across the
room toward her, a silent plea. The sympathy in her blue
eyes was devastating. O'Gorman began hoping it would
take the Cubans several weeks to deliver their marvelous
weapons.

A MAN FOR ALL SERMONS

Head down, legs pumping in the wet sand, Father Philip Hart jogged into the relentless northeast wind. Above him, light seemed drained from the gray sky. With the windchill factor the temperature had to be twenty degrees below zero. His body was a piece of frozen meat; a curiously satisfying thought. Father Hart jogged every day, regardless of the weather. Yesterday he had jogged in driving, stinging sleet. He had loved it.

His numbed ears were filled with the rush of the wind and the boom of the surf. The waves towered to incredible heights and then crashed straight down when the wind caught them, creating explosions of angry water. Beneath the gloomy sky, the foaming combers seemed doubly berserk. Warnings from an angry God?

Another jogger came toward him, accompanied by a frolicsome Airedale. It was the Jewish girl, Jacqueline Chasen. She waved cheerfully to him. They often met in the dawn and occasionally in the twilight. She jogged on doctor's orders, to regain her muscle tone after months in hospital beds, recovering from an automobile accident.

"How do you like this weather?" she called to him as they passed.

"I like it," Father Hart said, slowing down.

"Me too," she said, jogging backward. "Last year at this time, you couldn't have gotten me out in this weather without a regiment of marines. Maybe there's something to be said for almost killing yourself."

"Maybe," Father Hart said, jogging backward too.

She had an incredibly good figure, which was extremely visible in her jogging suit. Suddenly Father Hart's body was no longer a frozen piece of meat.

"See you later," she called, and continued up the beach toward her house on Leeds Point.

He would dream about her again tonight. Why had she become the object of his lust? Was it simply her figure, or was it her Jewishness? His lust, which Father Hart disowned, was feeding on myth and erotic hearsay, on vile jokes about the Jewish obsession with sex. Jacqueline Chasen was not a person to him.

Reprehensible. Father Hart gazed at the raging surf, the immense expanse of black, whitecapped ocean beyond it. He might have been jogging along the rim of eternity. That made his lust for this woman even more reprehensible.

In spite of this noble attempt to evade it, last night's dream floated into his head. It had a lot to do with the confession he had heard earlier in the day. *Bless me, Father, for I have sinned. I went to Atlantic City and won a thousand bucks and got laid at Billy's. After I got laid, she asked me if I wanted a blow job and I said okay.*

In the dream, Father Hart was at Caesars. He was lying naked on a huge roulette wheel and Jacqueline Chasen was smiling down at him. *Ohhhh, Phil, you won,* she said, and took his penis in her mouth. *Lucky, Phil,* she said, and slowly wiggled out of her jogging suit and mounted him. *Let's go for a ride.*

A grinning crowd surrounded them. Someone spun the wheel and they whirled around and around, his hands on her breasts. He had awakened with his pajamas soaked with semen. He had had to take a shower and was sleepless for the rest of the night.

Damn Atlantic City. It was Sodom and Gomorrah rolled into one city of sordid glitz. He heard a dozen confessions like that a month. Married men who swore they were sorry, who vowed they would not do it again. Yet they did it again and again. He tried not to associate names and faces with the shape of the head, the sound of the voice that penetrated the confessional screen. But it was hard not to make the connections in a small town. It was hard not to remember what was happening, night after night, only fifty miles away.

Out on the frothing ocean, Father Hart saw the white hull of the SS *Enterprise* emerging from Pochank Inlet. The sixty-foot fishing boat was rolling violently as the fifty-mile-an-hour gale struck her on the beam. The Vietnamese refugee Phac, abuser of his delicate, tragic-eyed wife, was on board that ship. Father Hart had not heard from him. He had been hoping he could solve that problem with a warning. If Phac proved defiant, the situation could become messy.

Father Hart jogged down Delaware Street to St. Augustine's two-story, brown-shingled rectory. Next door, the church, a vine-covered stone rectangle with a stubby Romanesque tower added as an afterthought, was dark and silent. It would remain that way for the rest of the day. Father Hart had said mass at 8 A.M. for a half dozen aged women. A meeting of the Sons of the Shamrock was scheduled for seven-thirty tonight. At least the basement lights would be on for a while.

Father Hart hated to see the church empty. It reminded him uncomfortably of the slipping attendance at Sunday mass, the even steeper decline in daily massgoers. That was why he made the basement hall available to organizations like the SOS, even though they were not religious.

As he jogged up to the gate, a big man got out of a car and walked toward him. It was Mick O'Day, the cop. Not one of his favorite people.

When Hart had come to Paradise Beach in 1972, Mick's grandfather, Dan Monahan, had been the town's reigning patriarch. With money he had stolen during his years of power in the corrupt big-city machine that had dominated the state's politics for the first half of the century, Monahan had bought fishing boats, saloons, and other businesses for his daughters and sons-in-law and nephews and cousins and taken over the town's power structure.

Hart had been invited to pay his respects to the old man, as priests had paid obeisance to him and his cohorts for generations. At dinner they had gotten into a discussion of the presidential election and the war in Vietnam. When Hart had said he was voting for George McGovern and began denouncing the war, a chilly silence had enveloped the table. He had not been invited back.

Mick had not been at the dinner. He had been in Vietnam. That year he had been dishonorably discharged from the marines for committing an atrocity. Old Monahan was getting senile now, but most of the family remained surly and even hostile to Father Hart. Mick came late to Sunday mass and left early. If he ever went to confession and Communion, it was not at St. Augustine's.

"Say, Father. Could I talk to you for a couple of minutes?" Mick said.

"Sure."

In the rectory, the priest slipped out of his sweaty running suit and pulled on a pair of chinos and a sweater. "Some coffee?" he said to Mick, who was waiting in the small parlor.

"No thanks. Listen, Father. You got to lay off Phac. His wife called me. She says you're gonna give him a hard time for beating her up. Stay out of it, Father."

Father Hart bristled. Where did this Neanderthal get off giving him advice? "Why is this any of your business?"

"I knew them both in Nam. I was stationed in their village."

"I'm amazed they'd ask you for help. They probably saw you gun down their brothers, sisters, cousins. Didn't you get a dishonorable discharge for doing something like that?"

Mick's fair-skinned face flushed. Guilt. If ever Father Hart, who considered himself an expert on guilt, saw it. "Let's forget about what I did. I'm here to protect Trai. If you push Phac over the edge, he could really hurt her."

"That's a hell of an attitude for a policeman to take. Aren't you supposed to protect women against wife beaters?"

"Sure. But Phac isn't some Irish drunk, Father. This guy's been through a lot. Don't put any more pressure on him. Let me talk to him instead."

"Now you're really being ridiculous. Are you setting yourself up as a marriage counselor?"

"No. But I know the background, Father. Phac trusts me. I'm the reason he came to this crummy town—"

"Haven't you and people like you caused enough pain and suffering to him and Trai?"

Amazement flickered across Mick's wide face. "You don't know what the hell you're talking about, Father."

All Father Hart could see was Trai's plaintive, innocent eyes, her trembling lips. Here was the antidote to the lust Jacqueline Chasen stirred in him. Here was innocence betrayed by a vile warmongering power elite. Here was their spokesman, with the blood of other innocents still on his hands.

"I do know what I'm talking about! I marched against the war. I went to teach-ins where they told the truth about it. I know exactly what went on out there in Vietnam. Exactly what people like you did to innocent men and women trying to live in peace in their own country."

"Live in peace! There hasn't been any peace in that country for a hundred years. Look, Father. Phac is a tough guy. Awful tough. He was the police chief in Binh Nghai."

"Did he shoot people like that police chief in Saigon shot the man they caught during the Tet Offensive?"

"No. Usually Phac hanged them. It made more of an impression."

"You helped him?"

"I didn't stop him. I couldn't have stopped him if I wanted to. He was in charge. I've seen him beat people up too. I mean really beat them up. I don't want him to do that to Trai."

"This is the sort of war criminal we've brought to our country? I'm going to write to the head of Catholic Relief and get him deported."

"Then he really will kill her. He might kill you too."

"I'm not going to let you intimidate me!"

"I'm not doing anything but telling you the truth! Now that he's gotten Suong to this country, Phac doesn't care whether he lives or dies. He's told me that more than once. But he won't let you disgrace him. He's a proud son of a gun."

"Well, I'm going to humble him. I want you to bring him down here tonight after work in your car."

Mick stepped back two paces. "Father, I heard from a lot of people that you were more or less an asshole. But I didn't realize how big an asshole you were."

Father Hart trembled from head to foot. He was face-to-face with one of the helmeted killers he had marched against in 1969 and 1970, his first years as a priest. One of the military murderers who had a lot to do with sending him to this obscure parish on the freezing Atlantic. The archbishop had made it clear that he did not approve of his priests becoming radicals.

It was incredible the way the Irish could close their minds by an act of the will. Here was a man who had committed a crime so vile his militaristic government could not condone it. Yet he refused to admit his guilt. He defended one of his fellow killers and dismissed his pastor's condemnation.

"I'm giving you an order, Mick. Bring Phac down here."

Mick strolled to the door. "You go get him. That's the only way you're going to see him. I told Trai to forget the whole thing."

Fuming, Father Hart took a shower and poured himself a dish of cornflakes. He could not believe that Trai would listen to Mick O'Day and ignore his offer to help. Should he drive to the house tonight? No, that could create an ugly scene in front of the boy, Suong.

As he finished his cornflakes, Father Hart felt, not for the first time, a sinking sensation. Around him, the rectory creaked in the March wind. Outside, on street after street, his parishioners lived their impenetrable, entangled lives. Not singly, like him, but as part of families, as fathers, mothers, brothers, sisters. Too often, he felt like a space traveler, marooned on an alien asteroid.

Father Hart had joined the priesthood in the euphoric days of the early 1960s, when the Vatican Council was supposedly transforming the Church. Priests were going to be permitted to marry, they would share power with the bishops. Now, in the year of our Lord 1984, it looked more and more like the Catholic Church of the 1950s. The difference was, there were fewer priests and a lot less respect for them. In 1962, when he had entered the seminary, no one would have talked to a priest the way Mick O'Day had just talked to him.

Father Hart struggled for equilibrium. He must not yield to the winter blahs. Spring and summer were just around the corner. He had a family, even if they were scattered now, his father and mother in a retirement village in Florida, his older sister living in Seattle, his two brothers pursuing the almighty dollar in Chicago. He was not as lonely as he sometimes felt. They were all just a telephone call away.

In spite of the knock the Monahans had put on him, he had some supporters in the parish. Now that he had learned to keep politics out of his sermons and his conversations, he would have more. With some prodding from the archbishop, he had accepted the sad fact that no one in Paradise Beach (or in the whole diocese of Trenton, for that matter) cared about the need for a nuclear freeze or a reduction in the arms race.

The front doorbell rang. There stood a medium-sized, sandy-haired man in a black suit and black overcoat and round collar, with a suitcase in his hand. He had the saddest eyes, the most hangdog expression, Hart had ever seen. "Father Hart?" the man said in a soft Irish brogue that somehow added to his mournful mien. "I'm Dennis McAvoy. Archbishop Cardigan thought it might do me good to stay with you for a few days."

"Come in," Father Hart said.

McAvoy gratefully accepted a cup of coffee. It did not take him long to tell his story. He was a graduate of the Irish seminary at Maynooth. With Ireland's declining population and steady supply of vocations, priests were one of its main exports. Half the American bishops wrote letters to Maynooth, begging for one of their products. But Father McAvoy had run into trouble in his tour at St. Patrick's Parish in posh Tenafly, in suburban North Jersey.

He had asked for volunteers to join him on a trip to the UN to protest British policy in Northern Ireland. Not a soul had come forward. When he tried to organize a poverty kitchen in nearby Union City, he had been similarly ignored. When he preached a sermon against America's imperialist policy in Nicaragua, people had walked out of the church. He had had a terrible row with the pastor.

"I'll tell it to you straight, Father. I went on a bender. It's a weakness in my family," McAvoy said. "Maybe in the race, God knows. I've been drying out for the last six weeks at a sanitarium in Flemington. The archbishop thought I might be happier down this way 'with your own kind,' as he put it. I'll try not to be a burden to you. I'll try to be some help."

Father Hart's eyes misted, his throat filled with sympathy. Here was a fellow priest struggling to save his vocation, his soul. A fellow wayfarer in late-twentieth-century American Catholicism. Perhaps a partial answer to his loneliness. "Welcome to St. Augustine's Parish," he said, holding out his hand.

It seemed more than a coincidence that Father McAvoy had arrived in time to join Father Hart at seven-thirty that night for the monthly meeting of the Sons of the Shamrock. Hart told him about the SOS at supper and was pleased by the way McAvoy's wan face came aglow. The Sons usually mustered about a hundred people for a meeting, about two-thirds of their membership. They were a modest organization, compared to the Order of the Friendly Sons of the Shillelagh, forty miles up the coast in Madison township. The Shillelaghs had a sumptuous clubhouse and a membership of four hundred. Like them, the Sons were dedicated to keeping Irish culture alive in New Jersey.

Some 1,440,000 New Jerseyans reported themselves to be of Irish descent in the census. But most of them had lapsed shamefully from their heritage if not from their faith. "My family's one of them," Father Hart ruefully admitted. "I grew up in Metuchen, a typical suburb. We knew nothing about Ireland. My father said he was sick of Mother Machree and just ignored the whole subject. He was reacting against the god-awful songs and Irish jokes at parish smokers when he was growing up in Jersey City."

"What a pity," Father McAvoy said.

"Every year on the first of April the Sons of the Shamrock stage a feis. Authentic Irish dancing and piping, sports like hurling, Gaelic football. We attract about ten thousand people."

"I can hardly wait," Father McAvoy said.

Mayor Desmond McBride, who doubled as *taioseach* of the Sons, greeted Fathers Hart and McAvoy as they entered the parish hall. "What a coincidence," he burbled, pumping McAvoy's hand after Hart had introduced them. McBride led the priests over to a corner and introduced them to two smiling strangers. One was as tall and elegant as the other was squat and ugly. "Meet Dick O'Gorman and Billy Kilroy, just off Aer Lingus. They're here to lecture on Irish culture. Every cent they raise is going to a home in Belfast, where children orphaned by the violence are being raised by nuns."

"How wonderful," Father Hart said.

"That isn't all, Father," McBride said. "Dr. O'Gorman here's agreed to supervise our feis. He and Billy will live here and work with us."

"It was the least I could do, in return for such hospitality as Desmond's shown us," O'Gorman said. "Right, Billy?"

"Yah," grunted Billy, who did not look very bright to Father Hart. He warned himself not to allow stereotypes to influence his thinking.

"We're planning to lecture around the state. It's easy to reach almost any part of it from here."

"Yah. Like the fookin' airport," Billy said.

"The what?" Father Hart said.

"Davenport," O'Gorman said. "For some reason Billy's always wanted to go there. I've had a hell of a time convincing him it isn't in New Jersey."

"Ah," Father Hart said, totally bewildered. "Where will you be staying here in town?"

"They're going to stay with old Dan. They've got lots of room. There's just Barbara and Mick in that big house with him now," McBride said.

"What part of Ireland are you from, Father?" O'Gorman asked McAvoy.

"Mayo, God help us," McAvoy replied with his wan smile.

"You don't say. What town?" O'Gorman replied. "I'm from Castlebar."

"Cong."

"Oho. You got so rich on the American tourists at Ashford Castle you've come to America to buy real estate?"

"My father's a gardener there," McAvoy said.

Father Hart was puzzled by the rasp of hostility in O'Gorman's voice and touched by McAvoy's humility.

The meeting began with the usual ritual. Father Hart said a brief prayer. They saluted the American flag and the Irish flag. Then their best tenor, Donal Finch, sang the Irish national anthem in Gaelic. Father Hart was puzzled by the Irish visitors' silence. Neither sang a note of their country's song. But Dennis McAvoy caroled it in a lovely tenor voice. The meeting buzzed quickly through the plans for the Sons' annual trip to Ireland. Then McBride introduced Richard O'Gorman, repeating the information he had already given Father Hart.

O'Gorman told them that he and his assistant, Billy Kilroy, were here to spread the good news about Ireland's return to the family of nations. After fifty years of independence, Irish culture was flourishing. All that was needed to complete the nation's happiness was the recapture of the six lost counties in the north. Then a united Ireland would resume its historical role as the cultural leader of Europe. He descanted on how the heritage of Greece and Rome had been kept alive in Irish monasteries during the Dark Ages, when Germans and Frenchmen and Italians were drawing pictures on rocks.

Best of all, a united Ireland would permit young exiles such as Kilroy to return to Belfast, where his father and mother had been murdered by British special agents. Resisting the assassins, Billy had brained one of them with a hockey stick and was wanted for what the British called murder.

"When Billy came to my door," O'Gorman said, "he looked like a victim of the famine. I've adopted him as a son. No one has revealed a deeper enthusiasm, a greater pride, in Ireland's culture. He was like a man who had been deprived of solid food since birth, which in fact he had, under British rule. No Irish writer, no Irish song, no Irish dance, is permitted in British Belfast. With God's help and yours, we may someday change that."

The entire meeting was on its feet, applauding. Father

Hart's throat was so full, he could hardly breathe. My God, the man rang true. He was the quintessence of the modern resistance fighter, modest, generous, patient. Hart turned to Father McAvoy and said, "What do you think?"

Tears were streaming down McAvoy's face. "Would to God I had the ability to preach such a sermon."

Desmond McBride rose to ask the members to contribute to the orphanage that Messrs. O'Gorman and Kilroy were supporting in Belfast. Watching the $10 bills tumble into the collection basket, Father Hart wondered if he too should take some speech lessons from the Ould Sod.

MICK OF THE WOODS

The car pitched and rolled on the makeshift sand road like a small boat in a gale. Mick ignored the jolts and kept his foot on the accelerator. Around him were mile on mile of pine and cedar trees. He was deep in his favorite refuge, the 650,000 acres of wilderness that stretch across the narrowed peninsula of South Jersey, from the Atlantic shore almost to the Delaware River. Geographers call them the Pine Barrens, a name that reflects the opinion of their early discoverers. The sandy soil made farming impossible so the land was never cleared. Even the original inhabitants of New Jersey, the Leni-Lenape, shunned the Barrens.

Ahead of Mick the woods suddenly opened and a house stood in the bright March sunshine. It was not much of a house. Most of it was a porch, with three rocking chairs on it. Behind that was little more than a shack, with two dirty windows staring into the woods. Tufts of grass grew on what might charitably be called a lawn. On the left, water sparkled in acres of cranberry bog. In the center of the yard was an ancient brass water pump. Around it sprawled no less than eight automobiles.

One, a green and white 1955 Chevrolet V-8, was upside down, its tail fins invisible in the sand. Two other cars were on their sides. One of these was a light blue '56 Chrysler 300-B with its split grille gone but most of its 4,600-pound body intact. Its 355-horsepower engine, which had won first place in the Daytona High Performance Trials that year, was long gone. Beside it was a 1949 Hudson Hornet step-down chassis car with its famous 7X flathead six engine also long since cannibalized.

Around them squatted muscle cars of the sixties, upright but with their tires missing, their big bumpers half-buried in the sand. A red Ford with a bubble in the fiberglass hood for the 427 high-riser engine, a white '66 Pontiac GTO, a blue Mercury Montego, and a bright Orange Judge model Pontiac with wild spoilers and faded decals still in place.

Parts of all of these cars were in Mick's white 1970 American Motors Rebel and in the only operating car in the yard, a dark blue Studebaker Hawk GT, with white-wall tires and flaps. Its small, square grille, Thunderbird roofline, and clean flanks made it look as if a piece of Europe, or at least a snooty part of Long Island, had somehow dropped uninvited into this wilderness junk-yard.

Mick got out of his car and strolled onto the porch. Through the open door he saw a man in red flannel underwear standing at a stove, cooking something that crackled in hot grease. He had a spatula in one hand and a raw onion in the other hand. He was in the middle of biting into the onion when he saw Mick. "Jeeesus Christ," Gamaliel Oxenford said. "Look what the gale blew in. Look what the gale blew in."

"Hello, Pops," Mick said.

Gamaliel Oxenford stood about five feet ten in his flannel-shod feet. He had solid shoulders and remarkably thick muscular legs. His hair, once blond, had turned as white as a cumulus cloud, but there was not a line in his ruddy, sharp-featured face to reveal that he was eighty-six years old.

"Want a drink?" the old man said, and without waiting for an answer handed Mick a jug of applejack. Mick took a swallow of the clear, brown fluid. Inside the kitchen, he discovered another man sitting in a chair: Joe Turner. As usual, he sat on the end of his spine with his legs stretched halfway across the room, no expression worth mentioning on his mournful ebony face. He wore a leather hunting shirt that might have belonged to Daniel Boone and homemade canvas trousers.

Joe was a black marine veteran of the Korean War. He had been born in Camden and hunted in the Pines with his father as a boy. When he came back from Korea, he found his father was dead and his mother had married again. Joe had moved into the Pines, built himself a one-room house about a mile from Oxenford's, and had rarely emerged from the woods for the past thirty years. He made a living as a guide for hunters—he knew every sand road and dirt track in the wilderness's thousand square miles—and as a cranberry grower. He had built his own four-acre bog.

"Hello, Joe," Mick said.

Joe said nothing. He seldom had anything to say. That was one of several reasons why Mick found him good company.

"You seen anything of my next-to-worthless son lately?" Gamaliel Oxenford said.

"Now and then in the Shamrock," Mick said.

The Professor, as Mick and everyone else called Alex Oxenford, had always been easy to talk to, in school and out of it. After Mick came back from Nam, the Professor was one of the few people in town outside Mick's family who tried to help him, taking him into the Pines to meet Gamaliel ("Pop") Oxenford and Joe Turner. Together they had worked on these old cars, which Joe and Mick drove on dirt tracks in rural counties in Pennsylvania, New Jersey, and Connecticut. Mick had revealed an astonishing aptitude for understanding how an engine worked, almost by divination, it seemed at times. Alex Oxenford had spent hours urging him to do something with this talent, to no avail.

"I saw a big buck out in the yard last night," Pop Oxenford said. "He had velvet on his horns. Them horns is soft when he's in velvet."

Mick said nothing. Often there was no need to reply to Pop Oxenford's comments. That was one reason why Mick liked him. Another reason was the Medal of Honor he had won in the Argonne in 1918. He had the medal framed and hung in the outhouse. He said that was the best place to hang a medal, because they were mostly shit.

"Want a chop?" Pop Oxenford said.

"Yeah."

Pop went into the next room and came back with another chop, which he threw into the crackling pan. Above the stove on the wall was a framed poem.

> God hath not promised
> Sun without rain
> Joy without sorrow
> Peace without pain.

Pop took a sip of applejack and flipped the sizzling, sputtering chops. He took another chomp of the onion. "What are they after now?"

"Nothin'," Mick said.

"They always seem to be after somethin' in Paradise Beach. Remember when they was after the jetport?"

"Yeah."

The year after the bearer bonds had disappeared into the federal treasury, the state was supposed to build a jetport in the Pines. It was going to turn Paradise Beach into another Atlantic City, and Atlantic City into Miami Beach and Las Vegas rolled into one big pile of money. Mick's grandfather and his uncles had sat around nights figuring out how much they could get for their oceanfront property in Paradise. They were going to be millionaires after all. But something went sour in Trenton. Instead, the legislature voted to keep the Pines forever wild. So here they were in Hog Wallow, population forty-five, one of the bigger towns in the woods.

Pop Oxenford claimed he was the mayor of Hog Wallow. No one argued with him because he was the oldest resident, as far as anyone knew. No one had elected him either, but no one ever voted for anything in the Pines. They regarded those "outside" as slightly crazy, with their worries over voting, making money, getting married. All the things Mick's mother and aunts and uncles talked about all the time.

Maybe he liked the Pineys because they reminded him of the way the Vietnamese were when he first came to Binh Nghai. At least, the way he thought they were. Mick let the Pineys stay the way they were in his head by not getting to know them well, except for Pop Oxenford and Joe Turner. Some people might say Mick did not know Joe well. Mick had probably said no more than a hundred words to him in the past ten years. But in another way, a marine way, Mick knew him very well.

Oxenford threw the chops onto plates and set them on a rough board table. He handed Mick a baked potato from the oven of the stove and a pitcher of melted grease to pour over it. "I can't understand why my son don't get married. When I was his age, I had seven children mustered and grown. Two of them got killed in the wars. Did I tell you that?"

"Yeah," Mick said.

Mick chewed on the crisp pork. It was delicious. His favorite food, these days. Maybe that was why he came over here.

"Did I show you my new girlfriend? I've been meetin' her every night down by Apple Pie Hill. She enjoys it so much she left me her picture."

From a drawer in the table the old man pulled out a picture of an Arab girl wearing a veil and nothing else. "She wears that rag on her face 'cause she's afraid I'll brag about her to someone she knows like maybe Mrs. Rockefeller."

"Nice," Mick said.

"How about you? Gettin' much?"

"A little here, a little there."

"When I was your age, I kept three women busy. That's the only way to do it. Otherwise women get involved with you and vice versa. Women like to mix up sex with all sorts of crazy things. I was the best jig dancer in these woods. That got me into a lot of women. I had one who was sixty-four. She was the hottest of them all in bed. But she couldn't cook worth a damn. I'd puke up the breakfast she fed me every time. I never found a woman who could cook as good as me. I think that's why my wife died. She died of shame, I really think so. She died of mortification because I was such a better cook."

"No kidding."

"Why should I lie to you?"

"What about the air tune?"

"Oh, that was my fallback. If I couldn't get nowhere with jig dancing, I'd try the air tune. That was surefire, but you couldn't overuse it, don't you understand? You couldn't overuse it. Women do a lot of talking between themselves. I used to say, if you could stop women talking between themselves, this world'd be a paradise."

"If you could just stop them talking, period."

"No, I like to hear women talk. They talk the damndest nonsense. It's entertaining. You got to learn to listen to women. It's good entertainment, it really is. Did I ever tell you about El and Will Williams?"

"I don't think so."

"I laid El many a time before she married Will. That woman was so damn mad at me for not marryin' her she vowed to get rich. Know how she did it?"

"Nope."

"Three nights runnin' she and Will had the same dream. It was right after they found Jesus for the thirty-second or thirty-third time. Will was the biggest drunk in Hog Wallow, and El wasn't far behind him. Anyway they both dreamed there was an iron-handled drawer buried up by Tulpohocken Creek, on the road that goes by Joe Holloway field and comes out at the High Crossing. They went up there on the third morning and dug up a box full of buckskin bags full of gold coins. It went back to pirate days or maybe '76 when people buried money all over these woods."

"What did they do with the money?"

"Oh, they moved to Atlantic City and became the two biggest drunks there. That was long before they brought in the craps. Where do you think El got that dream?"

"Search me."

"Will told me before they left for Atlantic City, them three nights he heard the air tune. He heard it clear."

"Hey. I hope I hear it some one of these days. I'm sick of livin' on a cop's salary."

"I told you a long time ago a salary's a bad idea. It eats a hole in your belly."

"Feel like a roam, Joe?" Mick asked.

Joe nodded. Mick thanked Pop Oxenford for lunch and walked through the pines to Joe's house. There was no furniture in it, except for a table, a kerosene lamp, a sleeping bag, and a huge Bible. Joe took correspondence courses in the Bible. He stayed up nights studying it by the light of the kerosene lamp. The courses had convinced Joe that the world was coming to an end soon. They were in the final days.

"How's the bog doin'?" Mick said.

"Okay," Joe said.

They walked to the edge of the bog. Mick had helped him dam and dredge it. They had hauled tree stumps the size of armchairs out of its freezing depths. One of the cranberry companies had given Joe the land. Eventually, when the bog began to make money, Joe hoped to build a bigger house and marry someone. Who that would be, it was hard to say. There were no black women in the Pines, as far as Mick knew.

They set out along one of the twisting sand roads, two marines going no place in particular. Mick did not know why Joe had moved into the woods. It might have something to do with coming home and finding his mother in bed with a stranger. It might have had something to do with what happened to him in the marines.

Joe had been in the retreat from the Yalu River in 1950, one of the roughest fights in the history of the Corps. Mick did not know what had happened to him there. He did not want to know.

Just being with Joe, not knowing, made Mick feel better. He could let the movie of the day he had volunteered for Binh Nghai unreel in his head as they moved along.

It was a beautiful day, that morning in Nam. Like this one, here in New Jersey. Mick let the woods absorb his mind for a while. The sun glistened on brooks the color of dark tea, where buried cedars lay. On nearby hills, files of white cedars paraded against the blue sky. Mick knew these woods almost as well as Joe Turner and Pop Oxenford. He knew the stories, the place names. He could hear Pop's voice, telling him he had planted those pines on the bank of Wading River.

Look at them big pines. You'd never think I'm as old as them big pines, would you? I seen all of these big pines grow. All around here was cut down for charcoal.

Mick recognized Dan Dillet's field, overgrown now with blueberry bushes and scrub oaks, where Dan had made charcoal. The Hocken Lowlands near the creek, where rattlesnakes by the dozen gathered. Bony Hole, where a man named Bony used to water his horse.

I want volunteers for this job, the colonel had said. Sergeant O'Day had been the first marine to step forward. Some people thought it sounded too hairy, but Mick thought Binh Nghai sounded a lot better than life at the firebase, with the colonel pulling chickenshit inspections and Charlie firing mortars and rockets into your lap at all hours of the day and night. Binh Nghai meant you were on your own, without an officer within ten miles. It meant you could make your own rules, fight your own war.

Wasn't that what the Corps wanted us to do? Mick asked Joe Turner in the silence of his mind. He looked across another creek at a red cedar that Pop Oxenford said he had planted. *I went to school there, by that red cedar.*

On another day like this they had come to Binh Nghai. They had been dumped out of the truck before the fort, Sergeant O'Day, Corporal Lummis, and ten other marines to live and perhaps die with the five thousand people of this village on the Tra Bong River, near the coast of Quang Tri province.

The fort looked like something out of a movie of Arizona in Wild West days, with some Vietnamese touches. It had whitewashed brick walls and an inner courtyard. Beyond the outer walls was a moat. It had once been the home and headquarters of the French district chief. Inside they found twenty members of the South Vietnamese Popular Forces, who slept at the fort and only went into the village in daylight. The PFs were all marked men, and if they slept with their wives or girlfriends during the night, the VC murdered them. They had murdered one man in his parents' house the night before the marines arrived.

Mick and Joe hiked across the overgrown field where the town of Washington had once stood. *Jim Snow's was the last house. I was awful fond of his daughter Martha,* Pop Oxenford said.

They had sauntered into the market square of Binh Nghai, looking the place over. There sat Trai by a plate of fish her father had caught the night before. At Mick's suggestion, their Boston aristocrat, Belknap, had bought the whole plate. Mick would never forget the way Trai had wrinkled her nose and laughed when he had pointed to Belknap and said, "His name's Rockefeller."

No. The screen had gone dark; something was wrong

with the projector. There was Trai in the kitchen of that freezing trailer with the ugly black-and-blue bruise on her cheek, saying to him, *I know I deserve to suffer great beatings for my sins. But I am afraid of the difficulties that will arise for all of us. You must help us, Mick. For Suong's sake.*

Suong? That wiseass kid? Mick had tried to be a sort of American father to him. He had taught him how to surf, he had taken him fishing on the bay and the ocean. Now Suong had Uncle Mick sized up for the dummy he was. Suong talked about going to Princeton as casually as some city big shot on vacation from Bucks County or Morristown.

The hell with Suong. Mick wanted to touch Trai's battered face with magical fingers, he wanted to pick her up and carry her to his car and drive into the Pines and disappear with her forever.

Jesus, Jesus. Fix the projector, quick. Otherwise he was going to lose everything, he was going to lose the Pines, Joe, the Corps, all the things that held him together. He was going back to Paradise Beach and dismember Father Hart. He was going to put the barrel of his .38 in Phac's mouth and say, *Swallow it.*

The Corps wouldn't want me to do that, would they, Joe?

Of course not, Joe said in his own silence. That's one thing we both understand, Mick. Marines don't cry.

WHEN IRISH EYES START SMILING

"*Dinnseanchas*," Dick O'Gorman said. "That's what the ancient Irish used to call it. The poetry of place. A man or woman carried in his head an amalgam of history, mythology, and folklore connecting every piece of the landscape to the past. It's how they gained control of the unseen forces that could cure or curse them."

"You know so much," Barbara O'Day sighed.

"Tell us the one about the Belfast Express again," said Sunny Dan Monahan.

O'Gorman sliced into his porterhouse. "You tell it, Billy," he said.

"The blether blows up the Belfast Express and goes to confession," Billy said. "He blirts it and the collar tells him to recite ten Marys and do the stations."

"Oh, hoh hoh, do you get it, Mick?" gasped Sunny Dan, the loose skin on his neck bouncing up and down like the crop of a turkey. "Do the stations."

"I get it," Mick said, shoveling in the steak and potatoes.

"What's wrong with you?" Barbara O'Day said. "It's a joke."

"I know."

Mick chomped his last piece of steak, downed his coffee, and put on his jacket. "Gotta go to work."

"You don't go to work till midnight," his mother said. "Unless you call what you'll be doing between now and midnight work."

"Investigation," Mick said. "I'm investigating a mystery."

"What would that be?"

"Who put the chowder in Mrs. Murphy's overalls," Mick said.

"Ho ho ho," said Sunny Dan. "That's pretty good, Mick. The chowder in Mrs. Murphy's overalls. Do you get it Barbara?"

"I get it. But her name isn't Murphy," Barbara O'Day said.

Mick laughed and vanished into the night. Billy Kilroy glowered after him. Billy badly wanted to investigate somebody's overalls and he was getting no help from Mick. The dislike between the two of them had been instant and mutual. O'Gorman was beginning to worry about it.

Billy thought the whole deal was a right haun, as they say in Belfast when describing a mess, and Mick was the worst part of it. "What the fook are we dooin' livin' with a bloody B-Special?" Billy had demanded, when he awoke the day after his shooting contest at the Golden Shamrock, hungover and furious at his defeat.

A B-Special was a Belfast cop. It had taken O'Gorman another hour to convince the sod that Mick was not going to blow his whistle on them.

The whole deal was no great pleasure so far for Dick O'Gorman, he thought as Barbara O'Day served them big pieces of apple pie for dessert. But that could change soon enough.

"By God, did you make this too?" he crooned. "I'm

goin' to take you home with me, Barbara Kathleen."

They were first-naming it now. She still blushed like a schoolgirl when he looked at her, but it was a delicate come-hither pink now. Although she had to be over fifty, Barbara O'Day looked no more than thirty-five. She had kept her figure, and her red hair was still as fine and glossy as it must have been at eighteen. What was wrong with the American Irish, letting a flower like this woman go unplucked?

"When I was your age, I didn't pay no attention to Ireland," Sunny Dan said. "I should've, but we was up to our eyeballs in our own politics, you know? Were any of your relatives in the Easter Rising?"

"My father, God save his soul, stood with De Valera at the bridge," O'Gorman said.

"You don't say."

Barbara's eyes never left him as he recounted the wholly imaginary exploits of the O'Gormans in the Easter Rising of 1916. He almost gagged, praising Eamon De Valera and Michael Collins and others who ended up betraying the IRA and the Republic and setting up the vile capitalist state in southern Ireland that made up its deficits peddling Irish sweepstakes tickets in America until the Yanks started lotteries of their own.

He would be telling the same lies to Irish organizations in New Jersey, from the Ancient Order of Hibernians to the Sons of the Shillelagh. None of the Irish-Americans had the foggiest notion of the knotted, pitted hatreds that divided modern Ireland. It was necessary to pretend to love the pseudo-republic of the south in order to stir their sympathy and loosen their wallets on behalf of the persecuted Catholics of the north.

"Dick's done a lot more up in Belfast than those Easter heroes did in Dublin. He told me about it," Barbara said.

"In confidence, in confidence, Barbara Kathleen," he said. "The one thing I want them to say when they lay me in the grave is, he never hawked himself as a hero. There's too many others, such as Billy here, who've done far braver things."

Amazing, he thought, when you tell the truth, it can be stated with such conviction. Barbara of course did not believe a word of it. Jesus had the right idea when he forbade those he cured to tell anyone. Naturally they told everyone they met. In the crooked interior of the human heart, everything runs backward.

Upstairs after dinner, Billy Kilroy grabbed O'Gorman's arm. "You start fookin' her and I'm gonna put it in me book."

"Your book? That's news indeed. I didn't think you could write your name, much less write a book."

"I got orders to watch you close."

"What do you know? I've got orders to watch you. I guess they don't trust either of us."

"How long we gawn to hang around this fookin' place? Where's the fookin' weapons?"

"There's certain arrangements that have to be made. I'm going to a meeting with the police chief to see about them, tonight."

"I'm gawn along."

"Only if you promise to keep your stupid mouth shut."

"I'm gawn to make sure you don't start singin' the Ballymena anthem."

The *Ballymena anthem* was Belfast slang for "What's in it for me?"

"My God, take your bottle away and you're a regular ate-the-bolts," O'Gorman snarled.

An ate-the-bolts was a workaholic, the last thing in the world Kilroy was in danger of becoming.

Billy drew his Zastava autopistol, a small, extremely powerful gun made in Yugoslavia. "You can blether all you want, this has the last word. Remember that."

"I can use one of them too," O'Gorman said.

On this note of sweet harmony, they sallied into the night to the home of the chief of police, William O'Toole.

He greeted them with a glass of whiskey in his hand—not a good sign. "Come on in, we got the joint to ourselves. Mrs. Bigmouth is off runnin' the Rosary Society."

In the living room, Desmond McBride was already ensconced, grinning like a tourist poster as usual. They were a pair of contrasts. McBride was all light and air, the original smiling Irishman. O'Toole spoke and moved like a man carrying a thousand-pound weight on his back.

"Where's Leo and lovely Melody?" O'Gorman always liked to keep track of everyone in an operation.

Desmond McBride looked troubled. "Leo's stomach is bothering him."

"They don't want to have anything to do with the Mob," O'Toole said, his voice thick with sarcasm. "They wanna pretend they didn't find out organized crime was involved until it was too late."

"It's nice to hear someone in America has a worse political smell than the IRA," O'Gorman said.

"Here's the deal, from the Mob side," O'Toole said. "They're ready to put up a million and a half for the cocaine if the stuff's any good. But they wanna look at it first. They don't trust these Cubans. They don't trust anybody period."

"Fair enough," O'Gorman said, letting O'Toole fill half his glass with Irish whiskey.

"What the fook is this?" Billy said as O'Toole started to serve him. "I dawn't drink that piss. It's made by the fookin' Prods."

O'Gorman explained to their host that Billy was objecting to the label on the bottle. Bushmills was made in the north of Ireland. "I don't give a shit where it's made, it's the best," O'Toole said. "You want Scotch?"

"Bourbon," Billy said.

Back to business. "If the dope's okay, we run the dough out to the Cubans and get the guns and whatever else is in the shipment. Des here says the *Enterprise* can handle the load. We go up the Mullica into the Pines, and your guys meet us with the trucks to take the hardware up to Boston."

"Couldn't be smoother," O'Gorman said.

"Yeah, except for some details. Joey Zaccaro's godfather don't go for foolin' around with drugs. So this thing's got to be airtight, understand? Joey told me to tell you that before we meet him."

"Unless his godfather vacations in Ireland, which I doubt, he has little to worry him," O'Gorman said.

"You're gonna be movin' around the state. You're gonna meet a lot of people while you're passin' the basket."

"Hey, that's good stoof," Billy said, holding out his glass for more bourbon. "I drunk it in Sofia. I thought theirs was cow piss, but that's good stoof."

"Sofia?" Desmond McBride said. "Bulgaria? Didn't those fellows shoot the pope?"

"Yah, but the fooker they put on the job couldn't hit a van if he was sittin' in the driver's seat," Billy said. "He only plugged the Polock in the belly. You gotta go for the head. That's the ony sure ticket."

"You see how brutalized lads become in the north," O'Gorman said. "How ready they are to endorse random violence."

He was trying to get McBride's mind off Sofia. O'Toole looked at O'Gorman with incredulity plain on his face. He knew what the IRA did with guns. He did not care if they used one to shoot the pope. He was a desperate man. Exactly why, O'Gorman did not know. He could smell desperation in a man. It always made him dangerous.

"There's some more details. I ain't doin' this for dear old Ireland, like Des here. He's got plenty of dough from his goddamn fish. I want two hundred grand off the top of the take. Do I get it?"

The Ballymena anthem. "Sure," O'Gorman said. The actual price of the Cubans' weaponry was a million. The rest was to be used to finance the legal defense of several IRA gunrunners whom the FBI had recently arrested. But the weapons took precedence over all other considerations—and without O'Toole's cooperation they could never bring them ashore.

Billy Kilroy did not approve O'Gorman's concession to O'Toole. "What the fook kinda patriotism is that?" he snorted.

"It ain't patriotism, it's business. I gave up on patriotism a long time ago," O'Toole said. "Do I get the two hundred grand? If I don't, you might as well go back to Ireland tomorrow."

"I said it was okay," O'Gorman replied.

"What about this shrimp?" O'Toole glared contemptuously at Billy Kilroy. Was the basic division of the world between the large men and the small men? Could Marx have been wrong? O'Gorman wondered.

"He's not in charge of this operation."

O'Toole held out his hand. "We got a deal. Only one thing left to figure out. Who's gonna crew the *Enterprise?* The regular crew's mostly clam diggers."

"Mostly what?" O'Gorman asked, totally confused.

"Local men. Not Irish," McBride said. He thought for a moment. "I'd say our best bet would be that Vietnamese, Phac. He doesn't know enough English to figure out what's going on. And Mick. I've always had Mick in mind."

"Have you talked to him about it?" O'Toole asked, contempt still thick in his voice. O'Gorman sensed that Mick shared the police chief's opinion of McBride.

"No," McBride said.

"I'll handle it," O'Toole said. "He'll do it for me."

"Are you sure?" O'Gorman asked, remembering Mick calling Billy Kilroy a communist.

"I own Mick. It'll be okay," O'Toole said.

"I just thought—he seems a bit troubled. Is it because of his parents' marriage?"

"Mick's okay," O'Toole insisted. "He's better off with no father than with that weasel of a numbers runner. I'm as much his father as anybody."

"And we'll have you at the helm, Des?" O'Gorman said.

"You bet we will," O'Toole said with relish.

McBride looked as if he might get sick on the rug. "Yes."

A horn beeped twice outside. "There's Zaccaro," O'Toole said. "Come on."

They put on their coats and followed him out to McBride's car. This time Billy had no difficulty finding the bar in the seatback. "Hey, this is livin'," Billy said, pouring himself another glass of bourbon. Chief O'Toole helped himself to a lot of Irish. O'Gorman decided to keep his head clear and declined another drink.

They followed a long blue limousine into the night. After about twenty minutes, they pulled up before a white bathing pavilion with SURF CLUB in large red letters on it side.

Downstairs in the men's locker room, which had the dank cold of a basement in winter, they met Joey Zaccaro and a gigantic companion. Zaccaro struck O'Gorman as the sort of slime that would make any reasonable man turn against capitalism. His friend looked as tall as the Tuatha da Danaan, the mythical giants who had once inhabited Ireland. He was a helot with murder in his eyes.

"I like to meet someplace where the FBI wiseguys can't have thought of puttin' in a bug," Joey said. "It's a kinda game I play, and so far I ain't lost. I'm the only guy they ain't got a word on. Some agent I know told me that. They got old Tommy the Top doin' everything from baby talkin' his dog to orderin' hits. They ain't got nothin' on me."

"You're wonderful," O'Toole said. "Meet two guys who've killed more people than you've shaken down."

"Oh, yeah?" Joey said. "Meet Angie Scorsese. He don't get impressed easily by that kind of stuff."

"Okay. Now let's talk business," O'Toole said. "You gonna get up the money, Joey? I cut you in on this deal because I owe you one. But I hear you may have trouble raisin' the scratch. Your Big Macaroni'll blow you away if he finds out about it, right? That must make it tough for a two-bit loan shark and swindler like you to move up. Ain't Uncle Tom gonna smell something when you start callin' in all the loans in three states?"

O'Gorman thought O'Toole had lost his mind, insulting Zaccaro that way. But the police chief seemed to know exactly how much he could say. Was it his way of retaining at least a shadow of his integrity?

"After I pull this off, maybe I'll do the blowin' away," Joey said. "I got the dough. I got it right now."

"All of it? These Cubans don't go for down-payment bullshit. Neither do these micks."

Zaccaro flipped a briefcase onto a rubdown table. Click. They looked at wads of thousand-dollar bills. O'Gorman's stomach revolved, his mouth went dry. It was better than a naked woman, the sight of that much money. He could take that briefcase and disappear to South America, Thailand, Australia, for the rest of his life.

"That looks like all of it," O'Toole said.

They parted company with Zaccaro and his oversize goon and drove into the night. O'Gorman was still dazed by the money. He had never seen a million and a half dollars before. The weapons he had bought in other countries had been paid for in useless currencies. A million and a half dollars could be taken anywhere. A million and a half dollars could buy an entire country, in certain parts of the world.

Maybe that was why he dispatched Billy to the local pub without a keeper. He was gambling again, risking his life, his mission, for the touch, the consolation of beauty, of woman, breathing, sighing, surrendering in his arms as the world refused to surrender. He was like a man who had taken LSD or sniffed cocaine. The money created the need and the power for the fantasy of love.

There she sat before the television, with Sunny Dan snoring in his BarcaLounger. She was watching a movie from the dim past, something about the American Civil War. A city was burning, blacks and whites were running and screaming. "How was your meeting?" she asked.

"More of the same. There are times when I grow so discouraged I'm ready to walk into the sea like Cuchulainn."

"Who's he?"

"The greatest warrior of the ancient Irish past. Our Achilles. He died fighting the sea, the only thing he hadn't conquered."

She did not know who Achilles was. That was all right. She was innocent culturally as well as spiritually. Perhaps that was the best, the sweetest thing about her. She was unspoiled. They were always the ones who attracted O'Gorman. He yearned above all to touch innocence. He wanted to believe in his own innocence for a little while. He wanted to be told that he was not responsible for the dead children, the amputeed brides, the kneecapped teenagers. He wanted her to whisper admiration for an Ireland that never existed, an Ireland created by his rhetoric. He wanted her to convince him that his soul was not damned for all eternity, as Deirdre had told him more than once.

"You won't . . . do anything like that, will you?" she said. "I thought of doing it once, when I was pregnant with Mick. Somebody must have been praying for me. Somebody wanted me to stay alive. I don't know why, anymore."

He was staggered for a moment to find himself in depths he had not suspected.

"We all wonder that at times," he said. "Until we find someone that gives it all meaning. I've been searching for that person for thirty years now."

"I thought your wife left you twenty years ago."

"The previous ten were as empty, with her, as the next twenty without her."

"How sad."

"Can I come to you tonight? I have nothing to offer you but sadness. But I think you can turn it into joy."

"Yes," she whispered. "Yes."

Sunny Dan snored. On television the city burned. The

money burned in O'Gorman's mind, a golden flame. Tonight there would be joy. Tomorrow perhaps sorrow, perhaps something even more magical. Salvation?

He would come to her on his knees, like a pilgrim to the shrine of the Virgin at Knock.

Oh, oh, oh. You blaspheming bastard. You lost, dangerous blaspheming bastard.

AT HOME WITH MRS. LAZARUS

One-two, one-two, one-two-three. Push-ups, sit-ups, deep knee bends, Jackie Chasen finished her last exercises of the day, even though her body sent shock waves of pain racing up various ganglia to the cerebral cortex. She stopped, breathing heavily, and contemplated herself in the full-length mirror. The plastic surgeon had done a good job of rebuilding her face. She recognized herself. But there was a certain blankness, a lack of expression most of the time. The surgeons had removed some nerves that could not be replaced. Only when she smiled was there a resemblance to the old Jackie. So she smiled a lot, even when she did not feel like it.

Fortunately, most of the time she felt like it. Mentally, spiritually, she was no longer the old Jackie. During the months she had spent in the Atlantic City Medical Center, the New York Center for Reconstructive Surgery, the Leahy Clinic, and other hospitals, she had slowly escaped her previous self. She had been like a snake wiggling out of last year's skin, a soul groping for a new body. The new body that the doctors had given her, with its plastic kneecaps, aluminum hips, titanium elbows (all concealed by expert bone and skin grafts, of course), added reality to the vision. So did going blond.

Studying her sucked-in waist, her firm breasts beneath the leotard, Jackie decided it was still a good body. That was another reason not to abuse it. The new Jackie was off dope and booze and was resolutely opposed to junk sex with humanoids like Joey Zaccaro. Although she still despised her mother's liberal Democratic politics and her late grandfather's Goldwater conservatism, she now considered herself apolitical.

The new Jackie was in search of new values, new virtues. She was reading all the books she had ignored in college to protest the Vietnam War and establishment oppression. She had fallen in love with modern poetry, above all the vibrant chants of Dylan Thomas.

"And death shall have no dominion." That was her motto, her faith. Life could triumph over death. She had proven it in her own body, her own soul. "The force that through the green fuse drives the flower drives my green age." Like Dylan, she had awakened in her thirty-eighth year to "heaven hearing from harbor and neighbor wood the morning beckon."

Clatter. Clump. *What was that?* Jackie stumbled to the dresser beside her bed and pulled out a pistol. Tiptoeing to the door of her bedroom, she peered across the sunken living room. Her Airedale, Taffy, was curled up on the couch, snoring away.

Jackie's heart pounded, her hand shook. She wondered if she could use the gun if Joey Zaccaro or one of his hoodlums came after her. Mick had assured her that Joey would not have the nerve to try anything in Paradise Beach. Just in case, he had given her the gun and taken her out in the Pines one day and taught her how to use it.

Jackie refused to let fear of Joey Zaccaro drive her out of this house. This was where the transformation from self-destructive, out-of-control bitch to mature woman had begun, and this was where it would be completed. Not for the first time, she reproached herself for going to Atlantic City. That was the old cokehead Jackie, creeping back, contesting the new Jackie for possession of her restored body.

She was *happy,* Jackie told herself. She was happy running on the beach each morning and evening, reading her books, watching old movies on her VCR. Now she had Mick O'Day visiting in the dawn. It was great sex. He had a magnificent body. But he seemed to have no interest in taking her back to the girl in white. Whenever she tried to talk about the past, he changed the subject.

He would not tell her anything about himself, beyond minimum facts, some of which she already knew. He had been an athletic hero at Paradise Beach High School, all-state in football, basketball, and baseball. He had been in the marines and served in Vietnam. When she had begun asking questions, revealing her loathing for that war and all wars, he had told her to shut up.

Mick was only interested in athletic sex. Jackie wanted love from a man whose intelligence, whose soul, stirred a response in her battered heart. Where she was going to find this spiritual paragon in Paradise Beach remained a mystery. But she stayed here, determined, hopeful, prayerful, even if she did not believe there was anyone who listened to human pleas for divine help.

Squirming out of her leotard, Jackie stepped into the shower and turned on the hot water. As the jet hit her, she felt a shiver of nerves. When she was alone in the house, she felt jittery in the shower. Was it the scene from *Psycho*?

As if her mind had produced the reality, a hand reached into the shower and clutched her by the throat. It was attached to the black sleeve of a raincoat. Gagging, she was dragged into the bedroom by a behemoth in the rest of the raincoat.

There stood Joey Zaccaro. "How you doin', beautiful?" he said. "I'm in town on business. I thought I'd pay you a little visit."

"She's some piece," said the behemoth, who had now lifted her off the ground, his hand still around her throat. Jackie clutched at his wrist. The room began to grow dim.

"Put her down on the bed, you asshole," Joey said. "I don't wanna kill her just yet. First we're gonna have some fun."

They jammed a gag in her mouth—a foul-tasting hand-kerchief—and tied her down on the bed, her legs spread wide, her arms above her head. Joey began talking about what they were going to do. "First, we're gonna fuck you until you don't know who you are. Then we're gonna play some games with this."

He unfolded a long, gleaming knife.

Joey stood there, the knife in his hand, a sneer on his animal face. Jackie closed her eyes. It was impossible to escape the past after all. Impossible not to pay for her sins. She was going to die in this brutal, disgusting way. Death had final dominion no matter what Dylan Thomas said.

The silvery crash of breaking glass jerked her head toward the sliding door that led from the bedroom to the sundeck. A pistol gripped by a black-gloved hand appeared through the glass. The pistol did not go off. It just clicked. There was a chunking sound as if something heavy had dropped onto a pillow or into sand. A round red spot appeared on Joey Zaccaro's forehead. Terror flick-ered across his swarthy face. The knife slipped from his hand and he toppled onto the bed at Jackie's feet.

In front of the bathroom door, the behemoth was reach-ing for his gun when the pistol clicked again. Another chunking sound, another round red spot on the forehead. The bodyguard thudded to the rug with a strangled snarl of defiance in his throat.

The pistol, the black-gloved hand, hesitated for a moment. Then the barrel, which had an odd bulge beneath it, swung slowly toward Jackie. She watched, horrified, as it contemplated snuffing out her life too. But there was no click, no murderous bullet. Instead, the gun, the black-gloved hand, withdrew into the darkness. Jackie was left on the bed, shaking and sobbing with terror. She did not believe what was happening to her life.

But it was happening.

BURIAL PARTY

A quiet night—exactly what Mick wanted and needed. Absolutely nothing was happening in Paradise Beach. No aging boozers beating up on their worn-out wives, no kids taunting some retired bozo into threatening them with a gun, no complaints about loud televisions. In the winter, quiet nights were really quiet. Unlike the summer, with drunks galore on the boardwalk and attempted rapes on the beach and wild parties in every other house. Even the quiet summer nights were hairy.

As usual, Mick's visit to the Pines had calmed him down. The unreeling of Binh Nghai had stopped for a while. But he was left with a sullen wish to escape the whole lousy setup—his mother, Uncle Bill O'Toole and his crummy marriage, his grandfather with his old jokes—and now these two Irishmen who had suddenly settled into the house. He got a bad smell from them. His cop's nose did not buy O'Gorman's story that they were over here to raise money for a Belfast orphanage.

Jackie Chasen was Mick's only consolation. When he spun the police cruiser onto the road that twisted around Leeds Point, he saw lights still blazing in her house. She told him some nights she did not get to sleep until dawn. This must be one of them. Suddenly the thought of Jackie's terrific body beneath him or above him on the bed had irresistible appeal. Balling was a kind of escape, a trip into a world without faces, names, memories.

Mick raised Tom Brannigan on the radio and told him he was going to check out Leeds Point by foot. He had seen a shadow that might be a sneak thief. It was a well-established code for saying don't call me for a half hour. As far as Brannigan knew, Mick was taking a snooze.

He rang the front doorbell. Nothing. "Jackie," he called. "It's your friendly neighborhood cop." Nothing. Slightly alarmed, he went back to the car and found the skeleton key that worked for almost every lock in Paradise Beach. It was useful because so many houses were shut for the winter and they sometimes developed internal problems such as a burst pipe.

"Jackie?" he called when the door swung open. "It's me—Mick."

He flashed his light down the dark entrance hall. The Airedale, Taffy, was sprawled on the rug in the center of the living room. What the hell was wrong with the mut? Then Mick saw the puddle of blood beside the dog's slashed throat. "Holy shit," he gasped, drawing his gun.

He found Jackie spread-eagled on the bed, her terrified eyes bulging above the foul gag in her mouth. Beside the bed were Joey Zaccaro and a big guy with bodyguard written all over him, both dead with identical bullet wounds in their foreheads.

Mick untied the gag and the ropes and Jackie told him what had happened. "Put some clothes on. I'm calling Uncle Bill."

Jackie was in the living room, weeping over Taffy, when Bill O'Toole charged into the house. He glared at the two corpses and rushed out to Joey Zaccaro's car. He came back with a wild expression on his face. "Where's the goddamn money?" he roared.

"What money? Did you see any money?" Mick asked Jackie.

"No."

"Don't bullshit me!" O'Toole snarled, grabbing Mick by his shirt.

Mick tore himself loose. "I'm not bullshitting you. There's no money."

"These guys had a million and a half bucks with them. It's gone." O'Toole grabbed Mick again. "I'm askin' you one more time and I want it absolutely straight. I want it to be the straightest thing you ever said to me."

Mick disentangled himself again, totally baffled by O'Toole's berserk behavior. "There's—no—goddamn—money."

"Then she's gotta have it."

O'Toole glared at Jackie with murder in his eyes. She frantically shook her head, obviously thinking he was as dangerous as Zaccaro. "I didn't see any money. I don't know anything about it," she said.

"Are you goin' nuts?" Mick said. "I told you, when I got here, she's tied up on the bed." He picked up the knife and practically shoved it in his uncle's face. "That asshole was gonna use this to carve initials on her. I only wish I got here in time to shoot him first."

"It was a put-on," O'Toole insisted. "She tied herself up and you were too stupid to notice it."

"Yeah. And first she killed her dog to pass the time waitin' for these bozos to arrive, and she plugs them with one bullet each before they can move."

Mick took the Colt .38 he had given Jackie out of the dresser drawer. "I taught her to use this gun, which still has six bullets in it. I happen to know it'd be a miracle if she hit a battleship at twenty feet. Calm down, will you, Uncle Bill? I don't know what's happening, but I don't like it very much."

"Don't tell me to calm down! My life, your life, all our lives are on the line here. Including hers. I'm gonna search this house. Don't try and stop me."

Mick watched O'Toole tear the house apart for a half hour. He emptied closets, he cleared kitchen shelves, he peered into the stove, the oil burner. Outside, he tore apart Joey Zaccaro's car. He pulled out the seats, he exhumed the spare tire from the trunk. He came back, panting, his eyes even more berserk.

"Okay. It's not here. The guy who iced them must have known about the money. He wasn't just a Good Samaritan tryin' to protect Miss American Virtue here. I got a couple of other places to look. Meanwhile, you got a job to do. Take these guys and their car and lose them way back in the Pines. Put them into one of those cedar creeks where you can't see the bottom."

"You're not gonna report this?" Mick said. "I don't get it."

"I know you don't get it. But you will. As for you," O'Toole said, turning to Jackie, "you almost got hurt tonight. You know as well as I do that it was your own goddamn fault for screwing a scumbag like this guy in the first place and then takin' a walk on him. If you don't like the way you almost died tonight, just say something to a reporter or a state trooper about Joey Zip's brains gettin' splashed all over your bedroom. You'll die in a way that'll make what Joey was gonna do to you seem like a mercy killin'. I won't do it. I won't haveta do it. Joey was a scumbag but he was Tommy Giordano's nephew. His sister's only son. Do you know what that means? Do you know who Tommy the Top Giordano is?"

Jackie nodded numbly. Mick knew too. Tommy was the Mafia boss of New Jersey. Whatever was happening, it was starting to stink. It was starting to stink up the whole town.

"Okay. Then you got the message." O'Toole grabbed Jackie by both arms and lifted her off the floor. "Have you got it?"

"Get your goddamn hands off her," Mick snarled, tearing Jackie free.

"You've had a lot more then your hands on her," O'Toole raged. "Do you think I don't know that? Do you think I don't know all the games you midnight-to-eight assholes play? Get rid of these guys before it gets light. I'll see you at the house later. I'll tell you what's goin' on."

He left Mick staring at the bodies. "What is it, Mick? What's happening?" Jackie said.

"I don't know. But I think we better do what he says."

Jackie backed Zaccaro's Cadillac into the garage. Mick dragged the bodies through the living room and kitchen and shoved Zaccaro into the trunk and the behemoth into the backseat. He threw Taffy's body on top of Zaccaro. "You're gonna have to drive the hearse," Mick said. "Can you handle it? I'm gonna travel fast."

"I can handle it."

Jackie followed Mick's police car over the Bay Bridge and up the long, straight highway through the Pines. Mick hit ninety all the way until he signaled a right run and began lurching and bumping down a sandy track at fifty miles an hour.

They plunged into a hollow and over a hump that sent Mick's head up to the roof. Behind him he saw the Cadillac suddenly swerve to the right and disappear into the pines. As he slammed on his brakes, he heard it crash into a tree. Cursing, he got out and found Jackie sobbing hysterically, trying to disentangle herself from the dead behemoth. "His arm came into the front seat when we went over the bump!" she cried.

Belted in, Jackie was unhurt, but the impact had smashed the Cadillac's grille into the engine. "Get in," Mick snarled, dragging her to the police car. "We gotta get a shovel."

He drove with furious concentration, throwing Jackie all over the car, letting instinct, his knowledge of the Pines, turn them right, left, at twisting intersections in the inky darkness. Finally they hurtled into Pop Oxenford's clearing, with its littered corpses of old cars.

Mick ran up to the small house and burst in the door yelling, "Don't shoot, it's the cops!"

Pop was sitting in the easy chair listening to some late-night radio talk show. He gave Mick the shovel with no questions asked, of course, and followed him out to the car, although he was only wearing his red flannel underwear.

"This is her?" he said, shining a flashlight into Jackie's face.

"Yeah."

"She's a looker all right." He smiled at Jackie. "Oxenford's the name. I've been tellin' him to bring you out here. But I guess this ain't a social visit. I guess it ain't social at all."

"We got trouble, Pop. I'll tell you about it later," Mick said.

They roared back down the twisting sand roads to Zaccaro's Cadillac. Mick dragged the bodies out and shoved them into the police car. They plunged down the black, atrocious roads for another twenty minutes. Mick stopped, backed up, and turned the car at right angles to the road. The headlights revealed an oozing swamp. Stripping to the buff, Mick waded into it and flung muck over his shoulder for five minutes, then dragged the bodies into the pit and covered them with mud and dead tree branches.

Behind him, Mick could hear Jackie saying over and over again, "And death shall have no dominion. And death shall have no dominion." It was almost good for a laugh.

"Oh, Mick, Mick," she sobbed when he rejoined her in the police car. "Make love to me. Make love to me. I'm so scared."

"I'm covered with mud. We'll go back to the house and take a shower."

"No, I want to do it here, now. I need it now!"

Maybe he needed it too. He dragged her out of the car and practically tore off her clothes. They stood there, naked, in the dark. The cold wind was harsh on Mick's flesh but it did not chill him. He was numb, thinking and trying not to think about why Bill O'Toole was doing business with Tommy Giordano.

"Wipe me off," he said.

She used his shirt. The wind sighed through the tops of the pines. "Do you hear it?" Mick said, his hands on her breasts.

"What?"

"The air tune. The Pineys say it's the devil playing his violin. If he meets you and you can't outdance him, you lose your soul. I always thought it was bullshit. Now I'm not so sure."

Mick lay down in the backseat of the police car and Jackie mounted him. Up, up, up into her body slithered the tree of life, but this time there was no escape from what he was thinking.

"Death shall have no dominion," Jackie whispered. "It won't. It won't."

It was not good for a laugh. Mick was beginning to think from now on nothing in Paradise Beach would be good for a laugh.

MIDNIGHT MERRY-GO-ROUND

"Let's do it again," whispered Barbara Kathleen O'Day.

"My God, you're an earth mother, Astarte and Circe rolled into one," O'Gorman said.

"Roll me over, roll me over, lay me down and do it again."

"Shhh, for God's sake, are you drunk?"

"Drunk with love."

She was as sweet, as sad, as crazed, as any soul in the slums of Dublin. As any in the crooked streets of Derry and Belfast. Were you sent here, O'Gorman? Sent to lift her beyond sadness, beyond the blank monotony of her life?

She had told him everything in her breathy little-girl voice. The smooth-talking local who had filled her belly with Mick and then sailed away to fight in Korea, the forced marriage to the son of the city's chief bookmaker, who had slavered after her so long he had no compunction about taking damaged goods, the inevitable separation and the empty years as her parents' cook and bottle washer while Mick grew into a man who lived by the code of his generation.

Thirty years of the same same same. Thirty years of mass and Communion and confession with nothing to tell. Thirty years of waiting for something and getting nothing but the same same same. Now I know I was waiting for you.

He had listened as usual. Every woman a man laid insisted on telling her life story. It was part of the ritual. But this story tore at O'Gorman's tired heart in unexpected ways. He saw the tragedy of the diaspora, the agony of Ireland being repeated here in America, and no doubt in Australia and Canada and everywhere else the wild geese had wandered. The tragedy of Ireland ridden, ruined by her priests. While it shredded his heart, it gave him a new furious resolve to end it, with the gun and the bomb if necessary. End it for once and for all.

Yes, in the name of Barbara Kathleen Monahan O'Day he would be Ireland's new priest, his hands dripping with the blood of the sacrificed. He would resist the mad magic of Joey Zaccaro's money and continue the blind struggle in the dark.

Driving. Sometimes Bill O'Toole felt like he had spent his life driving. Forty years of driving these stupid streets as a cop. Driving anywhere, anyplace, on Sunday to get beyond the sound of his wife's voice. Yak yak yak. Singing that stupid song she had asked the band to play at their wedding: "Marie." Dancing around the living room half in the bag, trying to get him to dance too.

Marie, the dawn is breaking. Marie. Marie, your miserable neck will be breaking if you don't shut up.

Driving. Like his son, Jimmy: Ace. Driving his plane into the antiaircraft bursts over Hanoi. All right, he died like a marine, but what does that mean anymore? A year later, you had to stand there as chief of police and watch them piss on the American flag on the boardwalk. They did it again the next year. By that time Jimmy and his plane were junk in the jungle.

Part of the summer of protest against the war. Yeah. Part of making them feel virtuous. They screwed on the beach all night and pissed on the flag during the day. Now they were all on Wall Street making two hundred grand a year. Yuppies. Goddamned traitors making two hundred grand a year. The next thing, one of them would run for president.

Only the bearer bonds had kept Bill O'Toole sane. Knowing that $5 million was waiting there to be divided between the four daughters of Sunny Dan Monahan and their husbands, when the old gasbag got around to dying. When things got really bad, Bill told himself what he would do with that million dollars. He would quit this crummy job and head for California. Maybe buy a piece of a football team like the Oakland Raiders and meet some power players. Park Marie in some condo in Santa Barbara and spend most of his time in LA on business. Funny business.

The bearer bonds had been his consolation when he started thinking about all the money Desmond had made from his fish business and Wilbur Gargan had made from the Golden Shamrock while Bill O'Toole lived with Marie on his penny-ante salary.

The money. Where was Zaccaro's money? The micks must have done it. Who else knew it was there? Desmond? Gargan? Wilbur wasn't in on it. No one trusted him to keep his mouth shut in that bar after midnight, when he drank as hard as the customers. Leo McBride and his liberal slut? Where would Leo get the balls to ice Zaccaro and his bodyguard? He hid in Yale Law School, wetting his pants at the mere thought of going to Vietnam.

Mick couldn't come. They had tried everything. Jackie had gone down on him and he had gone down on her.

Now he had her up against a tree, stroking her from behind, wild, vicious thrusts. She was moaning and sobbing but he couldn't come.

The wind whined through the trees. Was it the devil playing the air tune? He thought of Jackie last Sunday after the pistol lesson, lying on the hood of the car, laughing, while he drove around and around the clearing looking up that beautiful snatch. She was the wildest thing he had ever seen. She had money. Why not marry her? he had thought. Why not let her set him up in a garage building custom cars?

Now this craziness, burying dead men in the Pines. Now he knew he could never marry her. It was the same reason why he couldn't come. The night, the dead, the darkness, had started the Binh Nghai movie unreeling in his head again. Trai was in his arms beside the river, murmuring pieces of words against his throat. Whispering in pidgin, *Me love you, marine*. Then some poem in Vietnamese. Something about flowers.

And all the time, the 409th North Vietnamese Army Battalion was moving into position to attack the fort. All the time while Trai was saying those things to him, she knew what was about to happen at the fort. She had said the same things and more to her Viet Cong lover, Le Quan Chien, earlier in the day in the safe hooch a mile down the river.

Mick had come that night. He had come like a fish at the bait. He had come and come and come until the darkness blossomed with flame and the explosions of the sappers' bangalores rolled across the rice paddies and the mortars crumped and the AK-47s chattered and the BAR, the fort's only BAR, clattered in reply.

His men, his marines, and the PFs were dying and he was out in the dark chasing pussy. That was why he could not come now. He could never come in the dark in the woods again. He went cold with the memory, the unreeling, maddening memory. His prick was a rod of cold iron forever in the dark woods listening to the air tune.

* * *

Desmond McBride was trying to make love to his wife,
Teresa. It had taken her by surprise. He had not touched her
for at least six months. Not since summer had faded.
Desmond was a summer lover. That was the only thing that
stirred his sixty-four-year-old blood, memories of strutting
down the boardwalk in 1946 wearing his white suit with
Teresa on his arm. One of Sunny Dan Monahan's daughters. Even then Desmond had been more thrilled by Teresa's
lineage than he had been by her shape and conversation.

The shape tended to be rounded, even then. Teresa had
taken after her mother. She had a tendency to gain weight.
Poor dear Mrs. Monahan had weighed 380 pounds when
she died. Teresa was pushing two hundred and she was not
as tall as her mother. What was sister-in-law Barbara's
secret? Desmond mused as he fondled and hoped for an
erection. She had never gained a pound. She had the same
svelte shape she had displayed when she was eighteen and
every male her age on Paradise Beach had panted after her.

Ugliness and fear were driving Desmond to this extraordinary (for him) winter excursion. These are not erotic
emotions and the net result of his fondles was zero. He
sighed and scolded his erratic member. It had failed him
on his wedding night. It had failed him frequently in their
thirty-eight years of wedded semibliss.

"That settles it, I'm going on a diet," Teresa said. She
always resolved to go on a diet when Desmond failed in
the bedroom.

"It's all right. I'm just tired," he said.

Tired of Black Dick O'Gorman and his slimy little
friend Kilroy, with his foul tongue. Tired of the swamp
into which his willingness to help Ireland, the land of his
ancestors, seemed to be leading him. His brilliant Washington, D.C., son and daughter-in-law with their heads
full of advanced political ideas had urged him to do it. But
neither they nor anyone else had told him about Joey Zaccaro. What was a respectable man, a patriot who loved

two countries, doing in the same room—or bathing pavilion—with Joey Zaccaro?

In the bedroom down the hall, Leo McBride was having a decidedly unromantic conversation with Melody Faithorne. "If you make another pass at that Irish charm boy, I'm through with you," he raged. "I'll file for divorce the day we get back to Washington."

Melody had telephoned O'Gorman, suggesting a lunch date at a restaurant in Atlantic City. He had turned her down, claiming jet lag was still debilitating him. She had called him again tonight. Barbara O'Day answered the phone. She said O'Gorman was out raising money for Ireland.

"Didn't you hear what I told you in the car?" Leo said. "I won't let you humiliate me in front of my family."

Melody's answer was a striptease, to a song Janis Joplin had made famous, "Love Is Like a Ball and Chain." It was marvelously ironic, from her point of view. She chanted other Joplin songs as the clothes dropped to the floor and that exquisite body, the coned breasts, the silken pussy appeared for his delectation.

Naked, she slithered around Leo, expertly undressing him. He knew what was coming next. That magical tongue was going to rove down his body until her lips found his penis. She would suck and suck until there was a pulsing rod that guaranteed satisfaction. Then she would fall into the bed, a mocking smile on her face, and await his delivery.

The tongue began its descent. Leo felt desire swelling in his belly. There was nothing, absolutely nothing in this world that could compare to the pleasure, the creamy, diapasonic delight of her lips on that priapic organ. But something else, something beyond pleasure, was thundering in Leo's soul. "No!" he snarled, and cuffed her in the face with his open hand.

She staggered back, amazed to find her patented for-

mula no longer worked. "No," Leo snarled again. "I mean
it, Melody."

Suddenly Leo began to weep. "We never should have
come here. You know why."

Pounding. Someone was pounding on the front door.
Kicking it. *Bong bong bong.* The intruder had found the
bell in the dark. Desmond McBride flung on his bathrobe
and rushed to the top of the stairs. "Who's that?" he cried.

"It's me!" roared Bill O'Toole.

Had he gone to Atlantic City with that mobster? Was
there another $10,000 loss to cover? Desmond had done
that once. Never again, he had told Brother (in-law) Bill.
He had forbidden Sunny Dan to lend Bill a cent. Sunny
Dan had wanted to mortgage his house. Without the
bearer bonds he was living on Barbara's teacher's salary.
But he still wanted to play the big shot.

"I'll talk to you in the morning," Desmond said.

With a tremendous crash the door flew off its hinges.
Up the stairs Bill charged shouting, *"Have you got it?
Have you got the money? Have Leo and Melody got it?
Are you in on it with them?"*

In his double bed, Sunny Dan was having one of his
golden dreams. It was 1940 or 1944. They were in
Philadelphia or Chicago and they had just nominated
Roosevelt. A band was playing "Happy Days Are Here
Again." Up and down the aisles they pranced, waving
their placards. New Jersey had just delivered her votes for
everybody's hero, the sure ticket and the straight ticket,
the savior who had led them all to the promised land of
the WPA and Social Security and jobs jobs jobs for leaders
like Sunny Dan to dole out to the faithful, the obedient,
the loyal.

*Roosevelt Roosevelt Roosevelt. The sweetest name this
side of heaven. You can have the pope, you can have St.*

Patrick, you can have Jesus Christ. I'll take Roosevelt.
Someone had screamed that in Dan's ear in Philadelphia
or Chicago while they were parading up and down the
aisles.

There stood the Big Man, their leader, Frank Hague,
shaking Roosevelt's hand, getting the okay for another
four years of jobs jobs jobs. The okay for the prosecutors,
the judges, all the guys who could make trouble. The fix,
the beautiful royal-flush guaranteed fix, was in for
another four years.

Afterward up in Sunny Dan's room there was Milly,
the sexiest little Polack in Chicago, or maybe Grace, the
slinkiest little Italian in Philadelphia. Now the band was
playing "There'll Be a Hot Time in the Old Town
Tonight." Sunny Dan was in the saddle, getting his reward
for all the hours in the clubhouse listening to the
lunkheads and the hours in the parlor and the bedroom
listening to Mrs. Two Ton, his wife.

Grace was wiggling and squirming under him telling
him it was the biggest, the best. They had told him the
same thing in Paris in 1918. Ooh la la, *mon Dieu.* Milly
was on top now, swearing it was as long as a Lake Michi-
gan ore boat.

Wham Thump Crash. The dream was in smithereens.
Sunny Dan sat up in bed, trying to pull his ninety-one-
year-old brain into some sort of working order. He stumbled into the hall in his nightshirt. There were his two
sons-in-law, Desmond McBride and Bill O'Toole, the
two lunkheads his money and political know-how had put
in charge of Paradise Beach, shouting curses and insults
at the Irishman O'Gorman, in his shorts and undershirt
outside his daughter Barbara's bedroom. Barbara was
screaming and sobbing inside. Desmond was peering into
the room, saying something to her about being shocked.

"Shut up," O'Toole roared at Barbara. *"I'm not interested in what you got to say. I'm not surprised you're up
to your old tricks with this guy."*

He grabbed O'Gorman and threw him against the wall.

*"Where's the money? You got the money? Someone blew
Zaccaro and his boy away and the money's gone."*

O'Gorman shook from head to foot like a gaffed fish.
"I was here all night. I haven't left the house since you
saw me in the door."

"Where's your wonder boy? Mr. Dead-Eye Dick?"

"I don't know. I'm not his keeper."

"He could be your keeper," O'Toole snarled. "He could
be running for the goal line right now. He could be
halfway to Mexico."

Sunny Dan got the football slang, but O'Gorman
missed the idea of a keeper play entirely. "I don't have a
keeper. I'm an officer of the Irish Republican Army," he
huffed.

"Kilroy's not in his room," Desmond McBride said.
"We already looked."

"How much money is missing?" Sunny Dan said.
Maybe he could put it all to rights by replacing it. They
could mortgage the house. The house was worth at least
two hundred thousand. He hated to see all this screaming
and yelling in the middle of the night. Poor Barbara
didn't know what was going on and was scared half to
death.

"A million and a half bucks," Bill O'Toole said.

"Jesus, Mary, and Joseph," Sunny Dan said. "Who
does it belong to?"

"Tommy Giordano."

Sunny Dan staggered back to his bed. He suddenly felt
191 years old.

Mostly snookered, Billy Kilroy staggered along the
beach. He had fallen off the boardwalk and lay uncon-
scious in the sand for a good hour at least. But that was all
right. That had happened to Billy before. It didn't matter
to the Yanks. They expected him to get drunk. They
thought it was funny. They thought he was something out
of a movie. Especially the big one, the Professor, they

called him. Billy didn't like him. He was a goddamned Englishman. Oxenford. An egg-sucking English name. He didn't buy him a single drink, typical English tight-wad.

The Irish-American Yanks paid for Billy's whiskey and listened to his Belfast bullshit. They were good enough sods, even if they didn't have the political education of a cabbage. They weren't like the wiseass B-Special he was living with, Mick O'Day. He looked at Billy like a cop. He was trouble; something in Billy's gut told him Mick was trouble.

The guns were the thing. Billy told them about the guns they were going to bring back, the right kind of guns this time. Handheld surface-to-air thingies that'd blow the British helicopters out of the air. Maybe blow up an Aer Lingus plane the same way. Show the fog-feeding southies their time was coming too. But he didn't tell them any of that, it was only what he wanted to say. He only told them enough to keep the drinks coming.

In his head Billy started hearing the clang of pans. It was the housewives whacking their pots to let them know a British patrol was coming. Jesus, Mary, turn it off! He didn't want to think about Belfast anymore. He only wanted to remember Sofia, where they had treated them as revolutionary heroes. These Yanks wanted a double-talking television show for their money.

Billy couldn't turn off the pans. He couldn't turn off the roar of the helicopter overhead. Or was it the roar of the motor of a Saracen in the narrow street? You can't believe the noise those motherless armored cars can make while you're lying facedown in a sewer drain with the shit floating past your nose.

Broad Daylight Billy they called him, but when you shoot them in daylight, you have to know where to hide. The last time they ran tear gas into the sewer and blinded his cousin Eddie. He lay there in the gas and let it eat away his eyes.

You can't tell the Yanks that kind of story. They only

want to hear the good ones, the wins. They think it's a stupid movie with a happy ending guaranteed.

"There he is!"

It was the big Yank, the police chief, charging at him across the sand like a runaway Saracen. He grabbed Billy by the back of the neck and started roaring about the money. The mollycoddle Mayor McBride and Slick Dick O'Gorman were with him, their faces lost in the dark.

"The money. You've got the money," they shouted, the waves half-drowning their voices.

It took Billy another minute to realize the gun money was gone. He swore he knew nothing about it. He told them about passing out. They didn't believe him. "What the fook would I do with that kind of money?" Billy screamed. "There's only one bastard in the organization who'd want that kind of money. You're lookin' at him."

Wishing it were a gun, Billy pointed his finger at O'Gorman. There was no question about it. Slick Dick was planning to sing the Ballymena anthem all the way to some bank in Brazil. He had the money. But Billy Kilroy vowed O'Gorman would not live to spend it.

On the second floor of St. Augustine's rectory, Father Dennis McAvoy, better known to others as Captain Arthur Littlejohn, sat at a desk writing a report to his superiors in London. He described how he had followed O'Gorman and Kilroy and the Irish-Americans to their rendezvous with Joey Zaccaro in the bathing pavilion, where he had no difficulty hiding in the cavernous men's locker room and hearing and seeing everything that transpired. Afterward, he had followed Zaccaro and his bodyguard to the house on Leeds Point, where he decided to dispose of them and seize the money.

I realize this is a bit irregular in the USA, but it's no worse than some of the things we did to the Germans over here before World War II. My father was attached to Intrepid's unit, you know, and I've heard a lot about his capers. Taking the money will, I think, put quite a dent in their plans, not to mention their confidence in each other's honesty, if I may use such an inappropriate word in this context.

I'm sending the money to our special address in Dublin where I trust it can be laundered into pounds. It should provide a nice boost to our Special operations in the Republic and in the north. I always thought it was a bit sticky, robbing banks in the Republic for our unattributable funds.

Behind him on the bed was Joey Zaccaro's briefcase, with the thousand-dollar bills in carefully counted piles. He left the letter unsigned and packaged the money in a cardboard carton he had obtained from Father Hart's cellar. He did not mention his exact whereabouts or his disguise. Even at headquarters, not everyone was trustworthy. People talked over cocktails, in bars. His disguise would make especially good telling. Could there be a better way to befuddle the Paddys?

Captain Littlejohn lay down on the bed and tried to sleep, but it was out of the question. He kept seeing Jacqueline Chasen spread-eagled on the double bed with Joey Zaccaro standing over her. It reminded him of a night when he was on reconnaissance in Belfast. He was in bed with his favorite informer, Maeve Flanagan, when two IRA gunmen burst into the room. He dove out the window although he was sure there would be another death squad waiting for him in the alley. But they had come for Maeve, not him, and let him go. Someone had tipped them that she was selling secrets as well as herself. They had tied her on the bed that way and done unspeakable things to her before she died.

Littlejohn's disguise somehow intensified his memory of Jacqueline Chasen on the bed. Did becoming a priest redouble the assaults of lust? An interesting question. Or was it a logical development in the soul of a man who was committing ritual blasphemy every day at the altar, consecrating bread and wine as the body and blood of Christ, distributing it as Communion, when he had no such powers? He was giving the faithful the equivalent of thinly sliced toast instead of the bread of heaven. He had told himself God would understand, but as he performed the rite each day, he had begun to grow indifferent to His opinion. He even began to think of his performances on the altar as acts of defiance, of accusation, to a God who allowed the atrocities the IRA committed in Belfast.

Toward dawn, Captain Littlejohn slipped into a light doze. He dreamt he was somehow soaring over Paradise Beach in the night sky, looking down on the rows of houses and the white surf breaking on the sand. To his amazement and delight, he had grown a pair of immense dark wings. He swooped down on the house where O'Gorman and Kilroy slept and on the nearby houses of the mayor, Desmond McBride, and the police chief, O'Toole. Then he soared skyward again and descended on Leeds Point. Into Jacqueline Chasen's bedroom he flew to softly, silently descend on her sleeping body and fold her in his winged arms.

Like a princess in a fairy tale, she did not awaken. She returned his passionate kisses, she opened her body to his thrusting maleness. Sated, the angel soared again toward the stars, exulting in the power, the freedom that God had bestowed on him. Only then, as he gazed down on Leeds Point, did he notice that his feet had become cloven hooves.

Captain Littlejohn awoke, trembling. Was it a warning, that dream, a warning against the pride that was festering in his soul? He stripped off his clothes and opened his suitcase. From the bottom he extracted a cat-o'-nine-tails. It was time to chastise the treacherous body, to do penance for deeds done on reconnaissance, for wishes that were equally sinful. He opened the window and allowed the cold March wind to chill his flesh.

Captain Littlejohn knelt in the darkness and raised the

whip to whirl its biting edges against his buttocks and back. But the pain did not create the penitence, the humility, he sought. Instead the defiant voice spoke in his soul again. He liked the image of himself as a dark angel, soaring above this tawdry American town, taking his pleasure where he found it, exulting in the power of his ingenious disguise, using his superior weaponry and intelligence to muddle the stupid Paddys and their witless American cousins. He liked it, and if God did not like it—that was God's problem.

STRANGERS IN THE NIGHT

"I know it sounds odious," Dick O'Gorman said, "but don't let it give you the nyrps."

In Belfast, *odious* meant "peculiar." The nyrps were nerves. O'Gorman was telling Hughie McGinty to keep calm. Was that all Black Dick was saying? That nickname was intended, as all Irish nicknames, to describe more than his appearance. In Belfast, McGinty's nickname had been Dink.

The telephone shook in McGinty's hand. "You can't tell me why the delay?"

"We're having some trouble with the Italians. The bastards aren't coming through with the cash. They want to go on credit. We're negotiating. It's a bore but what can we do?"

It didn't ring true. It didn't hit him right. But something else, something deadly, might hit Hughie McGinty in a day or two, if he was the reason why the Italians were stalling.

"I'll stand by," he said.

"Give Nora my regards."

"I can't do that. She doesn't know anything. She'd go crazy if she found out I was doin' this. After what happened to her father and brother, she'd go crazy."

"I just wanted to say hello."

"Well, you can't."

"Ah, poor Dink. Still jealous?"

"We've got two lovely kids. She thinks we've put Belfast behind us."

"So you have, up to a point. You're a lucky sod, Dinko. Let's hope your luck holds."

Click. The line was dead. Josh Moore was tapping his fingers on the counter. "Come on, Hughie. I want a dozen three-quarter-inch plywood cut to these numbers." He shoved the slip at McGinty.

"Right away, right away."

It was go go, rush rush, all day at Friel's Lumber Yard, where McGinty was assistant manager. Eric Friel spent most of the day on the telephone with his latest girlfriend. He had inherited the lumberyard from his father and let McGinty run it, but declined to pay him a salary in accord with his responsibilities. Not the sort of situation that won the heart, McGinty was fond of saying. It didn't stir admiration for American ways.

In Belfast, McGinty's father had worked in a lumberyard not unlike this one. It was owned by a Protestant named Dooley who treated his Catholic workers with uncommon generosity. That did not stop the IRA from burning the yard one night. It might even have impelled them to do it. McGinty's American boss, Friel, to make matters completely confusing, was a Catholic, an RC cheapskate.

McGinty had already joined the IRA when Dooley's Yard went up. He had been recruited in high school by Richard O'Gorman, who taught Irish history and culture to seniors. After hours, he taught them revolution until the authorities caught on and pink-slipped him. O'Gorman

had been McGinty's hero until the night the car bombs
started exploding. McGinty had managed to swallow the
lumberyard even though it put his father on the dole. But
he couldn't swallow the car bombs. They killed innocent
people. He refused to drive one of these rolling death
machines anywhere. He let them call him a coward and
threaten him with kneecapping. He still said no.

Go go, rush rush, shoving plywood and oak and cedar
into the trucks of builders who triple-charged their customers for it and got rich while Hugh McGinty struggled
along on $26,000 a year. It was twice as much as anyone
in Belfast made, but in America money came in and
money went out at a terrifying pace. He was a dishrag
when the day finally ended and young Friel tooled off in
his gray Jaguar and McGinty guided his Ford Escort
through the usual madness on S-3 to his split-level house
in Metuchen.

As he pulled off the highway and drove through the
quiet suburban streets, the rage began to thicken in
McGinty's chest again. By the time he reached his house
it throbbed there like a second heart. He was back in
Belfast, with the engagement ring for Nora in his pocket
and their emigration papers signed and approved, listening to Dick O'Gorman tell him about the night he went to
Nora's house to give her father and brother orders for the
London bombing campaign.

*I went back the next night when I knew she'd be alone.
I told her I just wanted to make sure she was all right. She
cried and I put my arm around her. Before you could say
King Billy we were in the bed screwing away. I came back
many a night after that for a good month. You've got
yourself a lively one, Dink me boy. A lively one.*

McGinty had known exactly what the bastard was
doing. He was dumping shit on his head. It was better
than kneecapping, better than gouging out an eye, to send
a man to America tormented by the knowledge that the
IRA had laid his wife. It was a way of saying, *See what
we can do to you? There's nothing we can't do to you.*

Thenceforth, they knew McGinty would be waiting for them, maybe hoping that if he did a job for them, they'd send word that it was all a lie. They might even send O'Gorman himself to apologize.

At least a hundred times, McGinty saw himself in a shadowy bar, not much different from the pub in which he had heard the original story. O'Gorman, his heroic head high, the magical smile glowing, clapped him on the shoulder and said, *I had to do it, Dink. It was orders. I had to tell you that awful lie. Can you forgive me?*

He did. In the bar scene McGinty always forgave O'Gorman. He wept and forgave the bastard who had poured cyanide into his belly ten years ago. He knew the scene was ridiculous. He knew it would never happen. The story was true. Nothing but the truth, the cyanidal truth, could cause such pain. That was why, when the sweet little thing from the Irish Mission to the UN had walked into Friel's Lumber Yard and told him in her soft Dublin brogue what they wanted him to do—and added with shining eyes that Dick O'Gorman was going to be in charge of the mission—he had instantly vowed, before God and Satan, to betray him.

The money was not important, although it was not unimportant either, McGinty told himself. He had heard about the federal witness program, how they paid plenty of money to a man for his services and then set him up in another part of the country with a new identity and a business of his own, maybe a liquor store or even a lumber-yard in Arizona. They were doing a lot of building in Arizona.

Ah. It didn't matter what they did for him. It was hatred, nothing but hatred, that had sent McGinty to the telephone to offer his services to the U.S. government because he wanted to reduce the level of violence in Northern Ireland.

He had made the call to the FBI before he stopped to figure out what he would tell Nora, if they asked him to testify. He had swallowed the awfulness of that possible moment by convincing himself that would be the time to fling all the cards on the table. To find out from her if the story O'Gorman had told was true and, if it was—he knew it was—offer to forgive her in return for her forgiveness. It would be a scene drenched in sanctifying grace, in sacramental beauty. Nora Collins, the daughter of the IRA, a woman with a father and a brother serving life sentences in British jails, forgiving her husband the informer.

Was it possible that Nora knew already? Was he talking in his sleep? Crying out to the FBI to protect him? Had O'Gorman called to check him out and she told Black Dick everything? Worst of all, was she in on the secret from the start? Did she know what O'Gorman had told him? Was she keeping him the way that Russian woman had kept Lee Harvey Oswald until the moment came for him to pull the trigger?

"Shewy darlin', what's wrong?"

Nora had her arms around him, her blond head on his chest. The tender sensuality in her voice, the use of Shewy, an affectionate version of Hughie, stunned him. He had opened the door and stepped into the house without realizing it. His rage and fear were turning him into a robot.

"What the devil are you talkin' about?" he said.

"You had the most awful skelly, I was sure you got pinked."

For a moment he had to stop and think to remember that a skelly was a fixed look. He was losing touch with Belfast slang.

"Pinked? That twit Friel wouldn't last a week without me."

Brian, seven, and Bridget, nine, both as plump as any Protestant brat in Belfast, came rushing in to search his pockets. They were tremendously disappointed to find nothing. Most nights he stopped to buy them some gum or candy and they had great fun going from pocket to pocket, while he whooped and yelled and claimed they were tickling him to death.

"Come on," he said. "We'll play dropsies. Tonight I'm going to win."

Brian got out his collection of baseball cards and they started playing the old Belfast game. The contest was to land a card so it touched or covered another card. If you covered more than half, you kept the card. Nora went back to the kitchen to cook dinner. They played dropsies for a half hour and McGinty let them win all his cards. According to the rules, they got a nickel a card. They came to dinner delighted to have an extra fifty cents to spend on candy in the school lunchroom.

McGinty said grace and sliced the pork roast. Nora sighed and wondered where in the world he had learned to carve meat so beautifully. They never had anything worth carving in Kilwickie. For a moment a surge of love overwhelmed the rage throbbing in McGinty's chest. She was always giving him little compliments, trying to tell him how grateful, how happy she was to be living in this land of plenty with a husband who went to work every day, even if it was to a job he disliked. She was so gentle, so tender, so different from hard-edged American women who treated a man as if he were a walking cash register.

Nora chattered gossip from the block, mostly news about pregnancies and job changes. They were all around the same age, all in the great American race for the dollar. At times McGinty wondered if it made sense, to work so hard. He remembered the lyrical descriptions O'Gorman had given them of a socialist Ireland, where every man would share equally in the riches of their green island. It was believable, almost touchable. A life of ease and plenty for every man, without the grinding competition of capitalism.

The vision made no sense on this churning, surging continent with its rivers of cars and hundreds of millions of people. America was a thousand Irelands. She was too vast for comprehension. All you could do was dash into her future until you ran out of luck or strength.

"That young fellow called today. Houlihan. You haven't been able to get the poor lad a job?"

"No. What's he doing calling here?"

"I don't know. Maybe he tried you at the yard and the line was busy. He said to tell you he needed word because he might have another job."

"He did!"

"What's it to you?" Nora said, baffled by his tension.

"Nothing I suppose. But I've got a builder all warmed up to give him one. It'll make me look a bit of a fool."

"Oh, dear."

Anxiety mingled with sympathy on her waif's face. She still found it hard to believe that a Catholic would not get fired for the smallest mistake. "It's nothin' for you to worry about," he said.

But it was something for him to worry about. He would have to go see his two patriot boys tonight. He cooked up a story about getting behind on the books at the lumberyard and drove south to Madison Township, calling from a highway phone to make sure both Houlihans would be home. Jerry, the older brother, met him at the door.

"What's happenin'?" he said, peering past McGinty into the night, as if he thought there might be an army of policemen right behind him.

"Not a thing. That's what I came down to tell you. We'll have to stand by for word from our commander in chief."

Houlihan invited him into a slovenly living room. Children's toys and last week's newspapers were all over the place. It made McGinty doubly grateful for Nora's housekeeping. Houlihan's wife was a nurse who worked nights. Maybe that was why she never found time to clean the house.

"What's this about another job?" McGinty said.

"It isn't me. It's Larry. He's turning flooter-futted," Houlihan said.

"Get him out here."

Larry Houlihan shuffled from his bedroom in response

to his brother's call. He was as tall as Jerry but much thinner. On his emaciated face was a haunted look. He had spent eighteen months in Long Kesh, the special prison the British had built for the IRA in Belfast. For his last two months he had participated in an attempt to launch a hunger strike, a tactic that had scored a propaganda victory a decade ago. The experience seemed to have left him a permanent skeleton.

"What's wrong with you?" McGinty demanded.

"I can't sleep thinkin' about what could go wrong. I got enough bad dreams about the Kesh."

"I thought you were the one I could depend on," McGinty said. "You were the one who saw what they're doin' to our best men. You saw the beatin's. You saw your friend Joe Walsh go to the limit in the strike. You didn't, for reasons no one holds against you. But here's a chance to redeem yourself completely. To strike a blow that will maybe free your friends."

"Yeah, yeah," Larry said. "But I couldn't take another stretch in the jug. Any jug."

"Even if the worst happened, if you did have to go back, you could look people in the face," McGinty snapped.

"He's right," Jerry said. "We'll stick with you. But tell them it can't drag on forever. We can't sit here eternally on day wages. My wife and I are thinkin' of goin' to California. Takin' Larry with us. Maybe he wouldn't be so jumpy in the sunshine. Maybe he'd get his appetite back."

"Maybe you'll be able to go back to a new Ireland," McGinty said.

He almost gagged on the manure he was shoveling down the throats of these two wet-eared donkeys. He was recruiting them for nothing but prison, nothing but rage and hatred at Hugh McGinty and his kind for all eternity. When it was O'Gorman, no one but Slick Dick and his irresistible prick, that he wanted to put behind bars. Maybe he could persuade the FBI or the judge that the Houlihans were innocent.

"Come on now. Let's go over to the clubhouse and hoist a few."

He drove them to the headquarters of the Friendly Sons of the Shillelagh and they stood at the stupendous bar and drank whiskey with beer chasers until midnight. Larry told more stories about the things the British did to people in Long Kesh. How some of the hard core were beaten for hours at a time to crack them. Eventually he got to the hunger strike. He always got to the hunger strike. How Joe Walsh told him as he was dying that he wanted Larry to quit. He wanted one of them to live and carry on the fight.

"It was a right haun," Larry said, his eyes wild. "The leadership admits the whole thing was a right haun from go. What did it accomplish? Who remembers Joe now?"

"Mistakes get made. God knows we've been makin' mistakes since the battle of the Boyne," McGinty said. "But does that mean we should give up on Ireland?"

Yes, whispered Nora's sweet voice. Yes. McGinty could hear her telling him what a mess Ireland was, how wise, how brave he was to get himself and her out of it. Jesus God, why hadn't he told that Dublin bitch from the UN mission to go jump in the Hudson? Why had he made that call to the FBI?

It was 1 A.M. by the time McGinty stumbled through the door of his own house. Nora was waiting for him, watching some movie about the American gangsters of the 1930s. One of them got shot and died on a church's steps as she turned off the set.

"You ran off before I could give you the good news," she said with a weary smile.

"What's that?"

"I'm pregnant again."

"Holy Mother of God."

NOW WE ARE ENEMIES

"Yes, many a night I spent with Dylan in Dublin," O'Gorman said. "After a pint or two he'd recite that wonderful poem about refusing to mourn the death of a child killed in a Nazi air raid."

"Really!" Jacqueline Chasen said.

They were sitting in a booth in the restaurant half of the Golden Shamrock. Jackie was wearing gray slacks and a peekaboo nylon blouse. While his eyes admired the flawless face and marvelous body, O'Gorman sensed something had gone wrong inside, something was broken. Jackie was looking for someone to fix it, someone with wisdom and courage.

It was a role Dick O'Gorman always liked to play. With a minimal effort, he could bed her before the end of the afternoon, he was sure of it. But two sleepless nights and the memory of Barbara O'Day's tears of shame made that a less than enticing idea.

One of O'Gorman's conceits, like his refusal to carry a gun, was the idea that he never left a woman weeping. He wanted them all to believe in some starry future when Black Dick would return with renewed ardor. In part it was sentimental, a desire to maintain a high opinion of his benevolence, in part practical. More than once in his unpredictable travels he had discovered the usefulness of having an O'Gorman worshiper stashed and waiting. He had to repair the damage with Barbara Kathleen before anything else could be put on his agenda.

Anyway, it was hard to think of Jacqueline Chasen as a sex object. She was too much a part of the incredible tangle of suspicion and rage and fear that was clotting his brain. The money had disappeared in her house. He was much more interested in talking to her about the money than about a drunken twit like Dylan Thomas. But how?

He had drawn up a list of potential suspects. Only a handful of people knew the money existed. O'Toole and his bastard of a nephew Mick O'Day were high on the list. So were McGinty and his two boyos. And the two operators from Washington, Leo McBride and his oversexed wife. But what could he do to extract the truth from any of them?

A lot was at stake for Dick O'Gorman as well as the IRA. If he blew this operation, he would be demoted and suspected forever. Kilroy would spread the slander through the ranks that O'Gorman had stolen the money, and that would give the chief of staff a good reason to eliminate Dick O'Gorman from contention permanently with a bullet. What better way to make sure that the traitor would not get to Switzerland to invest his stolen cash in a villa on Lake Lucerne?

Beyond the Irish-Americans and the Irish, of course, there was the gray, amorphous world of the Mafia. O'Gorman could not take it seriously, if Joey Zaccaro was a sample of its leadership. Morons like Joey Zip were able to accumulate millions because the Americans had so many trillions floating around they scarcely noticed the detachment of a stray million or two. It was part of their capitalist system, a permanent state of banditry and warfare among all comers. Even if some of the Mafia's top men were intelligent, it made no sense for them to shoot Zaccaro and steal their own money.

O'Gorman decided he would have to take some chances—with juicy Jackie here and with the others. "I gather you had a less than peaceful night before last," he murmured.

"Who told you?"

"We're thick with the police chief, O'Toole."

Effortlessly he began weaving his favorite persona, the wary romantic revolutionary on his last mission. He told her what Zaccaro had planned to do with the money and asked her help to recover it. Her lovely brown eyes widened, her breathing grew deeper. If she was acting, it was a first-rate performance. By the time O'Gorman finished his story of the mission, he was satisfied that Mick had not blundered into Jackie's house by chance, shot the two Mafiosi, and decided to steal the money.

She told him everything, including the trip to the Pines to bury the bodies. As intelligence, it was more or less useless, until she described the gun again. "It had a big bulge below the barrel. It clicked. That was the only noise it made."

O'Gorman felt a chill penetrate his flesh. It had nothing to do with the brisk March breeze that was whipping against the windows of the Golden Shamrock. One of his last assignments in Belfast had involved identifying British officers who were operating as part of their Secret Intelligence Service while ostensibly on staff duty at division or regimental headquarters.

They all had private guns beside their official Browning automatics. Some preferred German Lugers, others Spanish Stars. One had somehow acquired a Chinese Type 64 silenced, a gun that the IRA had been trying to buy for a decade. It was easy to identify because it fired a special subsonic 7.65x17mm rimless cartridge. Autopsies of three IRA leaders recently assassinated in the Irish Republic had produced these cartridges.

Was there an SIS agent—possibly the same man—in Paradise Beach? If so, he would have to be a recent arrival. He had killed a man in County Armagh less than two months ago. The SIS did not operate like the Russians, who planted agents in countries like the United States for a decade without using them. SIS did not have that kind of manpower. They were mostly volunteers on temporary duty. But they were a daring, deadly foe. It was certainly not beyond their imagination to send an agent here in disguise, if they had somehow picked up the news of this operation.

"Do you have any British friends?" O'Gorman asked Jacqueline Chasen.

She shook her head.

"Any British neighbors on Leeds Point?"

"Only the devil."

She told him the story of the British camp follower who had given birth to a creature with cloven feet during the American Revolution. Although he laughed heartily, O'Gorman did not find it amusing. There was still enough Catholicism in his blood to make him uneasy about Satan. One of his Jesuit teachers at Clongowes, the Irish college, had been fascinated by the devil. He had collected stories of satanic possession.

Jackie had nothing more to offer except her lovely self. For the moment, survival was more pressing. Borrowing Desmond McBride's car, O'Gorman drove north to Madison Township with Bill Kilroy beside him in the death seat muttering insults about melodeon-legged Dubliners. He was a marvelous example of the basic north-south hatred and suspicion that sprang forth whenever anything went wrong. It was enough to make a man despair of a united Ireland.

"Shut up and get ready to play a part you're born for," O'Gorman said.

"What's that?"

"Killer."

They pulled into the Houlihans' driveway at three

o'clock. Larry, the younger of the two, the one who had turned skite-the-gutter in the hunger strike, opened the door. O'Gorman threw him inside with a shove that sent him flying down the hall on his back. Billy pounced on him, the muzzle of his Zastava under his jaw. "Where's the yella man? You've got ten seconds to tell us."

Houlihan's death's-head face was blank with terror. It was incredible. The man had no more flesh on him than he had the day the British let him out of Long Kesh because they were afraid he might die on their hands.

Jerry Houlihan came rushing from the kitchen wearing an apron over his jeans. "What the hell's this?" he cried.

Billy kept a knee in Larry's chest and turned the Zastava on Jerry. "Shut yer yap."

"We're lookin' for the money you stole two nights ago down in Paradise Beach," O'Gorman said. "This is Kilroy. You've no doubt heard of him. I'm O'Gorman. Black Dick."

"We didn't steal a penny of it," Houlihan said.

"Oh? But you know it's gone. How did you manage that? Are you a mind reader?"

"McGinty told us."

"You're a bloody liar. He doesn't know it's missing."

"He told us. He came down last night and told us there was trouble about the money!"

"You know what we do to liars. And informers. And thieves who steal from the people."

Houlihan backed away from the Zastava. "Jesus Christ, it's the truth. Call him off. It's the truth."

"We're goin' to search the house. If we find anything, even a single bill, you're dead men. Tell us the truth and we'll let you off. It was McGinty's idea, wasn't it?"

The brothers Houlihan shook their heads in hysterical denial. It was convincing.

They tied their hands and feet and left them on the living room rug like a couple of trussed sheep while they tore the house and garage apart. There was no money.

"Either you're lucky or smart," O'Gorman said.

"What about loyal?" Larry Houlihan said. "Why the hell do you think we volunteered?"

Tears ran down his cheeks. He was shaking all over. Just the sort of man they needed to drive weapons through five states to Boston.

"I always heard you was a bastard. Now I know it," Jerry Houlihan said to O'Gorman. "His nerves is shot. Can't you see that? He won't sleep for a week now."

"If I'm a bastard, it's because we've got crybabies like you in the ranks," O'Gorman said.

Warning the Houlihans to say nothing and await orders, they freed them and drove on to McGinty's house in Metuchen. Billy was impressed to find McGinty inhabiting what was, on Belfast terms, splendor. He stared at the green lawns, the old trees, the comfortable split-level house.

"Does everybody in this fookin' country live this good?"

"Except in New York. Most of them are in tenements worse than Belfast's Blacks."

"Whyn't they bomb the bejesus out of the Prods like we done?"

"They're Prods themselves. They're undeveloped politically."

It was just five o'clock when they knocked on McGinty's door. Nora answered it. "Hello, sweetheart," O'Gorman said, pushing her back down the hall.

"Dick?" she said, her pliant, kissable mouth a twisted *O*. "What are you doin' here?"

"I wish it was a friendly visit. But it isn't. Maybe you can make it one, by answering a few questions. You might even save Hughie's neck if you tell the truth."

He told her what Hughie was doing for them and what had happened. "Just give us back the money or tell us where it is. Hughie's got to be in on it. No one else outside our little circle knew about it. We've checked out everyone else."

"He promised me he'd never go near you again!"

"A man will say almost anything to get you to drop your knickers, Nora dear," O'Gorman said.

"There's no money. He would have told me about it. He tells me everything. We made a promise—"

Her eyes went blank realizing that Hughie had already broken the promise.

"Was Hughie doing some gardening by any chance, yesterday?"

"No."

"You're sure? If we find it without your help, punishment becomes a necessity."

"There's no money. None!"

The doorbell rang. In bounced a bonny boy and girl, prime young American heifers. Nora shooed them into a back bedroom. O'Gorman thought of the scrawny Catholic children of Belfast and said, "Get rid of them."

She sent them back to the neighbor's yard where they had been playing. As at the Houlihans, O'Gorman and Billy went through the house like a pair of hurricanes. No money. Nora sat in the living room, weeping.

"Tell Hughie his luck is holding so far," O'Gorman said. "How about a kiss for old times' sake?"

"I'd rather die."

"Ho ho," chortled Billy. He liked seeing O'Gorman get a turndown.

"Maybe you'll oblige Billy here before we go, in that case. He's been as celibate as St. Patrick since we got to this godforsaken country."

"I'll kill myself first," Nora said.

"Aw, come on now," Billy said. "It'll be so quick y'won't scarcely notice it. They called me Gary Cooper in Sofia. Wham bum, thanks, mum."

"Get out. I'm goin' to write my father and tell him about this. He's still got influence."

"With whom?" O'Gorman mocked.

"Oh God, oh God, oh God."

Nora buried her face in the chair. They left her that way and headed back to Paradise Beach, Billy smacking his lips over what he would have done to Nora in bed if she had said yes. O'Gorman was beginning to think Billy couldn't get it up for anything but a Saracen tank. Talking about it day and night was a sure sign. It had to be the origin of the platitude about all talk and no action.

Billy's sexual fantasies did not distract his tiny brain from the main point. As they zoomed over the causeway to Paradise, he growled, "That was a good act, O'Gorman. But it don't change me mind. I'm gonna search your digs the way we just tore apart them sods' the minute we get back."

"You will like hell."

Billy took out the Zastava. "I give you this argument once before. But it don't make much sense to shoot you before we land the fookin' weapons. Just get it through your fookin' head that I'm in charge of this thing."

"Prove it, you squirmy little asshole."

From his wallet Billy fished a letter. He handed it to O'Gorman as they rolled to a stop in front of Desmond McBride's house. It was Billy's orders. It yammered on about the purpose of the expedition and finally got to the meat: "In all decisions which involve political considerations, you will exercise final authority."

There it was. They were putting this Bogside twit whose education consisted of a month's brainwashing in Bulgaria in command of Richard O'Gorman, graduate of Clongowes and the University of Dublin. "I was supposed to show this to you on the fookin' plane and tear it up. But I decided it'd only string y'out and we wouldn't get nothin' done. Now drive me over to Monahan's and you go for a walk somewheres while I do the lookin'."

Speechless with fury, O'Gorman obeyed and drove back to McBride's. He left the car keys with Desmond's pachyderm of a wife and stalked up Delaware Avenue toward the beach. If he had the money, he'd go to Barbara Kathleen Monahan O'Day and say, *Run. Run with me for the far horizon. Run with me to Shangri-la, if it only lasts a month or a year. Run with my life in your arms to some-*

*place where happiness is still possible, where treachery
and hatred and betrayal are unknown.*

Simultaneously he imagined himself on the beach,
hurling invectives across the ocean at those swivel-
headed patriot morons on the IRA's ruling council. Jesus
God! Here, if ever, was the end of faith, the end of hope.

But not the end of O'Gorman, perhaps. Instead it might
be his liberation. It might be the end of dear Deirdre's
moon face and perpetual affirmations of the cause, the
end of her idiotic image of herself as Queen Maeve in a
scullery, perpetually sending forth her errant warrior to
battle for Ireland. The end of her stupid forgiveness and
the beginning of O'Gorman's apotheosis as a free man.

Maybe he would run for the far horizon with Barbara
Kathleen, money or no money.

"Mr. O'Gorman."

It was Father Hart on the porch of his rectory. "What
luck. I've just been going over the plans for the feis with
Father McAvoy and Desmond McBride. I was going to
show them to you tomorrow. Would you like to take a
look at them now?"

"Why not?"

Desmond McBride was looking haggard. He wasn't
sleeping nights either. Father McAvoy gazed at O'Gorman, the priest's potato face more than justifying the
famous phrase "I come from Mayo, God help us." The
Irish countryman was unquestionably one of the most
stupid beings in the history of creation, and an Irish country priest was one notch lower on the scale, below stupidity in a boggy region where brain cells did not even exist.
Why had he spent twenty-five years of his life trying to
free these people from their spiritual chains? It was hopeless.

They presented O'Gorman with the plans for the feis.
They were going to have clog dancing and step dancing.
Irish and Scottish band music, and pipe-band competi-
tions. There were three Irish harpists he had never heard
of and the likes of Joe Burke, Jack Conn, Mike Rafferty,

Maureen Doherty, and a dozen other fiddlers, pipers, and singers whose names were equally mysterious. Liz Carroll had *Chicago* in parentheses next to her name as if that proved some sort of authenticity. In the mood he was in, O'Gorman would not have been impressed by the immortal John McCormack himself on the roster.

"It looks grand," he said. "All you need is a bard."

He was being sarcastic but they took him seriously. "We were hoping you could recite some poetry in Gaelic. Or perhaps young Kilroy could do this and you could translate it," Hart said.

"A capital idea. Except that Kilroy's Gaelic consists of untranslatable epithets," O'Gorman said.

He finally agreed to recite in Gaelic and translate too. He devoutly hoped to be long gone by the time the festivalists began their spurious jigging. Over the hills and far away with Barbara Kathleen. They could have their stupid culture, which had been effectively aborted in 1690 on the Boyne. He was through with this ridiculous artificial respiration of a ghost. He would thumb his nose at the whole thing and go to Hollywood and write movie scripts. He would lie beside his swimming pool in the sunshine and hump Barbara Kathleen and dozens of starlets until the San Fernando Valley was home, as the song promised it would be.

Father Hart was pouring whiskey, a beatific smile on his adolescent face. O'Gorman noticed that the other priest, McAvoy, was drinking ginger ale. "To Ireland," Hart said, raising his glass.

"I don't need whiskey to drink to that," Father McAvoy said, his potato face bright with equally brainless patriotism.

O'Gorman raised his glass and drank off his dollop. But he was toasting a little bit of heaven named Barbara Kathleen Monahan O'Day.

THIS IS THE END MY FRIEND

"Car twenty-six," Tom Brannigan said in his official voice. "Prowler reported at two three five Maryland Avenue."

"Roger," Mick said. "I'm at Baltimore and Virginia. On my way to investigate."

Maybe this would be some real police work, though Mick doubted it. Twice so far tonight he had made speed runs to Leeds Point in response to frantic calls from Jackie Chasen. She was spooked by every noise. He had gotten her a new dog, a Labrador retriever the size of a Honda, but she was still spooked.

The prowler on Maryland Avenue would probably be imaginary too. It was funny, the way people were jumpier during the winter, when the town was practically deserted, than they were during the summer, when the crowds poured in and it was much harder to keep track of what Bill O'Toole called "potentials." During the winter no stranger could drive into Paradise Beach without a readout of his license plate within a half hour.

Still it was good to get his mind off the mystery of what had happened to Joey Zaccaro and his money. As far as Mick could see, there was only one explanation. Joey had been shot by a fellow member of the Mob who had heard about the money he was carrying around. By this time, Bill O'Toole had explained what was cooking between him and Joey and the two Irishmen.

Uncle Bill too was inclined to think it was a Mob double cross. But he was keeping an eye on the Irishmen, especially the older guy, Tyrone Power, as Uncle Bill called him. He was too smooth for Uncle Bill. He never liked smoothies. He was a rough diamond himself.

The explanation had restored some of Mick's confidence in Uncle Bill. He was not selling the town out to the Mob. But Mick continued to have grave doubts about helping the IRA, even if they were Irish. The Professor kept telling him they were no different from the Viet Cong, guys who shook down civilians at gunpoint and shot their enemies in the dark in the name of some crazy vision of communism.

At 235 Maryland, Mick loosened his Colt .38 in his holster and slid out of the car. He had checked the block as he came down it, and no strange vehicles were in sight. Most sneak thieves were outsiders who arrived on wheels to loot the summer houses that were closed for the winter. It was unusual for a thief to try to break into an occupied house. In fact, it did not make much sense. The stuff people left in their summer houses was amazing. Silver and TVs and stereo sets. A fast worker with a van could make three or four thousand dollars if he hit the right house.

None of the houses on Maryland, especially 235, looked right to Mick. They were all four- and five-room shacks, most of them occupied by retirees who had winterized them. At 235, white-haired Joe McCaffrey met him at the door gripping a baseball bat. "I heard a noise in the backyard. Somebody bumpin' into a garbage can. I went on the back porch and there's this guy in a black suit tryin' to jimmy the lock on the screen door. I asked him what the hell he thought he was doin' and he dodges toward the garage. I'm afraid he's stealin' the stereo out of my van."

"I'll take a look."

Mick moved up the driveway staying close to the house. The guy could be a psycho with a gun. They had a half dozen active nuts in Paradise Beach, guys who'd been let out of mental hospitals ahead of time. One or two were dangerous.

The garage door was closed. If the guy was trying to steal a car stereo, he was doing it the hard way. McCaffrey was on the back porch now. "You got a remote for the garage?" Mick asked.

"Yeah."

"Hit it."

The garage door rattled up to the roof. Mick crouched beside an azalea bush and waited. Nothing. He beamed his flashlight into the garage. Only a 1985 Chevette and the Volkswagen van McCaffrey used to run day-trippers to Atlantic City during the summer.

Mick checked the backyard next door and several nearby yards. He could remember playing ring-a-levio in these yards when he was a kid. In those days the houses were closed for the winter and there was no end of places to hide. Now all these old people were living in them. Bill O'Toole said sometimes he wondered if they were running a two-mile-long old-age home. The golden-agers were always calling the police. If it wasn't a stroke or a heart attack, it was an argument in which the husband had whacked the old lady with a skillet or vice versa.

It was amazing how many of them didn't get along. Uncle Bill said the only thing that had kept them married was the job that separated them for most of each day. Mick thought they were just bored. Getting old was boring. No more sex, your stomach starts to go and you can't drink, you can't afford a fast car and can't drive one anyway—no wonder they whacked each other around.

Mick got back in the car and spent the rest of the night

on the usual rounds. Out to Leeds Point and back along Ocean Avenue and up to Jorgenson's Pavilion to make sure nobody was stealing the soda fountain and down to the inlet to make sure all eighteen holes were still on the miniature golf course. Around 3 A.M. he got a call from the Golden Shamrock to collect Billy Kilroy. The guy was turning into a permanent nuisance, drunk every night.

Billy was teaching the regulars a Belfast song when Mick arrived. It was called "The Ballad of William Bloat," about a Protestant who cut his unfaithful wife's throat with a razor blade and then decided to hang himself with one of the shccts on their bed. He died cursing the pope, naturally. Eyes dancing, Billy bellowed the last verse:

> "But the strangest turn to the whole concern is
>   only just beginnin'.
> Bloat went to hell but his wife got well and
>   she's still alive and sinnin'.
> For the razor blade was German made but the
>   sheet was Belfast linen."

Billy got a big hand and Mick good-naturedly joined in the applause. "Come on, Kilroy, I'll take you home."

Mick poured Billy into the front seat of the squad car.

"Marine, huh?" Billy said. "Them's the best in America, they tell me."

"Yeah."

"Me old man was the best in the fookin' British army. Was in the Irish Guards he was. Soldier of the fookin' queen."

"No kiddin'. Where'd he fight?"

"Fookin' Korea."

"He buy the farm?"

"What? We never had a pot to piss in much less a farm."

"I mean, did he get killed?"

"Nah. Died of fookin' pneumonia."

"Rough. How old were you then?"

"I dunno. A wee brat. I don't even remember him."

"I guess we're about the same age. I was born during the Korean War."

"Where's your old man? Did he get it in the head out there?"

"Nah. He lives in Jersey City. My old lady didn't get along with him."

"And they just split up? You're no different from the bloody Prods."

"We don't curse the pope. We just ignore him."

"I'll buy that, true enough."

"What do you think happened to that money?" Mick asked.

"O'Gorman's got it. I'll bet my eyes on it. He's got it somewhere. But he's afraid to run because he knows I'll follow him."

"Sing me another Belfast song."

Billy let his head fall back on the cushion. In a wailing voice that seemed about five years old, he sang:

"I am the wee falorie man
A rattling roving Irishman
I can do all that ever you can
For I am the wee falorie man."

"That's the first song I learned. My mother taught it to me."

"What's *falorie* mean?"

"How the fook would I know?

Mick helped Billy into the house and upstairs to his bed. As he went back down the hall, he noticed Richard O'Gorman's bedroom door was half-open. Odd. Where would he go at 3 A.M.? Mick edged the door open a little more with his foot. The bed was empty. He checked the bathroom. No one there.

As he went past his mother's room, he heard a sound.

A kind of cry-sigh, long and breathy. Mick felt his hands go hot. O'Gorman was in there with his mother. Suddenly Mick was back fifteen years, listening to The Doors sing "The End," one of their super-sicko specialties. It was about a hophead who wanted to kill his father and make out with his mother.

Mick remembered how weird he felt when he heard that song. Sometimes in those years a blind anger at his father would surge through him. Why had he left him at his mother's mercy? She was always hanging all over him, wanting to know the names of his girlfriends, hinting she'd like to hear a lot more than their names.

Weird. He didn't like feeling weird. He had stopped listening to The Doors after that song. For him that song really had been The End. Now he felt weird again. Was he angry at Dick O'Gorman? No. But it made him feel weird.

Mick finished his eight hours at seven forty-five. He wrote up a report of the prowler but did not mention carrying Billy home. He piled into his Rebel and drove up Ocean Avenue toward Leeds Point. If everything was on schedule, Jackie would be back from her jog on the beach. She would be out of the shower, lying on the bed in her terry-cloth robe, waiting for him. He had made up for that problem in the Pines the other night. More than made up for it. They were back on that nice even keel where she liked it and he liked it and afterward they felt good.

Nothing sensational, just good. They were no longer trying to set the night on fire. Afterward they would eat breakfast and play some of the old music, the kind Jackie liked now and swore she had hated in 1969. Maybe "Bridge over Troubled Water" or "The Boxer." She said he was her boxer. He sort of liked it. He liked the idea of "standing in the clearing a fighter by his trade." The guy sounded like a marine.

As Mick passed the intersection that led to the causeway, Phac came rattling by in his 1974 Fairlane, on his way to another day aboard the *Enterprise*. Mick waved to him and suddenly he no longer saw Jackie, he saw Trai. He had to check out that situation. He had to do something about that birdbrain Father Hart. Maybe the Professor was the answer. He at least understood Mick's connection to Trai. But not even the Professor knew the whole story.

At the house, Jackie was looking wan. She had not gone jogging. She had seen a stranger wandering along the beach and was afraid it might be a hit man. Mick told her she was being ridiculous. She cried and said she hadn't slept more than an hour all night.

"Come on," Mick said. "Let's take a shower together."

She wanted to and yet she didn't want to. She wanted Mick to feel sorry for her, to tell her it was awful, what Joey Zaccaro had tried to do to her. But he was not in the mood for sweet talk. What he had heard in his mother's bedroom made him want to do it like a machine, no words, just bang bang bang. It was wrong, but they took a shower together and Mick lathered her dark pussy with that sweet-smelling violet soap she used and slipped his finger in there. By the time they got to the bed she was wild and it went just the way he wanted it.

But when it was over, he could see she was unhappy. She wanted something more than a banging. She wanted someone to tell her how to get away from death. The crash in the Miura had not been death, the months in the hospital had not been death. Joey Zaccaro had been death.

Mick did not know how to tell her that death was bullshit. It was nothing. In Nam he had seen so many guys go from life to death in a second. It wasn't death that worried Mick. It was how you died. That was crucial. He was convinced that if you died like a man, like a marine, your soul went straight to some kind of heaven. He didn't know where it was or what it would be like, but you went there. He was absolutely sure of it.

He didn't know how to tell that to a woman because

death was a different game to them. Death was operations, a breast gone or a hysterectomy like his aunt Helen Gargan. Death was slow and ugly for a woman. For a man, if he was lucky, death was clean, fast, easy.

He was going to die that way, Mick was sure of it. He did not know when or how, but he knew that he had to die that way eventually to balance things out for the night the 409th NVA blew apart the fort in Binh Nghai while he was down by the riverside with Trai.

"I swear, there's nothing to worry about. The mafiosi don't know a thing. It's been almost a week now."

"Just long enough for them to figure out something's gone wrong."

"So? They're not mind readers. They don't know what happened."

The telephone rang. Jackie answered it. "Your uncle," she said.

"Get down here," Bill O'Toole said in his chief's voice. "Get down here right away."

"What's up?"

"Your ass may be up. Get down here."

Still with no breakfast, Mick drove back to headquarters. Uncle Bill was in his office, walking up and down. He looked like he had just swallowed a quart of paregoric.

"Bo Fallon took your car out."

"Yeah?" Bo Fallon took Mick's car out every day. Bo had been taking it out every day for five years.

"He opened the glove compartment to get the book for a parking ticket. He found this."

Uncle Bill handed Mick a thousand-dollar bill. It didn't look real. It had some walrus-mustached guy on it.

"What does it prove?"

"I don't know what it proves. But it raises a hell of a lot of questions about you and that Jewish broad."

"If we took the dough, would we still be around? We'd be on our way to Mexico or Hong Kong."

"You could be playin' a smarter game. You could be

lettin' one of us, your uncle Des or me, take the fall."

"Don't you know me better than that, Uncle Bill?"

Bill O'Toole looked at Mick with his police chief's face. Or maybe his marine's face. "I thought I did."

"Someone planted it. Someone's trying to frame me—and maybe you."

"Who? Who was in that car last night besides you?"

"The Belfast runt. He said he thought the other guy had the money. Tyrone Power. Why would the runt drop this on me and say that? He sat in the front seat and I didn't see him go near that glove compartment. He was drunk and sang some song his mother taught him."

"What else happened last night?"

"Not a damn thing. Except a prowler call on Maryland Avenue."

"You got out of the car there?"

"For about ten minutes."

"Who called?"

"Joe McCaffrey."

"We can forget that pinhead."

Bill O'Toole paced the small rug. On the wall behind him were plaques and awards from various organizations. He was a good cop. He had worked to make Paradise Beach the best-policed town in New Jersey. It was incomprehensible to Mick that Uncle Bill had allowed this Mafia garbage into their lives, even for dear old Ireland. He didn't believe Uncle Bill gave a shit for dear old Ireland. Only assholes like Uncle Desmond liked jigging at the annual feis.

"I wish I could believe you're clean. But I don't," Bill O'Toole said.

"Do you want my badge? You can have it right now. I didn't buy this kind of bullshit when I took this job. Here's my badge."

Mick held it out to Chief O'Toole. His shield. His ridiculous proof that he was trying to play it straight after Binh Nghai. He had evened part of the score there. He had taken the dishonorable discharge without a word.

Maybe this was another step to squaring it once and for all.

Bill O'Toole sank into the swivel chair behind his desk. "Get out of here. Get out of here and let me think."

IRISH EYES UNSMILING

"The senator called. He wants to know what's taking us so long," Melody said. They were on the second-floor sunporch of the McBride house, just off their bedroom, five days after the money had vanished. A northeast wind buffeted the windows. Beneath a sky of unrelenting gray, the Atlantic heaved beyond the breakers. On the horizon, Leo could see the flagship of his father's fleet, the SS *Enterprise,* heading for the inlet that led to the Great Bay and the McBride marina.

"What did you tell him?"

"I said I had a virus."

"I told the congressman the same thing. At least they'll think we're sleeping together."

"Who took that money?" Melody said. "They're your relatives."

"I don't think any of them took it. They may not like each other very much, but they're basically loyal."

Melody, scornful as usual of Leo's attempts to find

some shreds of virtue in Irish-Americans, dismissed this as nonsense. "I'm betting on Mick. He's a dead shot. And a trained killer."

"The little Irishman isn't a bad shot either."

"Mick could be working with O'Toole. The screaming and yelling about the money could be an act. Mick took the money and buried it in the woods, the night he got rid of Zaccaro and his bodyguard."

"I doubt it," Leo said. "I know Mick. He'd never inflict this humiliation on his grandfather. The old man isn't as gaga as he looks. He's horrified by what's happening. He knows what the Mob is likely to do."

Melody ignored this lamentation. "It doesn't make any sense for Kilroy or O'Gorman to take it. They know the IRA would find them, wherever they ran."

"Mick told me Kilroy thinks O'Gorman may have done it."

"They're your *relatives.* Can't you find out *anything?* If you hung out at the Shamrock a few nights, you might pick something up."

Leo shook his head. "Nobody likes me down there."

"Why?"

"Because I'm a big brain. I got high marks in school. And I didn't go to Vietnam."

"What a bunch of Neanderthals."

"Patriots," Leo said. "Neanderthal patriots."

His stomach throbbed. Pain curled into his chest. He had been a mess for the last two days, unable to eat any solid food, existing on milk and Maalox. Although they were sleeping in a double bed, they had not touched each other since the night the money vanished. Melody never said a word about him hitting her. In an odd, subliminal way, Leo sensed she liked it. Was there, deep in her Marxist psyche, some residual Christian guilt for her sexually liberated lifestyle?

Melody had not tried to call O'Gorman again. But Leo was not at all sure it was in obedience to his order or because she feared another rejection. She had yet to utter a word of sympathy for Leo's tormented stomach.

More and more, whenever they discussed the money, Melody talked to Leo as if he had become a stranger. She felt menaced by his relatives, even by O'Gorman and Kilroy. She was like an explorer surrounded by vaguely hostile natives a thousand miles up the Amazon.

For Leo, the vanished money created a special agony. He had to listen to his father and mother lament the loss of the bearer bonds. If they were still in Sunny Dan's cellar, this upheaval would never have happened. Bill O'Toole would never have headed for Atlantic City to make a million at the craps tables. He would never have let a thug like Joey Zaccaro into Paradise Beach. Even if some other more obscure need had driven Bill to do business with Zaccaro, they could have paid off the missing money, told the Mafia what happened to Zaccaro, and sent O'Gorman and his friend Kilroy back to Ireland without their weapons.

It was even more agonizing for Leo to listen to Sunny Dan talk about the bearer bonds when they went to his house for a family conference last night. A dozen times Dan had wished he could solve the whole thing with a quick trip to the cellar. Leo had seen how much the old man's lost munificence meant to him. Without the money he was powerless. Without power, his existence had lost most of its meaning.

Barbara, Mick's mother, had insisted on everyone staying for dinner. Leo managed to choke down enough food to escape attention. He had never told his mother and father about his ulcer. He did not want anyone else in the family to know about it, especially Mick and Bill O'Toole. They would regard it as further proof that Leo was a wimp.

After dinner, Barbara tried to cheer Dan up by leading them to the piano for some Irish songs. When they got to "The Kerry Dancers," Dan broke down in the middle of it and had to be put to bed. Leo went home and vomited his dinner. Melody, watching a movie on TV, told him to close the door—he was drowning out the dialogue.

Melody was unmoved by their close-up of Sunny Dan's misery—and the perturbation of the rest of the family. But massive waves of guilt surged through Leo's already ravaged stomach. He loved his grandfather. He remembered the expensive birthday presents he had gotten from him—a six-speed racing bike, a top-of-the-line Sony Walkman, a Leica camera. Leo's father, determined to plow every cent back into his fishing fleet and cannery, seldom gave Leo anything more than a $50 savings bond. Leo remembered trips with other grandchildren aboard the cabin cruiser Sunny Dan had kept in the McBride marina—how the old man had baited their hooks and offered a $25 prize to whoever caught the biggest fish. He had been a kind of royal personage in their lives, dispensing gifts and cheer.

The contrast between Sunny Dan and his tightwad father had always troubled Leo. He had wanted to love this remote, diffident, evasive man, who had scarcely said an intimate word to him since he was born. Only when Leo brought home A-pluses from his various schools had Desmond McBride loosened his wallet.

High marks were a sign of the one thing Desmond wanted to prove—that the McBrides were several cuts above the rest of the family when it came to brains and ambition. For all his churchgoing and his befriending of clergymen, Desmond was incapable of seeing himself as guilty of the first deadly sin, pride. Or of the second, for that matter—covetousness.

At times Leo wished he had never had a Catholic education. Although he was no longer a believer, he had a large amount of residual Catholicism in his psyche. He had embarked on his political career as a kind of substitute for a religious vocation. He saw himself as spiritually superior to most of the people his age in Washington— because he was acutely aware of the moral shortcomings of American society. But ten years of enjoying the perquisites of power in Washington—the hundred-thousand-plus congressional salary, the junkets, the lunches and dinners—had forced him to confess his hypocritical elitism.

Melody, on the other hand, viewed all the freebies as her due. She had the mind of a commissar. In her view, a consuming resolve to change the world entitled her to a lavish lifestyle. It also had a lot to do with being a Faithorne—a sense of belonging to a branch of the American aristocracy.

Leo had moved far beyond the world of Paradise Beach, but when he came home for a visit, it claimed him in ways that were too subtle, too invisible, to elude. His mother's aimless chatter about her bridge club often wandered into Marie O'Toole's unhappy marriage and the peccadilloes of Wilbur Gargan's numerous tribe, all of whom seemed to have gotten jobs in Atlantic City. That had led them to alcoholism, drug addiction, and the other charming vices of the gambling metropolis.

Wilbur's habit of pouring free drinks at the Golden Shamrock and letting his bartenders steal half the receipts while he got snookered had left his kids with nothing but their severely limited talents to face America's cold, cruel capitalism. In Jersey City, Sunny Dan would have gotten them all on the public payroll as cops or firemen or schoolteachers. But Paradise Beach's minuscule budget left no room for such largesse. Even putting Mick O'Day on the police force had stirred ugly comments from the voters.

Once, Leo had managed to look on these family trials and traumas with mild, distanced amusement. But these days a return to Paradise Beach seemed to rivet him to their anguished bodies and afflicted souls with an intensity that approached the supernatural. Was this a foretaste of hell? Leo wondered.

The telephone rang. Melody answered it. They were alone in the McBride house. "Oh, I'd love to. . . . No, he couldn't possibly. His ulcer has him in agony. When? . . . A half hour? I'll be ready."

"Who's that?" Leo said.

"O'Gorman. He wants to see us. I told him you were sick."

"Tell him you are too. You have a virus. You can get a note from the senator, proving it."

"He says he has important information the senator might want to hear. He's afraid to talk about it on the telephone."

"Tell him I have a virus. A virulent dislike of him and his crony Kilroy."

Melody was pulling off her slacks and sweatshirt. She rouged her cheeks and coated her lips with about a pound of lipstick. It was the call-girl look—very popular in Washington these days. She dropped a crimson Givenchy dress with a pleated skirt over her head.

Suddenly Leo McBride was saying words that seemed to be thrust into his body by some external power. "If you ball him, I'll tell Bill O'Toole about the bearer bonds. You won't get out of this town alive."

There it was, the spoken and unspoken part of the dirty secret they had been sharing for the last five years. But Melody did not beg for mercy. She simply stared at him. Leo realized how much he had revealed with that threat. She saw that he wanted to confess their betrayal and blame her.

"I believe we've shared that reward money more or less equally," Melody said.

"It was never my idea," Leo snarled. "You sucked me into it literally and figuratively."

"Maybe I can suck O'Gorman into protecting me from your adolescent guilt trip."

Leo McBride floundered, aghast. He should have known he could not penetrate Melody's armored self-righteousness. She was simply refusing to remember how it had happened—and succeeding—while Leo McBride could not forget every word, gesture, expression, every snarl and plea and sob of the nightmare.

He and Melody had been slugging down martinis, cel-

ebrating the passage of the treaties on Panama, the sum-
mit of Jimmy Carter's presidency. It was such a noble
deed, worthy of Thomas Jefferson and Woodrow Wilson
and Franklin Roosevelt, the blessed trinity of the Democratic Party. The stolen canal had been returned to its right-
ful owners.

Destiny seemed to be playing a searchlight down the
coming years, in which a new Democratic Party, created in
the 1972 convention, would continue to lead the world
toward peace and justice. Unfortunately, after his fourth
martini, Leo had grown sentimental and began defending
the old Democratic Party. He tried to argue that the new
one had grown out of the old one. The old party had the
same desire to see justice and equality triumph at home and
abroad.

Melody had scoffed. For her the 1972 convention was
part of the ongoing revolution. The word *new* was a door
slamming on the stupid, corrupt past. Irked, Leo had told
her she was ignorant. She had no idea how much money
the old political machines had generated—money that
had sent children and grandchildren to the best schools
and erased NO IRISH NEED APPLY signs in banks and corpo-
rations.

Melody had expressed mild surprise. As far as she
could see, everyone in Paradise Beach except Leo's parents seemed to be living only a few inches above the
poverty line. That was when Leo, with a hiccup of pride,
had told her about the bearer bonds.

"How can you sit there and brag about something like
that?" Melody had screamed.

For the next week, she had harried him like a tigress
toying with her prey. Every night there had been a lecture
about the stench of corruption in his blood—and no sex.
Finally she told him what he should do: report the bonds
to the Internal Revenue Service. He had been suitably
horrified and refused to do any such thing. "Then I'll do
it," she said on the fifth night.

Leo had shouted, cursed, gotten drunk. But he could

not stop her. Nor did he refuse to help her spend the reward money, which blended with her righteousness to create an irresistible motive. The IRS paid informers 10 percent of all the tax money they recovered. Five hundred thousand dollars was a nice little nest egg. It had paid for the Ferrari and a vacation house in Virginia, complete with Jacuzzi and basement pool.

But the toll the betrayal had taken on Leo McBride's nervous system turned out to be a negative tax of sizable proportions. He had developed a peptic ulcer and sleeping problems that left him feeling like a dishrag on legs most days. Visits to Paradise Beach became a torment. Everyone, including his father, subtly blamed him for the lost bonds, though they never dreamt he was actually guilty.

His mother, his aunts, even his uncle Bill O'Toole, seemed to imply in looks and remarks that his Washington connections should have prevented the raid. They seemed to think Washington was organized like the Jersey City of old—nothing happened without an okay from someone on top.

Leo had in fact used all his Washington connections to quash any attempt to prosecute Sunny Dan Monahan for income tax fraud. Congressman Mullen, the recipient of at least $200,000 in donations from Dan in his twenty years in Congress, threw all his considerable weight behind the effort, and even Senator Kennedy, over Melody's violent objections, was prevailed upon to make a phone call to the commissioner of Internal Revenue.

But no one in the family gave Leo any credit for this achievement, and he began finding reasons to avoid visiting Paradise Beach. Melody, indifferent to his feelings as usual, had insisted their presence was a necessity at this conjunction of the Cubans and the IRA, to make sure his relatives performed up to par. Only when Leo had seen the CIA printout on Black Dick O'Gorman did another reason for her insistence occur to him.

Outside, a car horn beeped. Melody pulled a wide,

shiny leather belt around her slim waist. It had an oversize gold buckle. For some reason the buckle made Leo think of the incredibly fine blond hair of her pussy. It made him want her. What was happening to him?

Melody walked to the door. "I wasn't going to touch O'Gorman," she said. "Believe it or not, I have some consideration for your feelings."

As usual, she had an uncanny instinct for exactly how to subdue him. "I'm sorry!" Leo wailed. "I'd never tell them. Never!"

He saw Melody did not believe him. They had gone from strangers to enemies.

LOVE IS A SOMETIME THING

Dick O'Gorman knew he was in trouble the moment Melody Faithorne emerged from Desmond McBride's front door. Her cheeks were as rouged and her lips as red as a face on a piece of Wedgwood pottery. Her crimson dress was one of those silly little things that cost $3,000 in Paris. Maybe she'd gotten it from Senator Ted, although it was obvious that she could terrorize her husband into giving her anything she wanted. How American to think she could glamorize Richard O'Gorman, the IRA's quintessential idealist, into bed. When it came to understanding foreigners, Americans did not have a clue.

"Sorry to trouble you so early in the day," O'Gorman said. "But there's a bit of pressing business I think we should discuss."

"You've rescued me from terminal boredom," Melody purred with her brightest smile.

There was no doubt what she had in mind. To make it clear that he did not have it in mind, he drove to the

Golden Shamrock. The dismay on Melody's face was almost amusing. O'Gorman had to remind himself that he needed this woman's help. Could he keep her at arm's length without antagonizing her? Perhaps not. But he was going to try—for the sake of Barbara O'Day.

O'Gorman was in the sentimental phase of his fling with Barbara. She would be humiliated beyond measure if she found out he was also boffing Melody. It would cheapen him forever in her eyes—and in his own. But O'Gorman regretfully recalled that he had cheapened himself more than once in his checkered past for reasons all too similar to the ones that might require him to satisfy Melody Faithorne.

"Can't we go someplace more entertaining?" Melody said. "I've heard the food here is awful."

"They serve a very good fish-and-chips," O'Gorman said. "It reminds me of Dublin days."

"I thought fish-and-chips was an English dish."

"You'd be surprised how much the English and the Irish have in common, after a millennium cheek by jowl."

Wilbur Gargan, the Shamrock's outsize proprietor, greeted them at the door and led them to a booth with a nice view of the ocean. Melody ordered a vodka martini. O'Gorman chose Jameson. When her drink arrived, in an outsize cocktail glass that made it a double, she downed half of it in a single gulp.

"Even Atlantic City would be more enticing," Melody said.

"Possibly a good deal more dangerous," O'Gorman said. "Chief O'Toole tells me if the Mafia decides we had anything to do with the disappearance of Joey Zaccaro and his million and a half dollars, they may be in a very ugly mood."

He could see that Melody did not believe any mafioso in America would have the nerve to touch her. How wonderful it must be to have such a sense of invulnerability. It undoubtedly came from associating with power— although anyone who worked for Senator Ted Kennedy ought to remember every day that power can attract its own brand of deadly lightning. But Melody had probably been about ten years old when Castro's marksman blew off Jack Kennedy's head. It was a montage on television to her. The reality was Senator Ted's bulky potency—in more ways than one, no doubt.

Melody ordered another vodka martini. "I thought this whole thing could be accomplished in forty-eight hours," she said. "I have things to do in Washington that can't wait."

"We all have things that can't wait."

"I was looking forward to meeting you," Melody said, demolishing the second martini at the same pace as the first. "You were going to be my compensation for enduring forty-eight hours with my in-laws."

"Why do they distress you so?"

"They're so mindlessly, relentlessly stupid."

"Perhaps you're too hard on them. They have willing hearts—some of them at least."

"I can't believe it. Richard O'Gorman, the sentimental revolutionary. But I guess that's how you got your reputation."

"Oh? I didn't know my fame had traveled to America."

"I got your profile from Interpol. They have reams of data on you. 'Irresistible to Women' was the heading on one chapter. Another one suggested you could become prime minister of a united Ireland, if the IRA won."

"I'm afraid such rumors are more than a little dated—and could get me killed if some of my Irish friends read them."

"I must confess I don't think much of the IRA as a terrorist organization. You seem so mindless. England get out of Ireland. But then what? You never say. You have no program."

"If we revealed our program, the Prods in the north and the Catholic capitalists in the south would fight to the death. We intend to annihilate both of them."

"That's what I've been hoping to hear."

"I trust it won't go beyond this booth."

"Don't worry."

"What would the senator say, if he heard it?"

"He'd be horrified. He's the sort of brainless liberal that Lenin mocked—and then exterminated."

"What about your husband?"

"I thought I'd convinced him that there was no compromise possible with capitalism. Now I'm not so sure."

"Why?"

"It's a very personal quarrel."

O'Gorman sensed she was about to tell him something he did not want to hear—something that would obligate him to break those unstated promises to Barbara Monahan O'Day. Fortunately, Wilbur Gargan arrived with menus and recommended the crab cakes as the dish of the day. By the time they acceded to his spherical authority, the moment of intimacy had passed and O'Gorman got down to the business he wanted to discuss with her.

"I've picked up some rather disagreeable information. There's a British SIS agent operating here in Paradise Beach. I suspect he killed Zaccaro and stole the money."

He told her about Jackie Chasen's glimpse of the Chinese Type 64 silenced. It did not register. He could see Melody thought this was another romantic O'Gorman notion. Like most Americans, she had no idea of the savagery of the war the British and the IRA were waging in Northern Ireland.

"Couldn't someone else have the same gun? Mick O'Day? Bill O'Toole? Some mafioso enemy of Zaccaro?"

"Extremely unlikely. We've been trying to obtain one or two of them for five years. They serve only one purpose, assassination. The Chinese are not mass-producing them."

She remained stubbornly skeptical. "What am I supposed to do about it?"

"I was hoping you could mention the probable presence of this fellow to Senator Ted. As coming from me, through IRA intelligence. A little pressure from him might persuade your State Department to protest to the Brits. If the Brits are as obnoxious or deceitful as I expect they'll be, the Senator might become irate enough to urge the FBI to flush him out."

"That makes no sense whatsoever," Melody said briskly, her Washington persona suddenly in place. "The last thing we want is a squad of straight-arrow G-men messing around here while we're trying to get the guns ashore."

"I don't mean literally flush him. I mean the FBI might leak to the senator and then to you his cover. Billy and I would take care of him pronto."

"I thought you understood the senator has to *distance* himself from this business."

"Exactly. But for certain people, I would think he might feel obliged to reduce the distance somewhat."

"What do you mean?"

"We have a dossier on you too. We have our own version of Interpol. Hamas, the IRA, the Red Brigades, are constantly exchanging information. You were on Chappaquiddick Island when the unfortunate Mary Jo Kopechne took a nap in the backseat of the wrong car. I would imagine you know things that Senator Ted would do almost anything to keep secret."

Melody's blond good looks seemed to darken, as if a cloud had passed over the sun. "I suppose he'd do a great deal for me. But I've never asked him for single favor."

"Isn't this whole thing a favor? The warehouses in Boston? The names of the right customs inspectors?"

"I got them, using his name. If anything blew, he would have been able to say he knew nothing about it."

"Isn't this more of the same? You can call the State Department in his name. They must be used to you throwing his weight all over Washington."

"Maybe I could, maybe I couldn't. I'm not sure I see the necessity."

"It's very simple. If we don't get the money back,

there'll be no weapons. The Cubans are not altruists. They're donating the cocaine because they have it coming out their noses. But weapons are another matter entirely. They're also desperate for dollars. Their revolution is falling on its ass, thanks to Castro's arrogance. They have a bigger, fatter *nomenklatura* than Moscow. That's one thing we'll never tolerate in a socialist Ireland."

There was not a flicker of agreement in Ms. Faithorne's cold blue eyes. It occurred to O'Gorman that Melody considered Ireland not worth even a dollop of censoriousness, even if they *nomenklatured* every member of the IRA and their uncles and their cousins and their aunts. In her global revolutionary view, Ireland was more a nuisance than a vanguard nation. Was that opinion rooted in her obviously low tolerance for her relatives—and other Irish of the American branch? Or did the roots go deeper, to the first encounters of the Boston aristocracy with the horde of starving Irish who poured into their pristine metropolis in 1847?

"I don't see much point to this conversation. It's so one-sided," Melody said. "In Washington, when we ask a favor, we're usually in a position to do one in return."

"If ever an opportunity arose. . ."

"My husband and I have just had a very unpleasant quarrel. He's threatened me with deadly force."

"Why in the world?"

"Because he's apparently regressing to the same level of stupidity as the rest of the family."

The crab cakes arrived, along with a bottle of white wine. The cakes were surprisingly good and so was the wine, an Australian chardonnay. Melody ate them without comment and drank quite a lot of the wine. O'Gorman barely had a chance to refill his glass.

"I did something five years ago that seems to bother him. I presume it won't bother you."

She told O'Gorman how and why she had informed the Internal Revenue Service about the bearer bonds—and her husband's skewed reaction to this act of unquestionable justice against an Irish *nomenklatura* that had ruled and looted the state of New Jersey for decades.

"Now Leo's threatening to tell Bill O'Toole. I have to confess I'm more than a little frightened. Can you help me?"

O'Gorman ordered another bottle of wine. Maybe it was time for them both to get drunk. He saw what she wanted him to do. Arrange for an IRA hit man like Kilroy—but somewhat more intelligent—to remove Leo McBride from the scene. Was it her way of validating her revolutionary credentials with him? If so, it was a total failure. Her story of the betrayal of the bearer bonds was causing a tidal wave of revulsion to thunder through O'Gorman's Irish soul. It was such an English thing to do—the Anglo-Americans were at least as morally smug and uncaring as the English English when it came to the Irish. The micks were a lesser breed beyond the law, to be dealt with as carelessly—or ruthlessly—as the African Hottentots or the Australian aborigines or the American Iroquois.

With a supreme effort, O'Gorman concealed his revulsion behind the mask of the gunman. Her revelation had altered the balance of power between them. He was no longer the supplicant. He was the favor grantor extraordinary, with a godlike ability to solve her marital unhappiness and her fears of sudden death with a nod of his head.

"I think what you're suggesting could be arranged," he said. "Provided our gratitude for your extraordinary efforts on our behalf runs deep enough. I can promise you that I'll do everything in my power to make sure it does. Assuming that your efforts reach that extraordinary level."

"I'll call the State Department this afternoon."

The second bottle was almost gone. He let his hand wander across the table to rest on Melody's slim fingers. "May I also say my heart goes out to you. It wasn't easy for you to do what you've done—about the bonds. It testifies to a remarkable ability to face history's demand for justice, no matter what it costs you personally."

Melody's eyes filled with drunken tears. She was snookered. "The moment I saw you, I said to myself, 'There's a man I want to hold in my arms.'"

"You shall, my dear, sooner rather than later."

Not for the first time, O'Gorman amazed himself by his ability to assume the role that a woman wanted him to play. It was especially remarkable here, dealing with a woman whose exquisite Wedgwood face he wanted to smash to smithereens. Perhaps he could arrange for others to do the smashing. Mick O'Day or Bill O'Toole or Leo McBride. But first he had to play the romantic gunman until he got what he wanted from this Anglo-American slut.

THE REVENGER'S TRAGEDY

At midnight in his office at police headquarters, Chief William O'Toole stared at the whirring tape recorder on the wall, his brain a chunk of polar ice. He pressed a button and the tape reversed. He pressed another button and he heard the blustering voice of his nephew Leo McBride.

If you ball him, I'll tell Bill O'Toole about the bearer bonds. You won't get out of this town alive.

A pause and then the silky, sullen voice of Melody Faithorne.

I believe we've shared that reward money more or less equally.

O'Toole stared at the $1,000 bill on his desk. He had been tapping every phone and house in Paradise Beach that might possibly have a connection with this remnant of Joey Zaccaro's million and a half dollars. He had found nothing even faintly resembling a lead. Instead, he had listened to Trai Nguyen Phac sob while her husband belted her around their trailer and their son, Suong, cried,

"Stop! Father! Please!" He had listened to Mick's heavy breathing and Jackie Chasen's gurgles of delight. He had listened to Desmond moaning to his wife about his slack member and his fear of the Mafia. He had listened to Billy Kilroy berate Richard O'Gorman and tell him who was running their sorry show. He had listened to Barbara Monahan O'Day telling the two-faced Irishman that she loved him.

How did a small-town police chief lay his hands on such sophisticated surveillance equipment? When Atlantic City surrendered to the mafiosi and the gamblers— largely one and the same—O'Toole had persuaded his nephew Leo McBride to persuade Congressman Mullen, the Appropriations Committee chairman, to come through with several million dollars for crime-fighting equipment to make sure the surrounding towns were not contaminated by this inundation of moral sleaze into South Jersey. Leo made sure that Bill O'Toole got his hands on a major slice of this cash. In Jersey City, tapping phones and bugging houses had been a way of life for the organization. O'Toole made it the leading edge of his crime counteroffensive.

There was not a motel room in Paradise Beach that did not have a connection to headquarters—or to a police car parked outside the place. Wilbur Gargan's Golden Shamrock had a half dozen booths with microphones in the table lamps that captured every word on tape recorders in the basement.

O'Toole rewound the tape and listened to Leo and his wife again. He put on a tape from the Golden Shamrock and heard Melody and O'Gorman discussing the existence of an English SIS agent in Paradise Beach. But that startling fact remained almost irrelevant in Bill O'Toole's rapidly thawing and soon seething brain. What mattered was Melody's confirmation that she had betrayed the bearer bonds. Not even her suggestion that O'Gorman eliminate her whining husband to guarantee the secret stirred outrage comparable to the thunderous fury that consumed Bill O'Toole's soul when he realized how and why this righteous bitch had destroyed his inheritance.

Only one idea permeated his flesh: revenge. With shaking hands, O'Toole began loading his police .38. He would kill them both, now. He would kill Melody first, while whimpering Leo, the ultimate draft dodger, watched. Then he would blow him away. He did not care what they did to him afterward. The death penalty would be a pleasure. Nothing could alter the stupendous satisfaction of seeing them dead.

The telephone rang. O'Toole heard Tom Brannigan, the night sergeant, answer it. "You called his house, his wife said he was here? Just a minute."

Brannigan's squat physique filled the doorway. "A guy named Nick Perella."

The consigliere of the Giordano family. O'Toole had met him several times in Atlantic City. A lean, sallow face, hooded, angry eyes, a habit of clenching his back teeth as he talked, so his words seemed squeezed out of his mouth like toothpaste.

"Bill, how's it going?"

"Not bad, Nick. How's it going with you?"

"Okay, okay. Haven't seen you at the tables lately."

"I'll get there one of these days."

"I got a problem, Bill. He's named Joey Z."

"Oh?"

"I keep thinkin' you could help me solve it. Tommy Giordano ain't heard from him in almost a week. Nothin' from his muscleman, Angie Scorsese, neither. They both walked off the planet, you know? There's big money missin' too."

"How much?"

"A million and a half."

"What am I supposed to know about this?"

"Joey said he had a deal with you and some Cubans to bring in a couple of hundred kilos of cocaine."

"So?"

"Did it come off? Have you seen him? The last anyone

heard of him, he and Scorsese were on their way to your place."

"I saw him. We clinched the deal. But the Cubans haven't shown up yet. I don't know where Joey went with the cash."

"Bill, I hope you ain't lyin'. He's Tommy's only nephew. He ain't got no kids of his own."

"Neither have I. You learn to live with that. You learn to live with a lot of things, Nick."

"Bill, I'm startin' to sort of dislike your attitude, you know what I mean? You don't seem to give a shit what happened to Joey and the money. Where's the deal if the Cubans finally show up? You ain't stringin' together a good story, Bill. If you double-crossed Joey, I hate to think of what Tommy would do to you—and everyone else in your fuckin' family."

"I can tell you one thing on my mother's grave, Nick. I didn't double-cross Joey."

"But you know someone who did?"

"I don't know who did. I don't know what happened to the money either."

"I think maybe you better come see Tommy for a talk. Face-to-face stuff, you know. He's not gonna believe anything else."

"I'm pretty busy, Nick."

"Bill, this is good advice. Very good advice. You know what I mean?"

"I'll think about it, Nick."

"Think real hard, Bill. And fast. I'll call you tomorrow."

Bill O'Toole sat staring at the loaded .38. He still wanted to drive to Desmond McBride's house and kill Melody Faithorne and her whining weasel husband. But other ideas were churning through his head now. Other ideas about Tommy Giordano and the possibility of doing the deal with the Cubans and laying his hands on his $200,000 slice of the action. A million and a half bucks could easily be replaced by Tommy Giordano. He would drive a hard bargain, but O'Toole was not worried about that. All he wanted was his slice, his getaway wedge of happiness.

What about revenge? That could wait a day or two or three. Why commit suicide for it—when it might be possible to enjoy it and go cruising off into the sunset. Laughing all the way to some South American bank.

An even better idea occurred to Chief O'Toole. Why not go for more than his slice? All they had to do was mess up the heads of Kilroy and O'Gorman a little more. They were already threatening each other with gunfire. If they lost control and did something crazy, O'Toole could sell the cocaine to Giordano for a million and a half and let the IRA suck wind for the weapons.

O'Toole picked up the telephone and told Tom Brannigan to get Mick O'Day out of his squad car. In ten minutes Mick was in his office. O'Toole handed him the $1,000 bill. "I checked this out seven ways from Sunday. I've decided Tyrone Power or his little pal Kilroy stuck it in your glove compartment. I think they've got the goddamn money somewhere."

Mick shook his head. "I don't get their angle."

"Here it is. They figure we'll get another pile of stash from Tommy Giordano and go through with the deal. They walk away with a nice bonus."

"How are we gonna get it from Tommy Giordano?" Mick said, his eyes widening. He had heard Bill O'Toole denounce Giordano as the worst slimeball in America.

"We're either gonna get it from him—or get something else. Something like this."

O'Toole picked up his gun and placed it against his temple. For a moment he was tempted to pull the trigger. It would be easier than going to see Tommy Giordano. It would be easier than lying to Mick this way. Mick—the substitute son who thought he could play it straight in Paradise Beach under Uncle Bill's guidance.

Revenge steadied O'Toole. He was not going to die until he had killed Melody Faithorne and Leo McBride.

"Here," O'Toole said, handing Mick the $1,000 bill. "Take Kilroy to Atlantic City to get laid and work on him. Tell him how O'Gorman laughs at him behind his back. Treat him like a piece of shit—as if you think he's no more of a hero than Leo McBride. Get him drunk and see if he spills anything about where they've stashed the money."

"What if it's some sort of Mafia double cross, Uncle Bill? They blow Joey away and we've got to cut a deal with them that will give them half the town."

Mick was not stupid. Bill O'Toole kept forgetting that. Mick was troubled, depressed, unhappy, but he was not stupid. He saw exactly where they were going. But it was too late to worry about Mick. It was too late to worry about anything anymore. Bill O'Toole only wanted two things out of life—his slice of happiness, and revenge. He was going to get both, no matter who got hurt on the way.

"If you get that shrimp to talk, we won't have to go near Tommy G. Do it tomorrow. That's an order."

The haunted, hunted look was in Mick's eyes. Bill O'Toole was not the only one who thought about getting far far away from Paradise Beach and life with one big unhappy family. But Mick was still a marine. He obeyed orders even when they did not make sense. He grabbed the $1,000 and stalked out of headquarters. He all but stripped the squad car's gears as he pulled away.

BY THE WATERS OF BABYLON

Over the causeway into the Pines drove Father Dennis McAvoy, better known elsewhere as Captain Arthur Littlejohn. His position was more and more precarious and he knew it. There had to come a time when Father Hart would chat on the telephone to someone in diocesan headquarters in Trenton and casually mention how well Father McAvoy was coming along. They would inform him that Father McAvoy was an impostor. Hart would tell his friend O'Gorman and the guns would be on the table.

Yet the risk continued to be worth the chaos Littlejohn was sowing among the Paddys. Planting the $1,000 bill in the young cop's car was only the beginning. He wanted to turn them into a mare's nest of raging suspicion. Eventually they would start shooting each other, as the Irish were wont to do. After five centuries of informers betraying Ireland for British gold, every man was suspect.

Meanwhile, he had to pretend to be the eager collaborator with Father Hart in his pastoral tasks. He had begun making calls on the housebound and bedridden—most of them old. He had listened to litanies of complaints against visiting nurses, overcharging doctors, absentee daughters and sons. He took their minds off their troubles by talking about Ireland. SIS had supplied him with dozens of Irish jokes. Many were drawn from newspaper clippings of pithy comments by public figures, such as the outspoken bishop of Galway, a fierce critic of the IRA, among other things.

Father Hart heaped praise on McAvoy's visits. Hart had received telephone calls telling him that the "little Irishman" was the best thing that had happened to St. Augustine's Parish in a decade. This unsought praise had a strange effect on Father Hart. He began to confess his deep feelings of inadequacy as a pastoral visitor. He was no good at making small talk. He had lost the Irish gift of gab. This morning Father McAvoy had received a more serious assignment. Hart had asked him to visit the Vietnamese woman who was being abused by her husband.

Littlejohn-McAvoy remembered that Desmond McBride had suggested the Vietnamese husband, Phac, as a crewman on the boat that was going to bring the guns ashore. Maybe he would find an opportunity to include him in the web of suspicion. Father McAvoy, aka Captain Littlejohn, had another $1,000 bill in his wallet.

Following Father Hart's directions, he found the mobile home in the trees without difficulty. But a knock, a second knock, a third knock, went unanswered. He walked around the house, if it deserved to be called that— it looked more like an abandoned railroad car—and peered in a window. A Vietnamese woman was kneeling in the middle of a small room before a crucifix. The woman's arms were outstretched, her head flung back. Her oval face was blank with ecstasy.

Littlejohn-McAvoy stood there for at least five minutes, transfixed. St. Teresa of Avila, St. John of the Cross, St. Thérèse of Lisieux, the greatest mystics of the Catholic Church, had prayed that way.

Finally, almost embarrassed, he tapped on the window. The woman sprang up, saw him, and rushed to open the front door. "Good day, Father," she said with an atrocious accent.

"Hello," Littlejohn-McAvoy said. "I'm sorry to interrupt your prayers."

"Oh, that not prayer. Please do not tell anyone about that, Father. My husband be . . . angry."

"Why should he be angry at you praying?"

"He say I too bad—too unclean to pray. I only make God more angry against us. So I don't pray, Father. I close my eyes and say nothing, think nothing. Sometimes Jesus come to me and I ask him to ask God for mercy, forgiveness. I let him pray for me."

"For what?"

"Oh, forgiveness for many sins, Father. Many bad sins. Come in."

He found himself sitting in the minuscule kitchen while she fixed him a cup of tea. "You priest—from Catholic relief?"

"No. I'm from the parish. I'm a friend of Father Hart. Staying with him for a few weeks."

She sat down and forced a smile. After another struggle, she managed a whopping lie. "Good, Father Hart. Good priest."

"Oh, yes," Littlejohn-McAvoy said, mentally adding, *good and stupid*.

"You—no like?"

Was she a mind reader? "No, no, he's been very kind to me. I'm . . . a sinner too."

Suddenly the words echoed as if he had shouted them in the middle of York Minster, the great cathedral in the city of his birth. I'M—A—SINNER—TOO. The echoes rolled out beyond the confines of the tiny kitchen, beyond the surrounding forest, beyond this strange American continent. They reverberated through vast reaches of outer space.

"Woman?" she asked. "In Quang Tri province, some priests . . . have woman."

"No," he lied, trying to deny the prostitutes he had screwed in Dublin and Belfast on reconnaissance. That was not Captain Arthur Littlejohn RA who had done those things. That had been the other self he assumed in defense of the realm.

"In Binh Nghai, my village, our priest—good. Father Nhu very good. Very angry against sinners like me."

"What did you do?"

"Oh—Father." Across her face passed an expression that could only be described as totally feminine. "I was . . . unclean. Like Mary Mag—Jesus' friend?"

"Mary Magdalene?"

"Yes. Like her."

"Jesus loved her very much."

"Yes. I hope he love me too."

"He does."

"Oh, no, Father. Not yet. I have much more pain to suffer. For my country, for Suong. For Phac."

"Is that why you let him beat you?"

"I let him because I sin against my country. Against him and Suong. Phac was . . . how you say . . . patrit?"

"A patriot?"

"Yes. He fought communists. I foolish, stupid woman. I let love—and obedience to father—ruin my patrism."

"You worked for the communists?"

"Yes. Now I see how bad that was, Father. I see what they do to my country. It was a bad sin, Father."

"Why did Phac marry you?"

"Oh. After my father . . . die, he marry me to show his good heart. To show he could rally me."

"Rally?"

"Yes. That what government call it. To rally people against communists. You went for education. You heard how bad Viet Minh were. That when I see how bad I was, Father. That when I say, yes, I will marry Phac."

"Why does he beat you?"

"Oh, I think his heart cannot love, Father. Before he came to Binh Nghai, Viet Minh kill his wife and three sons. Only Suong escape. Also—another reason."

"What?"

"I save Phac, Father. I save him and Suong. That wounds—"

She pointed to her heart. "If he saved me, all would be okay. But I save him. Unclean woman save him. I sinned to save him."

Suddenly there were tears pouring down her face.

"You were one of the boat people?"

"Yes. Boat. Pirates capture us. I save him and Suong. I let them . . . do me. This many, Father." She held up the fingers of both hands. "They do me again and again. Before they finish, British boat come and shoot them."

Littlejohn had heard such stories from one of his SIS friends who had become station chief in Singapore. They were all enraged by the bestialities inflicted on Vietnamese refugees on the high seas. But the Royal Navy had nothing east of Suez now except a few frigates at Hong Kong. The days when the British enforced law and order in the Pacific were gone, and the Americans, as usual, did nothing to fill the vacuum.

"Oh my dear," he said, and took her hand. "And you went on loving Jesus."

She looked at him with a new expression on her face. Was it condescension at his stupidity? The memory of her rape by the pirates had shattered her surface calm. She told him the truth now.

"Oh, no, Father. You no understand. Until then—I hate him. I hate Jesus. I think he kill my father. I hate our priest, Father Nhu. I . . . hate Phac. I marry him only because when Mick leave Binh Nghai, Phac will kill me. Only when pirates are doing . . . to me . . . Jesus came. He came into me, Father. I hear his voice and my father's voice whispering together. I hear their saying, 'By waters of Babylon. By waters of Babylon.' I don't know what it mean, Father. But it fill me with . . . happiness, Father. Do you understand?"

"Yes—and no." Littlejohn-McAvoy suddenly had an

overwhelming desire to fall to his knees and kiss the sandaled feet of this tiny, weeping woman. He wanted to cry out, *O Lord, I am not worthy*. He wanted her to lift him up in the name of Jesus and the Virgin and Mary Magdalene, in the name of all the impossible contradictions that lived together in the world's tormented heart.

"What 'waters of Babylon' mean, Father? Will they make me clean?"

"Yes. It's from a psalm of King David. About the Jews living in captivity in Babylon. He asks God how he will sing the Lord's song in a strange land."

"What . . . God answer?"

"He didn't answer. Later, much later, He destroyed Babylon. Maybe that was an answer."

"Ah. God is . . . angry, I think. Like Father Nhu."

"Sometimes."

"But Jesus, no. Jesus love, Father."

"Yes. Yes. Trust in his love, Mrs. Phac."

"Oh, Father. You understand. Will you explain to Father Hart?"

"Yes. I'll explain. Don't worry about it anymore."

Littlejohn-McAvoy stumbled to his car and sat behind the wheel for a long time. He took out the $1,000 bill and stared at the portrait of some nineteenth-century American president in the center of it. It would have been simple to ask to use the bathroom and leave it there. Or to pretend an interest in her marooned railroad car and tuck it between the cushions of the couch while she was showing him around, then make an anonymous call to the police chief. Now it was impossible.

What was happening? Was she a precursor? Was she telling him that beyond the veil of tomorrow there was similar suffering, similar humiliation for him? Why else had he understood, why else had he seen the beauty of her soul? She had entered the kingdom that he had once dreamt of entering. A kingdom that his father with the voice of God had denied him, when he ordered him to join the army instead of the priesthood. Was she telling him that the kingdom still awaited him? Or was she informing him that it was irremediably beyond him now?

Captain Littlejohn thought of Maeve Flanagan and Jackie Chasen spread-eagled on their beds. Why did that image fill his soul with dark pleasure? The same pleasure that bubbled like witch's brew when IRA men in Armagh cried no, no while the Chinese Type 64 silenced clicked death. Sullenly, bitterly, Littlejohn refused to disavow that pleasure, to exchange it for pain.

Trai Nguyen Phac had not sought the pain, of course. She had begged God to prevent it. But God had not listened. He had a hearing problem. He let Jesus take care of the suffering. Captain Littlejohn wasn't sure about Jesus. He was even less certain about Mary Magdalene and the Savior's enthusiasm for a woman of the streets. His soul was filled with angry doubt as he drove back over the causeway to Paradise Beach.

That night at dinner, Father Hart virtually levitated when Littlejohn-McAvoy told him that he had talked to Mrs. Phac and her husband, who happened to be at home, ill, and he had contritely promised not to abuse his wife anymore.

"You obviously have a gift when it comes to dealing with third world people like that," Father Hart said. "I guess it comes from growing up in a simple world like theirs. In contrast to our overcommercialized, machine-made world, with a television set blaring nonsense in every room."

"Perhaps," Littlejohn said. One of the first things you learned in the intelligence business was to bear fools patiently.

"Have you read Gutierrez or the other liberation theologians?"

"I'm afraid not."

"You should read them, Dennis. They're the hope of the world. They show how Marxism can be reconciled with Christianity. How Marx, in some views, may even be a reincarnation of Christ."

"Doesn't that fellow Marx preach hatred instead of love?"

"Class hatred is not the same as personal hatred. Class hatred is really a hatred of injustice, which every Christian ought to have. Once you see the world from the viewpoint of the oppressed, all sorts of things change. There's no such thing as individual guilt, for instance. The poor don't sin. The revolutionary doesn't sin when he strikes at the oppressors. The sin is on the other side."

"I see."

"I've been thinking of volunteering for missionary work in South America. We send priests to several parishes in Guatemala and Brazil."

"I admire your courage. I don't think my nerves could handle such a challenge, at present."

"You're happy here, aren't you? The people are happy with you. They like you more in a week than they've learned to like me in twenty years."

"Now, Philip. If I stayed here twenty years they'd find plenty of fault with me too."

"I doubt it. I need a challenge to make my priesthood meaningful. You should have been over here during the Vietnam War. That was a meaningful time. You felt a moral purpose in your life, every day. A sense of mission. I'm dying of boredom here, if you want to know the truth."

"A pity. Maybe you should apply for the missions. But I'd think it over for a week or two."

"No. I'm going to call the archbishop tomorrow to see if there's an opening. He may be a lot more amenable when I tell him how well you're doing here. I've got a ready-made replacement!"

"I wish I could say I was ready, Philip."

"You will be in a month. It'll take a month for the archbishop to make up his mind. It takes him a month to decide anything."

As he spoke, Father Hart's face had undergone a remarkable transformation. He seemed to grow younger and younger before Littlejohn-McAvoy's eyes. Soon he was facing the boyish seminarian who had pleased his mother so much by becoming a priest and disappointed his father by becoming an antiwar protester.

"I'm flattered by your confidence in me," Littlejohn-McAvoy said.

It was time to move Father Hart offstage. It had always been a possible if extremely risky option. In Littlejohn-McAvoy's suitcase was a variety of potions that could remove him permanently. But that would cause severe complications. For the time being, it would be better if he simply fell ill. A raging fever and other debilitating symptoms. Father Dennis McAvoy would become the acting pastor of St. Augustine's Parish.

Acting pastor. Littlejohn rather liked that. Too bad there wasn't someone with whom he could share the joke. If it was a joke.

GLITZ

"Come on," Mick said. "We'll live it up."

"I don't want to go near that place," Jackie said.

"Joey Zip's not gonna bother you anymore. Nobody's gonna bother you with me around."

That was undoubtedly true. But Jackie still resisted the idea of going to Atlantic City. The stage shows were too boring, the food too bland, the gambling tables too seductive.

"Come on. We've got a thousand bucks to blow. You can hear all about guerrilla war in Belfast from Kilroy the great."

Mick had told her they had found one of Zaccaro's $1,000 bills on the beach. He had orders from Chief O'Toole to get rid of it and keep Kilroy happy in the bargain.

Jackie sensed that Mick was not really enthusiastic about going to Atlantic City. He was in one of his who-gives-a-damn moods. She did not like him around in one of those moods. She especially did not like making love to him. All he wanted to do was tricks, the more outrageous the better. That was not the kind of sex that satisfied the new Jackie, the woman the girl in white wanted her to become.

But Jackie was tempted by her old fascination with wars of liberation. When she had gone to Hanoi with the student peace delegation in 1969, she had bedded a North Vietnamese colonel after listening to him tell her over dinner how he had annihilated an American outpost in Quang Tri province. It had been one of the most unforgettable experiences of her life. Not that he had been very great, sexually. She barely felt him inside, compared to Mick. It had been the idea of connecting with the world revolution that was being created out there, the apparently irresistible force that was destroying the American war machine.

Now Jackie was not so sure about apparently irresistible forces or the march of history. Instead of marching, history seemed to lurch through time like a drunk with the blind staggers. Vietnam had turned into another boring communist dictatorship. Four or five million Cambodians were dead, thanks to a communist maniac. Russia was revealing the horrors of Stalinism, and China was confessing Mao was a first cousin to a monster.

It was time to disengage from history, Jackie had decided. That was what she was trying to do in Paradise Beach. Find her personhood, her individual soul, and nurture it for a while.

Still, she was tempted. Belfast. Bombs and gunfire in the night. It would be interesting, even if the rest of Atlantic City was a bore. It would be a break from another evening in front of the television in Paradise Beach.

"Is Kilroy for real?"

"You bet he's for real. He's killed more limeys than George Washington. Wait'll you hear his stories."

"Okay."

She almost changed her mind when she got a look at Kilroy. It was hard to believe this prematurely wizened little man was a hero. She sat in the back of Mick's car and listened to him chirp about birdies in Atlantic City.

"Yah, we heard all about'em in Belfast. They say it's better than New Yawk," he said in an accent that did not sound Irish to her. "They say you can pick'em off the boardwalk as you please. You can't do nothin' like that in Belfast with the fookin' Prods on your back all day and night. They wouldn't know a good time if it ran over them like a fookin' locomotive."

"Tell her how good you are at pickin' off the paratroopers, Billy," Mick said.

Billy aimed an imaginary rifle ahead of them down the Garden State Parkway. "I can knock the head off a para at thousand yards. I done it more times than you can count."

"Than you can count, anyway, champ," Mick said.

"What's with this boyo? He's always full of back talk."

"I'm just kidding, birdbrain," Mick said.

"We dawn't kid that way in Belfast."

"Tell me more about Belfast," Jackie said.

Billy told Jackie the way the IRA operated. They were a real army, with generals, colonels, majors. They issued orders for operations. Nothing was done accidentally or on impulse. It was all controlled and planned, all aimed at the expulsion of the British and creating a united Ireland.

"Once that's done, we get rid of the fookin' Catholic Church and start enjoyin' ourselves," Billy said. "We'll have a socialist paradise, where nawbody has to do a lick of work if he dawn't feel like it, and a man can enjoy a woman without havin' to get a bloody marriage license."

"Hey, I'm gonna emigrate," Mick said. "Want to come with me, Jackie?"

"Sure. Make me an offer." She always tried to get in the spirit of a party, though it was not easy to join this one, with Kilroy as master of ceremonies.

"Jackie's big on revolution," Mick said. "She helped North Vietnam win the war. Set off bombs, marched to

Washington, balled fellow revolutionaries. Even went to Hanoi. Did you ball anyone there?"

"Yes," she said, old anger stirring. She could easily learn to dislike Mick O'Day.

"Naw kiddin', you got to Hanoi?" Billy said. "I've been to Sofia. I was gawn to Moscow but they quit the revolution business. How'd you like Hanoi?"

"Nice," Jackie said, deciding not to describe the atrocious food and worse service at the former Imperial Hotel.

In Atlantic City, the casinos blinked their neon invitations on the boardwalk's skyline. They headed for Caesars, easily the gaudiest of the bunch. In the lobby, a black bellman grinned when Mick slipped him $5 and asked for Arlene. The bellman led them to a corner where a blonde with her hair teased into a birdcage was waiting. She was wearing a gold lamé dress with a slit skirt; on her face was a pound of rouge and a quart of eye shadow. "Hi," she said.

"Let's go for the Bacchanalia," Mick said. It was the most expensive of the casino's eight restaurants. The interior was an orgy of mirrors and gilt and silver glitz. A dwarf in a toga escorted them to their table. "Hey, Billy," Mick said. "Why don't you hire that midget for the IRA? Then you wouldn't be the shortest guy in the army."

Billy glared. Jackie wondered if Mick was being indiscreet, but there was no need to worry. Arlene had never heard of the IRA. She had barely heard of Ireland. She was Polish, from Camden, and had been "working" in Atlantic City for three years. She was twenty-three and was not a little pleased that Jackie was fifteen years older.

Arlene watched a lot of television. She treated them to a long appreciation of *Dallas,* her favorite TV show. She adored Lucy Ewing, who specialized in seducing cowboys. She even liked old J.R., the ruthless patriarch. Meanwhile they ate and drank. The courses all had Roman names but it was basically American meat and potatoes. The Bacchanalia served a different wine with each course and Billy drank plenty of it, as well as most of a bottle of Irish whiskey Mick had ordered when they sat down.

What the hell, Jackie thought as the wine began to hit her. It was only one evening. It was funny. Arlene talked about *Lifestyles of the Rich and Famous*. Billy said he had seen it at the Monahans and thought it sucked. "Who gives a fook about a lot of capitalist assholes?" he said.

"Hey, what is this guy, some sort of communist?" Arlene asked.

"He's a revolutionary," Mick said. "But only in Ireland. Here he just wants to get laid."

"I don't like communists," Arlene said.

"Come on, relax," Mick said.

Arlene gave them a lecture on politics. The communists were against the Americans because they were rich. "That's right," Billy said, amazed at her perspicacity. "It's a fookin' British idea, one percent of the fookin' realm drinkin' champagne and the rest fookin' swill."

"Hey, this guy really is a goddamn communist," Arlene said.

"Have another drink," Mick said.

"I'm not lettin' any goddamn communist touch me," Arlene said. "I got my principles, you know."

"We'll play switchees," Mick said. "You and me. Jackie here can swing with Billy. She goes for revolutionaries, right, babe?"

He was needling her about Vietnam. It was a fairly serious needle, Jackie thought, finishing her fifth glass of wine.

"That sounds good to me," Arlene said. "Is it okay with you, honey?"

"You bet your fookin' capitalist ass it is," Billy said. His hand crept up Jackie's thigh. She shoved it away.

"How about some dessert?" Arlene said. She took a packet of cocaine out of her purse and poured it on a plate, along with a silver sniffer.

No, Jackie thought. She had vowed not to touch that

stuff again. But Mick's needle was under her skin. She
really did care about the revolutionaries of this world,
even if they were no longer the unblemished heroes of her
youth. She was not going to let Billy Kilroy touch her, but
maybe some cocaine would make him more tolerable for
the rest of the evening.

Wham, it was good stuff and it hit her like a blast from
Cape Canaveral. Smooth, spacey soaring into a high that
made even Mick look enticing. They drank some more
wine and Billy persuaded Jackie to try Irish whiskey.
They went downstairs and gambled away most of Joey
Zaccaro's $1,000. Jackie had a run at the blackjack table
that almost doubled it for a while, but it did not last. Billy
was a disaster at everything, roulette, craps, the slots. He
must have put $100 into the slots, with Mick laughing at
him.

"I'm beginnin' to think O'Gorman's right. You've got
bad luck comin' out your ears. No wonder he wants to
ditch you."

"He told you that?" Billy said.

"He said he'd pay me a year's salary if I blew you
away. Where would he get that kind of money? Anyway,
I told him you were too small to hit in the dark."

It was rotten, the job the marine hero did on Billy. Mick
never let Billy forget he was half Mick's size and could
barely read and write. After they ran out of money Jackie
charged everything on her American Express card. They
adjourned to a bar and Arlene passed around the cocaine
again. Mick said no, which only made him more con-
temptible. When Billy's hand crept up her thigh, Jackie
did not push it away.

In the bar's half-light Billy looked small and pathetic;
he was one of the little Vietnamese whom the huge Americans thought they could step on the way the Russians had
stepped on the Jews. The way the Americans had stepped
on the Indians and the Mexicans.

Wham, Jackie was really flying now. They were all in a
bedroom somewhere in Caesars' stratosphere. Billy was

on top of her but he couldn't do anything, and Mick was in the other twin bed making Arlene squeal like a Miura cornering at 105 miles an hour. Mick was laughing at Billy, telling him O'Gorman said he couldn't get it up, and Billy was cursing until Jackie offered to play Lucky Pierre and Mick took her from behind while she sucked Billy off, and Arlene watched saying that was the most fun she had ever seen, and she insisted on doing it while Jackie watched and then there was more coke and more booze until everything blurrrrred.

Jackie woke up with someone snoring in her ear. She was back on Leeds Point. *The Collected Poems of Dylan Thomas* was on the night table, only inches from her head. She turned over and there lay Billy Kilroy with his mouth a round *O,* looking like Popeye the Sailor. Snores came out of the mouth. In a fury, Jackie pushed him out of bed onto the floor.

Billy struggled to eye level. "How did you get here?" she cried.

"Fooked if I know. But it's all right anywhere with you, Jackie me darlin'."

"It's not all right with me," cried the new Jackie, clutching the sheet around her bare breasts like a Victorian maiden. "Get out of here before I call the police."

"What the fook are you sayin'? I thought we was good for another roll or two."

Mick appeared in the doorway, looking as fresh as a man who had slept at a spa for the previous week. "Hey, what's wrong with the lovebirds? Has the revolution gone sour?"

"You get out of here too, you bastard," Jackie said. She was crying and shaking all over as memory restored last night. She picked up *Dylan Thomas* and threw it at Mick. She threw an ashtray, her slippers, the lamp, at Billy.

Billy could not figure it out. "What'd we do wrong?"

"You didn't do anything wrong, champ," Mick said. "I

think you can chalk it up to your friend O'Gorman. He's put the knock on you with her. She forgot it for a while with some help from Monsieur Cocaine."

Kilroy looked ready to murder Jackie along with O'Gorman. Was Mick trying to get even with her? What else explained the way he was acting? Mick hated her now. He hated her for Vietnam, for playing games with Billy. He knew exactly why she had done it. She wondered, as she saw the contempt hardening his mouth, if he was measuring her against someone else, someone she could never match. Who could it be?

"Get out," Jackie sobbed. "Get out of my life!"

PILGRIMAGE

"We gotta go see him," Bill O'Toole said. "There's no other way."

"I'm not going," Desmond McBride said. "I refuse to have anything to do with it."

"We're all in this together, Desmond old friend," Dick O'Gorman said.

"Stayin' away might be a lot more dangerous than comin'," O'Toole said.

"What's the fooker gonna do, kneecap us?" Billy Kilroy said.

O'Toole ignored him. "We'll take Sunny Dan with us. He knew him in the old days. And Mick, for some muscle. And Melody and Leo to let him know how high we go in Washington."

They were back in the locker room of the Surf Club where the nightmare had begun a week ago. O'Toole had called Nick Perella and told him they were ready to go see Tommy the Top Giordano. Now O'Toole was laying it on the rest of them. Mick's trip to Atlantic City with Kilroy had produced a lot of expletives on O'Toole's bugging tapes, but O'Gorman had managed to convince the shrimp that he knew nothing about the money.

O'Toole could see Mick was still against going anywhere near Giordano. Was it possible that Mick had the money? For a few seconds, O'Toole thought about throwing him to Giordano. Tommy had ways to make people talk. But O'Toole decided against it. Mick was straight, as straight as you could expect anyone to be after what the marines had done to him in Vietnam. If anyone was guilty, it was the Jewish broad or Tyrone Power.

O'Toole had already gone to Sunny Dan and told him what they were going to do. Sunny Dan had gotten the general idea. That was all he needed to get. He said sure, he'd be glad to go see Giordano. He knew him when he was a numbers runner after World War I. Ho ho ho.

It was like digging up the centuries, talking to Sunny Dan. He was a walking history book. Too bad he was a talking one too. He talked almost as much as his daughter, Mrs. O'Toole, and said about as little.

Nick Perella gave O'Toole a number to call. It went through about six dummy companies and guys in phone booths in Jersey City before he finally got Tommy on the telephone. "What the fuck's happened to Joey?"

"I want to talk to you about it."

"Is it bad?"

"Very bad."

"You know who did it?"

"That's what I want to talk to you about."

"Where's the fuckin' money?"

"I wanna talk to you about that too."

"You better have a lot to say."

"Maybe you can tell us somethin' too, Tommy."

"You bet I can."

"Where do you want to see us?"

"There's a guy who'll meet you on the corner of Arlington and Carteret in Jersey City. You still know where that is?"

"Sure," O'Toole said.

"I thought you might have so much fuckin' sand between your ears by now, you forgot."

"I remember all right. I grew up a block away."

"Yeah? Nothin' but niggers there now. The guy'll be wearin' a tan coat and readin' a newspaper. The coon can't read but that don't matter. Don't talk to him. Just listen. He'll tell you where to go."

"Okay. I'm bringin' along the IRA guys. And Sunny Dan. And my nephew Mick. He saw what happened. And our Washington contacts."

"Bring along the whole fuckin' town if you want to. They probably won't even fill my livin' room. How many people you got down there in the winter? Twenty?"

"A few more than that."

"Joey's dead?"

"Yeah."

"Make sure you're here tomorrow."

They drove north up the Garden State Parkway and the New Jersey Turnpike in Desmond McBride's Cadillac. Leo McBride and his wife rode in the back with Sunny Dan. Mick rode up front with O'Toole and Desmond McBride, their designated driver. O'Gorman and Kilroy occupied the jump seats, which was fine with Billy. It gave him easy access to the bar.

Melody had wanted to know why she and Leo couldn't drive their own car. "Because I say you can't," O'Toole snarled, barely controlling his hatred. He got the underlying message—the WASP bitch was horrified at the thought of spending four or five hours in a car with her Irish in-laws.

As they rolled along, O'Toole could sense every square inch of Melody Faithorne's treacherous flesh. His hands opened and closed in his lap, imagining themselves around her throat. He wanted to do unspeakable things to her while she died.

Sunny Dan told them what a wonderful road system New Jersey had. He told them how much the Big Man,

Frank Hague, got under the table to build it. He told them
jokes. Like the line his Irish mother, Lord rest her soul,
had unleashed as they passed Moscato's Dump on the
outskirts of Newark Airport. "Me nose is in Jersey City."

Ho ho ho. Sunny Dan laughed alone. He was in his own
world most of the time. A wonderful world where being
Irish meant something in New Jersey. Where money
jumped into people's pockets because they were Irish.

O'Toole debated one last time whether to tell Giordano
about Mick and the $1,000 bill. No, he told himself, a
thousand times no. But it was tempting.

Soon they were twisting through the westside streets of
Jersey City, which still had a few traces of civilization.
Over the hill they went to Carteret and Arlington. "By
God, it's the old neighborhood," Sunny Dan said.

That was all he said. That was all anybody said. There
wasn't a white face in sight. The porches were falling off
half the houses. Blacks hung out windows and yelled
messages and insults. There was Sunny Dan's house on
the corner. The big bay windows were still intact. But the
place had not been painted in twenty years. Someone had
sprayed MALCOLM along one wall in six-foot letters. The
lawn was littered with beer bottles and milk cartons and
broken toys.

"Me nose—and me eyes— is in Belfast," O'Gorman
said.

"You sure these fookers aren't RCs?" Billy said.

On the corner, the big black in the tan coat was pretending to read a newspaper. He opened the back door
and jammed onto the jump seat beside Kilroy. "Follow
them guys," he said.

Halfway up the block, a gray Mercedes pulled away
from the curb and headed north. In an hour they were in
Bergen County. They drove down winding roads lined
with budding trees. "There's where shitface Nixon lives,"
said their guide.

"Hey, I voted for him twice," O'Toole said. "First time
I ever voted Republican. But not the last."

"A shame, a shame," Sunny Dan said as if he were lamenting the fall of Rome. In a way he was.

The Mercedes slowed and the driver blew the horn. A set of gates opened, revealing a winding road that seemed to vanish over the horizon. "Looks like the Oregon Trail," O'Toole said.

Eventually they reached a house that seemed to be mostly gray fieldstone. It hugged the ground and spread up a hill and down a slope. O'Toole had never seen a house quite like it. He had never been to Saddle Brook before. In the back, Melody Faithorne was telling everyone how many parties she and Leo had attended around here. She claimed Giordano's house was small compared to some of the mansions of the top political moneymen.

The big black took the wheel of Desmond's car and drove it away. Two large guys got out of the Mercedes and waved them into the house.

Giordano was waiting for them beside his indoor swimming pool. He was wearing nothing but a towel. Black hair bristled on his bulky chest. Another big guy with a bald head was giving him a massage. Giordano let them stand there beside the steamy, overheated pool until the job was finished. He got up, put on a bathrobe, and told them to sit down.

"Tommy, remember me?" Sunny Dan said, putting out his hand.

"Siddown," Tommy said.

Erect, he looked like a bulldog on hind legs. A massive jaw, a wide, scowling mouth, protruding eyes. The body was pure gorilla. He was the old school. He had gotten where he was by breaking legs and arms and killing people. He looked it.

"Tell me what happened."

O'Toole told him, while Tommy the Top paced up and down beside the pool. O'Toole let Mick supply some of the details. Giordano paced for another minute and a half. Finally he stopped in front of O'Toole and glared down at him. "I don't believe you."

"It's the truth."

"Then why'd you bury him in a fuckin' swamp, without a priest, without a mass? How am I gonna tell my sister that?" Giordano roared.

"We were shook, Tommy. We weren't thinkin' straight. We didn't want to blow the whole setup."

"We wanted to get our fookin' guns," Billy Kilroy said.

"I'll show you what you're gonna get, you fuckin' Irish midget," Giordano shouted. He grabbed Billy by the front of the shirt and threw him into the pool.

"Halp," he spluttered. "I can't swim."

"Did you hear him?" Giordano shouted. He grabbed Desmond McBride by the collar and slung him into the pool on top of Billy. Whirling, he seized O'Gorman and threw him in headfirst. Next went Sunny Dan, with a croak of terror. He couldn't swim either. Mick jumped in to help him. Leo McBride jumped in to help his father, who was also not exactly Johnny Weissmuller.

Giordano headed for Bill O'Toole. He rose to his full six feet four. "You touch me and I'll kill you," he said.

The two bozos from the Mercedes drew guns. Giordano swayed in front of O'Toole. Off to the right the chief glimpsed Melody Faithorne's wide-eyed face. He reminded himself of his determination to stay alive until he had the pleasure of killing her. "I mean it, Tommy."

"They're gonna stay in there till you tell the truth. You're gonna be with them, face down, if you don't tell me the fuckin' truth. Who hit Joey?" Giordano screamed.

"I told you we don't know!" O'Toole roared. "I personally think it was one of your guys."

Mick was keeping Dan's head out of the water. O'Gorman towed Billy to the side of the pool where he hung on like a water-soaked rat. The Irish matinee idol was trying to look tough, but it wasn't easy to do in a pool with all his clothes on. In spite of Leo's arm around him, Desmond McBride looked as if he might drown from fright.

Mick wanted to climb out of the pool and dismember Tommy the Top. The rage on his face finally convinced

O'Toole. He would not, he could not, throw Mick to this wop slime.

Giordano swayed back and forth, from heels to toes. He still looked like he might try to get his hands around O'Toole's throat. They were not friends. O'Toole had stopped Tommy at the boundaries of Paradise Beach. Tommy had never gotten a single prostitute, a single after-hours club, a single card game, into Paradise Beach while O'Toole was chief of police.

"You were always a fuckin' wise guy. If there's anybody with the balls to try a double cross like this, it's you," Giordano said.

"You don't have any guys with balls? What kind of a show you runnin' these days? A fuckin' seminary?"

Tommy the Top glared at the waterlogged sextet in the pool. "Get these guys dried off. I'll see you all in my office," he snarled.

He vanished through a swinging door. The two bodyguards stashed their guns and helped O'Toole haul the others out of the pool. Poor old Dan was in bad shape. He was coughing and choking. His face was purple and blue. The bodyguards led them into a locker room and told them to take off their clothes. They left them sitting there naked until Mick found some robes in a closet. Melody joined them, but she had nothing to say. No one had anything to say.

An hour later, their clothes dried but not pressed, they trooped into Tommy Giordano's office. It was as big as the entire ground floor of the Paradise Beach police headquarters. Bill O'Toole's office could have fit into it about twenty-eight times. Row on row of leather-bound books rose to the ceiling. On the wall was a huge painting of a castle in Italy.

This time, Giordano sat down. Nobody asked them to sit down. Standing beside Tommy's desk was Nick Perella, the consigliere. He never looked happy. Now he was looking unhappy in capital letters ten feet tall.

"Okay," snarled Giordano. "You come up here to tell

me your story because you want to keep walking around
on this fuckin' planet, right?"

There was no need to answer.

"If I found this out from someone else, none of you
would have lived another twenty-four hours. Joey was a
shit but he was my flesh and blood, you get it? Another
reason, that fuckin' money was mine. It wasn't Joey's."

"I thought you were shootin' people for foolin' around
with drugs," O'Toole said.

"That was five years ago, wise guy. That million and a
half was my money. Joey couldn't raise that kind of
money without robbin' the fuckin' Federal Reserve. So
now you want another million and a half for the fuckin'
Cubans?"

"We have to get it somewhere," O'Gorman said.

"What about makin' sure Joey's dough isn't in the
pocket of one of your underbosses?" O'Toole said.

"Nick here says it didn't happen. But he's gonna check
around some more anyway. In the meantime I want mortgages on every fuckin' piece of property you guys own in
Paradise Beach. That includes Grandpa Gumbah here.
We got a very good line on what you got, so don't try to
hide nothin' under the table. That especially goes for you,
McBride. We want all them boats and that fuckin' fish
factory and that marina. We can do a lot with that
marina."

"How can you issue a mortgage?" Desmond McBride
said.

"Through a fuckin' bank, asshole!" snarled Giordano.
"We own three of them."

"What kind of terms are you offering?" Desmond
whined.

"You want to go back in the fuckin' pool with fifty-
pound weights on your feet?" Giordano roared.

"Tommy, wait a second," quavered Sunny Dan. "I done
you some favors in the old days—"

"Yeah, and I thought you was a pile of Irish shit then.
Shut up. We're runnin' this fuckin' state now."

Bill O'Toole drove home. Desmond McBride was in no shape to do anything. The police chief drove slowly down the winding lanes of Saddle Brook past the invisible houses to the Garden State Parkway. No one spoke until they had crossed the Raritan. For Bill O'Toole that river had once been a dividing line between North Jersey and its cities and its corruption and the south with its beaches and its mythical simplicity and purity.

"*Jesus!*" Bill roared. He pounded the wheel with his huge fist. "*Jesus!*" He pounded the wheel again. "How did you let slime like that take it all away from us? How did you do it?"

He turned to glare at Sunny Dan in the backseat. "*You want to know?*" Bill roared. "You weren't tough enough. You were too busy listenin' to the goddamn Catholic Church. Too busy dippin' your miserable ass in holy water. Those guys don't give a shit about holy water, they don't give a shit about anything but money."

Sunny Dan said nothing. He just stared between his two sons-in-law in the front seat. He stared down the Garden State Parkway with its budding trees and greening fields at a vision that had turned into a nightmare. "We didn't shoot people," he said. "We didn't blow them up. We didn't do that kind of thing."

"You give me a fookin' map and some money for gelignite and I'll blow that fooker from here to Canada," Billy Kilroy said. "I'll put a bomb under his fookin' swimmin' pool that'll blow him higher than fookin' Westminster Abbey."

"I'll go with you," Mick said. "Give me an M16 and a dark night and I'll take on that whole lousy setup. I'll blow every one of them away."

"That won't get us the money or the guns," O'Gorman said.

"We was tough," Sunny Dan said. "We was as tough as them once. I remember in 1928 they tried to bring some hooch through the city. The Big Man had searchlights above the railyards. We turned them on and told them through a megaphone to leave the stuff and start runnin'. You shoulda seen the party we had with that stuff. It was the best. Straight from Scotland."

"They're going to take it all away," Desmond McBride said to O'Toole. "Everything we worked for all these years. Because you thought you were Mandrake the Magician in Atlantic City."

"You put together this Mickey Mouse deal, not me." O'Toole snarled. "You thought you were St. Patrick and Eamon De Valera."

"We was tough," Sunny Dan said. "But we didn't kill nobody. We didn't blow people up. That wasn't the way we played the game. You had to go to confession eventually, you know. You didn't want to confess things like that."

"Gentlemen," Dick O'Gorman said. "It seems to me our one hope of salvation is to find the original money. I have reason to believe it's still in Paradise Beach. Reason to believe it was stolen not by one of Mr. Giordano's thugs, but by the British Secret Service."

He told them about the Chinese Type 64 silenced that Jackie Chasen had seen shooting Zaccaro and his bodyguard. Bill O'Toole managed to subdue the rage that was engulfing his brain and pretend to be interested in this revelation, which he had already heard on his surveillance tapes. He also knew something O'Gorman did not know. Melody had called the U.S. State Department about the SIS man and they had told her there was nothing they could do about him, if he existed—a fact they obviously doubted. In the era of Ronald Reagan, Senator Ted was not as powerful as Melody wanted everyone to believe.

Over the causeway they rolled into Paradise Beach at last. But it did not look like the same place. The clean streets, the neat houses, the fresh, salty air were all superfluous now. The safety, the peace, the quiet, all the contrasts to the city for which they had spent twenty-five years congratulating themselves, had vanished. All O'Toole could see was the sneer on Tommy Giordano's face. All he could hear were the words *We're runnin' this fuckin' state now.*

Something similar was happening in the soul of Sunny Dan. It blended with the water in his lungs and the memories of the old days. It was a deadly combination. In the house he said, "I'm goin' to bed."

"Don't you want any supper, Papa?" Barbara O'Day asked.

"No. I'm goin' to bed."

"What did you do to him?" Barbara said as Mick helped Sunny Dan up the stairs.

"I didn't do anything to him," O'Toole said.

"The hell you didn't," Mick said, coming back downstairs. He was glaring at Bill O'Toole without an iota of respect or affection on his face.

A twisting regret clutched O'Toole's chest. He was losing another son. A son he had never quite accepted because he had never accepted the death of his real son. But a son nevertheless.

Mick, give me a chance to explain, somehow explain everything, a crazy voice inside O'Toole's head pleaded. While his real voice snarled, "Shut up. You're in no position to start callin' anybody names."

Kilroy and O'Gorman watched them, baffled expressions on their faces. They could not begin to understand this American brand of Ireland's sorrows.

PRAY FOR US SINNERS NOW
AND AT THE HOUR OF OUR DEATHS

Sunny Dan Monahan was terribly confused. There was an awful racket in the next room. The place was full of echoes, as if people were shouting in an empty convention hall. Were they in Philadelphia, picking out good seats for the New Jersey delegation? The Big Man always had the kind of clout that got them right in front of the podium. They had been in all the newsreels at the last convention.

Suddenly a voice snarled, *We're runnin' this fuckin' state now.* Who the hell was that? Giordano, the wop numbers runner. He remembered him because he always wanted a bigger cut and if you didn't watch him, he stole it. He was a nasty ginzo, the type you had to let the cops beat up now and then to keep him in line.

Sunny Dan never went for beating people up. He never went for a lot of things the Big Man did. Dan was for Al Smith in 1932; it was rotten the way the Big Man dumped Al and switched to Roosevelt. It was rotten to do something like that to your own kind. But it turned out to be a smart move.

What the hell? There was Barbara, crying her eyes out. Ohhh, Bobbie, I hated to see you cry. I'd give you anything to stop you from crying. You were my sweetheart, Bobbie, Daddy's sweetheart. I couldn't believe it when you let that Piney knock you up. Why are you crying now?

Dying? Did someone say that? Was that happening? He used to wonder what it would be like. Then you saw people die and you stopped worrying about it. In France guys died without a sound. His father just drifted away like a boat that had parted from its mooring. He had a smile on his face. Dan wanted to die that way, with a smile on his face. He wanted to live up to his nickname, Sunny Dan.

He gave his mother and father credit for it. They were the happiest people. They cried when they lost his brother Bill in the trolley car accident, but they were smiling a week later. Dan wanted to die like the old gent with a smile on his face, but it wasn't there. Why?

It was that voice: *We're runnin' this fuckin' state now.* Did they lose it because they weren't tough enough? No, they lost it because they got old. They got old and fat and self-satisfied. They lost it because they started fighting among themselves. They started double-crossing each other, they had double-crossers like Barbara's husband, that scrawny bastard O'Day, in their own families. I never should have let you marry that scumball, Bobbie. It would have been better to put the kid out for adoption. Have it in upstate New York and give it away. But then we wouldn't have Mick. What a hell of a mess life can be.

There was another reason why he wasn't dying with a Sunny Dan smile on his face. The bearer bonds. What did he have to leave anybody now? Especially poor Bobbie. She'd been supporting him for the last five years. How could that have happened? Who knew about them, outside the family? No one. Did that mean someone in the family had ratted? Why? Everyone lost on the deal. Especially him. He had lost his interest in living. Now he was dying and everyone was saying good riddance. Instead of being surrounded by gratitude, love, it was good riddance.

There was Leo, his favorite grandson. The only one with enough brains to go into politics. What a charmer he had been when he was a kid. Not much guts but a charmer. Still a good-looking boy, even with tears streaming down his face. "Grandpa, I'm so sorry, so sorry," he whispered.

Sorry about what? Dan almost quipped. You're not the one who's dying. But it wasn't an appropriate thing to say. Especially with Leo's WASP wife frowning behind him. So Dan just reached out and touched his cheek. "It's all right, Leo, it's all right," he whispered.

What was that sound? Like a car motor that wouldn't start in January. It was his own breath. Who's that now beside Barbara? The little guy in black—the priest. The Irish priest. Better him than that mealymouthed wimp Father Hart. He wouldn't confess his sins to him. Had he told someone that? Maybe.

"Papa," Barbara was saying between her sobs. "Papa. Here's the priest. Father McAvoy. Father Hart's sick. Father McAvoy'll hear your confession and give you Communion."

"Hello, Father."

"Hello, Mr. Monahan," McAvoy said. "Are you sorry for all the sins of your past life?"

"Oh, yes, Father. I've committed some lulus."

What were they? The women at the conventions? They were the only ones, after he married Helen. He hadn't touched Helen before the wedding. She barely let him kiss her. The ones in France, did they count? When you're fighting a goddamn war, the rules are different, aren't they? He had never felt bad about the women at the conventions. They had helped him put up with Helen's big mouth. Without them she might have driven him nuts. A man needed some consolation for a mouth like Helen's. He could swear she didn't talk that much before they got married. He would never have married her.

"Say an act of contrition now."

"Bless me, Father, for I have sinned."

Father McAvoy was raising his hand to bless him. Suddenly an awful thing happened. McAvoy's face turned into Giordano's. Instead of saying the words of forgiveness, he was saying, *We're runnin' this fuckin' state now*.

Then something even more terrible happened. Giordano's face turned into the face of a creature with blackened skin and ghastly fanged teeth and glowing green eyes. The face of a movie monster, an outer-space alien, Satan.

He saw Leo's face going the same way. The two of them side by side, a twin horror show. Why? What was God trying to tell him? Was it all his fault, this evil nightmare? Were those sins he committed that serious? Could being on the take all those years lead to this?

"Oh my God," Sunny Dan cried, and reached out for Barbara's hand, her arm. He crawled up it toward a memory of happiness. He curled his trembling old arms around her neck. "Oh, Bobbie, Bobbie, oh my God," he cried.

He let go and fell back on the pillow, dead.

Without a smile on his face.

MARCHING ORDERS

Clanging through Mick's brain was the old Rolling Stones song about a guy who had nothing in his head but the four letter word that rhymed with luck. He nipped at a pint of Southern Comfort as he drove through the night to Jackie Chasen's house. He had to tell somebody. He had to talk to somebody.

"You're drunk!"

Jackie sat up in bed, those lovely breasts lifting their nipples to his hungry hands like young deer welcoming the dawn in the Pines.

"Aw, Jackie. I jus' wanta—I mean—"

"Get out. I don't let anybody touch me while he's drunk."

Jesus, who could he tell? Who would believe they killed poor old Sunny Dan? Who could believe what these IRA communist bastards were pulling off? A million and a half Mafia bucks worth of heroin or cocaine or some goddamn thing. To buy missiles to shoot down

British planes and helicopters. His Uncle Bill, his Uncle Desmond, up to their eyes in a deal like that? Bill said it was to clear his goddamn gambling debts, he didn't give a shit for the IRA. So what? So you cleared your lousy debts and gave Ireland to these communist bastards?

Except they weren't bastards. His mother was in love with that smoothie, Tyrone Power O'Gorman. She was in the sack with him every night. The other guy, Billy Kilroy, he was like Minus One Haines, the little marine in his Parris Island company. Minus One had been a loser from the start. He tried so goddamn hard but he never made it. You could see why. Someone had told him he was a loser from birth. Kilroy was a loser from Belfast.

Mick reeled back to his car. Who could he tell? No one left now but the Professor. You couldn't tell the FBI. You couldn't tell the state cops. They'd put Uncle Bill in jail. He didn't want to see Uncle Bill go to jail. He didn't want to see him go down for the count. He just wanted to tell someone. It was exploding inside him.

He found the Professor at the Golden Shamrock, half in the bag as usual, holding forth on the failure of Western civilization. Mick tried to tell him what was happening. Alex Oxenford was not having one of his better nights. Instead of listening to Mick, he started telling him to stop drinking, to straighten out his head once and for all and do something with his life beside drive around in that stupid patrol car.

"Listen," Mick said. "Somethin' really bad's goin' down, you get me? It's so bad I need advice."

"You've never taken any advice from me before," Oxenford said.

"I know. Because I thought you were full of shit most of the time. But now I need to talk to someone."

"Try Father Hart. Or your mother."

"My mother!"

Mick drove into the Pines to Pop Oxenford's. He got the old man out of bed. He had done it before, when he first came back from Nam and thought about killing himself. He'd go out there and sit and talk to him with the gun on the table. Pop was the only one who knew the whole story of him and Trai and the court-martial. Pop was the only one who knew what had happened when the photographers and newshounds had come rushing to Binh Nghai to tell everyone how the Viet Cong had overrun the fort.

As if the VC had ever overrun anything. They shot people in the dark, but it was the NVA, the goddamn North Vietnamese, who did the overrunning. Anyway, it didn't matter, six marines were dead, his men, and he should have died with them. The next day Phac told him about Trai and her father. It drove him crazy. He told the reporter from the *LA Times* to hang around, he'd see some fireworks tomorrow.

That night Mick and Phac waited in the safe hooch down the river where Trai met Le Quan Chien and blew about twenty holes in him. The next day at noon Mick walked up to Trai's hut with Le's head in his hand and threw it in the door and asked her how much she was going to pay him.

The reporter took it all down, his cameraman took pictures. It didn't matter, Mick was crazy with grief and revenge. That night he watched Phac hang Trai's father in the ruins of the fort. Next Phac started tying a hangman's knot around Trai's throat.

No, Mick had said, no, and backed it up with his M16. He had let her live for some crazy, romantic reason. For the way she had cried and followed him into the lane saying, "I didn't love him. I loved you."

A month later with the fort rebuilt and the VC on the run—without Le Quan Chien they fell apart—the big shots in the dry-cleaned uniforms arrived from Saigon with the reporter's story in their hands. They asked people in the village if it had happened, but no one remembered anything. No one but Trai. She told them it was true. She tried to tell them it was her fault, but that was the last thing they were interested in hearing. They just wanted to confirm that Sergeant Michael Peter O'Day was guilty as charged of mutilating an enemy corpse.

"Mutilating?" Mick said. "Mutilating? I cut off the son of a bitch's head and I should have cut off his balls too and made her cook them for supper. I hung his goddamn corpse in the village square and let it rot there for a week. What else do you want to know?"

It was perfect. He got exactly what he wanted, what he deserved, a dishonorable discharge. It was for the wrong reason, of course. But if they had given it to him for the right reason, he would have shot himself in Nam instead of waiting to think about it until he got home.

The unreeling stopped. Mick stared into Pop Oxenford's lined, solemn face in the lantern light. He felt as if he had been underwater for an hour. As if he had drowned and been pumped out and brought back to life somehow.

"Aw, Pop, Pop, why am I tellin' you all this again? You've heard it."

"Hey, Mikey, a man my age don't sleep worth a damn. It's the most entertainin' story I've heard since Alf Burns shot twenty-two holes in one of them goddamn Navy blimps during World War II. Thought they was lookin' for his still. Alf hadn't even heard about the war. He never read a newspaper in his life."

"Pop, what the hell do you make of all this?"

Mick had told him the story, somewhere between the time he had said good-bye to the Professor and the unreeling of Binh Nghai. "What the hell should I do?"

"Nothin'."

"Nothin'? The Professor says they're goddamn communists."

"The Professor always was full of shit. Funny how you can spot that. I saw he was full of shit when he was six years old. I spotted that exactly right. I spotted him from the start."

"Nothin'?"

"Just play the game through. You owe that much to your uncle Bill. He took a lot of heat when he put you on the force. You owe him somethin' for that. You don't owe the Professor nothin'. He's never done a thing for you but shovel shit in your ears. That's all he's good for. So bring the stuff ashore. Finish the job. But when it's done, get the hell out of here and take that Jewish piece with you. Maybe marry her."

"She hates my guts, Pops. She's still fighting the goddamn Vietnam War."

"So are you. Maybe if you stop, she'll stop."

"I don't love her, Pops. There's only one woman in this lousy world I love. You know who she is."

"I was the same way at your age. Loved a married woman. But I didn't let it stop me from livin'."

"You're not Irish, Pops."

"Thank God for small favors."

A SLIP OF THE TONGUE

Wearing his best black suit, a red rosary entwined around his bony old hands, Sunny Dan Monahan lay in the parlor of Corrigan's Funeral Home in a steel-lined mahogany casket that was worth $6,000. The undertaker had rearranged his face to remove the terrified expression he was wearing when he died. He looked contented, as if he were thinking back over his long life and finding little to complain about.

The old and the middle-aged Irish-Americans of Paradise Beach and a few of the young turned out to pay their respects to the fallen chieftain. Dick O'Gorman sat beside Barbara O'Day and listened to endless anecdotes about local and national elections that meant nothing to him. The stories were mostly about stealing votes in clever ways, by bribing or intimidating election officials.

This was apparently a form of heroism among the American Irish. The more votes they stole, the greater the feat. It was amazing how they had carried intact to

America the corrupt habits they had acquired from English landlords in the eighteenth and nineteenth centuries.

Another set of stories was less surprising to O'Gorman. These were tales of largesse, of money loaned and favors done, a son placed in a government job, a brother-in-law rescued from a jail sentence, an aged mother admitted to the city hospital free of charge. They might have derived, with the details changed of course, from the Ireland of the fifteenth and sixteenth centuries, when the heads of great Irish families presided over miniature kingdoms, with hundreds of relations, followers, poets, musicians, in their retinues.

Sunny Dan had no poets, but the people who sang his praises in the nasal accents of North Jersey were sincere. It made O'Gorman wistful that he had been born too late to witness and perhaps enjoy this chapter of Ireland's diaspora. While he listened and smiled, he kept seeing and hearing Tommy Giordano's loathsome face. To O'Gorman it was the face of capitalism in all its naked venality. The Irish-American political machines had been a feudal interlude that the ruthless who-gets-what of capitalism had swept away.

What would Barbara O'Day think of him if she discovered he had sacrificed her father to this Sicilian Moloch? She must never find out, as least as long as Dick O'Gorman was in America. And in Barbara, of course. She had fled to him for solace last night, when they were alone in the big house. Solace and something deeper, something unspoken that he was uneasily waiting to hear tonight.

"I don't think much of this fookin' wake," Billy Kilroy said. "You can barely find a drink."

By Irish standards, Billy was right. Corrigan's Funeral Home had no facilities for serving liquor, and it was considered unseemly to drink in the same room with the corpse, a prohibition that astonished Billy. But a steady supply of liquor was supplied to all comers in Corrigan's office, where Wilbur Gargan, gigantic proprietor of the Golden Shamrock, had set up a temporary bar.

At 9 P.M. Father McAvoy arrived to say the rosary. His pants were a size too large for him and so was his coat. He was a makeshift priest if there ever was one, with his wan, humble face, his routine pieties. Father Hart was still a sick man. He sent his apologies. Father McAvoy would say the funeral mass tomorrow.

At ten, after the last of the mourners had departed, Barbara and her sisters said a final prayer before Dan's bier and then went home. Once more, Billy and Mick continued their drinking at the Golden Shamrock or elsewhere, and O'Gorman had Barbara Kathleen to himself. She was as wild as a teenager until he subdued her. For a few minutes she lay contentedly in his arms. Then came the unspoken thing he had sensed, between the wildness and the final surrender.

"I have enough money now. Enough for both of us. This house is worth two hundred thousand dollars. He's leaving most of it to me. My sisters don't need it. We can go away. You can get a divorce in Nevada for almost nothing."

A cold wind blew in O'Gorman's mind. What would this woman say and do when she found out that Dan had mortgaged the house to Tommy Giordano? She would kill him and he would not blame her. She would order her behemoth ex-marine son to kill him. Strenuous efforts had to be made to prevent her from finding out this appalling truth until O'Gorman had left America with the weapons, the wonderful weapons that would shoot down British helicopters and, if this failed to produce a troop withdrawal, British commercial planes.

"How I'd love to go with you tomorrow," he whispered. "But there's something I must do first. I think I'd better tell you who I really am. I'm a colonel in the Irish Republican Army. Billy and I are here to buy guns that will be smuggled ashore here in a few days. A week's time at most."

"You lied to me?" she cried, sitting up in bed, her fists clenched. He had never seen such ferocity in a woman. "That stuff about your wife was a lie?"

"No," he said, drawing her down against him again, confident of his mastery of the female. "That was true and now I'll tell you another truth. I'll go with you. Wherever you say. I'm sick of the killing. I'm ready to quit the business. But I have to fulfill this last contract. Otherwise they'd come after me. They'd track me down and kill us both."

"You're not lying?" she said, almost hysterical. "I couldn't stand it if you lied to me too."

Thirty years apart, the two loves, one American, one Irish, were still fused in her mind. The female of the species was far more incomprehensible than the male.

"I'm not lying," he said, and almost believed it. O'Gorman had told so many lies to so many women, he no longer thought of them as untruths. They were gifts, lovely illusory pearls of hope with which he draped their willing bodies for a while. Only much later would they perceive their beauty.

Oh. Oh. Oh, spoke Deirdre in the eternal silence. You faithless bastard.

Hearts were made to be broken, O'Gorman replied. Your IRA heroes have broken my heart and I am breaking yours. It is a triumph of justice, not revenge. Yes, when you considered the size of O'Gorman's heart, its desire to embrace not merely Ireland but the whole battered, bleeding world of the poor, the hungry, the oppressed in its thwarted embrace, a thousand broken female hearts were justified. None of their little hearts or minds nor all of them together, including yours, my sowish wife, can approach the power and the glory of the revolution Dick O'Gorman dreamt and lost.

Yes, lost. He faced in the silence the other thing he had seen when he'd confronted Tommy Giordano. The knowledge that the IRA were turning into thugs just like this man, extorting money from businessmen, taxi drivers, even the working poor, and spending it as they pleased. They were a long way from living in Giordano's Italianate splendor, but he saw in communist Ireland's future the same corruptions that had made the revolution a bitter joke in Russia, China, Cuba. Limousines and vacation houses and seven-course dinners for party members, hovels and gruel and ten-hour days for the rest.

Maybe, incredible thought, he was telling Barbara Kathleen the truth. Maybe he was truly sick of it all. Maybe he was ready to go with her to Bermuda or Miami or Los Angeles and spend the Mafia's million and a half dollars. Maybe Deirdre and the IRA deserved this ultimate act of unfaith.

He grew hard again at the very thought of it. He placed Barbara's hand on his pulsing member and whispered one more O'Gorman truth. "There's your promise. Your promise and your fulfillment, my darling." With exquisite care, he slipped it into her depths, into the inner world of pleasure and pride that obliterated for a little while the outer world of humiliation and frustration.

As he stroked her, another meaning grew in O'Gorman's mind. He was fucking them all in this supremely symbolic act, not merely Barbara Kathleen's innocence, which deserved to be fucked because it was innocence, but the Irish-Americans who had fled the challenge of agonized Ireland to make money in America; fucking America too because these fugitives and their progeny were no longer Irish—the immense quantities of money and meat and milk and sweets they had consumed in a century had turned them into Americans, quantifiers of greed in the name of more greed and power and pleasure.

In his Irish soul O'Gorman fucked all these things, invented by England and reinvented, polished, emblazoned, perfected, by their American capitalist descendants. He fucked this daughter of Moloch on behalf of the wretched of the earth, but ultimately out of an ancient Irish refusal to accept the world as created because in his soul he envisioned an immensely better one, a world of exquisite purity and perfection inhabited by saints.

Ahhhhhh. His semen gushed into her body, the second

coming, the best, the most prophetic kind. There you are
Kathleen, there's O'Gorman's promise.

The next day, Billy Kilroy groaned and whimpered about
his hangover. Mick glowered at O'Gorman, making him
regret he had not taken the precaution of retreating to his
own room last night. The limousines ferried them to Corrigan's for one last look at Sunny Dan. Barbara and her
sisters wept and the coffin lid came down. They drove to
the packed church and stood, sat, knelt, as Father
McAvoy droned through the mass.

He continued to confirm the impression O'Gorman
already had: the fellow was a hopeless clod. He had
trouble finding some of the prayers in the big, gold-
trimmed altar missal. He knocked over the chalice and
spilled some of the wine on the altar linens. But his sermon was touching; he pictured Dan before the bar of
heaven, telling God that he had done his best to practice
the theological virtues, faith, hope, and charity, especially
charity.

The interment was in a cemetery in the city, where the
Monahan family had a plot. O'Gorman and Kilroy rode
with Barbara, Mick, and the priest, McAvoy. No one had
much to say until they wound through the city's black
ghetto again. Barbara said the littered streets and wrecked
houses made her glad they had fled to Paradise Beach.
Mick said nothing.

The cemetery itself was a dismal sight. Many of the
tombstones had been knocked over or defaced. Especially shocking was the desecration of the mausoleum of
the city's erstwhile leader, Frank Hague, who had built
the political organization that had once ruled the state.
The stained-glass window had been smashed, the sides
spray-painted with incomprehensible slogans such as
77X-YANI. O'Gorman asked Mick what they meant and
he just shrugged.

At the grave, a thin, balding, sour-mouthed man in unpressed corduroys and a dirty sweater approached Barbara. "Sorry for your trouble," he said.

She stepped back as if she was afraid he might touch her. "Thank you," she said.

"You too, Mick," he said.

Mick looked at him as if he were an insect he might squash. "Thanks," he said.

Afterward, rolling back to the shore, O'Gorman asked Barbara who he was. "My husband," she said.

"He's Mick's father?" O'Gorman said, pretending he knew nothing about the true story.

"Yes," Barbara said in a small voice, almost a whisper.

"He must have inherited all his muscles from your side of the family."

"I guess he did."

Trying to restore or create some cheer, O'Gorman asked Mick what he had done in the marines. Getting nothing but surly monosyllables, O'Gorman soon gave up. That left no one but Father McAvoy. He began talking to him about Maynooth Seminary and the church in Ireland.

"I almost went there myself," O'Gorman said. "My best friend at Clongowes was going and almost succeeded in talking me into it."

"Really," Father McAvoy said.

"Yes. He's now the bishop of Galway."

"Oh, yes. Monsignor Finnegan. A wonderful man."

"He is indeed. But not terribly bright, Father. It makes me wonder if I shouldn't have gone to Maynooth. I think I could have beaten him out for a job like that. It must be a pleasant life, with hot and cold running cooks and butlers and your car and chauffeur."

Father McAvoy nodded and smiled feebly, granting him the jape. It was all perfectly jolly, but behind the smiles Dick O'Gorman's cold brain was at work. The correct name of the bishop of Galway was Flanagan, not Finnegan. Wasn't it a bit odd that a priest would forget the

name of the bishop who had probably paid his tuition at
Maynooth?

Joey Zaccaro had been killed and his money stolen by
someone who had recently arrived in Paradise Beach.
Father McAvoy had been there exactly ten days.

Maybe Billy Kilroy would have some use for his Zastava after all.

SPIRITUAL TRANSACTION

"If you weren't in Paradise Beach in the fourth week in March, I'd swear you had malaria," Dr. Vincent Butler said to Father Hart.

"It isn't just the flu?" Father Hart said, wiping the sweat from his streaming neck.

"It must be the flu. It can't be malaria. But the way you've been sweating, the way it goes away for about eight hours and then returns. . . ."

Butler had been a doctor on Guadalcanal during World War II and had seen a lot of malaria. He was a big, gruff man, married to a Monahan cousin. Something of a hypochondriac, Father Hart had gone to him four or five times over the previous ten years, convinced he was dying of illnesses as various and fatal as nephritis, cancer of the bladder, and a tumor on the brain. Dr. Butler had briskly dismissed Hart's symptoms and told him he was the healthiest priest in the diocese. Nevertheless they got along fairly well as fellow professionals who shared a common task with the local sick.

Butler had surprised Hart by approving his attempt to launch a healing ministry at St. Augustine's. But only a handful of people showed up at the Wednesday-afternoon service, and they soon dwindled to eighty-six-year-old Emma Murtagh, who wanted God to heal her arthritis of the spine to prove Dr. Butler did not know what he was doing. Father Hart had prayed fervently for her, but by the time Emma died she was bent almost U-shaped.

Dr. Butler left Father Hart to the gentle ministrations of his nurse, Father McAvoy. For dinner he served Hart a delicious clam broth and well-fried scallops. Hart dutifully consumed the food, even though his appetite was nil. "Can you believe it?" Father Hart said. "Dr. Butler says I've got malaria. We need a decent doctor down here."

"Maybe you can get one from Ireland. They have a surplus there, along with priests. It's the sweepstakes money. They put so much of it into medicine, there's a saying, if someone in Connaught sneezes, they build a hospital around him."

A violent hand seemed to be crushing both sides of Father Hart's skull. Never in his life had he had such headaches. He found himself wondering if he really wanted to go to the tropics and actually get malaria, if this flu was an imitation of the real thing.

He turned on the television to listen to the McNeil-Lehrer report. At least he would try to keep up with the state of the world. Downstairs, he heard a thump and a strange cry. Heavy feet pounded up the stairs and along the hall to Father McAvoy's room. Hart heard angry masculine voices. Clutching a blanket around him, he opened the door of his room and found himself face-to-face with the lecturer on Irish culture, Richard O'Gorman. He had a gun in his hand and an enraged expression on his face.

Father Hart recoiled. "What's going on?"

"Your friend Father McAvoy is a fraud, Father. He's a British agent. You haven't got the flu. You've got malaria—and he gave it to you."

"I don't believe you."

"Come take a look." O'Gorman half dragged Hart down the hall to McAvoy's room. The man was sitting on the bed, blood streaming from a gash beneath his eye. Kilroy, the little Belfast freedom fighter, was holding a snub-nosed gun to McAvoy's head. Police Chief William O'Toole was going through McAvoy's suitcase. Mick O'Day stood by the window, watching the street. He too had a gun in his hand.

"He doesn't believe me. Show him," O'Gorman said.

O'Toole picked up a small bottle of clear fluid. On the label was written in precise script *Falciparum Malaria*. On several other bottles more grisly words were written: *Doexpin, Resorcinol, Nitroprusside*. "There's enough germs in these bottles to wipe out the state of New Jersey," O'Toole said.

"I still don't believe it," Father Hart said. "Can you explain these bottles, Father?"

McAvoy just looked at him. It reminded Hart of the contemptuous stare he had received when he had tried to defend his antiwar sermons and marches to the archbishop. "Is your name Dennis McAvoy?" Hart asked.

"I'm Captain Arthur Littlejohn of the Yorkshire Rifles, Father, on detached duty with the Secret Intelligence Service. Your Irish friends here aren't using their real identities either. You've been talking to Black Dick O'Gorman, one of the leaders of the Provisional IRA. His little friend Billy Kilroy is wanted for at least a dozen murders in Belfast."

"Is that true?" Father Hart asked.

"Pay no attention to him," O'Gorman snarled.

"If you want to obey the law, you will go to the telephone and call the state police to report a conspiracy to smuggle drugs and guns into this country," McAvoy/Littlejohn said. "You might also report a soon-to-be-committed murder."

O'Gorman smashed Littlejohn in the face with the back of his left hand. He hit him on the other cheek with his right hand. Littlejohn made no attempt to evade the blows. "Not murder, you limey son of a bitch. An execution. You will be tried and executed, according to the international code of military justice, which stipulates death for spies and traitors."

"Are you going to let him stand there and mouth such nonsense, Father?" Littlejohn said. "He has no claim to being a soldier. His army is a vile fiction, a collection of Marxist thugs."

Billy Kilroy smashed Littlejohn in the face with his pistol. "That's for me pal Brian Slattery you killed with his gun in his hand last month. Show me a fookin' limey who died better than him."

Littlejohn fell back on the bed semiconscious. O'Toole grabbed Kilroy by the back of the neck and threw him across the room. "I told you not to do that! You can't find out where the money is from a dead man."

"He's a long way from being dead. But he'll soon wish he was," O'Gorman said.

He turned to Hart. "Who's side are you on, Father? We can't stop you from calling the state police. If you call them, Billy and I will simply disappear. Chief O'Toole can do what he pleases with this limey scum. The men he's assassinated in Ireland—I have personal knowledge of at least three—will go unavenged. The weapons we came here to smuggle to Belfast will be dumped into the sea."

Father Hart's head pounded with pain; sweat soaked his pajamas; his fever was rising again. He stared down at McAvoy/Littlejohn on the bed. This was another imperialist killer, the same loathsome tribe he had risked his career in the Church to attack in 1969. This killer had given him a possibly fatal dose of malaria and simultaneously tricked him into humiliating gullibility.

Suddenly all the hours Father Hart had spent reading liberation theology, dreaming of himself as a leader of the poor, committing terrible but necessary acts of violence against the rich, all his theorizing about personal and collective guilt, converged in this small room full of angry men with guns in their hands.

"You can do whatever you want with him," Father Hart said. "What you have to do."

"Can we work on him here?"

"Of course you can."

Father Hart stumbled back to his bed and shivered and shook through the long night. From the room down the hall came unearthly cries of agony as O'Gorman and Kilroy attempted to persuade Littlejohn to tell them what he had done with the money. At first they did not believe him when he told them that he had mailed it to London. Then O'Gorman wanted the address in Dublin where the money was being laundered. Father Hart heard only fragments of this contest between a man who was prepared to suffer the worst torture and men who were ready to inflict ingenious pain on his flesh.

More than once as Hart sweated and trembled with alternating bouts of fever and chills, he imagined himself rushing into the room to gather McAvoy/Littlejohn into his arms like a lost tormented sheep. Was that what Jesus would have done? Or was the real Jesus the infuriated guerrilla leader who drove the money changers from the temple?

Shouts of anger now; the torturers were arguing among themselves. "I've had enough of this shit!" Mick O'Day roared. He stormed out of the house; his uncle Bill O'Toole pursued him to the stairs snarling curses at him.

Then it was almost dawn and Bill O'Toole was snarling at the Irishmen, "Look. He ain't gonna tell you. The money's gone. I don't give a goddamn where he mailed it. Let's kill him and get him the hell out of here."

"Father Hart!" Littlejohn cried. "I want to see Father Hart."

Hart stumbled out of bed again and down the hall to the room where Dennis McAvoy, the wan, humble Irishman who had somehow given Father Hart renewed confidence in his priesthood, once lived. Richard O'Gorman met him in the doorway. "Stay out of here, Father. You're not ready for this."

The room smelled of burnt flesh. Over O'Gorman's shoulder Hart could see McAvoy-Littlejohn tied to a chair. Blood was all over his face. "Father," he gasped. "I'm a Catholic. I would like to confess my sins before I die."

"Go back to bed, Father," O'Gorman snarled.

Billy Kilroy had another gun in his hand, with a strange bulge in the bottom of the barrel. He was looking at it with something close to joy on his wizened face.

Yes, Hart thought. Yes. Go back to bed before you look at the awful meaning of the word *necessary*. Go back to bed before you disappear into the depths of McAvoy/Littlejohn's mournful eyes, which were unchanged. The sorrow you saw in them belonged to both men, the priest and the secret agent. What did that mean?

O'Gorman pointed to the gun in Kilroy's hand. "He doesn't deserve absolution. You see that? It's the gun he used to kill God knows how many innocent Irishmen. Now we're going to use it on him. That's all he deserves."

Wasn't that decisive? Wouldn't that persuade Jesus, the guerrilla leader? The fever burned in Father Hart's body, the pain slammed in his head. Yes. It would convince Him. It would convince anyone.

As he stumbled away, Littlejohn cried out, "Father!"

Hart looked over his shoulder, seeing nothing but O'Gorman's saturnine face in the doorway, surmounted by Bill O'Toole's heavy cheeks, sagging his mouth into a caricature of a tragic mask from Aeschylus.

"Into thy hands I commend my spirit," Littlejohn said.

Father Hart fell into his bed and drew the covers up to his chin. He lay on his side, curled into a trembling fetal ball, waiting for the blast of the pistol. It never came. Instead, a new kind of cold seemed to gather in his body, a cold deeper than the chill of malaria. It seemed to be in his body and in the room too, an intense, pervasive heatlessness that extinguished his fever like a hand snuffing a candle.

"We're just going, Father," O'Gorman said at the door. "Going to bury him in the Pines. I'll speak to you later in the day."

"He's dead?" Hart cried, sitting up. Why didn't O'Gorman notice the cold in the room?

"He's dead—without telling us what we wanted to know. Billy's cleaning up the mess in the room."

Hart lay there listening to the footsteps on the stairs. O'Gorman said something about Mick O'Day. "I'll calm him down, don't worry," O'Toole said.

The priest heard Billy Kilroy cursing to himself as he went down the hall to the bathroom. He returned, still cursing, and a scrub brush soon slithered back and forth on the floor of the room where Father McAvoy had slept in supposed celibate sanctity. The cold gathered beside Father Hart's bed like a hooded presence, a being with zeros for eyes, an empty triangle for a nose, a larger zero for a mouth. Was this Jesus the guerrilla leader? *Have mercy on us,* Father Hart prayed.

A waste of spiritual energy, that prayer. Mercy was not in this god's vocabulary.

POSSESSION

"Father. I missed you on our jogging route and heard you were sick," Jackie Chasen said. "Here's the Jewish equivalent of penicillin—chicken soup."

"Oh—thank you," Father Hart said, taking the plastic container. "Come in, come in."

Jackie had never been inside a Catholic rectory before. A new experience. She was in search of new experiences. Last night, Mick had turned up at her house drunk again, trying to tell her he was sorry for being such a bastard that night in Atlantic City. She had thrown him out again. Obviously the magic was gone from that relationship. Maybe the magic was gone from Paradise Beach. The little Irish creep Kilroy called her two and three times a day. He was getting nastier and nastier, calling her a fookin' capitalist cockteaser and other charming names.

Father Hart invited her into a living room that looked as

if it had been decorated by Bob Cratchit: faded brown wallpaper full of butterflies, harps, and birds, ancient stuffed chairs with lace doilies on their arms, a red rug with a flowered pattern that was almost obliterated by age, over the fireplace a portrait of Jesus ascending into heaven. The priest looked almost as blah as the room. His smile was forced and dim, his eyes lackluster. He wore a red sweatshirt with BEAUTIFUL NEW JERSEY in white letters across the chest.

"What's wrong, the flu?"

"Yes—the flu. You might call it the flu."

"What did the doctor call it?"

"Flu. But he said it reminded him of malaria."

"In Paradise Beach?"

"A lot of strange things come to Paradise Beach."

"Like me, for instance."

"Yes. You did seem strange to me at first. I'd never known a Jewish person before, believe it or not. We all live in ghettos in America. Sometimes golden ghettos, but still ghettos."

"Yes," Jackie said, not sure what was coming.

"But we grow—less strange, we even become friends— through gestures like this. Through . . . learning about each other. Your enthusiasm for Dylan Thomas, for instance. I got out some of his poetry and read it for the first time. Magnificent stuff."

"Oh, I'm so glad."

"I told you I was familiar with him. I was ashamed to admit I wasn't. I'd only heard one of his poems sung by Joan Baez at a peace march in 1970."

"You marched against the war?"

"Yes. Did you?"

"I did everything against the war. Including some things you wouldn't approve, Father."

"How do you know? I hope you don't think I believe in that insipid figure over the fireplace, ascending into a heaven that makes a mockery of the real world. I believe

in another Jesus, a guerrilla leader who pledged himself
and his followers to a revolution on behalf of the poor, the
victims of imperialism."

Amazing things began happening to Father Hart as he
said this. His slumped chest vanished, his shoulders
seemed to expand to fill the sweatshirt to its full dimensions. His head no longer drooped, the line of his profile
acquired Roman nobility, which his high forehead and
balding head accentuated. He was still not handsome, but
Jackie suddenly found him attractive—incredibly attractive.

When was the last time she had loved a man whose
mind she admired? Jackie asked herself.

The word *love* seemed to flip automatically into her
head. It was not forbidden in these sacred precincts. Yet it
was illicit, a word that always stirred warmth in Jackie's
body. She listened while Father Hart told her how he sat
here through the long, lonely winter nights—his visiting
priest had apparently departed—and thought these revolutionary thoughts that he could not express to the Irish-
Americans of Paradise Beach.

He poured her a glass of Chablis and one for himself
and asked her to describe Chicago in 1968. He had been
locked in his seminary, hearing, reading about it from a
frustrating distance. Jackie left out nothing. The mari-
juana and the sex in the park, the stoned crazies charging
the helmeted police, the smashed windows of the days of
rage. Father Hart's face grew flushed; he confessed his
secret wish to go to Guatemala and launch a revolution
there, in the name of Jesus the guerrilla, to be the Che
Guevara of his time.

"Go," Jackie said.

"Would you come with me?"

"Sure," she said, sensing for the first time in years what
she once called a flow. The wine, the conversation, was
unreal, surreal. It was rushing toward an exquisite
moment, a desire that was a marvelous mixture of sex and

politics and poetry, the way she had always imagined love and so seldom found it.

"I'd need someone like you—to give me the courage," he said.

"I'm not brave," she said, remembering her terror the night Joey Zaccaro had visited.

"Yes, you are. You've proven it. I know—what you did the night those mobsters attacked you. I know what happened."

"Everything?" Jackie said, remembering the wild lust with Mick in the Pines. Was that where she had lost the girl in white?

"I mean, helping to bury the mafiosi. Helping the Irish gunrunners. I'm helping them too."

"You are?"

"Yes. The other priest who was here . . . was a British agent. They killed him here . . . last night."

"My God. You helped them?"

"I gave them permission."

"Oh, Father."

A murderer. This sallow-faced, boyish man had committed what Norman Mailer called the ultimate act, the only act that defined and proclaimed absolute freedom. He had murdered a fellow human being. The girl in white could never understand such a person. But the old Jackie understood him. So did the new Jackie.

"Stop calling me Father. My name is Philip."

"Philip. Yes, Philip."

"I have to tell you something else. I'm a virgin."

"That makes me . . . almost cry. It makes me feel . . . honored."

It was incredible how much she wanted him. She felt creamy inside at the thought of him entering her. It would be like making love to a piece of God. Embracing something old and sacred. The girl in white would understand that, even if she did not completely approve it. Some lines from Dylan Thomas leaped into Jackie's mind.

A process plows the moon into the sun
Pulls down the shabby curtains of the skin
And the heart gives up its dead.

Yes, perhaps she could give up the dead at last, Great-grandfather Yid and Grandfather, aka Ronald Colman, give up bitchy mother and chastened father, who were as good as dead, give up all the years of garbage sex for a new beginning with God.

Breathlessly, almost strangling on the words, Jackie told him about the girl in white. He wept. She touched the salt tears with her fingertips, then with her lips. Never, never, had she wanted a man so much, never had she wanted to give a man so much.

He was so shy, so naïve. He undressed first and then undressed her, an unbelievably bad tactic for a seducer. But it didn't matter. Her body blazed with wanting; she lay on the bed, ignoring the chill in the room, and watched him strip. She raised herself on one elbow and took his penis in her mouth—a completely spontaneous gesture. It simply seemed right to her. He gave a little cry, of pleasure or of fright. Her tongue explored the head as it swelled; she seized one of his hands and placed it on her breast.

An oddity: the penis was cold, icy cold. It had to be the terror of the first time, the dread of damnation still lurking in his Irish-American soul. There was an answer to that problem. She fell back on the bed and opened her legs. "Now, Philip, now," she whispered.

He entered her and she knew, somehow, what he was thinking and feeling. He was entering freedom, entering the America that his priesthood had denied him for so many long, dry years. He was entering woman, the other half of the known world, after so many years trapped in the arid dungeon of maleness. He was entering triumph, ascension, Moon-Mars-Venus walking, the starry reaches of outer space. He was entering life, love, courage.

She soared with him. It was so different from Mick; there it had been surfing. No flight, simply the mounting wave, the spasm of release, the long ebbing ride to the beach of satisfaction. Surfing or a whirling ride around a track in a souped-up Audi 5000S or Acura Integra across a finish line to the blare of a brass band.

Yes, there was more than one thrill in Mick's repertoire, but none of them equaled this transcendent ascent. Up, up, in wild, ever-widening spirals until the whole sky, sun, moon, and stars were in her, she was the universe and the universe was her and him and God in an ecstasy of oneness beyond anything she had ever known. How could she ever come down? How could she ever walk the humdrum streets again?

When it finally ended, they lay there for a long time in silence. If they had returned to earth, it was a remarkably soft landing. Perhaps they were on an asteroid somewhat south of Venus. Finally, he spoke. "The mafiosi—when they were going to hurt you—they tied you to the bed?"

"Yes," she said, shuddering involuntarily at the memory.

"That must have been terrifying."

"It was. I get sick to my stomach every time I think of it."

"Horrible," he said, cradling her in his arms. He pressed her against him, as if he wanted to squeeze the evil memory out of her body. Jackie trembled and almost wept.

"What if we did it that way? What if I loved you that way? It might heal the wound."

Enormously touched by the word *heal,* Jackie agreed. She let him tie her arms and legs to the ends of the bed, exactly as Joey Zaccaro and his bodyguard had spread-eagled her that awful night. Philip Hart knelt beside her, his long, bony body trembling. Was it that cold? He should have gotten over the shock of desire. She decided it was that cold in the room. Hunched beside the church, the rectory did not get much sun.

Philip's hands traveled down her body. He knelt between her legs and she watched him grow hard. Then, with both hands on her breasts, he entered her. Jackie looked into his eyes, expecting to see concern, tenderness, adoration. Instead she felt as if something were sucking her soul out of her body down a long, terrifying tunnel toward a tiny pinpoint of light, like the twinkle of a single infinitesimal star. Inside her his penis was incredibly cold, like a tube of icy steel. On her breasts she could swear she felt the furry sensation of an animal's paws.

From Philip Hart's mouth came a guttural laugh that was totally out of character, a chortle of pleasure she might have expected from Joey Zaccaro. "I've got a wonderful idea," he said in a strange croaking voice, as if the cold in the room had settled in his throat.

He vanished and in a few minutes returned wearing the outer vestment of the mass, the long green garment with a golden cross on the front and back. "Holy, holy, holy, Lord God of Fucks," he croaked as he mounted her again.

What was happening? Suddenly all Jackie could remember was a prayer Great-grandfather Yid had taught her when she was four years old. *Open to me the gates of righteousness, that I may enter through them and give thanks to the Lord.* It did not make any sense but it was the only prayer she had ever learned, and prayer, nothing but prayer, seemed vital at this terrifying moment.

She did not know why. Was it because she was encountering another face of God, the side that was adored in darkness and fear? Was this the murderous Philip Hart, the worshipper of Jesus the guerrilla?

"I don't like this. It's not helping," Jackie said as the icy penis stroked her. She twisted and turned but the knots were well tied.

"Say the prayer after me," Hart croaked. "Holy, holy, holy, Lord God of Fucks."

"No. Untie me!"

He withdrew, reared back, and crouched above her. She stared up the green vestment and the gold cross to the sallow face above them. It swayed there like an unfinished moon, strained by bewilderment. "I'm sorry," he said. "I don't know what's happening to me."

Suddenly a round stain appeared on his forehead. Exactly like the stain on Joey Zaccaro's forehead. The bewilderment on Father Hart's face became absolute, final. His eyes careened to the left and he fell forward on top of Jackie. She twisted her head and saw Billy Kilroy in the doorway, the gun with the bulge beneath the barrel in his hand.

"You fookin' capitalist bitch. Seducin' a fookin' priest," he said.

He stifled her scream with a handkerchief jammed in her mouth. Then he went downstairs and came back with two bottles of Irish whiskey. He poured them all over Jackie and Father Hart and the bed and dropped a burning match beside them. Everything—flesh, vestments, sheets—exploded into flame.

To Jackie's amazement there was no pain. Or perhaps the pain was so total, nothing else existed for comparison. Like absolute cold the flames extinguished everything, obliterated opposites, annihilated possibilities. The universe was on fire and Jackie only had time for one last prayer. *And death shall have no dominion.* It was a poem but it was also a prayer. Great-grandfather Yid's prayer had made Dylan's poem a prayer.

Was it heard? Was it answered? Did Great-grandfather burst through the flames to gather the girl in white into his arms and stagger, smash, bang his way through a thousand million stars to eternity? I hope so.

LOVE AMONG THE RUINS

For the last ten days of March the bomb had been ticking away in the bedroom, in the kitchen. Nora Haines McGinty knew it was going to explode. Bombs always exploded. They had torn apart the Belfast of her youth. Was it so surprising that they should follow her to America?

Part of the bomb had already gone off. The shock of learning that Hughie was working for the IRA again had lost the baby. It had been a simple miscarriage, the doctor said in his cheerful way. He was a Protestant and didn't think Nora should have gotten pregnant in the first place. Two children were enough. It had left her feeling unbearably sad, thinking about the little life that the war for Ireland had claimed.

Weeping, she labored over a letter to her father. Because of the bombing campaign, Nora had seldom gone to school. Her mother had kept her home because the streets were not safe for anyone, much less a girl.

Dear Da: I'm sorri to heer you are still sick. Can't you get your lawyer to stop them from putting you out of hospital that way, even when you have a fevir? It's terible the way they mistreat you and Eddie. I lie awake at night thinking of the good old days before the Trouble started. When you had your job at the shipyard and you'd get out your fidle and play for us when you come hom. Eddie was such a good dancer. I bet he could have gone on the stage. The bulet in his knee ended all that, alas. The way things are makes me glad Mother is gone from us. She'd have never been able to bear the thot of you and Eddie caged for life. It would have driven her mad. She'd have shot a policeman or something. I'm sure she's praying for you wherever she is. I pray every night too and so do the kids. Hughie doesn't, he says he doesn't believe in God anymore. He's a good man in spite of it. We're still hapy and the kids are thriving. Your loving darter Nora.

You're becoming a liar at all points, Nora thought, mournfully sealing the letter. Maybe you get like the people you live with, as the Americans say.

In the cellar, in the attic, in her mind, the bomb ticked. Something was wrong. Hughie was not telling her the truth about working for the IRA. She sensed it constantly, in the way he talked about it, in the way he looked at her across the supper table with a strange anger on his face. She had been horribly upset by the discovery. Even more upset to see that slimy bastard O'Gorman again.

But the job did not seem that dangerous, compared to duty in Belfast. There she had watched men go out to risk violent death night after night. She had watched her mother's heart falter under the strain. Compared to that, the danger of arrest, perhaps a jail sentence, was mild. She had calmed down and made Hughie promise it was the last time.

Then the bomb began to tick. It started in the bedroom.

Hughie tried to make love to her that night. She had encouraged him, she had worn the shocking pink nightgown he had given her for Christmas, the chorus-girl special, she called it. She liked the way he wanted her. He was not her heart's desire, but he was a good husband and she liked to make him happy.

Hughie couldn't do it. She had heard of it happening to men, but it was the first time it had happened to them. He said he was tired and flung on his pajamas and hurled himself into bed with his back to her. That was when the bomb began to tick.

After that it was the silence. Hughie was a talker. He was always spouting his opinion about President Reagan or Margaret Thatcher or the pope. Now he said almost nothing. Then he stopped bringing candy to the kids. He barked at them for playing the TV too loud and yelling in the house when he used to make more noise than both of them, romping around like a ten-year-old.

What was it? Nora could only think of one thing—the job was a lot more dangerous than Hughie had told her. They were going to kill somebody, kill an informer. The IRA never forgot or forgave an informer. They hunted them down around the world. More than a few of them were in America, men who couldn't stand the bombing campaign, the maximum war they had launched in Belfast.

Nora felt sorry for them, mostly. She could barely stand it herself and all she had to do was live with it. She did not have to drive those ticking car bombs through the British roadblocks, break into Protestant houses in the middle of the night and shoot a man with his wife screaming beside him in bed.

It was terrible but what the British had done to Ireland for four hundred years was a lot more terrible. What the Protestants had done to the Catholics in Belfast was part of it. Nothing in this world was achieved without suffering. Even the priests admitted that much. So it had grown clearer and clearer to Nora over the past ten days that

Hughie was going to kill somebody and he was afraid, he was sick with the fear of it.

That was the bomb, trying to find a way to tell Hughie she knew he was afraid and understood it, that she forgave him just as she forgave him for running to America in the first place. There was nothing left for her in Belfast once her father and brother got those life sentences. Nothing but being screwed around by black-eyed bastards like Dick O'Gorman. She had told certain people about O'Gorman, and they had assured her that one of these days they would deal with him.

The telephone rang. "Nora. Come on next door for a cup of real coffee."

It was Suzanne Conti, her best friend on the block. Suzy was Italian and a talker beyond belief almost. Nora put on a sweater and slipped out the back door. The cappuccino machine was smoking away in Suzy's kitchen. She claimed only Italians knew how to make coffee, and Nora was inclined to agree with her whenever she tasted a cup of her cappuccino. Suzy's husband had given her the machine for Christmas last year. It cost $650. The presents that American husbands gave their wives left Nora breathless sometimes.

The wives were hardly ever impressed by them. They talked about their husbands in such condescending ways. Suzanne called Joe Conti "the Raging Bull," after a character in a movie. He was actually a big, easygoing fellow who worked as a salesman for Merrill Lynch, a stockjobbing company.

This morning Suzanne was off on her latest obsession. She was going to start an interior-decorating business and she wanted Nora to join her as an equal partner. Nora would be the salesperson, calling on people; Suzanne would handle the decorating. Her sister had started a similar business in Connecticut and was getting rich. It was an exciting idea but Nora thought her brogue and her lack of knowledge of decorating were severe handicaps.

"Nuts to that," Suzanne said—her favorite exclamation. "The brogue is cute. It makes you sound honest. As for the decorating, I can teach you enough to sell our approach in twenty minutes. The idea is not a complete overhaul, see? We're going to specialize in accessories, rugs, paintings, draperies. Things that will make a room go from a four to a nine or ten."

Ten was perfection, Nora knew that much of Suzy's slang.

"You're serious about this?"

"Am I ever? I got the Raging Bull to put up ten thousand dollars to get us going. He's coining money over there on Wall Street."

"It's a deal," Nora said, holding out her hand. It would be exciting to have a job, like so many American wives these days. With both children in school, she had plenty of time on her hands. Maybe a job was better than a new baby. Maybe Hughie would take heart and not be so terrified of the killing he had to do if he knew she could support herself and the children should the worst happen.

But it wouldn't, it couldn't happen. She had paid her price of admission to a little happiness. Leaving Suzy's, Nora walked to the corner in the spring sunshine to mail the letter to her father. Tonight she would defuse the bomb. She would give Hughie the courage he needed, somehow.

He was barely in the door when he blurted the news: "Tomorrow's the day."

"I'll be so glad to get it over with."

"You're to call me in sick. The flu or some damn thing."

"Can't you tell me what you're going to do?"

"No."

"My brother Eddie used to tell me. Da stormed his head off when he found out. But Eddie kept on tellin' me. I wanted to know. It made me feel better."

"This won't make you feel better."

"It would. No matter how dirty it may be, I'll find a way to be proud of you, Shewy dear."

"Oh, you will," he said with a strange bitterness that she took to be fear of admitting his nerves.

"Yes. I didn't marry you for your courage, but it would be a reason to love you so much the more."

"What did you marry me for?" he snarled. "A ticket to America?"

"I married you because I thought we could love each other as well as any man and wife in the world. It's turned out a good deal better than that. I love you tremendously, Shewy. You know that."

"Do I? After Dick O'Gorman comes to visit?"

"What's that slick blatherskite got to do with us?"

"More than you'd think. A lot more. He told me about the two of you. He told me everything, laughing in my face, the day before we sailed."

"The bastard. If I see him again I'll kill him. I'll stick a knife in his heart."

"That won't be necessary. I'm going to do that, tomorrow."

"You're going to kill O'Gorman? Is that the job?"

"I'm doing better than that. I'm turning him and that little ferret Kilroy in to the FBI. They'll get ten to twenty years and we're going to get forty thousand dollars and a new life, far far away from this coast, where no one's ever heard of the IRA. We're going to Arizona and I'm going to own my own business and never take another lousy order from the likes of Friel."

The bomb had gone off. The explosion was tearing through Nora Haines McGinty's life, ripping it into a million bloody fragments. She felt her body, her soul, catapulted into a black oblivion infinitely worse than on the day she had heard about her father and brother receiving life sentences in England. That bomb had left her clutching love to her breasts like a frightened child, the one possession she had left, but a precious one. This bomb annihilated love and loyalty, its blast left her naked, bereft, destroyed.

It was so terrible to see the knotted tangle of hate and

profit on Hughie's face, to see the countless times that Ireland had been betrayed by these twin motives recapitulated before her eyes. "How could you do this without consulting me?" she cried.

"Consult you?" he shouted. "Is that all you've got to say? Not a word of shame, of pleading for forgiveness?"

"It happened before you came near me," she cried. "When I was in need of comfort and the lying bastard knew just how to offer it. Why didn't you put it out of your mind? It had nothing to do with you."

"Is that so? A man finds out his wife's a whore and it has nothing to do with him?"

"I don't deserve that name and I won't let you use it. And I won't let you do this thing tomorrow. Oh, Shewy, Shewy, can't you see what you're doing? You're killing us all. If I don't die from the grief of it, I'll die and so will you and the children in a year or two or ten. It doesn't matter where we go. They'll find us, and all the time while we wait, there'll be the terror shriveling our hearts. For God's sake don't do it, Hughie."

"They'll never find us. The FBI has a program. They change your name and give you a whole new identity."

"Dear God, you'll risk your wife and children and your own life on the strength of those kinds of promises? Look at the South Vietnamese. Where are they, trusting to American promises? They're using you, Hughie, using you as truly as if you were taking British gold."

"I'll not only risk all that, I'll win the game and so will you and like it. That's the price you can pay if you want my forgiveness for O'Gorman."

"I won't. I won't ask your forgiveness for that. I'll leave you. I'll take the children and leave you! Tonight!"

"You try that and I'll arrange for you to spend some time in jail along with O'Gorman. I'll take the children and you'll never find me or them."

"Oh, you bastard. You bastard."

She picked up a Waterford glass vase he had given her for Christmas and threw it at him. It smashed against the wall near his head. He rushed at her swinging his fists. She crashed to the ground, her mouth bloody, and fled sobbing to the bedroom. Raging, he pounded on the door and demanded her surrender, but she refused to unlock it.

The children came home and he fed them. She heard him explaining that Mother was sick. At nine o'clock he put them to bed and knocked on the door. This time she opened it. "I'm going," he said. "I've got to dress."

He put on rough clothes, corduroy pants and a checked shirt. To her relief, he did not try to kiss and make up. "You'll see I'm right when you think it over," he said. "We couldn't have gone on with the thing eating away at me. This will end it."

It was hopeless. He could not see the way his greed and fear of failure in America had twisted his mind. All he knew was the satisfaction of his revenge. She lay on the bed, her head turned away, saying nothing until his car drove down the block. Then Nora began to think about life after the bomb.

There was only one way to protect herself and the children. She had to turn him in. She had to betray Hughie. Otherwise she would be considered as guilty as he was. Even if they gave her the benefit of the doubt, there was always the chance that the men who came to kill Hughie would be careless. The car bomb might blow up her and the children instead of Hughie. The bullets sprayed in the dining room window might kill all of them.

There was only one way to save her children's lives. In the back of her dresser drawer, behind the sexy black underwear Hughie liked her to wear to parties so he could take it off when they got home, she found the telephone number the IRA Council had given her before she left Belfast. "Call this if you ever need help," the colonel who had brought it to her said.

They were telling her that they had no great opinion of Hughie. They were telling her that she was a daughter of the IRA, one of their own, and they would do everything in their power to assist her and her children if she asked them. All by itself, the telephone number made it impossible to let Hughie betray Dick O'Gorman, no matter how much he deserved it.

She dialed the number, which was in New York. A woman said, "The judge isn't home."

"My name is Nora McGinty. I have a message for him. I may not be able to call him again. Can you give it to him?"

"Yes."

"My husband, Hugh McGinty, is working for the FBI."

She hung up and sat there. Without the bomb it was so quiet it seemed as if the whole world had stopped breathing. Nora turned on the television and stared at it for the rest of the night, seeing nothing.

COME ALL YE

On April 1, Patrolman Mick O'Day stood in the center of the intersection of Ocean and Atlantic Avenues, directing traffic. It was a beautiful spring day but he was not enjoying it. He was not enjoying much of anything these days.

"Great!" he yelled when a Toyota Celica liftback driven by some bald-headed jerk from the suburbs stalled in the middle of the intersection. A glance in the window revealed that the hotshot had bought the five-speed manual gearbox instead of the three-speed automatic, and he was unable to cope with the notches in the first-second and second-third shifts.

"Get an automatic, you asshole," Mick bellowed into the closed window, causing the hotshot to slam the accelerator and send the motor roaring to its 2410 rpm cruising speed. He lurched out of the intersection and Mick blew his whistle and tried to get some movement into a line of cars stretching back to the causeway. Each had fluttering green flags on the fenders to celebrate the Sons of the

Shamrock's annual feis. Not until July 4 would they have this many cars in Paradise Beach again. By that time, Mick hoped to be far far away from his hometown.

When he went off duty at four, he was going to take off his uniform for the last time. At midnight he would make a final installment on the debt he owed Bill O'Toole. He was going to help smuggle dope and guns into the country. It was a beautiful way to end his policeman's career. It fit the ugly pattern that had taken shape in Vietnam. Someone or something must have put a curse on him a long time ago.

Mick had become a cop because Uncle Bill O'Toole and others told him that if he kept his nose clean for five years, he would be able to join the FBI or maybe get back in the marines. That turned out to be malarkey. But he had told himself he would go on being a good cop and maybe make sergeant and eventually forget Nam. In spite of his back talk to his mother, he was not opposed on principle to finding a wife and settling down to a nice boring life by the sea.

Then Trai and Phac had arrived and Nam became impossible to forget. It kept unreeling, night after night. Now it was mixed up with Joey Zaccaro and Tommy Giordano's *We're runnin' this fuckin' state now* and the British SIS man. Tyrone Power and the pint-size killer he had brought from Belfast no longer trusted Mick because he had refused to stay there and watch them torture the Englishman. He could not explain that it had triggered memories of watching Phac work on captured VC.

In Nam he had never seen much point in torturing people because most of the time they died before the information they gave you could be checked out. Only with Trai's father had it really worked. He had told them exactly where to find and riddle the famous Le Quan Chien, but Phac hanged the old man anyway.

"Move it, move it, assholes," Mick shouted to the cars as they turned right onto Ocean Avenue and headed for the feis on the football field beside the high school. On top of everything was Jackie Chasen's death in Father Hart's bedroom. The coroner said it was accidental, but why were Jackie's hands and feet tied to the bed? It looked like murder to Mick. But no one was interested in his ideas. Everyone, including Chief O'Toole, was a lot happier with them dead.

The priest did not bother Mick, although there was a certain amount of shock in the idea of someone murdering a man who was, theoretically at least, close to God. Father Hart's obnoxious ignorance about Vietnam more or less canceled that emotion. But Jackie was another matter. He had almost loved her. She was like him, messed up at an early age. She had paid her bitter dues and was trying to make a fresh start. You had to grieve for a woman you had held in your arms, especially when she died an agonizing death.

Only a scumbag like Tommy Giordano would kill a woman that way. It could not have been Tyrone Power or Kilroy. No one with Irish blood could do that to a woman and a priest. Maybe he would buy himself some weaponry with his final paycheck and wait in the woods on the Top's estate until his limousine came down that curving drive to the main road. It would be simple to shoot out the tires and hit the gas tank with a grenade launcher. Tommy would find out how it felt to die at a thousand degrees Fahrenheit.

By 10 A.M. the traffic had dissolved and there were only random arrivals, who could make the turn with the light on automatic. Mick drove down Ocean Avenue to the feis, as ordered by Chief O'Toole. The entire Paradise Beach police force was supposed to spend the day there. Beer would flow like Niagara, and with a lot of first-generation Irish from different counties, that often meant trouble. It was amazing how much guys from County Mayo disliked guys from County Cork and vice versa. No wonder the British had been able to divide and conquer them for the last four hundred years.

Who should come staggering at him the minute he

stepped onto the football field but Kilroy. He was drunk and looking for an argument. "They tell me you played fookin' football here marine," he said. "Scored more fookin' points than God. How come y'dawn't have the guts to make that fookin' SIS man squeal?"

Mick ignored him. That only made Kilroy madder. "I dunno what's it with the marines. Maybe the fookin' VC cut off your fookin' balls. Is that how they run you out of Vietnam? We're gonna run the fookin' British out of Ire- land the same way. We don't give a fook if the Rooshians and the Bulgarries and everyone else in the world turns quitter, we'll do it alone!"

Mick kept walking. Who should he meet, a few yards away in the crowd, but the Professor. "I guess I didn't do you any favor, making that little IRA man your enemy," Oxenford said.

"I can handle him," Mick said, stifling an impulse to tell the Professor the real reason why Billy was on his back—and why Mick was finally going to take the Pro- fessor's advice and get out of Paradise Beach. Maybe Pops Oxenford would explain it to his son eventually.

"I'm surprised you haven't had a visit from the FBI about him," the Professor said. "He and his smoothie friend sure as hell aren't hanging around here to promote Irish culture."

"Maybe the big chief's heard something. He didn't mention it to me," Mick said.

Strolling past was Mick's mother and her sister Marie O'Toole. His mother was wearing a new green dress; her red hair was all fluffy and shining. She was looking around, an eager smile on her face, as if the feis was a world's fair.

"I wish I could figure out your mother's secret," Oxen- ford said. "She's as beautiful as she was when you were a kid."

"She's in love with the Irishman O'Gorman," Mick said. "It's put her in a great mood. She's stopped bugging me about getting married."

"Has her husband—your father—died?"

"Nope. He was at Grandpa's funeral."

"What's going on? I thought the Catholic Church didn't let her do that."

"I guess she's decided to tell the Church to get lost. She's talking about going to California with him."

"I'll be damned," Oxenford said. "I would have been at your house with a bouquet every night if I'd known . . ."

"I thought Oxenfords never got married."

"The smart ones didn't. But I'm one of the dumb ones. I've always . . . been very fond of your mother."

Mick was amazed. He seldom heard the Professor talk so personally about anything. "You've missed the boat. Look."

O'Gorman had emerged from the crowd. Marie O'Toole did a vanishing act. The Irishman was holding Mick's mother's hand, smiling, whispering something in her ear. She laughed and pretended to slap him.

"I guess I have," Oxenford said, turning away as if the sight was too painful for him to look at. He blundered through the crowd and headed down Ocean Avenue toward the Golden Shamrock. Mick could only shake his head in amazement.

Ten minutes later, Mick found O'Gorman talking to Bill O'Toole, resplendent in his gold-braided trousers and coat with the shoulder boards of stars on it. "You better do something about Kilroy," Mick said. "He's mouthing off to the whole goddamn feis about the SIS guy."

O'Gorman muttered a curse and dove into the crowd in search of his wonder boy.

"Be at the dock at eleven-thirty tonight," Bill O'Toole said. "You pick up Phac."

"Yeah."

"I know it's a mess. But we gotta go through with it. Don't you fink out on me like Desmond."

"What's wrong with him?"

"He's havin' dizzy spells. We gotta line up another captain for the *Enterprise*, fast. Got any ideas? He's gotta know the bay and the Mullica River inside out in the dark. And he's gotta have a little larceny in his heart."

"Only guy around who adds up that way is the Professor. He learned the river from his old man. When it comes to breaking the law, he's still a Piney."

"I'll talk to him."

Mick strolled toward the main tent, from which the music of fiddlers and fifers was squealing. He stood in the entrance, watching a bunch of kids step-dancing on the stage. They wore Irish-peasant costumes, the girls in white aprons and long green skirts, the boys in green velvet pants that buttoned over their shoulders like overalls. Pretty dumb dancing, Mick decided. They had tried to get him onto the stage at the first feis and he had refused. But it was lively music. He found his feet shifting to the beat.

"Oh, Mick, isn't this nice?"

He turned to find himself staring down at Trai and Suong. She was wearing an *ao dai,* white silk pants, and a long silk skirt. He had seen women wearing this outfit in Saigon, but he had never seen one in Binh Nghai. Trai had put a little makeup on her face. Her long black hair gleamed in the sun. She looked incredibly beautiful.

"Do you like my outfit?" she said in Vietnamese. "Suong gave it to me for my birthday. He spent his own money that he won for a prize in an essay contest at school."

"You look great," Mick said.

"I want to thank you for helping me with Father Hart. He sent his friend Father McAvoy. He was so understanding. Is he here today?"

"No. He . . . went back to Ireland."

"Oh. It's so terrible about Father Hart. I can't believe it."

"Yeah."

"There was something strange about Father McAvoy. He was very kind. But I thought he was troubled. Perhaps he knew about Father Hart and the woman."

"Maybe," Mick said.

"Mother says this reminds her of market day in Quang Tri City when she was a girl," Suong said. "Except there aren't any fire walkers or sword swallowers."

"They'll be here next year," Mick said.

He had to get away from Trai. In some ways it was worse seeing her happy than it was seeing her sad. The happiness started everything unreeling again.

"Gotta get to work," he said with a forced grin. "Gotta keep these Irish lugs from slugging each other. Tell Phac I'll pick him up for that special job tonight around eleven o'clock.

Mick strolled down the midway, where the usual pitchmen were selling games of chance. Wherever possible, they gave their scams an Irish flavor. People were invited to throw baseballs at little stuffed leprechauns, for instance. The pitchmen didn't look very Irish, but Mick bought a round and knocked three leprechauns off the top shelf. He won a stuffed dinosaur and gave it to a little blond girl in the crowd.

At the southern end of the football field, on a stage where the goal posts usually stood, a pipe band started playing "The Kerry Dancers." Mick could hear Sunny Dan's husky baritone.

Oh the days of the Kerry dancers!
Oh the ring of the piper's tune!
Oh for one of those hours of gladness
Gone! alas, like our youth, too soon.

Suddenly Mick was back in Binh Nghai kidding with Trai and her girlfriend Missy Thinh. He was giving candy to the village kids, letting them crawl all over him, as he sat in front of Trai's house. He was in the fort selecting the night's patrols, solving quarrels, calming fears. He was gliding along the village lanes and across the rice paddies with death out there in the dark, but that did not matter, that did not change what he felt inside: gladness. He was the protector, guarding these defenseless people in their fragile huts from midnight assassins.

Gladness. Those were his hours of gladness. Gone like his youth too soon. Gone into a beer belly that would eventually bulge like Bill O'Toole's if he stayed around here. Gone into endless midnight hours in search of imaginary prowlers, into arresting drunks on the boardwalk, into beery arguments about the Giants and the Jets in the Golden Shamrock, into this ugly deal to turn smuggler to rescue Bill O'Toole from his gambling debts.

Jesus. Was this part of his punishment, part of the dishonorable discharge for those deaths in the fort? The dishonor, the humiliation, went on and on? Wasn't there someplace, sometime, when God said enough? You've paid it off, you can try feeling glad again somewhere, somehow?

A hand on his shoulder. It was Bill O'Toole with Nick Perella, the consigliere of the Giordano family. "He's here with the money," O'Toole said. "I asked him about the Chasen thing. He says they had nothin' to do with it. He swears on his mother's grave."

Mick stared at the crafty Sicilian face, the glittering eyes. "So who did?"

"I think it went just like the coroner said it did. They were drunk and playin' sex games and passed out with a cigarette burnin'. Set themselves on fire," O'Toole said.

Uncle Bill was lying. He was shaken by what had happened in St. Augustine's rectory. He had covered it up with some help from the county coroner, another Monahan relative. Someone had murdered Jackie and Father Hart. Mick was still inclined to bet it was Tommy the Top evening the score for Joey Zaccaro. The priest gave them a beautiful cover story.

He thought of Jackie's body shriveling in those flames. It filled Mick with fresh rage. He remembered the first time with her, how shy, how tender, she had been. For a second he was tempted to punch Nick Perella's shiny white teeth down his throat.

"I just told him I thought you oughta get somethin' out

of this thing tonight," Perella said. "If it all goes nice and smooth, you're good for five grand on our account. Your Vietnamese pal gets a grand."

"Why not five for him too?"

"He can't count that high," Perella said. "I hear you're pretty good with a gun. We could use a guy like you now and then. We'll pay a lot more than five for a job."

"I can hardly wait," Mick said.

"Hey, he's on the level," Bill O'Toole said.

"Give him my phone number," Mick said.

There would be no end to it now. They were all working for Tommy Giordano. There would be high-class hookers in Jackie's house on Leeds Point and floating crap games on the yachts in the marina and drug pushers on the boardwalk. Paradise Beach would be wide open. Why not stay around and get rich? Maybe that was the way to find some new hours of gladness.

The only way, now.

A TERRIBLE BEAUTY

He was in it now. He was in it for life, Dick O'Gorman thought, his hands on Barbara Kathleen Monahan O'Day's ripe breasts. He raised his head and sucked her nipples. She cried out with joy. Pleasure, he could still give pleasure, but the last of the taking was gone now. It had vanished with faith, hope, and charity in that room in St. Augustine's rectory.

That Englishman was different. O'Gorman didn't understand why until the very last moment when the bastard asked Hart to give him absolution. The usual Englishman's watery Protestant blood was easy to shed, his feeble faith even easier to shatter. Never before had O'Gorman failed to make a prisoner talk, whether he was an IRA informer or a British captive. Not for nothing was he called Black Dick. It was not a simple tribute to his complexion.

Barbara rose and fell on the long, supple limb of Ireland that grew from the center of his loins. She sighed and moaned with the length and fiber of it. O'Gorman used to imagine it as James Joyce's martello tower, where a new Ireland was being born. He used to think of it as running from the trunk of his body to the dark earth of the Curragh. He had imagined it producing a tribe of defiant heroes from its seed, socialist aristocrats who would emulate Yeats's long dead lords and ladies who drank and loved and laughed at fate.

Now he saw it, he saw himself for what he was, in the Long Kesh of his soul. A lifer in the service of death and more death. He could not turn back now. The Englishman had sealed his fate by betting his soul against O'Gorman's soul. He had committed sacrileges in the name of Mother England that were unforgivable to Mother Church. He had pretended to consecrate the host with his murderous hands, to drink the sacred blood of Christ with his lying mouth, he had consoled the dying with worthless absolution and useless extreme unction. If Captain Littlejohn was wrong, his soul was in hell. If O'Gorman was wrong, his soul was going to the same place.

Those who studied theology knew hell had nothing to do with flame or burning coals. Those images were for the infants, the peasants. Hell was a place that was not a place, a realm for which the explorations of outer space had suggested images, but only the Catholic mind, the mind that Joyce in his bitterness boasted of being steeled in the school of Thomas Aquinas, only that mind could appreciate the true meaning of hell, a place of virtual nonexistence, of absolute cold, of emptiness beyond all sensations, an abstract vacuum of untouch, untaste, unhope, unlove. An ur-place that negated every word, that became absence upon absence upon absence without end.

That was the hell to which Captain Arthur Littlejohn was sentencing Richard O'Gorman. If he was wrong. If the Ireland he worshipped was not a place where men and women could finally love each other without the disabling fear of this insipid, obnoxious being with the voice of thunder. If Ireland was not a place where finally knees bent only in reverence to the martyrs of the struggle for

freedom. If it was not a place where the ancient druids
would rise from their graves to bless a new generation
who welcomed on May eve the spirit of earth, joyous,
proud, and free.

Yes, O'Gorman vowed in his inner Long Kesh. Yes,
even now I am betting, I am breaking this woman's heart
in Ireland's name. I am condemning her to join the winding, wailing procession of broken hearts I have left
behind me, a procession that I now accept in the name of
our cosmic wager, Captain Littlejohn.

Ahhhhhh. She was coming there in the soft April twilight. His semen surged in her. The sea tumbled on the
beach a block away, the same sea that raised its blank,
black swells against the west coast of Ireland. Linked by
love and betrayal to her ancient history, so rich in both.

"We'll go away, you promise, as soon as the job is
done?" she whispered.

"I promise. I'm mad with the dream of it," O'Gorman
said.

A barbaric yawp shattered the seaside quiet. Once,
twice, three times. It was the Paradise Beach fire alarm,
summoning the volunteers to a blaze. The sound flung
O'Gorman back to the day he had heard it for the first
time. He had been in this same room, doing the same
thing with Barbara Kathleen. He had almost jumped out
of his skin at the sound. It had been a long night with Captain Littlejohn.

After the yawp, sirens and clanging bells had resounded
through Paradise Beach. The roar of a powerful motor
passed the house. Barbara had padded to the window.
O'Gorman was admiring the shape of her behind when
she cried, "My God. It's the rectory. The rectory's on fire."

O'Gorman felt a cold wind blow through the open window. A strange climate the Americans had. Such a mixture of cold and warmth. Like their women. The bizarre
deaths of the priest and the Jewish girl had troubled his
sleep for days now. He could see them in the flames, he
could hear their terrified cries.

He knew Kilroy had done it, well before the sod had told him the next day. He had followed Jackie to the rectory and found her in bed with the priest. Billy had decided it was a perfect opportunity to get rid of both of them. They were too undependable, too likely to talk.

Would they erect tablets to such unknown martyrs in O'Gorman's Church of Humanity? Would their names be placed in the tabernacles in place of the host? A lovely thought.

In the bathroom as he washed himself, O'Gorman heard on the south wind the sound of the pipe bands at the feis. He was scheduled to make the awards to the winners at 4 P.M. He would follow it with a fund-raising speech that should be good for two or three thousand, at least. Later tonight, the voyage. Then a farewell note to Barbara Kathleen, a rush to Kennedy to catch the next plane to Ireland.

By this time in two days, he would be walking the streets of Dublin. Would he stop at St. Patrick's Cathedral to formalize his wager with Captain Littlejohn and God? It had been a Protestant church for a long time, but in his student days it had been his favorite place of prayer. He had imagined himself reclaiming it for Catholic Ireland.

No, he would do it in a better place. From the top of Joyce's martello tower, on the shore of Dublin Bay. He would salute sea and sky and water and dare His Infinitude to do His worst.

"What are you thinking?" Barbara Kathleen asked.

"Of you. In California," he said, and did a little jig as the pipe band swung into "The Kerry Dancers."

VICTORY AT SEA

By four o'clock the feis was beginning to wind down. Mick had arrested two drunks and broken up three fights. Only the parents of the competitors in step dancing, piping, and other events of the day stayed around for the awarding of the prizes. Mick went home, drank a half dozen beers, and got five hours sleep. For supper he drank another beer with a double whiskey chaser. Perfect. He was smoothed out exactly right. At eleven o'clock he drove over the causeway and picked up Phac.

Trai was puzzled and a little worried by this midnight voyage. Mick told her some rich people from New York wanted to do some night fishing.

"What the hell's going on?" Phac asked in Vietnamese when they got in the car.

"A lot," Mick replied. "Cocaine and guns."

"Guns for who?" Phac must have thought for a moment he was back in Vietnam.

"For the IRA. The Irish Republican Army."

"Where are they fighting?"

"In Ireland."

"Is that a communist country?"

"Not that I've heard."

"Then they must be communists. Fighting the lawful government. Why are the Americans helping them?"

"They're not. This is strictly illegal. You get a thousand dollars for it."

Phac stared out at the waters of the bay. "I don't like this kind of shit."

"You want a job on that boat tomorrow, play along. If anything goes wrong, you didn't know a thing. Neither did I."

"We could get arrested?"

"Don't worry about that. Chief O'Toole is in it up to his big fat ass."

At the dock, O'Gorman and Kilroy were already aboard the *Enterprise* with their Washington pals, Leo McBride and his wife. A few minutes later Bill O'Toole showed up with the Professor. His appearance sealed cynicism into an icy block in Mick's chest. After all the bullshit the Prof had shoveled against communism being the worldwide enemy of freedom, here he was, selling out for a couple of thousand dollars, like the rest of them.

O'Toole took Mick aside and muttered, "Don't mention nothin' about weapons to the Professor. I told him we were bringin' in some dope in two shipments to help me pay off the Atlantic City stuff. When we go out again for the hardware, it'll be too late for him to start an argument."

Oxenford was drunk. "Ten generations of Oxenfords made their living as smugglers. Why shouldn't I join the procession?" he said to Mick. "I always knew Atlantic City would get to us eventually. How much are they paying you?"

"Five."

"I'm getting ten. That's enough money to get me far far away from Paradise Beach and Barbara Monahan O'Day.

Jesus, what a fool I've been! A nightlong, daylong, life-long fool."

Mick could only give him another amazed stare. He never knew the Professor had had so much as a single romantic thought about his mother.

It looked like a perfect night, no moon and calm seas. Phac cast off the lines and the Professor backed out of the slip, then shoved the throttle forward. The big Packard engines sent the sixty-foot boat briskly up the bay to the inlet that led to the ocean. A light southern breeze was carrying thick warm air up from the Carolinas.

"You can almost smell the magnolias," the Professor said.

All Mick could smell was dead fish. Phac squatted in a corner of the wheelhouse, his shirt open to the waist. Billy Kilroy nipped from a flask and bragged about what they were going to do with the surface-to-air missiles they were getting from the Cubans.

"What the hell's he talking about?" the Professor said.

"Never mind, just steer the goddamn boat," Bill O'Toole said.

"I'm talking' about shootin' down every plane and heli-copter that flies over Ireland," Billy shouted. "Whatya think of that, you fookin' English bastard? Before this night's over you'll have helped us get the stuff to do it!"

"That takes a lot of guts—to shoot down unarmed planes," the Professor said.

"Shut your goddamn yap," Billy said.

"Hey, why are you so uptight? Didn't you get anything at the feis?" Mick said. "I told about twenty broads you were a genuine heroic Irishman. I thought maybe one at least would have been dumb enough to believe me."

"You shut the fook up too," Billy screeched. He glared at Phac. "What's this fookin' cannibal got writ on his chest?"

"*Sat Cong*," Mick said.

"What's that mean?"

"Kill communists."

"What the fook we doin' with someone like that aboard?" Billy snarled.

"Relax, you asshole," O'Toole said. "He don't know ten words of English."

"I'll relax after we finish this fookin' operation. Just remember I'm in charge and if you dawn't like it, you'll be over the fookin' side."

"Is he gone nuts?" O'Toole asked O'Gorman.

"It's the truth. He's in charge," O'Gorman said.

"No wonder you guys can't win a war," O'Toole said.

"You didn't do so fookin' great in Vietnam. That's why you've got this bugger on your hands," Billy said.

"One more crack like that and you'll go back to Ireland in a box," O'Toole roared.

"Not as long as I've got this in me hand." Billy pulled out his Zastava pistol. "This'll blow a hole as big as a fookin' soccer ball in your belly."

Instinctively Mick loosened the .38 he was carrying in the shoulder holster under his jacket. Billy noticed the movement of his hand and pulled Mick's jacket open. "Why the fook is he carryin' a gun?" Billy raged.

"Because I told him to," O'Toole snarled, glaring at Mick. He had told him nothing of the sort. Mick could see suspicion flickering in his uncle's eyes. Mick stalked out of the wheelhouse onto the deck, gesturing to Phac to follow him.

"What's wrong with that little asshole?" Phac asked in Vietnamese.

"I'm afraid he's coming apart like Belknap."

Belknap was the Boston aristocrat who had cracked up in their fourth month in Binh Nghai. He had started talking bigger and bigger, insisting he had more nerve than anyone else in the squad. To prove it he always volunteered for the most dangerous assignments. Off duty he got into fistfights with the other marines and treated the Vietnamese with contempt. One night he got drunk and started shooting up the village. Mick had disarmed him at gunpoint. For a while Mick had thought he would have to kill him.

"I don't like this shit," Phac said.

"Me neither," Mick said.

In the darkened wheelhouse, O'Gorman was busy telling the Professor where to rendezvous with the Cuban freighter. Mick could see the Irishman's handsome face in profile by the binnacle light. He wondered if O'Gorman was really quitting the IRA and taking his mother to California. It would be nice to get his mother out of his life. But it left him with a lonely feeling. His world was turning inside out, upside down.

Above the wheelhouse, the *Enterprise*'s radar grid started turning. In an hour the freighter loomed up in the sea-lane, twenty-five miles out. At first no one could see it but Mick. With his exceptional night vision, he spotted it at five miles. In twenty minutes they were alongside.

O'Gorman shouted Spanish to someone on deck. A minute later, a steamer trunk was swung over the side on a wire cable. Phac and Mick grappled it onto the deck of the *Enterprise* and carefully lowered it into the hold. There was more conversation in Spanish, and O'Gorman and the Professor went over the charts to make sure they knew where the freighter would be at 4 A.M.

The Professor gunned the engines and the *Enterprise* headed back to Paradise Beach. Nick Perella, Giordano's consigliere, would be waiting at the dock with the money and an expert to test the quality of the cocaine. If the expert said go, they would get the money and rendezvous with the freighter again to pick up the weapons. By dawn they would have the hardware well up the Mullica River into the Pines.

Phac and Mick lashed the trunk down in the hold and climbed back up on deck. Kilroy was standing by the open hatch, his gun in his hand. Bill O'Toole and O'Gorman were a few feet away from him. Leo McBride and Melody stood in the doorway of the wheelhouse.

"You sure you got that fookin' thing tied down tight?" Kilroy shouted.

"Go down and add a few knots if you're not happy," Mick said.

"That's all the shit I'm gawn to take from you," Kilroy screamed. "You're a fookin' double-dealer. I think you and your cannibal friend here was in with that fookin' SIS man."

"You can think anything you goddamn want," Mick said.

"Oh, yah?" Billy snarled. "Well, here's what I want you to do. Blow him away."

"What the hell are you talkin' about?" Mick said.

"Blow the fookin' cannibal away!" Kilroy screeched. "In Belfast that's how we find out if a man's an informer. We set him to kill one of his fookin' informer friends. Even if it's his fookin' brother."

O'Gorman and Bill O'Toole said nothing. Mick realized Kilroy meant it. If he didn't kill Phac, Kilroy would do it. Those words, *Sat Cong*, on Phac's chest were his death sentence. He had beaten it once by getting out of Binh Nghai a half hour before the communist tanks arrived in 1975. Kilroy and O'Gorman didn't like that. They still saw the whole thing exactly the way the Marine Corps had said the communists played the game until they started losing it. The war was worldwide, using guns, words, politics—but especially guns whenever they had the chance to win with them. These guys were still fighting the war—and Phac was their way of getting even for the way their system was starting to fall apart.

Kilroy might kill him too, Mick thought in this brief yet somehow eternal moment. Maybe Bill O'Toole had told the Irishmen about the $1,000 bill in the glove compartment. Maybe Uncle Bill wanted to see Mick prove his loyalty to him too, by killing Phac.

There was no question that Phac deserved to die, if you looked at it from the communist point of view. Or almost any point of view. He had been a merciless bastard in

Binh Nghai. He had tortured and killed a lot of people. How many times had Mick seen him take a VC suspect upriver to district headquarters and come back in a half hour. It was a two-hour trip to headquarters. Everyone knew the man's body would wash up a week or two later, his eyes eaten out by the crabs.

Why not kill Phac? He did not really care whether he lived or died. He was still dying in that other village where his wife and sons had been murdered. Every day of his life he went back to that village and died there. In a way he was already dead in the frozen center of his soul. If Mick killed him, he would almost be doing him a favor.

Mick would be doing himself an immensely larger favor. He would have Trai. Suong and Trai would become his responsibility. He would care for them, he would love them.

For a fragment of this eternal moment, Mick thought of having Trai, night after night. Holding her small, tender body in his arms, feeling her breasts beneath his hands, her silky black hair against his mouth. Telling her he understood why she had betrayed him, telling her he forgave her. Telling her how many times when he was with another woman, he thought of her. Telling her so many things.

But he couldn't kill Phac. He couldn't kill a man who had fought beside him in his hours of gladness, who had saved his life in the dark a dozen times. He couldn't kill a man who had helped him redeem at least a piece of his shattered honor by helping him kill Le Quan Chien.

He couldn't kill Phac. Which meant he had to kill Billy Kilroy. The implications of this conclusion only brushed the edge of Mick's mind for the moment. It was all instinct now, like those milliseconds in the dark in Binh Nghai where you waited for a VC in the bushes twenty yards away to move first, knowing he was trying to decide which way you were going to move, both hands on triggers, both minds balanced precisely on the edge of eternity.

The difference here was a gun in Kilroy's hand and no gun in Mick's hand. But the rolling deck of the *Enterprise,* the darkness, tilted the odds the other way just enough to give Mick the sense that they were even. He remembered Kilroy's dislike of shooting in the dark. Until they got to the freighter, Kilroy had stayed in the wheelhouse, which meant his night vision was not functioning. Out on deck, Mick's night vision had been operating for an hour.

With a swing of his left arm, Mick sent Phac sprawling toward the stern. Simultaneously he dove to the right, toward the bow, reaching for his gun as he went down. Billy blasted two shots from his Zastava into the empty darkness. Mick's gun was in his hand by the time he hit the deck, and he came up shooting.

He fired three shots. Each one hit Billy in the heart. He uttered a cry that sounded curiously like the call of a gull and toppled into the sea.

"You no good son of a bitch bastard," Bill O'Toole screamed.

Would he have to kill him too? Mick wondered. Still in a crouch, he covered him and O'Gorman. Mick wanted to kill O'Gorman, but he did not want to shoot Uncle Bill. He would do it if necessary because he was no longer the tough, honest cop who had given him a chance to have a decent life after the dishonorable discharge. He was a mafioso stooge and Paradise Beach was mafioso property thanks to him. He deserved a bullet, but Mick did not want to fire it.

"See if they've got any guns," Mick said to Phac in Vietnamese.

Phac frisked them. They were unarmed.

"Check the other two," Mick said.

Phac frisked Leo McBride and his wife. "Get your slimy hands off me!" Melody shrilled.

She pointed a finger at Mick. "No matter where you go, the IRA or some other freedom fighters will track you down for that vile murder."

The Professor came out on deck to find out what the noise was all about. He was a bit nonplused but not especially alarmed to find Mick pointing a gun at him. "Have you gone nuts?" he said.

"Maybe," Mick said. "Help Phac lower the boat."

"What the hell are you going to do?"

"Put them in it," Mick said.

"Then what?"

"We're going into the cocaine business," Mick said.

"We're gonna kill you, Mick. No bullshit, we're gonna kill you," O'Toole said.

"I got a better idea. Let's kill him," Mick said, pointing to O'Gorman. "We've got the cocaine and we sell it to the Mob and tell them to get the hell out of Paradise Beach and forget those IOUs you made Desmond and Grandpa Monahan sign."

"No deal," O'Toole said.

Bill O'Toole's soul had gone rotten. He liked the idea of working with Tommy Giordano. He looked forward to having a hundred thousand a year to bet in Atlantic City. He didn't care whether the IRA took over Ireland.

"Get in the boat," Mick said.

"Which way is land for God's sake?" O'Gorman said as Phac and the Professor unlashed the lifeboat on the stern and lowered it into the water.

"Row west when the sun comes up," the Professor said.

"Are you in on this too?" Bill O'Toole raged.

"Not me," the Professor said.

"Maybe you better get in the boat, Prof," Mick said. "Maybe that'll convince them I'm doing this on my own."

"Thanks, Mick." Oxenford climbed into the lifeboat. He had no pretensions to being a hero.

"You too," Mick said, gesturing to Leo McBride and Melody.

"Five people can't fit into that little boat!" Melody cried.

"Give it a try. You've got ten seconds. Then I'm throwing you and Leo over the side."

Leo seized Melody's hand and dragged her to the railing. In another sixty seconds they were huddled on the boat's rear seat.

"If I can work it out, I'll make a deal with your mafioso friends before you bozos get back on dry land," Mick said.

"You're out of your skull. The deal's with me, not with a two-bit punk like you," O'Toole said.

"Then I'm headin' for the Pines with the stuff and I'll sell it on my own."

"You better have an army with you," Bill O'Toole said.

"I got two marines. That's better than an army."

Mick was thinking of Joe Turner. He was pretty sure he could talk him into helping them out. He would use the Oxenfords as go-betweens. He would sell the stuff in Philadelphia or New York and give Joe enough money to buy his cranberry bog and Phac enough to buy his boat. He would give the rest of the money to his mother and Desmond McBride. They would pay off Giordano and Mick would vanish. Maybe live in the Pines like Joe. Or head west to California.

Mick gunned the engines and the *Enterprise* headed for Paradise Beach, leaving O'Toole and O'Gorman, the Professor and Leo McBride and Melody Faithorne bobbing in the darkness twenty-five miles from shore. They would probably get picked up by a fishing boat in the morning. He had about eight hours to pull off the deal.

"What are we going to do, Mick?" Phac asked in Vietnamese.

Mick told Phac they were going to sell the cocaine and go to California, where Phac would have enough money to buy a boat twice as big as the *Enterprise*. They would take Trai and Suong with them. Mick was improvising the future. Phac was dubious. He had learned the hard way not to trust American promises.

"Isn't this against the law?"

"Sure," Mick said. "What the hell isn't these days?"

"I must think of Suong. We mustn't endanger his future."

"He'll be safe, I personally guarantee it."

"It is not safety that is the point. It is his reputation. He cannot be involved in this."

"He's a minor. No one's going to charge him with anything. He can stay with my mother. He and Trai can both stay there."

"They will be safe?"

"Sure. Uncle Bill may want to shoot us. But he won't go after a woman or a kid."

It was 2 A.M. when Mick eased the *Enterprise* into the inlet on a moderate swell and chugged down the channel to the Star of the Sea Marina. In the parking lot, someone flashed his lights. Mick didn't know the answer, but he decided it was probably simple. He flashed the *Enterprise*'s running lights. While Phac was tying up the boat, Mick jumped onto the dock and trotted to the parking lot. Nick Perella and two other men were getting out of their car. One was carrying a small black doctor's bag. He was tall and thin. The other guy, taller and twice as wide, was the bodyguard.

"Listen," Mick said, stopping about ten feet away. "The deal's changed. You can have the dope but you give me the dough. We're splittin' with the IRA. They're a bunch of lousy communists."

"What the hell do you mean? Where's O'Toole?" Nick Perella said.

"He's a couple of miles offshore, feeding the IRA to the fishes."

"You're full of shit. Without him there's no deal."

There it was again. They wanted the deal more than the dope, just like Bill O'Toole. They wanted to own Paradise Beach. The dope was incidental. Even the million and a half dollars was incidental. They could make twice that selling cocaine here during the summer.

"Then get the hell out of here. I got the dope and I'm sellin' it to some other guys."

"The fuck you are," Nick Perella snarled.

Nick and the bodyguard went for their guns. Mick shot

them both before their hands touched metal. It was not even a contest. He shot the bodyguard between the eyes and Nick Perella in the shoulder, figuring it was better not to kill him.

Whimpering, the cocaine expert fell to his knees begging for mercy. "I'm only a pharmacist," he wailed.

"Get yourself and them the hell out of here."

Mick wrestled the bodyguard into the backseat and shoved the groaning Nick Perella into the front seat. The pharmacist cowered behind the wheel and the limousine roared out of the parking lot, spinning up a shower of gravel.

Mick ran down the dock and helped Phac hoist the cocaine out of the *Enterprise*'s hold. They carried the steamer trunk up the dock to Mick's car and drove into town.

To Phac's horror, Mick stopped at police headquarters. "What are you doing now?" he whispered.

"Getting ready to fight a war."

Mick strolled up to Tom Brannigan, the night sergeant. "Give me the keys to the armory. We got some problems down in the marina."

"What the hell's going on?"

"It looks like the Mafia's trying to move in. Send both cars down there, fast."

Brannigan handed Mick the keys and he rushed to the armory. There, waiting silently on racks, were a half dozen M16 automatic rifles. Chief O'Toole had bought them in the early seventies, when it looked as if summer at Paradise Beach might turn into a replay of the Tet Offensive almost any night. A lot of local police chiefs had gone for heavy weapons in those days. Mick took three of the rifles and threw in forty or fifty clips in ammo pouches hanging beside them. He sprinted past the open-mouthed Brannigan to his car.

"I've got some bad news," Mick told Phac as they roared over the causeway. "I had to shoot the Italians. They're going to come after us now. We've got to take

Suong and Trai with us. Those guys are like the VC. They'll shoot anybody."

"Mick, you will destroy us all. Finally you will destroy us all!" Phac wailed.

"No. I swear to you, Phac, we're going to win this war."

Did he believe it? Yes. In a corner of his soul Mick believed you could not lose everything if you tried to play it straight. He was no longer playing it straight but he was playing it that way from the inside. He was trying to cleanse himself, his mother, Phac, Trai, of the putrefaction that was oozing into Paradise Beach.

If he knew how difficult that was, would he have tried it anyway? Probably. Beneath and beyond and around that noble dream rose the fierce joy of the warrior, the lure, the love of battle.

THE OPEN BOAT

Suddenly Bill O'Toole was in a twelve-foot rowboat with Melody Faithorne and Leo McBride sitting only inches away from him. Since O'Toole had learned about the bearer bonds, he had made a point of distancing himself from both of them—especially from Melody. Proximity for more than a few minutes led to thoughts of slaughter.

Now he had to listen to Melody unstrung. She swore like a longshoreman at her hunched, cowering husband. "Jesus Christ, why did I ever get involved with you and your fucking relatives? You're nothing but a tribe of motherless assholes. I'm beginning to think that term covers the entire Irish race."

"Shut up," Leo whined.

Did he sense what she was doing? Did he by some sort of radar of the blood pick up the rage building in Bill O'Toole's soul?

"I think your husband is giving you good advice," O'Gorman said.

"Shut your fucking Irish mouth too. When I get back to Washington, I'm going to make sure the senator never lifts another finger for you and your pea-brained movement. Why couldn't you stop that little twerp? I thought you were in charge of this operation."

"So did I."

"Why didn't you stop him anyway?"

"Because he had a gun and I didn't."

"Shut up, please," Leo McBride screamed. "If you say one more word—"

"You're gonna tell Uncle Bill about the bearer bonds," Bill O'Toole said. "How you and she squealed to the feds and walked off with ten percent—a half million bucks."

The silence in the boat was almost as thunderous as the quiet in Nora McGinty's house after the bomb went off.

"How did you know?" Leo quavered.

"I know a lot of things. That's a policeman's job."

"You knew all along?"

"If I did, you'd've both been dead a long time ago."

"You told him," Melody screamed. "You miserable piece of cowardly lying slime."

"He didn't tell me," O'Toole said. "He didn't have to tell me. I let you both tell me. I know what you've been sayin' to each other in your bedroom for the last week."

"It was her idea, Uncle Bill. I didn't want to do it. I couldn't stop her," Leo McBride cried.

"I know. She sucked you into it. I heard all about it."

More silence, broken only by the sea's sigh and Leo McBride's terrified breathing. Bill O'Toole loomed over him and Melody, hunched on the rear seat.

"How much life insurance has she got?" Bill O'Toole asked.

"What?" Leo quavered. "I don't know. About a hundred thousand dollars, I think. It's a government policy."

"You're gonna take that money and give it all to Wilbur Gargan. You're gonna sell your beautiful little country estate in Virginia and give the proceeds to my wife. Or I'll come to Washington and kill you too."

"You lay a finger on me and the senator will move heaven and earth to find out what happened," Melody screamed.

"I'm more inclined to think the senator goes to bed each night hopin' one or two of you Chappy girls are drivin' too fast or drinkin' too hard and maybe your number is up like Mary Jo Kopechne. You really think he cares enough to get his tit caught in this wringer? Smugglin' cocaine, shippin' ground-to-air missiles to the IRA? The senator may be a lot of things, but he ain't that stupid."

"O'Gorman. You won't let him do this. You owe me too much!" Melody cried.

"Give it to her straight. You know about the bearer bonds," O'Toole said. "What do you think, one Irishman to another?"

"She should unquestionably die," O'Gorman said.

"You'll have a witness. Are you going to kill Oxenford too?' Melody said.

O'Toole laughed. "He's a Piney. He ain't got the conscience of a ground squirrel. Just for the hell of it, we'll give him a vote. What do you say, Prof?"

Like everyone else in Paradise Beach, Oxenford had heard about the bearer bonds. He had grieved for Mick. The money would have given him a fresh start somewhere.

"Whatever you do, it's much too dark for me to see it," he said.

"Fucking bastards," Melody screamed. "If I'm going to die, you're all going with me."

She sprang past Leo McBride and clawed at Bill O'Toole's eyes. As he lunged sideways to escape her attack, his weight flipped the boat, throwing them all into the sea. O'Toole tried to hang on to Melody as they went over, but she slithered out of his flailing grasp. Blood streamed from his eyes. He could barely see. He floundered over to the boat. Leo McBride, O'Gorman, and Oxenford were clinging to it.

Something large and heavy zoomed past Bill O'Toole.

He felt a ripping pain in his right leg. A shark. "Get in the boat," he roared. With two sets of hands on each side, they lifted it out of the water, flipped it rightside up, and scrambled aboard.

"You've finished her?" O'Gorman said.

"No, but I think we got some help," O'Toole said.

"What do you mean?"

Whump. The shark bumped the boat. O'Toole tied a tourniquet around his bleeding leg. *Whump.* The shark hit them again. "He'll find her any minute," O'Toole said.

He shouted into the darkness. "Any minute you're gonna meet somebody you'll like even less than an Irishman."

"It's a shark!" Melody screamed, thrashing the water around her.

"About twelve feet long," O'Toole said. "A man-eater, just like you. Maybe God knows what he's doing, after all."

Melody swam toward the boat. "You can't do it. You can't leave me here to die. Stop them, Leo."

Leo said nothing. Melody screamed in terrible agony. The shark had struck. She screamed and screamed and screamed and thrashed the water. Through Leo McBride's tormented soul swirled a chaotic mingling of horror and terror. Whatever shred of manhood he had left after ten years as Melody's husband was being annihilated here. He gazed down a tunnel of gruesome future years.

Suddenly there was a brutally simple choice. A choice that declared his independence from the Monahan tribe and its tangled heritage of loyalty and greed and simultaneously confessed his unforgivable sin and performed his contrition. All his life, Leo had lived in a maze of words and ideas. Suddenly there was this act that simplified, purified, everything.

He sprang into the cold dark water. "I'm coming, Melody," he cried. "I love you!"

In some corner of Leo's ruined soul, those words still

rang true, a compound of febrile memory and doomed desire. It did not matter that they were as futile as the rest of Leo's intellectualized life. He had said those fatal words one last time.

He never reached Melody. She died alone, her final scream a gurgle as the shark dragged her under the surface. A moment later, one of his carnivorous companions seized Leo and dragged him down into the same watery darkness. Was there a tormented triumph, a hope of eternal peace amid the ravaging pain? Perhaps.

"Goddamn it," Bill O'Toole said. "I wanted that insurance money."

"It's simpler with them both out of the way," O'Gorman said. "What about Leo's father? Will he get hysterical and turn on us?"

"Desmond? He's got even less guts than Leo. He won't say a word."

"Let's talk business. How can we get back our cocaine?"

"We're gonna need reinforcements. Tommy the Top and his best guys."

"We can trust them?"

"Sure. Without me they don't have Paradise Beach. With me they got a fuckin' gold mine."

Capitalism at work, O'Gorman thought. If they could cling to power in a few countries like Ireland and Cuba, they would be ready when the merchants of greed drowned in their own putrefaction.

"We may have to kill them. Mick and Phac. You understand that," O'Gorman said.

"I spent four years in the U.S. Marines in World War Two. I know how to kill people," O'Toole said.

"I think Mick had the right idea," Oxenford said. "Kill this IRA bastard, sell the cocaine to the Mafia, and forget the rest of it."

"When I want advice from you, Professor, I'll ask for it," O'Toole said.

"Bill, you can't kill Mick. You couldn't do it!"

"I've already done a lot of things I never thought I could do, Prof."

The words swirled around them in the night like a phantom shark. That was when Alex Oxenford began to believe in the existence of evil. A moment later he was listening to it. Richard O'Gorman gazed at him, his opaque eyes reflecting alien starlight. "Maybe we ought to get rid of this fellow now. He doesn't seem to be on our side."

"We're gonna need him to reach Mick," O'Toole said. "He'll head into the Pines to get some advice from Pops Oxenford, this bullshit artist's father. I'm hopin' he and the Professor here can talk Mick into givin' back the cocaine."

"If they don't succeed?"

"We go in with the guns."

SUCH DEVILS ARE DRIVEN OUT
ONLY BY PRAYER AND FASTING

It was wrong, it was bad, it was evil, Trai thought as Mick and Phac bundled her and Suong into the car along with some hastily packed suitcases. It was just like Vietnam, people were being killed for political reasons, for ideas that dwelt in the distance like malign gods.

"Why are you doing this? Is there no other way?" she had asked Phac while he watched her collect clothes and food.

"I'm beginning to think Mick and I are bound to each other on the wheel of fate," Phac said.

"If you told me, I would have prayed. I might have been some help."

"If your God is so wonderful, why did he let you suffer those bestialities from the pirates?"

"So my heart would be torn open wide enough to hear my father's voice," she said.

"Your father!"

Phac raised his hand to strike her. Mick rushed into the kitchen to hurry them and Phac changed his mind. They drove deep into the Pines on the main concrete road and then even deeper into the trees along sandy roads that twisted and turned like corkscrews. Finally they reached a house surrounded by many ruined automobiles. An old man with a beautiful face met them at the door. Trai saw at a glance that he had achieved a rare thing: he had completed his soul. They sat at the table while Mick explained what he had done and what he hoped to do with the cocaine.

The old man shook his head. Trai had been praying he would dislike the idea as much as she did. "Get it out of here," he said. "It won't work, Mick. Get it out of here and get yourself out of New Jersey. The thing's gone sour."

"No, it hasn't!" Mick said.

"Yes, it has. You can't fight them and the whole U.S. government. They're going to be in this thing soon. You can't fight them. Hell, if you could, we would have declared Hog Wallow independent long ago."

"I'm tired of taking bullshit advice from you," Mick roared. "I'm doin' this my way. I'm gonna get Joe, and with Phac here and three M16s I can take on a regiment of those assholes. They've never fought in the woods."

"Even if you kill them, what can you do with the stuff? Go down to Chatsworth and open a store?"

Chatsworth was the main town in the Pines. Suong and his friends sometimes drove there to drag-race on the roads around it. He used Mick's car and always won.

"I'll sell it in the city. My father will help me sell it."

The old man shook his head. "The thing's gone sour."

"My whole life's gone sour, Pop. I'm going to buy it back this way or no way."

The words struck Trai's heart with awful force. She saw the desperation in Mick's soul. She also saw the battle fury turning his hazel eyes almost black. She had seen that in Vietnam and it had terrified her. Now it transported her. There was divinity in it; now she grasped the dimensions of Mick's warrior soul. A part of God was in that soul, working itself out here in this terrible way. Even if he died living out this divinity, she could no longer oppose him.

The old man saw it too. He sighed and ran his hand through his white hair. "What do you want me to do?"

"Talk Joe into it. Tell him to meet me at the head of Tulpohocken Creek. We'll camp there for the night."

"All right."

"I need some of those railroad flares and a couple of gallons of gasoline."

"You gonna burn the woods?"

"Only as a last resort."

"You could start a big fire. We haven't had much rain this month."

"We'll let the rangers worry about it, if we have to do it. They've gotten good at putting them out."

"Not the big ones."

"I promise you, it'll be a last-ditch thing," Mick said.

For the old man the woods were holy. It was a crime to burn them. Mick did not want to burn them. But he did not think anything was holy anymore. His belief in honor, in loyalty, in love, had been wounded by too many people. How could Trai give holiness back to him? The experience was essential for a soul to reach God.

Oh. Trai realized she did not want to save Mick's soul for God. She wanted it for her own sake, she wanted his love and her love to join again and never part for all of time and eternity. She loved him, sitting there, despair on his face, she loved him with all the wild, trembling desire she had known in Binh Nghai.

The old man gave them the gasoline and the railroad flares. He watched them drive into the Pines, hands on his hips, shaking his head, finally waving good-bye. Suddenly Trai saw him surrounded by a rainbow. She saw tiny figures dancing inside the colored stripes of the rainbow and she heard a marvelous humming song. She knew the old man was going to die.

Tears streamed down Trai's face. "What's the matter?" Mick said.

"He's so good."

"He's the best that ever was or will be," Mick said.

FATHER, OH, FATHER,
COME THROUGH FOR ME NOW

In his white 1970 American Motors Rebel, Mick roared up the New Jersey Turnpike in the dawn. The steamer trunk full of cocaine was in the backseat. Sleepy tolltakers let him pass without a glance, missing their chance to make headlines. In an hour he was rolling through the outskirts of Jersey City. Down the littered streets he zoomed to a house on Bayside Avenue, overlooking the cemetery where they had buried Sunny Dan Monahan. In the distance, the spires of New York City loomed in the 6 A.M. light.

Mick pounded on the door of 774 Bayside, noting the odd coincidence that they were the last three numbers of his marine dog tags. Buster O'Day spoke from somewhere inside the house. "Who the hell is that?"

"Mick. Your son."

It took Buster about five minutes to open the door. He had a half dozen bolts and locks and chains on it. He stood there shivering in his underwear, glaring sullenly at Mick. "What the hell do you want?"

"Some help."

"Find out if he's stolen anything. If he's wanted for anything," cried a woman's voice from the top of the stairs.

"Shut up," Buster said. He waved Mick into the house and spent another five minutes locking, bolting, and chaining the door again. The woman came down the stairs while he was doing this and glared at Mick. She looked exactly like Buster, except that she was not bald. The same button nose, sneering mouth, raw, reddish complexion.

"I tole you not to go that funeral. I tole you never to have nothin' to do with these people again. I knew he was gonna show up lookin' for you know what."

"Shut up and make us some coffee," Buster said.

Still in his underwear, Buster waved Mick into the living room, which was full of decrepit overstuffed furniture at least fifty years old. Springs popped through cushions, stuffing oozed from torn arms of the couches and easy chairs. "That's my sister, your aunt Mary," he said, pulling on a pair of pants he must have carried downstairs when he answered Mick's knock.

Aunt Mary served them coffee with the glare of hatred still on her face. Mick gulped his cup down, hoping it would fight the exhaustion that was drying out his brain.

"What's on your mind?" Buster said.

"Cocaine. I've got about ten million bucks' worth of it, street value, in the back of the car."

Buster spilled half his coffee on his undershirt. "What am I supposed to do about it?" he cried.

"Help me get rid of it."

"Where did you get it?"

Mick started telling him. When he got to shooting Consigliere Perella and his bodyguard, Buster spilled the rest of his coffee down the front of his pants. "Get out of here!" he screamed. "If you tell anybody you came here, I'll personally hire guys to blow you away!"

"Jesus Christ! You're my father. My whole life, I never asked you for anything."

"I'm not your father!" Buster screeched. "Your mother had you in her belly long before she married me. Nobody told me until after I married her. But I had to swallow it because her big-shot father said do it or else. Then suddenly he ain't a big shot anymore. He runs outta here with his money to that penny-ante suburb of Atlantic City and I'm supposed to go too? Give up the biggest numbers business in the state? A business my old man spent his life buildin' up? That's when I decided your goddamn mother wasn't worth it."

In a frenzy, Buster pulled Mick out of the living room through the kitchen into a connected garage. A green 1952 Studebaker sat there, all four tires flat; rust had practically consumed the rear fenders. Buster flipped up the trunk and Mick stared at money. Thousand-dollar bills. Hundred-dollar bills. Five-hundred-dollar bills. The trunk was crammed to the top with them.

"See that?" Buster screamed. "There's maybe two million bucks in there. Why should I give that up for her? When she wouldn't let me touch her nine nights out of ten. Tell your mother what you saw here today, big shot. Tell her how we could've been livin' in Saddle Brook next door to Tommy the Top if she stuck with me. Tell her!"

"I'll tell her," Mick said.

"Lemmy give you some advice. There's only one way to get rid of that cocaine. By givin' it back to Tommy Giordano. If you do that, maybe—and I can't guarantee it—he'll let you go someplace like California without a contract on you."

Buster wiped his mouth with the back of his hand. "Listen. Maybe in a couple of months I can talk him into payin' the hit guy off and pretendin' the punk did the job. Maybe you should tell your mother about this money and what I might do for you if she comes back to me. Here or in Saddle Brook or New York. I got the money to go anywhere she wants. I could set you up in California in a nice business."

On and off all his life Mick had imagined coming to

this man to ask his help for something. It was part of his struggle to understand why his father had turned his back on him. Why he had never said a word to him between the ages of one and twenty-seven, when they had met in Atlantic City at Caesars.

Now Mick had his answer. He turned his back on this nonfather, on this slime who had made his deal with the Mafia to pile up the $1,000 bills in the trunk of this rusting car.

Mick strode to the front door and started turning the locks. But Buster had the keys to the bolts and chains. "Open this goddamed door!" Mick roared.

"It's your only chance, what I told you," Buster whined.

Mick picked up one of the overstuffed chairs and threw it through the front window. "Call the cops!" screeched his bogus Aunt Mary.

"Shut up," screamed Buster.

Mick climbed through the shattered window and gunned his Rebel down Bayside Avenue. In ten minutes he was on the New Jersey Turnpike, heading back to the Pines. Thundering in his mind was the worst question a man could ask himself. Who was he?

THE IRON CHANCELLOR

"You're sure it was McGinty's wife?" O'Gorman said. "Absolutely sure?"

"She said it was. Why don't you call her?"

"No. It isn't necessary. It's all coming together now."

It was one o'clock in the afternoon of April 2. In his bedroom in the Monahan house, Dick O'Gorman hung up the telephone and gazed at himself in the mirror. The too handsome face, which he had always disliked, except when he was pursuing a woman, was seared and blistered by a half day on the ocean in the *Enterprise*'s lifeboat. His lips were so swollen it was painful for him to smile, even to talk.

So be it, he thought. Farewell to Handsome Dick. All his life the face had been an obstacle to other men taking him seriously. Perhaps to taking himself seriously.

It was time to change, he told the man in the mirror. Time to live up to that nasty swollen mouth. Time to prove there was iron in his soul. He had always admired Bismarck. As chancellor of a united Ireland, he planned to pursue similar brink-of-war policies, use every weapon from terrorism to piety to keep his enemies, above all England, demoralized. He would make Ireland more than an accidental island on the fringe of Europe.

For the moment he was in no danger of becoming chancellor of anything. The operation was a shambles. The Cuban freighter was pretending to have engine trouble off Cape May, seventy miles south of Paradise Beach. But this subterfuge was attracting the attention of the U.S. Coast Guard, which would soon make unloading the weapons out of the question. Coast Guard or no Coast Guard, the missiles would never come ashore unless they got the cocaine from Mick O'Day.

Now he had another reason for wanting to even the score with Mick. The $1,000 bill in his glove compartment was no accident. Nor was the gunfight with Kilroy. Mick was unquestionably working with McGinty and both of them with the FBI and the SIS, getting paid by the day or hour and making so much money Mick was careless with the take.

Where did that leave his mother, sweet Barbara Kathleen? Was she in with the son, laughing behind her hand at how easily she had seduced the Irish hero into smiling compliance?

Barbara burst into the bedroom. "What's happening?" she said. "I want to know what's happening."

"Maybe you can tell me."

"Mick telephoned me. He's in the Pines. He said there was a fight on the boat. You tried to kill him."

"That's hardly the truth. He's alive and poor Kilroy is dead."

He gave her a rapid summary of what Mick had done and why.

"He's become the three most despicable words in the history of Ireland: turncoat, traitor, informer."

She swayed there, wanting to believe both of them, seeing the impossibility, wanting, as O'Gorman accurately predicted, to believe him more than her surly, perpetually defiant son.

"He's going to get killed," O'Gorman said. "The Italians will kill him if we don't."

Perfect. Just the right degree of concern for the bastard's survival. Conscience soothed, Barbara flung herself against him. "No, Dick, no. Don't let that happen."

"I'll do my best, for your sake. What did he tell you on the phone?"

"He wants me to join him in the Pines. He's afraid you'll hold me hostage."

"You see how sick he is, how vicious?"

"He said I shouldn't trust you. He said you made my father sign this house over to a bank that's controlled by the Mafia. Is that true?"

"It was the only way to raise the money for the guns," he said, silently cursing Mick again in his mind. "Your father did it out of his love for Ireland."

"How can we go away? How can we do anything now?" Barbara cried.

"We can only do it by getting the cocaine from Mick. Will you go see him and try to talk him into giving it up?"

"He says you're going to use the money to pay for the guns."

O'Gorman picked up the telephone and dialed the safe number of the Cuban Mission to the United Nations in New York. "I'm sending the ship back to Cuba."

The operator came on the line and he spoke rapidly to her in Spanish. In a moment he was talking to the Cuban intelligence man who was handling the liaison. He told him in Spanish that there was a problem and the freighter should wait for a new rendezvous. Paradise Beach was blocked by the FBI.

He hung up and smiled at Barbara. "Does that convince you? Tell Mick I'll meet him anywhere he says and guarantee his safety with the Italians. We'll give them the cocaine and our money worries will be over."

"You promise not to hurt him?"

"All will be bygones. No one in Belfast will miss Billy Kilroy, believe me. He was a spent bullet."

As he spoke, O'Gorman saw himself placing the Chinese Type 64 silenced to Mick's head and pulling the trigger. Now you know the whole truth, he exulted, now you accept the ultimate meaning of your nickname. It's your soul that is black, O'Gorman. As black as Satan's and you're proud of it. Are you listening, Captain Littlejohn?

"Mick says he'll be at Pop Oxenford's house in the Pines. He says Alex Oxenford knows where it is. He can bring me there."

"He will, depend on it."

An anxiety that O'Gorman mistook for fear swept Barbara's face. "I'd rather go alone. But I'd never find it."

"Oxenford'll take you. And he'll behave. He knows the consequences if he doesn't. We explained quite a lot to him while we were bobbing around in that damned boat."

O'Gorman went down the street to Bill O'Toole's house. Giordano, the Mafia boss, was there, raging up and down the living room. The police chief slumped in a stuffed chair, his fair-skinned face practically raw from their sojourn on the ocean. He had a patch over his gashed eye. His damaged leg was laid across a leather footrest. He looked exhausted or disgusted or both.

"What the fuck do you mean you can't find him?" Giordano shouted.

"There's six hundred thousand acres of woods over there and Mick knows them better than anybody except a Piney," Bill O'Toole said. "They know him and they're not gonna squeal on him. Especially if he promises them a cut of the take. If you want my advice, make a deal with him. Take the coke and call it even and let the stupid Cubans rot out there on that rust bucket. Let this son of a bitch go home and try to explain it to the IRA."

"You do that and I'll see to it that you're both dead in a month," O'Gorman said.

"Blow it out your ass," O'Toole said.

O'Gorman saw that O'Toole's self-disgust and his disgust with the messed-up deal had blended into a massive indifference. He did not care whether he lived or died. If he had to die, he was going to go defiantly. It was the only piece of his manhood left.

Giordano blinked at O'Gorman, amazed. No one had dared to make such a threat to him for a long time. "Do you know who you're talkin' to?" he growled.

"I do. I know both your names. Let's keep our heads and our patience a bit longer," O'Gorman said. He told them about Mick's call to Barbara.

"I know where Pop Oxenford lives," Bill O'Toole said.

"Let's pay him a visit now. Maybe we can locate your double-crossin' nephew before it gets dark," Giordano said.

"Pop won't tell us a thing," O'Toole said.

"You give me five minutes with the guy and I guarantee he'll answer every question in the fuckin' catechism. Even if he's a fuckin' Baptist," Giordano said.

"Let's save that for later," O'Gorman said. "Let's see if his mother can arrange a meeting at which we promise to give Mick the money for the cocaine. That's when we strike. When he has the stuff with him."

"I like that," Giordano said.

"Where are your men?" O'Gorman asked.

"In Atlantic City. Twenty."

"They're well armed?"

"Uzis."

"A good gun. The Israelis make very good guns."

"Yeah. What do we do in the meantime?"

"You can watch television. O'Toole and I will go see the fellows with the trucks. Hughie McGinty and I have a lot to talk about."

O'Gorman's hand caressed the Chinese Type 64 silenced in his pocket. The Iron Chancellor was in charge.

SWEATING IT OUT

In the fire watchtower on top of Apple Pie Hill, FBI agent Aloysius Sweeney paced up and down in the suffocating heat. The April sun made the flat-roofed compartment almost as hot as it would be in August. George Petrie, the gray-haired, laconic ranger who shared the tower with him, seemed unbothered by it. His lined face and lean body looked as dried out as one of the ancient pines below them.

The radio on the table crackled. "This is Sunbeam Two. Any orders?"

"No," Sweeney said. "Something must have gone wrong. Just stand by."

Picking up his Zeiss 600 binoculars, Sweeney studied the two rented trucks at the empty boat landing on the Mullica River. McGinty's Ford Escort was still parked beside them. It was almost three o'clock. By this time Sweeney had expected to have the trucks, the Houlihans, O'Gorman, Kilroy, and the Irish-Americans in custody.

Not a single boat had gone up the Mullica for hours.

The river was an empty, shining swath in the brilliant sunshine. In a sixty-mile circuit around Apple Pie Hill, twenty FBI agents who could be doing a lot of other important things were baking in cars along with almost as many state police, covering every road out of the Pine Barrens.

Sweeney paced up and down, sweating. Why didn't those goddamn trucks move? Why didn't McGinty get to a phone and call him in New York, where they would relay the call to him?

Sweeney sighed. McGinty was afraid the Houlihans would start wondering about a double cross and panic. McGinty had his problems, the poor bastard. He had no guts in the first place. These double-agent deals were nightmares for everybody.

"What's the biggest fire you've ever had around here?" Sweeney asked Ranger Petrie.

"Nineteen sixty-three was pretty big. Burned out seventy-five thousand acres. That's the biggest I've seen."

By now Sweeney had become an expert on fires in the Pine Barrens. It was the only thing Petric wanted to talk about. He had no interest in sports or politics. Sweeney learned that a forest fire moves in a V, like the wake of a ship. The point of the V is called the head fire, and if it gets up into the tops of the trees, it becomes a crown fire. The sides of the V are called lateral fires, and they have to be fought just as hard as the head fire, because when the laterals reach out far enough, they become new head fires.

"We had two hundred fire trucks from all over New Jersey and Pennsylvania," Petrie said. "We tried everything. Backfires, bombing it with retardant from the air—nothin' worked. Spring is the worse time for fire around here. The vegetation is dried out from the winter. Cured, we call it."

Sweeney had been amazed to learn that a lot of the four hundred fires each year in the Barrens were the result of arson. The forest glistens with oils and resins; oak leaves are coated with oil that will burn at the touch of a match.

Teenagers drive through the Barrens and fling burning matchbooks out of cars. They are miles away by the time the woods begin to burn.

Some blazes were what Petrie called "grudge fires," set by Pineys. No one could touch them for the skill with which they created a conflagration. Generally their aim was not to kill, however. They just wanted to burn somebody's house down for insulting them or taking a woman away from them. They were confident that a fellow Piney knew how to survive a fire.

"How do you do that?" Sweeney asked.

"Get onto burned ground. It isn't hard if the head fire's not too deep," Petrie said.

Sometimes, of course, the head fire can be very deep, and then the runner for burned ground is in a lot of trouble. Pineys could arrange that too in rare instances, when they wanted to kill somebody. Pineys, at least the older ones, had a lot of experience with fire. They used to set fires in the blueberry lowlands because wild blueberry bushes yield more berries after a fire.

The radio crackled again. "This is Sunbeam Three. When do we eat? We're out of everything, including water."

"Soon," Sweeney said.

He studied the trucks and the Ford again. Something was wrong. There were no signs of life around the vehicles. Wouldn't McGinty or one of the Houlihans emerge from the trees to squint impatiently down the river? McGinty was not stupid. He should be able to invent an excuse to telephone by now. It would be a logical move, when the operation was twelve hours behind schedule. O'Gorman must have given him a number to call for further instructions.

"Sunbeam One. This is Central. Pick me up. I think we better move in for a closer look."

In five minutes Sweeney was driving toward the Mullica with agents Larry Pinna and Tom Clancy. "What the hell's going on, Art?" Pinna asked. "I thought guys from New York never made a mistake."

"Other people do."

"Yankee fans? I can't believe it."

Pinna was from Boston. He believed in the Red Sox and not much else. They swung the car onto the sand road that led to the landing on the Mullica. Clancy, at the wheel, cursed as the car slewed in the ruts. They bounced around a curve and Clancy slammed on the brakes so hard they almost wound up in the trees.

A man was on the road ahead of them. He was trying to crawl toward them, but the result was more like the motion of a snake. He was inching himself forward by pulling on the loose sand ahead of him.

All three sprang out of the car and raced to him. Pinna turned him over and Sweeney looked into the agonized face of Hughie McGinty. They had kneecapped him and then shot him in the belly. They wanted him to die slowly and painfully.

"When did it happen? Who did it?" Sweeney said.

McGinty shook his head. He had no time for trivial questions. "Tell Nora," he gasped. "Tell Nora I died for Ireland."

RENDEZVOUS

As Barbara Monahan O'Day slipped into the front seat of Alex Oxenford's battered blue Volkswagen, thirty-two years unreeled in his mind, twisted in his flesh. It was the first time he had been this close to her since the night of 1952 when he had seduced her in the Pines. The night he had discovered an invisible boundary between seduction and love that even an Oxenford could cross, unaware.

For all those years they had not spoken a word. Thirty-two years of icy glares when he passed her on the boardwalk or the street. Thirty-two years of living on the wrong side of that boundary. Now, surrounded by terror and death, he felt a need, almost a compulsion, to speak.

"It's been a long time," he said as he shoved the balky clutch into first gear and the old chunk of rust rumbled toward the Pines and her meeting with Mick at his father's cabin.

"Just drive the car," she said. "I have nothing to say to you."

"I have some things I'd like to say to you."

"I made a vow—a long time ago—that I'd never listen to another word from you."

"Was what I did so terrible? Part of the way things turned out was your fault. If you'd waited a few more months—"

"Shut up! You ruined my life! I would have had a perfectly happy life if it wasn't for you."

"Are you sure? When I look at your sisters, I wonder if you would have been happy marrying some Irish lunkhead and having six lunkhead kids."

"Why do you think what I did instead was better?" She was practically screaming now.

"You had Mick."

"Mick."

"I remember seeing you with him when he was four or five on the beach. I ate my heart out, envying you."

"You never ate your heart out for anyone. You have no heart. What have you done with your life? Chased women and corrupted kids' morals with your crazy ideas."

"Has it ever occurred to you that I might have been waiting?"

"For what?"

He kept his eyes on the road. He had no hope of being taken seriously. "You."

"Shit."

"I talked Mick out of the Catholic Church, true enough. But I was trying to talk you out too. I hoped he might take some of those ideas home."

"He did—and they only made me despise you all the more."

"But now, things have changed?"

"Nothing has changed—nothing will ever change as far as you're concerned."

"But as far as you're concerned—you and the Catholic

Church—you seem to have decided to give yourself a dispensation from perpetual chastity."

"I don't know what you're talking about. Why don't you just shut up and drive the car."

"I'm talking about you and that Irishman. Mick says you're in love with him. And you're proving it in very direct fashion."

"That's none of your business. None of Mick's either."

"I know. But for some improbable reason, it stirred hope in my skeptic's soul."

"It shouldn't. He's all the things you never have been and never will be. Kind, considerate, honest."

"I wonder. I just spent ten hours in a small boat with him. He didn't mention you once. He didn't say a word about retreating to California to bask in the sunshine of your love when this mess was cleaned up. He talked mostly about what he was going to do to Mick when he caught him—and what he was going to do to the British when he became the maximum leader of Ireland. He didn't mention you as his royal consort in that role."

"He wouldn't tell you what we're planning to do. He wouldn't tell anyone."

"He gave me and Bill O'Toole quite a lecture on the IRA. He said they sent gunmen to the ends of the earth to shoot people who double-crossed them. Will you be happy living with a man who dives under the sofa every time a car backfires?"

"I'd be happy with almost any man in the world—except you."

"I guess that's definitive."

They drove in silence the rest of the way. Jouncing into the Pines in the twilight, Oxenford remembered growing up in Chatsworth in the 1940s, prowling these woods with his father, listening to the same stories about their history the old man told Mick. The wind sighed mournfully through the tops of the taller trees.

"Listen," he said, unable to resist it, thinking in his

exhausted state he was saying something significant. "The air tune."

"Oh, you bastard, you rotten bastard." Barbara started to cry.

"I'm sorry."

"You were never sorry for anything you said or did."

"Generally that's true. You were the exception."

"Don't start that again," she raged.

They lumbered into the clearing before Pop Oxenford's shack. He met them at the door. "Hello, Alex," he said.

"Hello, Pops. This is Barbara Monahan."

"Mick's mother? Well, this is an honor. A long-awaited honor. I wish it was a happier occasion, I wish it was."

"Thank you," she said. "I wish it was too."

They sat down at the table. Pop Oxenford stayed on his feet by the sink. "Mick's given me a lot of hours of happiness. Not as many as you've had, watchin' him grow to manhood. But knowin' him, the last fifteen years, has made gettin' old a lot easier. It really has made it a lot easier."

"I'm . . . glad," Barbara said.

"He's turned out pretty good, considering his troubles. He really has. He ain't a henpecked husband or a burglar. Or a barfly like this fellow."

"Yes," Barbara said, accepting with relish the last designation.

"Things happen to grown men a parent can't do a thing about. I guess they happen to women too, but I'm more acquainted with men. Did Mick ever tell you I had two sons killed in the war?"

"No."

"Yeah. The big war. One was killed in the Atlantic and the other in the Pacific. All I got left is this fellow. The permanent bachelor. That's why I've been grateful for Mick, even though he's only partly ours."

"Yes," Barbara said, her voice growing smaller. She did

not know that Alex Oxenford had told his father about Mick.

A handful of pebbles rattled against the window. "That'll be Mick. He's too smart to walk in the front door. They could be out there with a dozen machine guns. Nobody followed you, did they?"

Alex Oxenford shook his head.

"I'll give him the high sign."

Pops lit a lamp and held it up to the window. A moment later, Mick loomed in the doorway. He had an M16 over his shoulder. Joe Turner was with him, also with an M16.

"Hello, Mom. Hello, Prof. Are you coming with us?"

"No," Barbara said. "I'm here to give you a message from Dick—Dick O'Gorman. He says he wants to forgive and forget this whole thing, Mick. The ship is gone. The guns are gone. All he wants you to do is give him back the cocaine so he can settle with the Mafia. Pay off our debts and have some money to send back to Ireland. So they won't come after him when we go away together."

"Is that on the level, Prof? Is the ship gone?"

"I don't know," Alex Oxenford said.

"It's gone. I heard him make the call to New York, telling them to go back to Cuba," Barbara said.

"What about Trai and Phac and Suong? Will they be safe?"

"Yes. They can stay here. But I don't think it would be a good idea if you stayed."

"I don't plan to. There's nothing to hold me here now. Nothing in this whole lousy state or country. I went up to the city to see the old man. Your husband. My father. I asked him if he could help me get rid of the cocaine. He practically went nuts. He said he wasn't my father. You just married him to cover up being pregnant. Who the hell is my father?"

The anguish in Mick's voice was unbearable. Alex Oxenford had to speak. In his father's name and his own name, they had to claim Mick now, when they were in danger of losing him forever.

"I'm your father, Mick. I left your mother pregnant and went off to Korea to fight a war."

Disbelief at first. Then a smile of comprehension spread over Mick's face. "No wonder you were always trying to change my mind about everything under the sun."

Alex Oxenford had hoped Mick would remember the days they had spent fishing on the Mullica or in the bay, the trips to New York to see the Yankees. Mick had been one of a group, of course. But Alex had made some feeble gestures at fatherhood.

"Mick," Barbara whispered, "Mick. I had to do it. The family made me get married. They made me keep quiet all these years."

"What do you think we ought to do, Prof?"

"Give the stuff back. But keep your guns loaded and be ready to fight. I smell a double cross."

"So do I," Mick said.

"That isn't true. Dick promised me. If anything goes wrong, it'll be your fault," Barbara cried.

"Tell them we'll meet them at the head of Tulpohocken Creek tomorrow at noon. The Prof knows where it is. The stuff is hidden near there. I'll show them where it is. I want five thousand bucks off the top for Joe here. Tell them to bring that along. And twenty for Phac. That's all he needs to buy his boat."

"You don't have any right—" Barbara began.

"The hell I don't," Mick said. "Tell them. We'll be waiting."

LOVE IN THE SHADOWS

Mick drove back to the base camp at the head of Tulpohocken Creek feeling dazed, bewildered. Who was he, now? All his life he had thought of himself as Irish first and American second. Now he had found out it could just as easily be the other way around. His blood was half-American and half-Irish. His real name was not O'Day. It was Oxenford or Monahan, take your pick.

He did not know, he could not know, the incredible tangle of Dutch, English, German, and Irish with whom the Oxenfords had intermarried during their twenty generations in America. He did not need to know. American was what registered, American was what had meaning to him. For the first time, he saw these silent woods, the white beaches of the shore, as his land by inheritance. He was not a recent visitor, tossed up on this continent by history.

He could make the same claim with his Irish-American blood, of course. It was 120 years since the first Monahan had staggered from the steerage of an English ship in

New York harbor. But the ghetto mentality into which his people withdrew for a century had forfeited this claim. Now nationality thundered in Mick's soul. It somehow made him calmer, more resolute, in his preparations for tomorrow.

First, they lugged the steamer trunk full of cocaine into the deep woods at the head of Tulpohocken Creek, known as the Hocken Lowlands. Around it in a hundred-yard semicircle they dug foxholes for Mick and Joe and Phac. Each man had twenty clips of ammunition for his M16 and Molotov cocktails, whiskey bottles full of gasoline. "We don't use these unless I give you the word," Mick said.

He hated the thought of setting the woods on fire as much as Pop Oxenford did. They gave extra firebombs to Trai and Suong and told them how and where to use them, to produce lateral fires beyond the battleground. On a sandy road a few hundred yards farther back, Mick parked his American Rebel. "If there's any shooting, start the fires and head for the car and get the hell out of here," he said.

"No," Trai said. "I am staying here as long as you stay here."

This declaration made Phac twitch. "You will go," he said to Suong in Vietnamese. "Let the whore stay."

"If she stays, I stay," Suong said. "Give me a gun."

"Order him to go, Mick. If he doesn't go, I will go now. I will quit this business now," Phac said.

"You've got an order, Suong. You take Trai with you."

"I'm a grown woman. I won't be dragged around by a boy."

"Let's get some sleep. We'll decide it in the morning."

Mick wrapped himself in a blanket and fell asleep almost instantly. He dreamt he was back in Binh Nghai and Trai was in his arms on the riverbank. It was dark and peaceful and her body felt like crushed flowers against his flesh.

A hand on his shoulder. Trai's voice whispered, "Mick."

"What?" His hand reached instinctively for his M16.

"Your friend Joe. He's gone. He ran away."

"I don't believe you."

Mick rushed to the foxhole on the left flank where Joe had bedded down for the night. It was empty. The gun was there but Joe was gone. Suddenly he knew, he understood, the reason for Joe's long years in the woods. He had committed an act of cowardice in Korea. It may have been the same thing he had done here—slipped away in the dark, leaving his friends exposed to infiltration and disaster.

For the first time Mick realized they all might die tomorrow.

"Maybe we should go away now," Trai said.

"No," Mick said. "They couldn't find the stuff. They might kill Pops Oxenford and the Prof. Maybe even my mother."

Trai put her arms around him. "Oh, Mick. I feel a great dark thing creeping toward us through the woods. Phac told me what you did, saving his life. It was noble, it was good. But he's part of the darkness. You were never part of it. You were always my white god. You still are."

"You're married to Phac."

"He's never touched me. He can't love anyone or anything, except Suong. Mick, tell me you forgive me for what I did in Binh Nghai."

"I forgave you a long time ago."

"That makes me so happy. But you can't forgive yourself. You still mourn your men."

"Yes." The truth fell between them, as lacerating and impenetrable as concertina wire.

"Give them to God, Mick. Give all of that terrible time to God."

He did not want to tell her he had lost God somewhere between Binh Nghai and Paradise Beach and Atlantic City. He did not want to add to her sorrow. "I'll try," he said.

"Le Quan Chien wanted to kill you too, that night. He wanted to send four men to kill you just as they attacked the fort. I threatened to betray the whole plan if that was part of it. I tried to hold back the darkness. Even then I sensed it rising toward us like a great wave from the sea."

Tears streamed down Mick's cheeks. "I forgive you, Trai. I really do. Except for that bastard Le Quan Chien. Whenever I thought of you kissing that communist pig, I went nuts."

"Oh, Mick. That was my worst sin. He made me do it. He said he would kill my father. I never loved him. I told you that in Binh Nghai."

"Then you forgive me—for what I did when I killed him?"

"There was nothing to forgive. I was glad to see him die."

"Trai, I still love you. I've never stopped."

"I've never stopped loving you. I never will."

Her lips found his mouth in the dark. A wind from the sea sighed through the tops of the oldest, tallest pines. American, on American earth, Mick loved the woman who had stirred primary love in his soul in tormented Asia. He had yearned to cherish and above all to protect her, and failed. He was amazed to discover that love survived failure, perhaps was even enriched by it. Thirteen years fell away from both their souls; for a little while time did not matter.

"You hear that wind in the trees?" Mick whispered. "The Pineys think it's the devil playing music."

"It's not the devil," Trai whispered. "It's God. I feel God all around us here. I saw him on your grandfather's face. He only jokes about the devil. You have to be holy to do that. For the rest of us, the devil is not a joke."

She wanted to tell him that she sensed, she almost saw, the evil wave rising from the shore of Paradise Beach, she saw the hooded figure, immense wings outspread, riding its crest, she heard his icy, guttural laugh. But Mick would think she was trying to frighten him. Trai could not offend what was divine in him, what she had loved from the moment she saw him: his warrior soul.

APOCALYSPE NOW

"We have to kill all of them. That's understood," O'Gorman said.

"Yeah," Bill O'Toole said in his heavy, bitter way. He looked at O'Gorman with total loathing. O'Gorman had seen his type in Belfast—the man who began the business with a heroic or at least proud view of himself. They were the ones who sickened of what they soon became. Either they sluffed off the sickness and accepted their new murderous selves or they died. They arranged for the British to kill them by bungling an operation or they drank themselves to death. O'Gorman suspected O'Toole would die soon, one way or another.

"Sure we're gonna kill all of them. What the fuck else we gonna do?" Tommy Giordano growled.

O'Gorman smiled. He was one with this capitalist thug, one with the scum of the earth. He liked it. Are you listening, Captain Littlejohn?

Last night he had enjoyed a farewell fling with Barbara Kathleen O'Day. He had made all sorts of promises to her that he had no intention of keeping. She would find out the truth later today. He had been in touch with the judge and his fellow politicians in New York, and they had arranged a new rendezvous with the freighter and a boat from Cape May.

The Houlihans, looking hangdog, followed O'Gorman and O'Toole and Giordano to the car. O'Gorman had interrogated them yesterday and decided they knew nothing of Hugh McGinty's treachery. He had ordered each of them to kneecap McGinty before he shot the informer in the belly, and they had obeyed with relish. They were second-rate cannon fodder, but they were loyal.

It was a gray, cloudy day, with a brisk wind blowing from the southwest. Over the causeway, they met three limousines with twenty of Giordano's thugs in them. They formed a procession and drove into the Pines over sand roads to Pop Oxenford's house. He met them at the door without his customary smile. "Hello, boys," he said. "Welcome to Hog Wallow."

The thugs got out of their limousines to stretch their legs and relieve themselves like dogs against the trees. One of them set up a target on a tree and fired a few dozen rounds from his Uzi machine pistol. The rest liked this idea and soon the tree and target were riddled.

O'Toole, Giordano, and O'Gorman went into the house with Oxenford. He had a map spread out on the table. "Here's where you'll find Mick," he said, showing them a road that ran well east of the Hocken Lowlands. "You got to walk from here. I hope you got a compass."

"We got one," O'Toole said.

There were other roads that ran much closer to Mick's camp. But Mick wanted to separate them from their cars.

"How the hell did you get mixed up in this, Bill?" the old man said.

"Shut up," O'Toole said.

"Is there a quick way to get out of these woods from there?" O'Gorman asked.

"No. You got to come back here," Pop lied.

"We'll wait here for you," O'Gorman said. "You're in charge of getting the stuff, Bill. You lost it."

"Yeah," Giordano growled. "I ain't up to hoofin' through a couple of miles of woods. We'll stay here and take care of grandpa."

"You fellows goin' to kill me?" Oxenford might have been asking them if they wanted coffee.

"You've got nothing to worry about if Mick cooperates," O'Gorman said.

"What've you got them twenty machine gunners out there for?" Oxenford said. "He ain't gonna shoot you. There's no percentage in that for him."

"I told you to shut up," O'Toole said.

"Let's finish him now," Giordano said. "I ain't gonna put up with his bullshit."

"Now wait a minute. I don't fancy goin' this way. I always hoped I'd die game."

As he said this, the old man backed into the shadowy rear of his cabin. Suddenly he had a gun in his hand, an ancient pistol that looked left over from some Western movie. O'Gorman could not believe his eyes. He dove for the door as the pistol thundered.

He heard a scream of rage and pain from Tommy Giordano and the crash of answering shots. The machine gunners practically trampled O'Gorman as they stormed the cabin. An Uzi chattered.

When O'Gorman got to his feet and stumbled inside, he found the Mafia leader slumped against the wall, blood spurting from a terrific wound in his throat. The old man was lying on the floor in the back of the cabin, riddled by a hundred bullets.

Giordano was trying to talk. On the brink of eternity, he was intent on passing on his power: "Car-lie. Car-lie."

A young swarthy brute with surprisingly intelligent eyes knelt beside him. Giordano dipped his fingers in his own blood and traced a cross on Carlie's forehead, in a parody of a sacrament. O'Gorman felt, no saw, an icy darkness swirl through the cabin. I'm watching, Captain

Littlejohn. Are you? he mocked. A moment later Giordano was dead.

Carlie stood up, the man in charge. "Let's go. Let's grab this goddamn stuff and get the hell out of these woods. Now we got a funeral to worry about."

Thrashing sounds in the thick brush, feet pounding on the sandy soil. Mick grabbed his M16. He had spent the morning repositioning his firebombs and teaching Trai and Suong how to shoot Joe Turner's M16. With only Mick and Phac to defend the perimeter someone might break through and get to Trai and Suong in the car. They might have to defend themselves as they fled.

Now these sounds. "Who's that?" Mick called, dropping into his foxhole.

"It's me—Joe."

In a moment the big black man was panting beside him. Tears drenched his face. "I'm sorry I ran away, Mick. I couldn't handle it. I'm a lousy marine. But I want another chance. They killed Pop. They're gonna kill you."

"Pop? Are you sure?"

"I was comin' down to see him, to tell him I ran away. I thought maybe he could talk me into comin' back. I didn't want to run, Mick. I couldn't help it. Just as I got to his clearing, they come in their cars and I hung back in the trees. They went in the house and there were shots. They dragged Pop's body out behind the house and left him there. They took another guy out too. He killed one of them. Mick, give me back my gun."

"You've got it," Mick said.

A wave of fury swept through his soul. He would kill all of them. Not one would get away. Above all he was going to kill that lying IRA bastard O'Gorman. Grimly, he summoned his little band and told them what to expect. They went back to the plan he had worked out last night. Suong and Trai would set their fires and retreat to

the car. But they altered the location of the steamer trunk.
They moved it into the middle of the fire zone.

"Anyone who gets this thing is going to have be made
of asbestos," Mick said.

"This is bullshit," Carlie Mammartino said as he trudged
beside Bill O'Toole in the woods. Carlie was the new don
and was almost overwhelmed with the sudden responsibility. There were a lot more important things to settle in
the family than this pursuit of a million dollars' worth of
cocaine.

Bill O'Toole and Carlie were the same age. They had
played football against each other in high school, back in
the city. He was the perfect choice for the new don; he
was cool, objective, not a wild man like Tommy the Top.
He didn't believe in shooting people if he could avoid it.
But he had to finish this job or lose face.

Carlie started dealing with Bill O'Toole as they plod-
ded along. "Screw these IRA guys. Let's take the dope
and blow them away. Nobody knows what happened. If
anybody from Dublin asks questions, blame it all on me."

"You got a deal," Bill O'Toole said.

"But we gotta kill these people up ahead. They gotta
go. They know the story, for one thing. This guy, your
nephew, shot two, maybe four of our guys."

"He goes, don't worry." O'Toole had acquired a strong
deep hatred of Mick O'Day.

"You talk to him. Get the stuff," Carlie said. "We'll fan
out in the woods on both sides of you. The minute you got
it spotted, start running. We'll blow him away. The others
should be easy."

"Sounds good."

In another five minutes they were close to where the
old man had located Mick on the map. "Mick," O'Toole
called. "Mick."

"I hear you, Uncle Bill."

Carlie Mammartino motioned to the Houlihans and his

men. They spread out in two arcs on either side of the leaders. It was hot and there were lots of curses as the mobsters tripped over fallen branches and stumbled into sudden dips in the sandy soil. Lousy infantry, O'Toole thought, remembering Guadalcanal. But there were enough of them to do the job.

"I'm here to get the stuff. No questions. No problems," O'Toole said.

"It looks like you've got an army with you."

"You've got some pretty good guns. We're not takin' any chances. Come on out, without a gun, and let's shake hands. Show me where the stuff is and it's all over."

"The stuff is about a hundred yards away, right in front of you. But you're never going to get it."

"Get down," Carlie yelled, and everybody dove for the earth, thinking Mick was about to open fire. Instead, puffs of smoke and flame appeared in front of them and on both flanks. The woods erupted into a roaring wall of fire. Behind it were glimpses of Mick and his friends, firing M16s at anything that moved on the other side of the flames.

"Run through it. Run through the fire," O'Toole roared. He had spent more than a few of the days of his youth fighting fires in the Pines and he knew the key to survival. But no one listened to him. Panic engulfed Carlie Mammartino and his troops. Firing their guns at phantoms, they backed away from the flames, which rushed toward them with the help of the brisk wind.

Men went down on the left and right and screamed for others to save them. But the fire was gaining momentum and no one tried to save anyone but himself.

Only one of the Houlihans showed some loyalty. When his brother went down, he tried to drag him to safety. But the head of the fire rushed toward them like the flash of a giant serpent's tongue. Suddenly they were both burning and screaming.

It was insanity. O'Toole could hear Mick shouting, "Kill Kill Kill." The mafiosi were being caught by the flames or falling in the hail of bullets Mick and his men were spraying through the woods.

Through a break in the fire O'Toole saw what he had come to find. The steamer trunk. The fire was rising on the wind into the treetops, turning into a crown fire that could devour all the oxygen around them. But it was vaulting over the trunk, which stood, scorched but essentially untouched, in burned-out ground.

O'Toole lunged forward, flames searing his face and hands. He burst through the head of the fire and was onto the burned ground, lumbering toward the steamer trunk, his holy grail, his salvation.

From behind the trunk rose Phac, his fellow police chief. He had his M16 leveled. He pulled the trigger but the gun jammed. O'Toole had heard Mick curse the weapon for jamming and killing marines in Vietnam. Maybe his luck was finally changing. He riddled Phac with a blast from his Uzi and crouched beside the trunk, glaring to right and left around the burned ground in search of another target. Maybe he could kill them all single-handed.

Behind him the fire roared out of control. The screams, the gunfire, died away. A plane came roaring in to drop chemical retardant on the head of the blaze. Out of the bushes beyond the burned ground stepped Mick and a black man, as big as Mick, with anger on his long, mournful face. "That's him," Joe said. "He went into the house and killed Pop."

O'Toole leaped up and poured bullets at them from his Uzi. They went flat and he heard Mick call, "You can't kill a marine that way, Uncle Bill. You should know that."

"Mick. Let's deal. You're gonna need protection."

"You got it wrong, Unk. Your pals are all roasted or dead. You're the one who needs protection."

"Remember what I did for you, Mick. I helped you when no one else would."

"I know you did. That's why I'm gonna let you gamble for your life, Uncle Bill. You can run back through the fire or stay where you are until we outflank you, which should take about five minutes. Or you can play roulette. You got your pistol with you?"

"No."

"I've got mine. Throw that machine gun over here and I'll give you the pistol. There's one bullet in the chamber. If you can beat the odds three times, you can go home to Paradise Beach."

His luck was changing. He had killed Phac, hadn't he? Bill O'Toole thought. Mick was right about the other two choices. Running back through the fire was hopeless. The head was a hundred yards deep by now. Looking over his shoulder, O'Toole could see the blackened corpses of the mafiosi and the Houlihans on burned ground. It was only a matter of time before Mick and the black guy worked their way around his flanks.

O'Toole threw the Uzi to Mick. He threw his Colt .38 to him. O'Toole broke it and made sure there was only one bullet in the chamber. Mick and the other man crouched, their M16s leveled. O'Toole spun the chamber and put the gun to his temple. He pulled the trigger.

Click.

"Looks good, Uncle Bill. Two more to go."

He spun the chamber and put the gun to his temple again.

Click.

"I always knew you were a lucky son of a bitch, Uncle Bill. One more."

One more and then what? More days and weeks and months and years with this thick, disgusting body? Probably some of those years in jail and the rest listening to his wife tell him what a fool he was?

Smoke thickened the air around them. The fire was a moving wall of flame, almost a quarter of a mile away, now. More planes were bombing it. Out on the main road fire trucks were wailing. One more for what?

"Bastard!" Bill O'Toole screamed. He threw the gun at Mick and ran toward the fire. Across the burned ground, across the bodies, he ran to catch up to the purifying flames. He knew he could not get through them. He knew and he did not care. Finally all he wanted to do was die the way his son had died. He wanted to be with Jimmy, with that red hair and those laughing eyes for a few seconds. He wanted to walk through purifying fire and somehow convince God that he should be with Jimmy for eternity.

Toward the end of the day, when they got the fire out, they found Bill O'Toole on his knees, embracing the blackened trunk of one of the tallest pines.

"Oh, Mick," Trai said. "That was so cruel."

"Yeah," Mick said, watching his uncle disappear into the wall of fire.

There was no love in him. He was all warrior justice now. He ordered Joe to guard the cocaine and Phac's body. He gestured Suong and Trai to the car. "I want to go get Pop's body," he said. He cleared the jammed round from Phac's M16 and threw it in the backseat beside Suong.

They drove down the sand roads, skirting the fire, and stopped near the mobsters' cars. Mick approached them through the woods, his M16 ready. They were empty. The gunmen were all dead or wandering, disoriented and terrified, in the pines.

In a half hour they were in the clearing. It was utterly still beneath the gray sky. An empty limousine sat with its doors open, like a looted tomb. Mick left Suong and Trai in his car and walked toward the house, his M16 ready. He checked the car and glanced in the open door of the house, then slung his rifle and went behind the house. He emerged with the old man's body in his arms. Death and war were all Trai saw on his face. Death and war and grief.

Out of the woods behind the house stepped a man with a once handsome face, burned raw by the sun. His teeth were bared in a grimace of diabolical rage. He had a pistol in his hand. He shot Mick in the back with it. The gun did not make a sound. It was like a gun in a nightmare. But the bullet tore through Mick's body. Trai saw the blood spurt on his chest, above his heart. It was a mortal wound.

Mick whirled and saw him, saw Dick O'Gorman. He saw his doom, hurtling toward him from four hundred tormented years of Ireland's history. Like a true warrior, Mick lunged at it, ready to grapple death itself with his bare hands, to fight the irresistible, the way Cuchulain in the ancient saga assaulted the waves of the sea.

Mick abandoned the burden of his American grandfather to grapple with this Irish death that had stalked him across two oceans. O'Gorman fired two more bullets into his chest from the Chinese Type 64 silenced and still Mick came at him. He seized O'Gorman by the throat and they both went down. The .64 clicked once more. This time the muzzle was pressed against Mick's heart. With a long, bitter sigh, Mick fell back, slain.

Slowly, calmly, O'Gorman stood up and reloaded the Type 64 silenced. Trai realized that he planned to kill her and Suong. "The gun," she said to Suong. "Give me Phac's gun."

"It doesn't work," Suong said.

"It will work for me," she said.

He slid the rifle over the seatback to her and she released the safety catch, as Mick had showed her last night. The evil wave had broken. They would have to learn to swim in its dark flood.

In a distant corner of his soul, Dick O'Gorman grieved. He had just destroyed a part of Ireland that he should have cherished, one of the sons of the diaspora whose body and soul spoke of ancient greatness. He had desecrated Mick's body and polluted his own soul in the name of the future, not the past, a future described by a bearded German Jew who had transformed economics into a philosophy of hatred and hope in a London tenement a century ago.

Whether it was true or false no longer mattered now. Only the blood mattered, the blood and torn flesh and shattered bone, the deaths on shell-pocked battlefields and greasy side streets and on gallows, deaths in ships beneath the sea and planes spilling more death from the sky. Only the darkness mattered; Mick's blond hair, his fair skin, were already obliterated by it, he was already vanishing in the onrushing wave.

Only The O'Gorman and a rare few like him could walk on these waters, could command death with a cold eye and pass by unafraid. A poet of death, he walked toward the woman and the boy in the car, ready to write the last stanza on this pasquinade. Like terrified deer trapped in the headlights of an oncoming automobile, they would sit there and await him.

Suddenly the woman sprang from the car and knelt on one knee beside it, aiming a rifle with a short stock and an ammunition clip beside the trigger. An M16, first cousin of the ArmaLite, the gun that the IRA had used to kill so many British soldiers.

For an astonishing moment, O'Gorman gazed down the barrel of the rifle into her eyes. They were blank. They were the staring eyes of the Virgin in a Byzantine painting. The eyes of Jesus the Terrific Judge in the dome of Santa Sophia in Constantinople.

Don't be an idiot, he told himself. Those are the ordinary eyes of a Vietnamese woman. The size of the eyes in the small face gave an impression of blankness, of false serenity, when she had the same gullible soul of any woman anywhere. There was a good chance that she would miss him with that formidable gun. Another ten steps and he would be close enough to finish her off with the Chinese silenced.

"Wait a moment," O'Gorman called, giving her his infallibly charming smile. "Don't shoot. I'm an officer of the law."

Trai pulled the trigger and dozens of bullets hammered into O'Gorman's chest. He reeled back, whirling in the blast of fire, trying to run. Instead he fell headfirst into the front seat of the limousine. It had looked empty to Trai and Suong, but it was actually a hearse. Tommy Giordano's squat body lay in the backseat.

Bullets shattered the rear window of the car as O'Gorman pulled himself erect behind the wheel. He tried to turn the key, the key to the kingdom of heaven, to escape to a hospital where lovely nurses would soothe his tormented body with kisses and caresses.

But the key would not turn. There was no life in his fumbling fingers. More bullets shattered the window beside his head. He slumped against the seat and watched the woman walk toward the car through the gathering darkness. She stood at the window and gazed at him. Through the shattered glass she acquired a terrific splendor. She was a being a thousand centuries old, surrounded by the aureole of sainthood. The boy stood beside her, his Asian face also partaking of eternity. They seemed immensely sad, immensely grave, these creatures from beyond time.

The car began to move. It hurtled through the blazing woods and caught fire. Looking over his shoulder, O'Gorman saw Giordano sitting up in the backseat, burning like a Roman candle. Flames poured out of every body orifice, his mouth was wide in a wild scream of pain. As he burned, he became more and more translucent and suddenly he was gone. His peasant soul was not worthy of damnation. Annihilation was his fate.

Over Paradise Beach the limousine soared to plunge into the deepest part of the sea. The flames vanished and O'Gorman felt the cold begin. Down, down he spiraled toward a frigidity that only the mind can conceive. Finally, beyond the uttermost depths of the deep, at the end of all dimension, he heard a voice, laughing.

A thousand welcomes, whispered Captain Arthur Littlejohn.

A CYNIC'S TEARS

Cynics are not ordinarily weepers. But Alex Oxenford wept the day Suong drove Mick's car back to Paradise Beach and asked him to help bring Mick home. Suong and Trai were afraid they might be accused of some of the crimes that had been committed in the war in the Pines. To calm their fears, Oxenford asked the night police sergeant, Tom Brannigan, to come with them.

They found Trai sitting on the mossy ground with Mick's head in her lap. Nearby O'Gorman and Giordano lay dead in the bullet-ravaged limousine. Pop Oxenford's body lay a few feet away. Alex Oxenford was struck by the extraordinary peace on his father's face—and Mick's face. It helped him to maintain a few shreds of self-control.

For the living, there was no peace. Alex Oxenford undertook the task of telling Barbara Monahan O'Day what had happened. Her grief was so terrible, he almost forgot his own sorrow. "It's my fault," she said. "It's my fault from start to finish."

"No, it isn't," Oxenford said. "Remember what my father said about things happening to grown men? What happened to Mick was beyond your control—or mine."

"No," she said, "No. I let that Irish bastard lie to me. I believed another lying bastard like you. I'm hopeless."

"No, you're not. A man in pursuit of a beautiful woman will always be tempted to tell lies. But some of them regret it."

"Regret," she snarled. "I'm supposed to believe that, now?"

"Yes, now!" Oxenford shouted. "Jesus God, don't you believe I loved Mick too? Loved him as much—maybe more than you?"

He blundered out of the Monahan house and almost got killed by a car on Ocean Avenue. For the rest of the day he walked the empty beach remembering Mick as a towhead of five, his chunky body already aglow with energy. Mick at twelve with the cloud of unease in his hazel eyes as he tried to comprehend his fatherless world. At seventeen, in his prime, the football and basketball star, the lifeguard emanating maleness, the year when the world belonged to him.

Oxenford brooded on his dreams for Mick—and himself, the artful invisible father. Mick was going to star for Notre Dame and then for the Jets or the Giants. Marry money and let the Professor help him manage it.

Then the war, Trai's dark wave, rolled toward them. History rearranged everyone's dreams. Oxenford remembered his numbing disappointment when Mick came home from boot camp in his dark green marine uniform and announced one night in the Golden Shamrock that he liked the Corps so much he was going to make it his career. For the first time Oxenford glimpsed the warrior who had been waiting beneath the swaggering boy. For the first time he realized Mick had escaped him.

The memories grew darker. He remembered the hours he had spent trying to rescue Mick from the tragedy in Binh Nghai. The struggle to plant some seeds of ambition in his wounded soul. To somehow obliterate the memory that haunted him. Oxenford found himself loathing his own boozy barroom lectures, his attempts to explain why this huge, voracious country has always been inept at fighting minor wars, why Americans worship patriotism and disown patriots. Trying to set a historical backfire to fight the blaze that was consuming Mick.

Remembering how many times he was tempted to assert his fatherhood and never finding the courage.

Remembering and weeping for his American-Irish son, betrayed by his parents, by his psuedoparents, by both his countries.

Eventually, the sun sank and Oxenford stared at the twilit sea and wondered if it held the answer to what to do with the rest of his miserable life. It would be simple to walk into the surf and let the Atlantic claim the last of the Oxenfords. It would prove his regret to Barbara Monahan O'Day.

"Alex."

It was a woman's voice. A voice he had never expected to hear again. Barbara was standing about a dozen feet away from him, speaking the words into the sea wind. "There'll be a wake tonight for Mick—and your father. I'd like you to come and sit beside me."

HAIL AND FAREWELL

These days, Paradise Beach is a prosperous, peaceful town. Yours truly Alex Oxenford is the mayor. Thanks to Police Chief Tom Brannigan, we have been able to resist the moral and political muck that oozes our way from Atlantic City with all the élan and not a little of the skulduggery that Bill O'Toole employed.

With a nice combination of public relations and legal maneuvers we were able to portray the Monahan clan as victims of Mafia pressure. We handed over the cocaine to the FBI, who were delighted to convict several of the survivors of Mick's conflagration for trying to smuggle it into the country. The demoralized Giordano mob were forced to surrender their mortgages and abandon their plans to take over Paradise Beach. Bill O'Toole and Leo McBride and Melody Faithorne emerged from our spin machine as heroes on a par with Pop Oxenford—all resisting the vicious scheme to sully our town with a tidal wave of dope. Black Dick O'Gorman and Billy Kilroy went unmentioned into the darkness.

I have been married to Barbara O'Day for thirteen years now. If we have not achieved happiness, I don't know what to call it. Out of the ashes of sorrow and loss has risen a veritable phoenix of our first love.

Not long after we married, we adopted Suong. Without the slightest prompting from us, he announced a determination to pursue a military career. A decade ago, he graduated from Annapolis. He is now a major in the Marine Corps, on his way to becoming our first Asian general. No one knows he is determined to review Mick's court-martial as soon as he achieves sufficient rank and power. I have no doubt whatsoever that he will restore Mick's good name.

Trai is no longer among us. She has joined a convent of contemplative Carmelites in Connecticut. They devote their days to meditation and prayer for the rest of mankind, who continue to demonstrate an egregious need for all the divine assistance they can get. Privately I believe she is waiting impatiently for the moment when her soul will join with Mick's for eternity.

Have I, the ultimate cynic, heir of twenty generations of indifference to law and morality, become a believer? At times I wake in the night beside Barbara and sense a hovering spirit in the room. Humming through the screens, the wind off the ocean almost becomes a human voice, crooning bittersweet words.

> *Oh the days of the Kerry dancers!*
> *Oh the ring of the piper's tune!*
> *Oh for one of those hours of gladness*
> *Gone! alas, like our youth, too soon.*
> > *Oh to think of it!*
> > *Oh to dream of it!*
> > *Fills my heart with tears . . .*